THE DECEIVER

THE DECEIVER

A Claire Roget Mystery

Priscilla Masters

This first world edition published 2017
in Great Britain and the USA by
SEVERN HOUSE PUBLISHERS LTD of
19 Cedar Road, Sutton, Surrey, England, SM2 5DA.
Trade paperback edition first published
in Great Britain and the USA 2018 by
SEVERN HOUSE PUBLISHERS LTD

British Library Cataloguing in Publication Data
A CIP catalogue record for this title is available from the British Library.

ISBN-13: 978-0-7278-8752-8 (cased)
ISBN-13: 978-1-84751-866-8 (trade paper)
ISBN-13: 978-1-78010-929-9 (e-book)

All Severn House titles are printed on acid-free paper.

Severn House Publishers support the Forest Stewardship Council™ [FSC™],
the leading international forest certification organisation.
All our titles that are printed on FSC certified paper carry the FSC logo.

Typeset by Palimpsest Book Production Ltd.,
Falkirk, Stirlingshire, Scotland.
Printed and bound in Great Britain by
TJ International, Padstow, Cornwall.

AUTHOR'S NOTE

The Chinese measure age from the moment of conception – not birth. Perhaps we measure it nine months too late? Obstetricians describe the weeks of pregnancy as 8/40, 10/40 and so on. Right up until 40+2 weeks, when it's really time the baby made an appearance! Whatever world it is born into.

ONE

Tuesday, 16 June, 4 p.m.
32/40

P erhaps it was her fault – at least partly for making the wish. 'Flaming June', she'd been scoffing as she'd peered out of her office window into an afternoon wrapped in a grey blanket of summer rain that blurred the sharp quadrangle which formed the centre of Greatbach Secure Psychiatric Hospital. Outside lines were indistinct, colours damped down, stones softened to cushions of grey, the walls weird shapes rising only to disappear into a fog, the familiar view lacking substance, form or definition. In her imagination, Claire was trying to replace the drizzle with something else. Something sparky and bright, dramatic and sharp. She badly needed some drama to break this monotony. Maybe a holiday? Hmm. She considered the option. Nowhere specific, just not here, not in Stoke-on-Trent, Central England, Land of the Potter, suffering a so-far disappointing summer. Somewhere bright, noisy and colourful, where the sun dazzled and the heat cooked her bones. She wanted to be in the epicentre of an adventure, witnessing a drama. Somewhere, something unpredictable, surrounded by excitement.

So she scanned the skyline of Hanley with mounting discontent, picking out the square, sixties' tower blocks, the spire of the church punching the skyline, stumpy bottle kilns stubbornly reminding her of the city's industrial past which refused to die, even with the challenge of cheap Chinese exports, but which constantly reinvented and revived itself. The city had pluck, she had to admit. But today, even the knowledge that just below her sightline snaked Brindley's Caldon Canal with its pretty, narrow boats decorated with roses and castles failed to inspire her.

Why? It wasn't just the weather.

She'd just left her afternoon outpatient clinic which had been the usual – streams of outpatients displaying strange behaviour, according to the referrer; the patients themselves invariably lacking the insight to classify their behaviour as abnormal. Most of them were, they claimed, perfectly rational, except . . .

It was her job to sort them out, like coloured wool in a workbox. Some aberrant behaviour was deliberate, some accidental, some the consequence of a chemical imbalance, others sequela of past abuse or a perceived slight. And some simply the result of an attention-seeking personality, folk so thirsty for the spotlight to stay on them and never ever move away that they would duck and dive, manoeuvre their position into illumination. This clinic had an even larger barrel load of neurotics, depressives, the anxious, the bipolar – people who capitalized on tragic circumstances, injustice shining through their stories.

They *wanted* to be well. They *wanted* her to heal them. They hadn't *earned* this. They hadn't *asked* for this. They *didn't want* it.

Take it away, Doctor. It was the subtext of all their sorry tales.

A demand rather than a request. An expectation. An entitlement.

That afternoon, she had seen two victims of real trauma – one a refugee from Syria, who had witnessed practically every friend and relation butchered in front of him and been powerless to prevent it. Even the murder of his three-year-old daughter, whose screams would echo in his ears for ever. That inability to have halted those dreadful events was paralysing him slowly. He was gradually withdrawing from life, oozing back into a protective shell. It would be more than a challenge to restore him. Possibly a challenge too far. Claire almost believed it would be cruel to return him to such a dreadful place as his real world.

Cognitive behavioural therapy, psychotherapy, drugs, ECT. All would be an ineffectual weapon, a pea shooter against an AK-47 or a Kalashnikov. Being aware of a cause is not tantamount to a cure. However much help Sharman El Khaled received, he never would be whole again. And she couldn't make him so. As she'd faced him in the clinic she'd recognized this. So had he. And that burden was adding to what should have been a bright summer's afternoon.

And wasn't. The rain continued to spatter on the windowpane.

The other patient who had added to her feeling of despair that afternoon was a twenty-three-year-old man, the victim of a vicious and unprovoked assault in the city centre eighteen months ago. A young man who had been left not only with permanent blindness in his right eye but also a never-ending escalator of flashbacks where the hammer which had robbed him of that eye's sight was raised over his head to strike again and again and again like some ancient Greek punishment for flirting with the gods. But Tomas Plant hadn't been flirting with the gods that evening – just the girlfriend of the wrong guy, who had then claimed provocation and been convicted of ABH, received an eight-year sentence and would be out in four. Claire doubted the assault on Tomas Plant would be Steven Hick's last crime. She knew too much about patterns of behaviour and recognized deep-set character traits. People were people – evil, good, cruel, kind, sadistic, their characters set in stone. They didn't change but remained in their allotted pigeonhole and would not fly out in spite of the interventions of psychiatrists like herself.

So, she was asking herself in a moment of self-doubt, what use am I? Do I ever save lives, prevent crime, alter a character?

Questions. And yet she continued like a wound-up automaton in her day-to-day work, arranging tests, dictating letters which would be typed up by her secretary. When she had corrected Rita's dubious spelling and juvenile punctuation, some of which could alter the meaning completely, she had to sign them with her still-childish scrawl.

Claire Roget (Consultant Forensic Psychiatrist)

So the roundabout went round and round and round. And she clung on because she had nothing to jump off for.

And then, into the bleakness the call came, as explosive as a rocket firing magnesium stars into a night sky, as demanding as an imminent suicide threat. A harsh bell shattering her thoughts and, behind that, the drama she had been seeking.

'Claire.'

'It's Charles.'

She was struggling.

'Charles Tissot.'

It took Claire a moment to remember who he was. Then she did. A local obstetrician. A colleague and, like her, an alumnus of Birmingham University.

'Claire. Thank God I've got hold of you.' His tone was desperate, hasty. *What on earth did he want?* Without waiting for a response, he plunged straight back in. 'Claire, you've got to help me.'

She could not have been more astonished, which raised her voice a pitch or two. 'Me? Help *you*? Charles, what on earth's going on?'

'I don't know where to start.' He sounded almost panicky now. 'Fucking evil, mad, insane woman. A patient.'

Evil? Mad? Insane? Strong words to describe a patient.

She thought quickly and took a running jump at a guess. 'I take it you want my help – an assessment, maybe – as a psychiatrist?'

'I want you to certify her fucking mad.'

She smothered a smirk at the idea of filling in the Section form with those two words: *Fucking mad.*

And still couldn't quash the surprise at the request from practically the most well-balanced, sure-of-himself, cocky, over-confident, sane man she'd ever known.

Tissot's rant continued. 'Deluded. Insane.'

Her response was guarded. 'Well, I will see her if you like.'

'Please.' He was beginning to simmer down a bit, sound a little more normal. 'As a forensic psychiatrist,' he emphasized. Before, interestingly, he backed down an inch. 'Well, of course, not so much for *my* sake, Claire. But . . .' He stopped, words eluding him for now. 'For hers. She's not right in the head. And then,' he added delicately, 'there's my career.'

That was easier and made much more sense. Charles was the leading local 'Obs' and 'Gobs' consultant – obstetrics and gynae-cology to the uninitiated. In other words, a ladies' doctor. In more ways than one. One can be a *ladies' man*. But a *ladies' doctor*?

She probed. 'Give me some background. Someone pregnant? A gynae patient?'

'Pregnant. Eight months. Thirty-two weeks. Eight weeks to go. Claire. Claire . . .' The desperation was returning to his voice, raising its pitch almost to a squawk. 'She's accused me of having sex with her. Of having some sort of bloody intense but clandestine affair. Claims I'm in love with her but we have to *keep it under wraps*.' She could almost see his fingers scratch out speech marks. 'She's saying that I'm the father of this . . . child. Mad.'

She picked up on the one verifiable point. 'Well, that should be easy to disprove with a DNA paternity test.'

'When she's delivered. There's no justification for taking cord blood. So we've got a two-month wait for my name to be cleared. But even then it won't absolutely prove that this whole fantasy love thing never happened. Bitch.' The last word had been spat out. Claire held the phone a little farther from her ear. 'She says that we've been carrying on – in secret, of course,' he mocked before the rant continued. 'None of it's true. It's all fantasy. In her sick, perverted little mind. She's off her trolley. She's mad. You have to see her, Claire, and certify her. Get her fantastic story discredited. Get her to confess she's made the whole thing up. She's nuts.'

Something in his narrative had stopped her heart. To a male obstetrician there is no worse allegation than having had sex with a patient. Promising careers, talented surgeons, brilliant practitioners – all had been cut short by a whisper of the dreadful words. But wait a minute. What was he expecting from *her*? What was *her* role in all this? Obvious: collusion. *She* was the one who could leap across the gap. Issue certification that the said woman was deluded, advise that this claim was to be ignored, the result of nothing but a kink in a blood vessel or a chemical imbalance in an already damaged brain. If she colluded with that, *her* opinion would be the one that counted. *She* was the forensic psychiatrist.

She hated having to do this, to put words into his mouth, but, 'So are you telling me that this patient is making the whole thing up?'

He came back fighting. 'Of course she is. She asked her GP to refer her to me when she was twenty-eight weeks pregnant, saying she was feeling anxious. She'd had two previous pregnancies but both times the child had died as a result of a cot death and she'd heard I was good. It's all a setup, Claire. Deliberate. The whole thing is a fantasy.' He paused for breath before getting right back in there and slipping back into character. Over-confident, cocksure, conceited. 'She wouldn't be the first patient to fancy themselves in love with me. Obstetricians are easy prey. All those hormones floating around in bloated bodies, believing their husbands are finding them unattractive and fat.' *Guffaw*. 'Which is probably true. They just thrive on the attention. But bloody hell, Claire. For *me* this is damned dangerous. Mud sticks, you know.'

'Yeah, I know, Charles.'

'So you *have* to help me.'

'Mmm.'

'You will *see* her?'

She'd meant for her response to be non-committal but his eagerness and panic punctured her resolve. 'Of course I will, Charles.'

She could see why he was so worried. But already she was beginning to line up some obvious questions. One doesn't see an obstetrician until one is *already* pregnant. So why was he so worried at a patient making this apparently wild claim? But before she could even start with a basic factfinder, he headed her off with, 'Of course I cannot possibly be the father of this child, and it will be easy to prove it. I did *not* have sex with the woman.' His Clinton-denial sounded very firm, very definite. Very clear. Very sure. Very like Clinton.

'But . . .' And then it came, dragging behind him like a leg iron. 'There's a complication.'

And instead of prompting him, she waited for the story to spill out, like the three-year-old Syrian child's guts on to the sand.

'Apparently she's claiming that we had some sort of drunken fumbling in the back of a car at a party last year sometime.' That was when a nail snagged on nylon, a shift in time as the rainy window receded, its image replaced by something else. A swirling vision of strange and drunken fumbling. It was that one phrase. *The back of a car.* Something buried deep in her own memory, out of focus now and elusive, that seemed to imprint itself over the present. Something in this memory felt like an electric shock as from a cattle prod. Something was warning her to be vigilant.

On the other end of the line, his pause was laboured. 'And her *sister*'s backing up her mad story.' This time he sounded exasperated.

'What?' She was struggling now to fit the facts together. An independent witness? To . . .? She checked the facts. 'She's saying she *witnessed* it?'

'No.' It was a careful qualifier. 'But there *is* a connection.' He was sounding glum now. 'The sister works for one of my colleagues. The alleged . . . act . . .' the disgust in his voice turned the word into a retch, '. . . is supposed to have taken place outside a party.'

'Ah.' From an impossible story, it was turning into something slightly more feasible.

'I *was* there.' The admission came out heavily.

She inched forward, hopping from ice floe to ice floe. 'The sister is . . .?'

'Secretary to Metcalfe. Thoracic surgeon.' The briefest of pauses before another denial. 'I don't even remember her at that party.'

But he was there. And this changed everything. 'Have the allegations been made public? Are you suspended?'

'No. She and her sister spoke to me at her antenatal appointment this morning. They don't intend going to the authorities. Why should they? We're in love. Heather – the patient – is convinced I'm madly in love with her, that I have divorced my wife so we can be together and is simply waiting for *our* . . .' he shouted the possessive pronoun down the phone, '. . . child to be born before I fall at her feet and beg her to marry me.'

It took a while for all this to sink in. Claire felt her eyes narrow. 'And you're saying there's *no* truth in this? In *any* of this?'

'Absolutely bloody well not. The woman's bonkers.'

He turned his anger on *her* now for trying to verify the facts instead of simply accepting his own version.

'So why . . .?'

'Not blackmail. She hasn't asked for money. She's just waiting for me to declare myself. Christ, Claire. This is awful. She just sat there throughout the consultation with this stupid, crazy smile on her face. When I told her, quite gently of course, that she's got the wrong end of the stick, she came back saying it's *me* who is mistaken. That she quite understands why I can't be more open about it. She says that she wouldn't do *anything* that would harm my career. That *our* baby . . .' he was shouting now, '. . . will be most welcome. She couldn't be farther from the truth. She is completely fixated on me. There seems to be nothing I can say to dissuade her. God, if word of this got out . . .' He dragged in a hoarse breath, tension in his voice speeding up the sentences. 'She seems to expect me to enter into this horrible and dangerous fantasy, and the more I try to tell her, quite politely, that she is mistaken, the more she appears to be convinced that I am doing this purely to preserve my professional integrity. She talked about a future together, about the child. She called it *our* child, Claire.' His voice was rising again. 'She is dangerous. To me. This could ruin my career.'

She brought the conversation back down to the role she was expected to play. 'And you want me to see her?'

'Make an assessment,' he begged. 'There's not a scrap of truth in these wild claims. But you know what the MDU are like.'

She did. The Medical Defence Union invariably guarded its members slightly less assiduously than the innocent general public it vowed to protect. But whoever's side they might be on, there were strict rules to be obeyed. 'Have you informed them?'

'Not yet, but time is of the essence. The longer this goes on the worse it will be for me. She makes me shudder, Claire. When I examined her this morning she just lay there giving me this doe-eyed look. Tried to stroke my hand.'

She was alarmed now. 'Please tell me you had a chaperone.'

'Of course. I'm not a complete idiot. But she spent half the time winking at the chaperone as though *she* was in on the act. The poor girl, first-year pupil midwife . . .' He couldn't resist tacking on, 'Pretty little thing with lovely, silky blonde hair and . . .' Before remembering. 'Poor girl. She didn't know where to look. What to do. It's embarrassing, as well as dangerous. The woman is seriously odd. When I tried to speak to *her*, her response was something about love. Love is patient or some such crap. Even her sister, who was with her this afternoon, put her hand on my arm and stroked it. Please, Claire. You've got to help me out here.'

He did sound desperate.

But she knew that before she got her hands dirty she had to ask again. 'I take it there's no truth in . . .'

He headed her off at the pass. 'Absolutely none. Have you been listening?'

She had to hear it just one more time.

'If you're asking did I shag her at this party, whenever it was, the answer is categorically *no*. It did not happen. Absolute balder-dash.' It was unfortunate that in that last word he had reverted to public school-speak. It sounded a tad too pat.

He continued in a calmer vein, reflecting now. 'Folk are often a bit funny about male obstetricians in the first place. Think we like firking around in—'

Claire cut in quickly, 'She will have to be referred to me.'

'Couldn't *I* do that?'

'No.' Already sensing conflict, she had to be firm about this. 'I think if we're going to have any chance of making this right and minimizing harm *to you*,' she emphasized, 'we're going to have to play it by the rule book, Charles. She's got to be referred by her GP. I think it might be an idea for you to have a word with her doctor to explain the situation.'

'The fewer people who know, the better.' He sounded alarmed. 'I don't want to tell the whole bloody world, Claire.'

'And there's no need to. You don't have to go into great detail. Just say that you think she's suffering from delusions and needs psychiatric intervention. You can say you've discussed the case with me and I've agreed to see her. That should help. I can take it from there. If she's not intending on going public about this you needn't elaborate on the claims she's making about you. Just give the bare essentials. *I* can be the one to unearth the detail at a later date, *after* something like a psychiatric assessment has been made. Then I can use it as evidence. But Charles . . .' She could practically see him sit up and take notice. And even though he wouldn't be able to see it, *she* needed the visual. Thumb and forefinger almost touching, even if only to illustrate the precarious predicament to herself, 'You're *this* far from being suspended pending . . .'

His response was understandably angry. 'I know that. Fucking GMC.'

Claire moved on. 'Who is her GP anyway?'

'Dagmar Sylas.'

Claire knew her vaguely. She had a blurred image of a young, homely woman, plump and secure in her own skin with magical cow-brown eyes. 'Right. I don't know her very well.'

'She's good,' Charles supplied. 'Works hard. Married. Couple of kids, I think. Special interest in breast cancer.'

'Well, I think *you* should be the one to speak to her without going into too much detail. What's the patient's name, by the way? So I recognize it when she's referred.'

'Heather,' he said with venom. 'Heather Krimble. K-r-i-m-b-l-e.'

Claire made a note on her pad. 'Suggest Doctor Sylas refer Heather to me for an initial assessment. Is that OK? Tell her to ring me first and tell me a bit about the patient. Off the record. I'll accept a faxed referral and assess Heather's mental state in the clinic.'

Charles scooped in a deep, relieved breath. 'Thanks, Claire, you've saved my—'

'I've saved nothing yet, Charles,' she said drily. 'Nothing. And you understand, once this . . .' She glanced down at her scribble to set the name in her mind. 'Once Heather Krimble has become my patient, I won't be able to discuss her mental condition with you except where it impinges on her obstetric well-being.'

'And mine,' he finished glumly.

'And yours,' she echoed, adding, 'and that of her unborn infant.'

But Charles had already put the phone down.

TWO

Claire was left searching the bare walls of her office with its bland colour scheme for a clue. What was it that was giving her this uncomfortable feeling that she had missed picking up on something significant? A vagueness where there shouldn't have been one. She frowned and half closed her eyes to blot out her surroundings – cream walls, electric light, background noise – until she found it and knew. She and Charles had history.

When they had been medical students together they had had a brief encounter. Strange, because he wasn't her type at all. *Let's face it, Claire, you know your type. The pirate, trimmed beard, ripped jeans, paint-spattered T-shirt look with a wicked gleam in his eye. Your type is Grant Steadman.* Whereas Charles was the Posh Boy. A bit preppy in trousers with knife-edged creases, collar and tie – even, on one horrid occasion, a cardigan. His sense of style proclaimed his background – public schoolboy with a plum in his mouth. Tall, overconfident, horribly sure of himself. Unlike her. She was half French. Unwanted. Damaged goods. The Frog. Yet there had still been that one brief encounter. Although, truthfully, she now acknowledged it hadn't been so much an encounter as a drunken fumble/one-night stand. To top it all, *in the back of his car*. And it was that phrase that had initially snagged her attention. There were parallels with Heather's story. But still, she was smiling with the memory of long-ago student days, days when drunken fumbling happened and ambition was the sun rising over the horizon. The MbChB they all strove towards.

Drunken fumbling? She blinked. Who was she trying to kid? It hadn't been that at all. Charles had been a big, strong guy, six feet tall; a fit, muscular rugby player for the varsity team, she a seven-stone girl with nothing like his bulk or musculature to equalize the competition. There had been no competition.

And there was something else.

In Charles's history, there had been what appeared to be deliberate vagueness. An avoidance of detail. The . . . *At a party last year some time . . .*

He was an obstetrician, for goodness' sake. Estimated dates of delivery, last menstrual period, date of conception. These would all roll off the tongue as comfortably and easily as the recipe for a Victoria sponge to a cook. Besides . . . how many parties did he go to in a year held by a specific colleague? So why was he muddying the waters? Why had he not been more precise?

The dark voice bouncing around her room reminded her that a few short moments ago she had made a wish.

Be careful what you wish for, Claire Roget. Sometimes, when the gods wish to cause mischief, they grant them.

So, she had been given her drama, handed it on a plate, but it had dragged baggage in its wake, evoked a memory she thought she'd buried deep enough for it never to resurface.

Never resurface? Mouth tightening, she mocked herself. *And you, a psychiatrist? Then you should have known there is no place that deep.*

Claire was thoughtful, twiddling her pen between her thumb and forefinger, eyes unfocused. These days, what had happened between her and Charles on that freezing November night in the back of his Vauxhall Astra would be classed as date rape. But of course, back then there was no such tidy phrase to describe drunkenness, reluctance, persuasion, fumbling, dominance and penetration. She couldn't even remember the exact sequence of events, whether she'd actually said no out loud, whether he had been too drunk to . . . She frowned back into the past, wishing she could erase even this vague memory, these fuzzy details. And acknowledged that even though she had believed the memory had been erased, like red wine on a plain, pale carpet, however hard you scrub, however many proprietary cleaners you apply, the stain is still there. Intermittently visible. You might forget it for a while and then one day you walk into a room and there it is, that irregularly shaped faint shadow, ambushing you.

Just like today.

She hadn't thought about it for years, had relegated it right to the back of her mind. But now she recalled that subsequently, after the *incident*, whenever she had been in contact with him, even at opposite ends of the same room, though the memories were always indistinct, she had experienced a very slight nausea. If accidentally alone in a room with him, she had checked for an

escape route, a door, even an open window, and with a sense of
panic searched for other people to join them. If he was at a mess
party she would leave early. And so, she had successfully avoided
him. And forgotten – or so she had thought. Now she realized she
had simply skirted round it.

They had reached their clinical years, he in a different set,
studying on another rotation, moving through the specialities under
different firms, often in different hospitals, so after that she had
hardly seen him. Through the Old Fellows grapevine, she had been
vaguely aware that he had married and some years later been
appointed as a consultant at the newly named University Hospital
of the North Midlands (to distance it from the ill-fated Stafford
General Infirmary). The paths of psychiatry and obstetrics don't
cross that often and so she had almost forgotten about the entire
incident and, until now, proceeded with her life, such as it was.

Not great.

Grant, her live-in boyfriend, had disappeared from her life,
only to reappear six months later with an explanation (of sorts)
of a demanding and manipulative sick sister and a mother who
couldn't cope. It had been their joint demands on him, he claimed,
which had led to his wordless abandonment of her. Reluctantly
she had reflected that he had probably been the best boyfriend
she'd ever had or ever would have. *Ce'est la vie.* Let it go. Float
downstream.

Nice, jaunty phrases. Harder than they sound.

Whenever she thought of Grant now, it was with an accompanying
sigh and a heavy heart, a memory of a dark beard and merry eyes,
someone who laughed often, was easy-going, lazy, a perfect foil to
her wound up, type-A personality. She wanted to move on. She
needed to move on. She had bought him out of their house and
waved him off. But he was still there, in her heart, in her mind.

Go away.

She had done everything she humanly could, filling her time
outside work with activities. She'd taken up running again, booked
a couple of singles holidays, met up with friends, even tried an
Internet date or two. And that wasn't all. She had deleted him
from her mobile phone and wasn't on Facebook or Twitter, though
that wasn't solely to avoid electronic contact with her ex. No
forensic psychiatrist in anything approaching their right mind
would risk exposure on social media.

But nothing had worked. So far, she was still a bit stuck in the past, with only the mantra that every day she was distancing herself a little further from Grant to act as a crutch.

So, *go away.*

The call came on the following day, via a penitent Rita.

Dr Sylas had a voice that sounded warm and quite friendly. A chocolate voice to match those chocolate eyes. Having introduced herself, she spoke in an only slightly embarrassed tone. 'I understand that Charles Tissot has already been in touch with you concerning a pregnant patient who is making claims about him?'

Claire kept it short. 'He has.'

'He's asked me to refer her to you.' There was a slight pause, which set Claire wondering. Was she sensing disapproval, or what? Dr Sylas continued, 'I can fax you over her details.'

'Thank you. Do you believe . . .?' She had been going to ask whether the doctor believed there could possibly be any truth in the allegations, but she got no further.

'Heather has had a traumatic life,' Dr Sylas said crisply. 'She has had her ups and downs. She has had two cot deaths in the past.'

This triggered a faint alarm bell in Claire. *Two* cot deaths were not impossible as had once been believed, to the detriment of innocent women. But they were certainly an issue.

Dagmar Sylas continued, 'Her family history is poor. Her father was a controlling man with strong religious beliefs. He believed in the *spare the rod* philosophy, you understand. Her mother appears to have been largely passive in her children's upbringing. But Heather does have a very loyal, balanced and sweet-natured sister, Ruth, who is a medical secretary.'

Claire was listening hard for undertones as Dagmar Sylas carried on. 'Ruth appears to back up Heather's allegations that somehow . . .' She couldn't resist shoving her own opinion in. 'I cannot believe there is any truth in this ridiculous story.'

So, Claire thought, she had declared herself. And privately, Claire agreed with her. People do change over the years. Medical students morph into respectable consultants or GPs. But when accepting a new referral it is never a good idea to form preconceived opinions. And if you *had* fallen into that particular pit then it was best to keep those opinions tightly to yourself, not share them when you make a referral and ask for a specialist's opinion.

'No,' she said, tentative and non-committal. 'So, give me a bit of background information.'

A heave of a sigh from the GP. 'She has a partner but Heather's husband is a very odd man. There is a spurious diagnosis of Tourette's but I don't think this is as a result of a formal assessment. He appears passive, quite fond of his wife, unable to hold down a job. He has intermittent problems with alcohol. Sometimes he appears inadequate and then at others he seems to pull himself together. I guess you'd say he's emotionally labile. Unstable.'

'You say she's had two infant cot deaths. Any *living* children?'

'No.'

'On what grounds are you referring Mrs Krimble?' She wanted to add *apart from a response to the request from Charles Tissot*, but it would have put the GP's back up. There was another longer pause before the doctor answered her question. Defensively. 'I suppose on the grounds of the allegations she's making. They're patently the result of a delusional state. I mean, she didn't even meet Charles until she was referred by me, already seven months pregnant.'

Claire's toes were tingling. That wasn't quite the truth, was it? Charles had already admitted it. They had met at a party. He was being selective in the facts he was feeding the GP. She listened harder to the GP, to seek out any undertones. 'She has previous history?'

Silence before the question was answered reluctantly. 'She has made allegations before along the same lines.'

'Allegations of affairs?'

'Yes.'

'Which were denied?'

'Yes.'

'And they proved to be false?'

'I would say so.'

It wasn't quite as firm an assertion as Claire would have liked. But there would be time enough to tease out and analyse the details at a later date. Check facts.

'Well, look at it this way,' Dr Sylas was on the defensive again. 'She asked to be referred to Charles when she was twenty-eight weeks pregnant. So for her to claim he is the father of this child is patently ridiculous.'

Claire was listening hard.

'Not only has she categorically assured me that *Charles* is the father of the child . . .' Her anger burst through then. 'She's convinced *he's* in love with *her* but is hiding it from professional consideration because he thinks he'll lose his job. It's just . . .' Again, she was searching for a phrase. 'Fantasy land. Particularly when you consider what sort of a man Charles Tissot is.'

There was a warning there that Claire picked up on. When you consider what sort of a man Charles Tissot is?

She would have liked to explore this phrase.

Claire's thoughts were twisting and turning. Yes. On the surface, she could agree with the GP. It looked like an obvious delusion. But she had already ascertained that Charles had edited the facts. What she wanted to know was what had he omitted from Claire's version?

More than ever, she realized she needed to see it all for herself – meet this woman, make her own decision, not rely on others' testimonies, all flawed and full of holes where Charles, clever dog, had deliberately left out facts.

And she felt a sense of resentment. She didn't like the way that Dagmar Sylas was putting words into her mouth, feeding her breadcrumbs like ducks in the park. Though Claire was honest enough to admit that perhaps somewhere in this resentment was a little too much ego. On her side. Even she was tempted to chin up to the GP and ask the question: *If you've already made your diagnosis, why collude with Charles and rope me in?*

Which would get her nowhere. But this whole situation was ice, and both of them knew this as they skated around each other in whirly figure eights. Claire was only too aware that the subtext of this phone call from GP to consultant was that Charles Tissot had requested the referral. He was spinning them around. Did he still believe, after all these years, that he could manipulate her with his charm? The Charles she'd known was certainly arrogant enough. If she declared Heather Krimble unreliable and sadly deluded, her allegations against Tissot would likely be dismissed without his suspension or any sort of enquiry or publicity. It would be swept under the rug, kept out of the press, the sister's account dealt with later. Because however sweet, nice, balanced and sane Heather's sister was, she would have been relying on Heather's version of events.

She must have been.

Claire couldn't resist asserting her position. 'So you're referring her as a . . .?'

The GP was forced to break cover. 'Look, I don't like this any more than you do, Doctor Roget. But . . .'

Claire was tempted to hold up a hand as a Stop sign to the doctor before she dug herself in any deeper.

Don't say it. Don't voice the fact that we have to protect one of our own. And as a reward for your silence, I won't ask whether you think it's possible her story – whatever it is, and I haven't heard a word of it yet except from Charles and the odd breadcrumb from you – just might be true.

The silence between them was growing uncomfortable. Neither knew the other well enough to be able to assess their response. On the phone, there is no body language to give you those vital clues. No flicker of the eyes, no jerk of the chin, no drop of the gaze, no sudden scratching of the mouth or rubbing of the nose, no tightening of the lips and no hand stealing over your mouth, smothering your responses. Over the telephone, even the tone of your voice is muted, strained through the mouthpiece like tea leaves.

'I'll see her,' Claire said finally. 'I'll ask Rita to send her the next available new patient appointment. You can fax through the referral.'

No hurry, she was thinking. This is not an emergency. It should be easy to unravel, simple to know where the truth lies and what was simply the result of a disordered mind.

THREE

Wednesday, 17 June, 12.45 p.m.

Dr Sylas wasted no time. The fax came through forty-five minutes later, buzzing through the machine like an impatient hornet, anxious for liberation, for attention, and at the same time with a sting in its tail.

Which Rita was unaware of when she brought the pages through to Claire's office. 'Sounds interesting,' she said. She never could resist the temptation to steal a peep.

'Substitute interesting for troublesome,' Claire responded, her eyes on Rita's pleasingly plump figure, 'and I might just agree with you.'

She scanned the pages and was impressed. Give Dr Sylas credit. Considering the short time she'd had to compose the referral, she'd passed on a detailed history and covered the salient points.

Her eyes slid down the sheet. From the desk drawer, she drew out a highlighter, fixed her elbows and hunched over the pages, ready to give it total absorption, shutting out everything else.

Grant used to tease her about it. 'You know, Claire, I think I could walk in here stark-bollock naked and do the rumba right in front of you and you wouldn't even notice.'

At which she'd looked up, laughing into those brown eyes. 'Try me.'

She bent even lower over the A4 sheet of paper. Shut out even this and read.

Dear Dr Roget,

Thank you for accepting this rather concerning lady with her potentially damaging allegations.

Heather is a twenty-seven-year-old woman, married for eight years to her husband, Geoff. It appears, if not a happy marriage, at least it is peaceful. She was, in the past, she claims, physically abused by her father, who had a 'short fuse' and was 'very strict'. According to Heather, he believed in the biblical teachings: spare the rod and spoil the child. No sexual abuse has been reported. The abuse took the form of systematic beatings.

Claire underlined the last sentence, reached for her highlighter pen and continued to read.

She has one sister, Ruth. She has a brother, Robin, five years older, but he left home when she was nineteen and she claims she has had no contact with him since. He has, to all intents and purposes, disappeared. No one knows what happened to him. I understand the police were informed and he's officially listed as a missing person.

Ruth is two years younger than her sister and unmarried. The two girls are interdependent, possibly bonded by shared negative childhood experiences and the loss of their brother, whom they both claim to have adored. The sisters are quite devoted. Almost abnormally so, to the exclusion of others, including Geoff.

Heather's father, Bailey, is a pharmacist who trained in Eastern Europe. Her mother is English and worked part-time as a school dinner lady. Heather's mother, Winifred, appears to have had a very passive role in her three children's lives and was either unable or unwilling to intervene when their father punished them. 'She never spoke up or tried to stop him. She seemed to accept that this was the way of things,' Heather said to me once. 'Even when Dad brought out the strap or his belt or anything else that came to hand.'

Her mother was addicted to prescription drugs – possibly supplied by the father? Heather doesn't know. She has little contact with either parent now.

Eight years ago, Heather married Geoff Krimble, a man a few years older than her who had lived with his widowed mother. He was trained as an electrician but, due to a diagnosis of Tourette's, has had little work during their marriage. I can't see that there has been a formal diagnosis of this Tourette's, which he could have slapped on himself. He certainly has an intermittent problem with alcohol and occasional anti-social behaviour but has never been in prison. Heather's husband's patchy employment has meant fairly abject penury and a dependence on handouts and income support which has, as you know, recently been withdrawn or at least reduced.

Heather has had two previous pregnancies. Both, unfortunately, resulting in cot death.

Eliza, born 2010, died when she was six months old of a cot death.

Freddie born 2012, died at two months old, also a cot death.

Claire marked the passages with her highlighter pen before reading on. For the time being, she was wondering many things: how had the two deaths affected Heather Krimble's already damaged mental state? She read on.

Each time, late in the pregnancy, Heather had doubts about the parenthood of the baby. On both occasions, she claimed she was coerced into having sex with the father of the child. When each child was born she had prolonged periods of puerperal psychosis, which have been largely controlled in the community with neuroleptics (haloperidol) together with chlorpromazine for the anxiety. In both cases, she was treated by the community psychiatric team under the auspices of the community psychiatrist, Dr Laura Hodgkins, while Heather's husband supervised the children. When Freddie died at two months old, questions were raised as to whether it was possible that Heather might have been responsible for her children's deaths.

There was a thorough investigation but no cause for concern was found at post-mortem. It appears she was one of those unfortunates who are unlucky enough to have had two cot deaths.

For a brief sentence, Dagmar Sylas stepped out of her role as GP. *Perhaps the cot deaths have contributed to her unstable mental condition?*

But this, Claire mused, could not account for any abnormality surrounding Eliza's birth and her initial allegation. Only with Freddie.

Claire read on: *Each time Heather appeared to recover and this pregnancy has been straightforward, until at around the twenty-eighth week when she asked to be referred to Mr Tissot. Naturally I obliged and the appointment was sent a week or two later. Initially she was seen by a midwife but asked to see Mr Tissot in person. That appointment, as you know, came through for yesterday and he saw her. But now he's made me aware that she alleged that he, her obstetrician, was her lover and the father of the baby. I need not point out to you that to my knowledge Mr Tissot has only seen her on this one occasion.*

Claire lifted her chin and stared out of the window. Why, Charles? Why be so secretive? What have you got to hide?

She continued reading. *Quite naturally, he is refusing to see her again and has requested that Heather be referred to you for psychological assessment.*

With her tragic history of two cot deaths, she does need to be under a consultant obstetrician and the child at least seen by a neonatal paediatrician, but obviously, with these stories, Charles can't continue to see her himself, even with a chaperone.

She still needed more detail about Heather's previous allegations. The bald truth. Nothing hidden or wrapped up. And she wondered how significant it was that Charles had kept secret the fact that he had met Heather socially, even if it was just that once.

She started making notes in the margin.

Who saw her through her previous two pregnancies? Another obstetrician?

Speak to Laura Hodgkins.

Interview paediatrician and pathologist re. previous cot deaths.

Get DNA results of both babies for paternity tests?

Heather should be under another consultant but could that result either in further allegations or in these original allegations spreading to someone else?

Look into the two men she accused previously of having been the fathers of Eliza and Freddie. The two doomed children.

What was Geoff Krimble's take on all this?

What influence has her parents' treatment had on her?

She looked up for a moment, still thinking furiously. This was going to be a challenging case and, in view of the circumstances, it was going to need kid-glove handling. But some things were already beginning to niggle her. And big among these was: if Heather had only ever met Charles Tissot once and at a party, why had she picked on him? How much contact had she had with the men she claimed had fathered her two previous pregnancies? She stared around the room, trying to recapture the thought that had just flitted in and out of her mind like a butterfly passing a window. Then gave up. No good. It had gone. Back to the letter.

Dr Sylas concluded with: *I wonder if you would assess her and consider admitting her, particularly if you believe the newborn could be in danger during the puerperium. Do we need to involve social services? In view of Heather's precarious mental state and the two previous cot deaths, should we consider making the child a ward of court? As well as an assessment and possible treatment for the delusional state of mind. I feel that this time it might be more appropriate for her to be admitted rather than managed in the community.*

Many thanks

With only part of the story, the GP's mind was already made up? She'd mapped out the entire case? There was a P.S. which emphasized this viewpoint, handwritten this time. *Please help, I hate to see a colleague put in this dreadful position, particularly Charles.*

Which planted another small seed in Claire's constantly sceptical and enquiring mind. Just what was Dr Sylas's involvement here? Charles . . . not Mr Tissot? There was some familiarity here. And knowing his way with women, had Dagmar Sylas come under his spell? Lost her objectivity?

She read the letter through three times, each time finding another point to highlight with her fluorescent pen so the final version looked more like a child's colouring book than a serious referral letter. Then she wandered along the corridor to Rita's office and asked her to send Heather Krimble the next available new-patient appointment. She was curious. What would she be like?

And it was as she was talking to her secretary that she realized what it was that was bugging her.

What had Charles Tissot said? Ruth, Heather's sister, worked for one of his colleagues. She scanned the letter again.

No mention of that one very significant fact here, that there was this prior connection, so important that it loomed large in her own mind. *Why not?*

The answer swam into view.

Because Charles Tissot, cunning little snake as he was, must have known it would come out at some point but he had, presumably deliberately, kept it back from the GP, hoping it would stay hidden? Some hope. Claire made a face to herself. On a scale of 1–10, that was a '1'.

She felt increasingly uncomfortable as she stepped across the shifting ice, listening out for that fateful, telling crack. Just because something couldn't be proved to be a lie or an omission, deliberate or accidental, it did not necessarily lead back to the truth. And that was what this case was all about, wasn't it? Truth and lies. And underpinning all this? A tangled web of professional loyalty and delusion, almost backed up by half truths. Into the pot she threw the supporting evidence of the sister, a sister whose loyalty was unquestioned. Unlike Heather, she had no history of mental pathology so the truth would have to be carefully unpicked.

With an effort, she pushed the fax and the new referral to one side. For now. Heather Krimble was not, literally speaking, one of her patients yet.

Others were. It was time to return to her current role and the questions she needed to respond to concerning her current caseload, the usual mixed bag of inpatient unsolvables.

What happens to an elderly schizophrenic when he develops dementia?

How do you deal with a fourteen-year-old girl who, at five-and-a-half stone, is convinced she is morbidly obese?

What happens to a young man with paranoid schizophrenia when his medication is stopped by a new, young and enthusiastic but misguided GP?

How do you protect the parents of a psychopath with severe personality problems who is not above inventing voices that order him to torture first his father and then his mother before turning on his sister?

And the two problems that were currently boring holes in her head.

Problem 1: Arthur Connolly.

Arthur's story was a sad one but not uncommon. His wife, Lindsay, had controlled every single tiny, dark corner of his life: control of money (he had no access to their joint bank account, had no cheque book and didn't even have a debit card or know their PIN), what job he did (shelf-stacker in the local B&Q), what hours he worked (anything that was going), what he ate, what he wore (generally ill-fitting suits that looked as though they came from a charity shop), what he watched on television (same as her: soaps, soaps and more soaps). The areas of Arthur's wife's control were endless: whether they had children (in this case just the one son, on whom Lindsay lavished all the devotion Arthur missed out on), what they did at weekends (she – shopping, he – DIY, polishing windows, ironing). And the more he did the more his wife despised him. Her control and disdain had spread like a virus, infecting their son, Saul, who also despised his father. Lindsay's rules even extended to the personal, as in when and how often Arthur took a bath (Saturday nights). And had a shower (every other day). Claire was only surprised Lindsay Connolly hadn't extended this control to how often Arthur opened his bowels. It appeared that Lindsay's husband had lost the ability to choose, to strike out on his own. Arthur made no decisions of his own.

Except one. And that only because Lindsay hadn't seen it coming.

In the months before the attack, Arthur had become increasingly unhappy and anxious. According to him, the pressure had built up very, very slowly over the years on this meek, obliging man with zero self-esteem. However hard he'd tried, it had not always been possible to please Lindsay, and when he had failed she had expressed her dissatisfaction with fury. She would punish him, slap him, belittle him in front of others and deprive him of his one pleasure in life: tobacco. Missing his cigarettes, the anxiety he had suffered had compounded, mingled with resentment, festering like a boil, angry, red and swollen, until one day it had burst in a cloud of red. Arthur had grabbed a kitchen knife and stabbed his wife in the chest four times, puncturing the lung three times and bouncing off the sternum on the fourth attempt but missing all the major blood vessels and the heart, which was a miracle. She might not have survived had a neighbour not heard the commotion and picked up on the strange fact that it wasn't just Lindsay's voice. There had been another. He said afterwards he couldn't work out who was doing the shouting back. Surely it couldn't be Arthur? Arthur who had no voice?

Bemused, the neighbour had knocked on the back door and taken in the bloody scenario. He had burst through and taken the knife from Arthur's hand. 'Gave it up like a baby,' he'd said later to the police. It had been the disarmed Arthur who had called 999 confessing to having stabbed his wife, which was one reason he had ended up at Greatbach rather than HMP Dovegate, one of the nearest remand prisons. The other reason was that his defence lawyer had raised the issue of Arthur Connolly's mental state.

And so, Claire had become involved.

She had decided to keep him here at Greatbach, not in the secure ward but loosely under lock and key, as the charge was GBH, the CPS having bargained with the police to reduce it from attempted murder. Arthur was lucky, the SIO said, not to be up on a charge of actual murder. Arthur had lifted his eyes to the detective and then dropped them again.

'No comment,' he'd said.

The problem for Claire was that as Arthur had acquired the habit of silence, keeping his thoughts and ideas firmly to himself, his mind and reasoning were a spiral proving difficult to unwind.

Claire heaved out another sigh as she moved along the corridor, passing another door, another patient here for assessment. But this person was someone for whom she had a little less sympathy.

Problem 2: Riley Finch.

Riley was a twenty-eight-year-old woman who had her own personal gay mantra: *I can have anything I want.* Which had morphed into a more petulant phrase: *Why shouldn't I have what I want?* But because Riley's tastes were for the upper end of the designer market, clothes, household goods and toiletries, combined with the fact that she worked on a zero-hours contract in an off-licence, with wages that scraped the bottom of the minimum wage barrel, her desires could only be fulfilled by shoplifting, for which she had had numerous previous arrests.

But that wasn't why Riley had been pushed Claire's way.

Goods were one thing. They led to fines and non-custodial sentences. But the latest item on Riley's shopping list had been a baby. Riley wanted a baby. And, as usual, she'd applied her tried-and-tested mantra. *If I want one, why shouldn't I have one? Other people do. So why not me?*

And when that hadn't happened for various reasons, the mantra had morphed into: *If I can't have a baby, why should someone else?*

That was when the real trouble had started.

Riley had had no current partner and she was far too particular and careful of the baby's parentage (*I want a perfect, blonde, blue-eyed, gorgeous little thing*) to risk a one-night stand. The one thing Claire had found in her favour was that not anyone would do to have casual sex with. She was very particular about not contracting any sexually transmitted diseases. The very words made her small frame shudder.

Another obstacle in Riley's quest was that men, Claire reflected, had proved surprisingly perceptive of her cold charm and steered clear of her even though Riley was, actually, an attractive redhead with delicate features, pale skin and witchy green eyes. Perhaps it was the temper that matched her hair colour and sprang as hot, dangerous and unexpected as a tropical storm. Or the selfish coldness at her heart which turned them away. But without a man Riley had to be resourceful and find another way of acquiring this blonde, blue-eyed baby. Besides . . . waiting nine months for what Riley wanted was not exactly on her agenda. She was quite likely to have got bored with pregnancy halfway through and decided to terminate it. Much easier to pinch the result of someone else's labour. Of course, to someone of Riley's particular morals, this was as easy as acquiring a Calvin Klein jacket, a Zandra Rhodes gown or Louboutin shoes. And so, just like before, she trotted around the shops, found a target, waited for an opportunity and stole one.

Simple. Except, fairly obviously, it was not.

Riley was arrested two days later, still trotting around The Potteries Shopping Centre, still doing her own brand of shopping which involved no money, the baby asleep in her arms. She hadn't got around to nicking a pram. Yet. The child had been returned to its distraught mother and Riley had been put on remand and referred to Claire for a psychological assessment.

Not very hard to do.

A first-year medical student with the barest knowledge of psychiatry could have arrived at the diagnosis. Claire had quickly decided

Riley was, to put it bluntly, a psychopath. You could call it a dissociative disorder. You could say she was antisocial, amoral or a
sociopath. Call it what you liked, but the result was the same. Riley's
mantra would remain firmly in place for the rest of her days. She
would always be a danger to society. Not in the way that she would
blast through a restaurant full of people shooting to kill, but she
would always lie, steal, take what wasn't hers if she wanted to. She
wasn't even an interesting case as she rarely moved on from her
simple code. *Why shouldn't I have what I want? Why should someone
else have it? If I want it, I can have it.*

Time to meet the psychopath.

Claire pushed open the door.

FOUR

R iley was lying on the bed, fingers flicking through a magazine,
eyes watching the television in the way that Riley did everything, with a sort of scornful half interest. Her gaze shifted
and flickered over Claire, but there was no welcoming smile. Riley
recognized the psychiatrist as an adversary. And so, she regarded her
with curiosity mixed with dislike, contempt and insolence. Underneath
that, she was guarded and watchful. Claire was perfectly aware that
her patient was sizing her up, wondering how she could manoeuvre
her into helping her achieve the best outcome for her: freedom. All
Riley wanted was to get out and back on the streets to fill her larder
and her wardrobe with anything else she wanted.

'Hello, Riley.'

The girl acknowledged the greeting with a wary staccato nod
before returning her attention to her magazine.

Riley was slightly built with a cute spattering of freckles over her
face and forearms. She had a trick of turning her head and lowering
her eyes to a shy, modest angle which gave her the air of an innocent,
forties' child star. She recognized a threat when confronted with one
and knew full well that Claire was a worthy adversary who stood
firmly between her and her desired freedom. She was equally aware
of the psychiatrist's influence and powers. Riley had considered her
predicament from all angles and come to the conclusion that the best

thing would be to try and win her psychiatrist over. And so now she smiled and laid her magazine down.

Claire sat down in an easy chair near the window, so the light fell on Riley's face. Two extra wards had been added to Greatbach in the sixties with the result that a wall was less than three feet away from the window. So instead of a landscape view you looked over an office, secretaries typing, a coffee machine. No one looked back at them. It was as though they were invisible, as insubstantial as ghosts. Riley's eyes followed hers, flickering over the brickwork, eyes glancing off the absorbed workers.

Claire studied her patient. Riley's make-up was skilfully applied: black eyeliner, mascaraed long lashes, thick pink lipstick on a rosebud mouth. She had been over-lavish with the perfume. But then, to her even expensive perfume would have been extremely cheap. Free, in fact. She was wearing tight-fitting jeans and a large, sloppy T-shirt, white with a spatter of small gold stars over one shoulder. Her feet were bare, her toenails painted the exact same colour pink as her lipstick. She looked like so many of her age group, the twentysomethings – streetwise, casual, alert, wary, expensive clothes, designer goods manufactured specifically for this discerning and particular market.

She did not look a danger. But Claire had to remind herself that this girl's actions had left havoc in her wake. The mother of the eight-day-old newborn had been distraught for the dreadful two days it had taken the police to identify and locate the woman a couple had described. The mundane details were much more poignant than the dramatic shrieking newspaper headlines: *Baby abducted on Mother's First Outing*; *Infant Snatched*, etc., etc.

The picture which took up most of the front page of the tabloids must have been taken immediately post-delivery. It showed a knackered Julie Alexander, still in labour-ward shift, holding an unmistakable newborn coated in vernix and blood. Six days later, mother and baby had been separated by more than a cord clamp.

Following the abduction, twenty-two-year-old Julie Alexander had sat at home, almost too numb to tearfully, optimistically express her breast milk every four hours day and night in the hope that her baby was still alive, would be returned and resume its place on her nipple. It had been her first trip out with her tiny baby. And it would be her last for almost a year. She would stay behind her front door, shopping done by family, friends and the Internet, baby bolted to her arms. The outside world had suddenly assumed the hostility and danger of a war zone. Because, like the shoppers in those Syrian markets, when horror had struck, Julie had been in familiar territory, at a convenience store she had visited almost every day for years.

And yet, she had not been safe.

Her last moment of peace had been as she had proudly wheeled the pram down to the store, strangers peering in and admiring baby Imogen on her first trip out. Not wanting to wake the infant, Julie had nipped inside, her eyes straying all the time back to the door. *For a second.* That was all it had taken. The pram *was* there but the baby was not. To add to her guilt, she hadn't even noticed until she had left the shop, because the cover was in order. Guiltily, afterwards, she would recall initial relief that Imogen was quiet at last, not crying. Seconds later, she had realized the baby was not there. Panicking, she had lifted the cover and searched beneath the sheets; even, stupidly, looked up and down the street. No baby. She had screamed and then fainted. Hit the floor while a crowd gathered around. Claire had read through the account. Not a mother herself, she could still imagine the poor woman's reaction, exhausted from the birth and the responsibility of looking after a new baby. That would have been worst of all. The heaviest burden – guilt. The word *neglect* hovering in the air like an infection. The finger-waggers were judgmental. She *should* have taken more care. She *shouldn't* have left the baby outside the shop. She *shouldn't* have taken her eyes off it. Not even for a second. That had been her furious partner's response. She should have kept a better watch on *their baby*.

Even in her grief and guilt, the phrase *their baby* had registered. So, for the first time, he wanted to be part of it?

Claire had known, as she had read through the report, what the fallout from Riley's crime would be. A traumatized mother, and trailing behind the unforgiving would be the lefties, the excusers, the people who always looked for a reason, who would say poor Riley with no baby of her own.

The fallout would continue. Julie Alexander would not be taking her new baby to the shops any more. There would be angry exchanges between her and her partner, he accusatory and she defensive. She would wake at night and relive this dreadful moment, see the empty pram again and again and again. And when her child had children of their own, she would still relive these moments and apply these neuroticisms a generation on.

It had been luck that the baby had been recovered without harm. Riley soon became bored with her acquisitions. Dresses, handbags, perfume, make-up, shoes, babies. Discarded. Chucked in the bin or stuffed in a black bin liner and abandoned outside the charity shop. Ill-gotten gains could soon be replaced. Why should a baby be anything different? Someone will find it and want it. Leave it outside a place where people care – hospital, medical centre, charity shop.

What would Imogen's fate have been when Riley had, inevitably, gotten fed up with the crying, the feeds, the dirty nappies? The sheer boring, fatiguing slog that is a new baby?

It had been pure luck that Imogen, only six days old, had been found before it was too late. Riley had no conscience about the things she had stolen, the people she had cheated, the woman whose child she had just taken.

That was her condition. And on the other side? The side of right and fairness and the law?

The police had flooded the entire area within minutes. They had swiftly collated witness statements and looked at the CCTV helpfully installed to watch the Co-op customers' comings and goings. They watched the woman lift the baby from the pram and replace the cover. But the angle was poor. They saw the baby clearly enough but only the top of the abductor's head. Then along came help in the form of an elderly couple strolling down towards the Co-op themselves, who had proved to have wonderful memories. They remembered. Oh, yes, they remembered: a slim woman in tight jeans and a blue fleece with a cigarette burn near the pocket clutching a tiny baby to her as she walked quickly up the street.

They had actually talked about it, hoping that she would not smoke when she was with the baby. Their tutting over this was what had led the police to such an early and satisfactory conclusion.

Then came a bit more luck.

Once this description was circulated to the team, one of the Specials, a young woman called Maud, had started to put two and two together. She too had had contact with a young woman only a week ago. She remembered the tight jeans and the blue fleece with a cigarette burn near the pocket. The girl had been lighting up in the doorway of Lewis's department store. She remembered the girl particularly because of the glare the woman had given her when she had remonstrated, heavy with hostility and hate. It had spooked her. And she remembered the name.

Riley Finch. A name well known to all the police who worked the Hanley area, particularly the officers who patrolled The Potteries Shopping Centre.

And so, Riley was eventually apprehended and the baby returned to its mother.

In fact, Baby Imogen would have been found earlier but for one fact: Riley had not returned to her own flat but decamped to a 'friend's'. A friend who appeared to swallow the fable that Riley was looking after the baby 'for a friend'. No name – simply 'a friend'.

But behind the scenes, the police were inching closer. The Special, Maud Stevenson, had passed on the information about the pretty little redhead with a killer stare. Riley's flat was searched. Without result.

They'd cast their net wider to trawl in her known associates, by which time headlines were spreading faster than a virus, reaching more people than an epidemic: *Midlands Today,* Twitter, Facebook, text message and any other method by which news can be spread. But the clincher was the £10,000 reward put up by a local billionaire. The 'friend' fancied the £10,000 reward so rang Crimestoppers, and within an hour Baby Imogen was safely back where she belonged, on her mother's luckily still-lactating breast.

When apprehended, Riley had not quite managed to act out remorse. Instead, rather grumpily, she had complained that babies were not all they were cracked up to be and that she had been getting bored with her. 'Bloody smelly thing and never stops bawling,' she'd said, opening her eyes wide for her final hit. 'Even at night.'

Many mums might have tossed their own comment in. *Welcome to the real world, Riley Finch.*

But of course, Riley didn't live in the real world. She lived in a place of her own manufacture. A place filled with provisions, designer luxury and crime without punishment, a world where nothing cost anything. A place where she had absolutely everything she wanted.

A substitute real world.

Riley's world.

And it was this world that Claire needed to explore if she was to convince the courts of the danger of Riley's condition.

She knew that, in one way, Riley had been telling the truth. To take the child had been an impulsive act. She hadn't gone out that morning to steal a baby. The opportunity had presented itself and, like an expensive handbag left on show, she had simply reached out and taken it. She hadn't prepared for the abduction with feeds, nappies and bottles – even a cot. Nothing practical, although Riley wasn't a great one for detail. Or planning ahead. It had been a spur-of-the-moment decision. Riley didn't do consequences. She would soon have needed to move on to something new.

Claire wanted her put away for a very long time but she doubted she would ever persuade a judge and jury to recognize the true threat that Riley's attitude posed. To see her as she saw her – a time bomb ready primed. With all this in her mind, Claire began with the blandest of questions. 'How are you today, Riley?'

The girl shrugged. 'Same as ever. Wondering when I'm going to get out of here.' There was a certain amount of indignation tucked into her voice.

Riley emphasized her eyes with black eyeliner which curved upwards at the outer edge. It gave her the look of a clever cat.

'I think you understand that we have concerns about the reasons why you took Imogen.'

Riley shrugged. 'Just wanted a baby,' she said, stifling a yawn, already disinterested. She'd been here before.

'Did you consider how her mother might feel?'

Riley's shoulders jerked and her head turned. For a moment, Claire could see the woman behind the facade. Riley Finch was genuinely puzzled, uncertain how to answer this simple question. Why on earth should *she* be considering the baby's mother? She just didn't get it.

She was devoid of empathy.

Claire knew the police and the CPS would like it better if she made this uncomplicated for them, if she asserted that Riley just wanted a baby, that her mind was temporarily disturbed and they could let her off the hook, send her home with a smacked hand. But Claire knew that was not the case. The way Riley had acted was not a temporary disturbance but a permanent fixture. This was who she was. It defined her. Riley Finch was, in her opinion, likely to reoffend. But what this reoffence might be was anybody's guess. It all depended on what she saw, what she wanted. But if what she still wanted was another baby, one day the outcome might not be so happy. Rather than smoothing over the cracks, Claire was determined to expose the true danger that currently lay dormant because she was being watched as an inpatient but which would, one day, cause real and even more permanent harm. Behind Riley's sweet countenance was something capable of true evil. So, ignoring the fact that Riley had not answered her question, she continued probing. 'You see, Riley, we worry that you might do the same sort of thing again.'

Riley sat up, tucked her T-shirt around her legs. She knew her lines all right. 'But I won't take another baby,' she said. 'They stink. They bawl. They want feeds.' Her eyes fixed on Claire's as she held her palms out to underline her next injured phrase. 'Like all the time. Night and day.'

This was the truth. Riley *had* tried having a baby. The experience hadn't pleased her. She might not repeat *that* performance. But what next?

Claire tried again, scratching a little deeper below the surface. What was the depth of Riley's detachment from society? She inserted a probe.

'How do you think Imogen's mother felt when she peered into the pram and her baby was missing?'

Riley looked bored. 'I don't know, do I? I mean, I haven't *got* a baby.' She paused. 'Any more.'

Thank God.

'What were you going to do with the baby?'

Riley stared at her. More confusion. 'Do?'

'Yes. Do. In the end. Keep her for ever? Have her for a test period then give her back?' Claire raised her voice a little, challenging her patient. 'What were you going to *do* with her?'

Riley was not stupid but she was stumped by this question. Again, she didn't know how to answer it. She hadn't thought that far ahead.

'I . . . I think,' she said finally, 'that I just wanted to try it out.'

Like a test drive?

Claire could have felt angry but that was not her job. Her job was to explore what Riley was likely to do next. Where the danger lay. And advise to prevent further harm.

'What were you going to do with her when you got bored with her?' she asked. This was the question she needed answering. This was the point of today's interview. How far did Riley's disdain for anyone else's feelings go? Would Imogen have ended up in a black plastic sack outside a charity shop? Would she have been dumped in a wheelie bin? Left on the side of the road? Abandoned?

Riley shrugged; her eyes flickered away.

Half an hour later, the interview was over. Time to make her assessment. Claire knew what the criminal justice system was like. She couldn't say that Riley should be incarcerated for the rest of her life. She probably wouldn't abduct a baby again. At least, that was Claire's judgement. But Riley would commit *other* offences that might have more serious consequences. Trouble was who knew what these might be?

She wrote her report knowing Riley Finch would go free. Free to do whatever. The law was not a sledgehammer.

The diagnosis here wasn't the problem. That was the easy bit. Riley Finch was a sociopath. A psychopath. Treatment wouldn't work. She might grow out of it – or become less of a danger to the general public. But Riley didn't really need a custodial sentence. It would achieve nothing. Her psychopathy was part of who and what she was, just as her red hair and sprinkling of freckles was also part of who she was. In her mind, she had done nothing wrong. Simply borrowed a baby. And it had been given back. No lasting harm done.

Her real fury was vented towards 'the friend' who had collected 'ten fucking grand'.

Claire dictated her report knowing that, however she worded it, Riley would be discharged. And there would be no custodial sentence. She would be free to commit whatever felon she felt like.

Claire left the ward.

FIVE

Wednesday, 17 June, 2.45 p.m.

Back in her office, a Post-it note in Rita's writing had been stuck to the front of her diary.

I've made an appointment for Heather Krimble on Friday. You had a gap in your clinic and a cancellation. I rang her and she's confirmed. R. X

So she had Arthur Connolly, Riley Finch and now another to

add to her motley collection. Heather Krimble, whom she would soon be meeting. In another two days, she would be tackling this almighty mess. She upgraded it to a dangerous mess for Mr Charles Tissot. There were plenty of warnings here that everything about this case had shifting sands. It might not be quite as straightforward as it had seemed. The GP hadn't referred her patient to her until prodded by Charles, who had plenty of reasons for wanting Heather's claims to be declared a fantasy, a symptom of psychosis. Questions were building up in her mind. It was in Charles's interest for Heather's story to be disbelieved from the start. And the previous allegations heaped doubt on any story Heather span. On top of that, Dr Sylas appeared to have personal admiration for the obstetrician. She hadn't questioned the request for a referral to her instead of to Laura Hodgkins again, so why had she escalated Heather's case from community to Greatbach? Purely because of the professional allegation? Had Charles told her that he had met her socially even if it was only on that one occasion? Had Heather mentioned to her GP that she'd met him, briefly, at a party? How well did Charles actually remember Heather from that party? How brushing or brief had their encounter been that night? Was Dr Sylas aware that Heather's sister worked for one of Charles's colleagues?

Four people were involved here: Heather, her sister, the GP and Charles Tissot.

She was the fifth.

The question was who knew what? Claire's thoughts chased each other round and round.

To unravel the claims and counter-claims, Claire knew she would need to plan her approach and assess her patient without prejudice. And to do that she had to begin with Heather's own version; not Dr Sylas's or from Charles, but the one from the patient herself.

There was another person to whom she could turn. Dr Laura Hodgkins, the community psychiatrist, who had dealt with Heather during her two previous pregnancies. There were distinct advantages here. Laura was a colleague who would use the same language as her and have the same perspective, unclouded by any fuzzy memory from years before.

Claire knew her vaguely – their paths had crossed on more than one occasion – and she had been impressed with Laura's competence, particularly managing difficult cases, elderly schizophrenic patients, patients with severe bipolar disorder and two or three cases of profound depression. All managed in the community? That was a challenge. And a risk.

On a couple of occasions, Laura had asked her to admit a patient to Greatbach and she had obliged. They didn't exactly work together – their roles were different. Managing a patient in the community as opposed to admitting them was a different skill. But each had a healthy respect for the part the other played, where they overlapped and how they could assist one another. So Claire was looking forward to an intelligent and impartial viewpoint. But she was in for a disappointment. When she rang the consultant's secretary, Faye, she was told that Dr Hodgkins was 'off sick'.

'Nothing serious, I hope?'

Laura Hodgkins was about forty. A bit young to have a serious illness . . . But then medicine, pathology, diagnoses, prognoses were all fickle entities, choosing their victims at random.

'I can't really tell you, Doctor Roget.' Even more concerning was that Claire could hear a catch in the secretary's voice. Shit. What was going on?

She tried another tack. 'Do you know when she'll be back?'

This time she could definitely hear the upset in Faye Gardener's voice more clearly. Claire was alarmed now. She felt concern for her colleague's health but she also needed Laura Hodgkins' notes on Heather. It was a difficult enough case without working blind. She needed the full history. And her colleague's insight.

Faye pulled herself together, clearing her throat. 'A locum is covering her work,' she said, her voice struggling to brighten. 'He's an Aussie. You'll like him, Claire. He's competent. He's different. And he's fun.'

But he doesn't know the patient was Claire's first thought.

She blew out her cheeks in exasperation. What she wanted was a clear, concise and truthful history of a patient's previous medical condition. Not bloody fun.

She tried to console herself. He might not know the patient but he would have access to Laura's notes. It would have to do. She just had to hope that all of Laura's observations had been recorded. But a locum covering such important work? So the holes in the NHS are patched and covered over, but they are still holes. Bits missing, gaps in histories, absences of knowledge.

'Was it anything really important?' Faye was doing her best to assist.

Claire hesitated. 'I need to discuss a patient of Laura's.'

'Which patient?'

'A Heather Krimble.'

'Oh?' There was definite concern.

'Yes.'

'I remember Mrs Krimble. A troubled soul,' Faye said. 'She's come your way?'

'Yeah.' Claire couldn't possibly explain the route which had dumped Mrs Krimble at her back door.

'Well, good luck with that one. I'll fish her notes out and ask Doctor Bracknell to take a look, shall I?'

But the phrase had stuck with Claire. *How much good luck exactly?*

'That would be brilliant. Just tell him she's now six months pregnant and making similar allegations to the ones made in her two previous pregnancies. I'm seeing her in my clinic on Friday to assess her mental state because of the potential seriousness of her current allegations.' There was no need to be specific.

'Not again.'

'I'm afraid so. I'm considering admitting her to Greatbach and could do with her past history to give me some perspective on her present condition.'

'OK. It's a pity Laura isn't here.'

Too right.

'I'll get her notes together and have Doctor Bracknell get in touch with you when he's read through them, shall I?'

'Yes, please. I'll be interested to hear his take on all this.'

'OK.' She didn't sound curious, which was good. It almost certainly meant that the word hadn't filtered through to her. For all its strict rules on confidentiality, gossip and tragedy spread like wildfire through the medical profession. No one was quite sure how it did when all were sworn to secrecy. It just happened. Through nods and winks like semaphore, leaked test results and the availability of scans and X-rays to anyone with the right password.

'And Faye, give Doctor Hodgkins my regards, will you? Wish her a speedy recovery.'

'I will.' *Sniff.* 'Thanks.'

Claire put the phone down. So she would have to be patient,

work blind with one arm tied behind her back and wait for this
Aussie locum, Dr Bracknell, to make contact.

In the meantime, Claire returned to another of her tricky patients.

Arthur Connolly. She was trying to tease out a little more of
his mental turmoil through the years. His case was up for review
in the following weeks and she wanted to assess him more thoroughly. The news on his wife, Lindsay, was good, in a way. She
had made a reasonable recovery from her husband's assault and
was currently back in the marital home, seething, no doubt, at the
harm her meek and docile husband had wreaked.

Resisting a smile, Claire made her way to Arthur's room.

He even *looked* the part of an abused and dominated husband.
He was short and slight with wispy pale brown hair and an unfortunately bristly, sandy-coloured moustache that did little to suggest
masculinity. He had a soft voice too and tended to look at the
floor when he was speaking, rather than at the person he was
talking to, as though he had no confidence in his own words. He
was a born victim.

He also had the unfortunate habit of rubbing his fingers together
while he spoke, accompanying his words with the rasp of dry skin.
A permanently apologetic look, eyebrows raised, forehead crinkled
and bent shoulders completed the picture. For the life of her, Claire
could not imagine him knifing Lindsay Connolly, who was a large
woman, plump to the point of obesity, with heavy, sagging breasts
which had been pierced by the knife. Claire had interviewed
Lindsay twice – once while she was still in hospital, the other
after she had been discharged to find out whether Arthur had shown
any sign that his tolerance was about to snap.

Lindsay's eyes had bulged with fury and self-righteousness.
'Just sat there, he was. Saying nothing.' She couldn't resist tucking
in a bit of spite. 'As usual. I was just telling him . . .' At that she
had gasped for air and pressed her oxygen mask to her face. 'I
was just telling him he'd spilt some coffee on the kitchen work
surface and he'd better wipe it up.' She coughed theatrically,
clutched her chest, groaned and gasped again. 'What's the problem
with that? I tell you, Doctor. After all I've done for him. The man
is mad. I cannot believe I have put up with him for all these years.
The man is mad,' she'd repeated.

Claire didn't think so. His patience had simply slipped.

She had visited Lindsay Connolly a second time at home and

received mostly the same response, but this time firmer. 'I'm not having him back, Doctor. Saul says I'm not to have him in the house again. Not ever. I want to see him go to prison. He nearly killed me, Doctor. I was nearly done for.' And behind the bravado, Claire had read real fright. Lindsay was used to being in control. Not a victim.

Lindsay had continued in the same injured voice. 'I don't understand why he did it. He wasn't strong and he had no direction. I had to tell him what to do, where to go, things like that. He wouldn't have known for himself. Not able to make decisions.' And in sudden viciousness, 'Gormless,' she'd spat out. 'Gormless. That's what he is. If I had him here I'd tell him, all right.'

Lindsay, it appeared, had not learned her lesson. And so Arthur would continue to be a danger – to his wife.

Her main reason for meeting up with Mrs Connolly had been to learn a bit more about their marriage pre-assault. Whether Arthur had shown any sign that he was about to rise up tall, like some monster from the deep. Had there been any build-up? Any planning in his actions?

When she'd put this to Lindsay, she had spent some time thinking about it before shaking her head, still bemused and unsettled by the turn of events. 'Nah,' she'd said. 'He was just sittin' there quiet as a mouse, looking at the floor.' She'd rolled her eyes. 'Like he *always does*. I told him. Arthur, I said, you've spilt some coffee. Now you go wipe it up. Then I follow him into the kitchen . . .' she'd tightened her mouth, '. . . to check on him and make myself a cup of tea, and he hadn't even picked up the dishcloth. "Arthur," I says, "you can see the mess you've made, now you go and wipe it up and be quick about it." But he didn't go to the sink. He walked towards the corner of the kitchen with this funny look in his eye, and before I knew where I was he's grabbing the bloody knife out of the block. "Arthur," I said, "what on earth do you think you are doin'?" Next thing he's sticking it in me, his eyes blood red like a madman.' Her own eyes were wide with disbelief. The shock was making her voice shake. Lindsay genuinely hadn't been able to believe what was happening.

'Blood everywhere,' she said, grabbing for the oxygen mask again, snorting in a noisy, panicky breath. 'I felt it go in, Doctor.' Claire could read the terror, the shock, the incredulity. 'I tried to get him to hear me, to scream out, *Stop!*, but he doesn't. Instead, he does it again. And again.' She clamped the oxygen mask tight over her face and took some deep breaths before continuing. 'I can't have him back, Doctor. He's not right in the head. Saul says if I had him back he'd just do the same again so I must never have him back.'

And that, Claire was thinking as she sat opposite the quiet, meek man that was Arthur Connolly, was what she was charged with ascertaining. Was Arthur 'right in the head'?

She smiled at him, ignoring the bristly moustache, the rasp of dry skin as his fingers rubbed together nervously. It was difficult not to feel pity for the man, not to say out loud, *Wrong wife, Arthur. Bad choice.*

Married to someone no more assertive than him, he might have had a happy life. Instead . . .

She substituted her thoughts for the psychiatrists' bland opening, 'How are you today, Arthur?'

In the weeks he'd been an inpatient, Arthur had been learning to trust her. Slowly.

He met her eyes and responded formally. 'I'm all right, thank you, Doctor.'

His voice was low and polite. His eyes immediately dropped back to the ground.

'You understand that we need to decide what to do with you?'

His nod was jerky, shoulders stiff. 'Yes.' The whisper was soft.

'What was in your mind when you followed Lindsay into the kitchen, Arthur? What were you thinking?'

'I—' He was struggling. 'I – I wasn't thinking anything.'

She couldn't leave it at that. 'You mean your mind was blank?'

He frowned. 'No,' he said, as though he was just discovering this. 'No. It wasn't a blank. I thought . . . I was thinking.' He tried again. 'I thought. I thought . . . I'd had enough.' The quiet words belied the action that had followed. Four stab wounds with an eight-inch blade. *Four.*

'When you picked up the knife, what were you planning to do with it?'

Arthur drew in a long, irritated breath. 'I didn't *know* it was a knife.'

A knife block that, according to Lindsay via the police, was always there? Claire could have asked what he had thought was in his hand but she didn't. She wanted Arthur to volunteer this information.

'I *didn't know* what it was,' he repeated. 'I just wanted her to stop being so . . .' he was fumbling for the word, '. . . nasty.'

'What was she saying to you? Can you remember?' She was always doing this, throwing him lifelines. But Arthur Connolly never picked them up. 'What was she saying to you?'

He looked at her then, and in that look was a weight of trouble. 'Telling me off,' he said, calm now. 'She was always finding something I'd not done right. Always telling me I'd done something wrong. Always angry with me.'

She had heard these words before. 'Why was she always angry with you?'

He gave a long, slow, thoughtful blink. 'I did tend towards clumsiness,' he said. 'My mother told me . . .' A pathetic attempt at a smile. 'I was born clumsy.'

'Oh?'

He nodded. 'And she were right. With me it obviously was so.'

She tried, gently, to draw him back to that moment. 'What happened then?'

'Lindsay asked me what I thought I was doing. I think I already had the knife in my hand by then. I think I didn't answer.'

It was a hollow attempt at bravado.

'So what *did* you say?'

'I wanted to say *just picking up the dishcloth from the sink*.' He looked pleased with himself at this clever invention. 'But I didn't get to say it. I tried to push her away but, of course, I had the knife in my hand and . . . There was blood.' He looked shifty, somehow. 'She were screaming.'

If there had been just one stab wound, Arthur might not have faced a charge of attempted murder. He might have just crawled under the radar with the fable, *I just wanted to push her away*. Not realizing what was in his hand. But there had been four stab wounds. Each one hitting deep; hitting home. He had struck again and again.

His eyes met hers and he nodded, knowing she was waiting for that explanation. 'I knew she wouldn't let it rest. I wanted her to stop making me feel so awful, Doctor.'

His pale eyes were pleading with her.

Temporary insanity would do fine for a diagnosis but that wasn't the end of the issue. It was just the beginning. What would happen to Arthur? A prison sentence for such a timid man would be hell.

And then where? What would happen the next time he met a situation he couldn't deal with? He couldn't fight, at least, not in a confident way. He could only explode when the pressure had built up sufficiently. Would he then be a danger to someone else? Her job was to protect the public.

She knew he wasn't wicked. He wasn't evil. But he was damaged. And she wasn't ready to release him to the authorities, although she knew she had already made up her mind.

She tried to flush him out. 'Lindsay has said you can't go home,' she said. 'And I understand your son, Saul, is in agreement with that.'

His eyes lifted for a moment and she saw a flash of red. He said nothing.

She needed to make him understand. 'She could have died, you know, and then you would have been up on a charge of murder.'

Something a little more cognisant passed across his face. He hadn't finished fighting yet. 'It's my house,' he objected. 'I paid for it.'

'That's something that will have to be decided through the courts and your solicitors.' She felt he still hadn't understood. Not fully. She needed to make him understand so addressed him directly. 'Arthur, you know you will almost certainly have a prison sentence once I've completed my assessment.'

Fight over, he nodded and then looked up, a brightness in his eyes, hope not quite faded. 'Maybe Saul will come to visit me?'

I wouldn't hold your breath.

He followed this up with, 'Has Lindsay forgiven me?'

There was no response to this except, 'I don't know, Arthur.' She felt compelled to add, 'But I wouldn't hold out a lot of hope. She was badly hurt, you know.'

She thought he had absorbed this quite rationally, until he added hopefully, 'I've written her a get-well card. Will that help, do you think?'

Her response was muted by the sharp summons of her bleep.

SIX

The bleep was from Rita's number and, when she connected, she was told that Dr Bracknell was waiting on the line to speak to her about Heather Krimble.

His response to her greeting was a jaunty, 'Hi,' his antipodean accent audible even in that one brief syllable.

He dived straight in. 'I understand that you need some details on a patient of Laura's, a Mrs Heather Krimble?'

'That's right. She's been referred to me by her GP. Thirty-two weeks pregnant. She's making a serious allegation against her obstetrician, and I understand this is not the first time.'

'That's right,' he said. 'I've been looking through her notes. She has quite a history of some very . . . imaginative . . . pregnancies.'

Claire smiled. His way of putting things made the episodes seem more like a fairy story than a serious psychiatric history with potentially serious repercussions.

'You want me to give you a brief precis?'

'Please – that would be really helpful.'

'Right, then. Here we go.' He cleared his throat, almost a drum roll for what followed.

'She first came to Laura's attention six years ago during her first pregnancy, referred by her GP, a Doctor Roy Barker, as she was claiming that her boss at work rather than her husband was the father of her baby and she wanted an HIV test. When questioned by Doctor Barker, she said she'd been having an affair with Mr Cartwright, who owned the printing works where she was employed. Doctor Barker reassured her but, as you know, HIV and hepatitis tests are routine anyway in pregnancy and they were negative. Trouble was her boss absolutely denied the whole thing. He said there was no affair, that he'd had *nothing* personal to do with Heather, that it was all fantasy. So . . . Doctor Barker asked Laura if she'd see her to try and find out the truth. That was the beginning of it all. She had some other delusions during the pregnancy – that the baby would reveal all when he was born and other stuff like that.'

He paused and she heard the sound of a page being turned. 'Laura made the diagnosis of puerperal psychosis, temporary schizophrenia and treated her with a neuroleptic. When the baby – a little girl, by the way – was born, Heather Krimble went home to her husband. She didn't return to work at Cartwright's. There's no more mention of him.'

Claire interrupted. 'Was the child's parentage ascertained?'

'You mean a DNA test for paternity?'

'Yes.'

'Well, I assume it was done, Claire, but I can't find a record. Anyway, Heather was treated and she gradually improved. She was discharged from Laura's care two months after delivery but four months later the little girl died. Cot death. Tragedy, eh?'

'Yeah.'

'There was a lot of discomfort about this considering Heather's previous psychiatric history. Doctor Barker wrote to Laura expressing his concerns, but she wasn't able to shed any light on the baby's death. There didn't seem a connection between Heather's allegations and the little girl's death. Plenty of questions were asked but there was no evidence that the child had died of anything other than natural causes. There were a few brief counselling sessions but Laura discharged her. Her mental state appeared to have stabilized, though she never appeared to accept that her husband was the father of her child. I guess the subject was dropped.'

Claire sat very still, focusing on the psychiatrist's words. This was true. This was what they did. They had enough work firefighting major problems. Subjects not considered pressing were just dropped.

'Well, that was it,' he said, 'until pregnancy number two a couple of years later, when again Heather claimed that the baby was not her husband's. This time her claims were even more bizarre – that the father was the window cleaner, a young chap named Sam Maddox. Incidentally happily engaged and just like Mr Cartwright before him, adamant he'd had nothing to do with the conception of her child. But Heather was sticking to her story that they'd had a long-term affair, that he was in love with her and was intending to leave his wife.' Simon Bracknell spluttered, 'Poor old bloody window cleaner hotly denied it, saying that he never even went *inside* the Krimble house, only did the windows from the outside – Heather was either out of the house or she stayed indoors. To cut a long and very imaginative story short, again there were lots of bizarre claims which continued right through the pregnancy. She was getting upset that the window cleaner wasn't spending enough time with her, saying that he wasn't showing enough interest in his own child. This time I did find a DNA report which proved that the baby, a little boy named Freddie . . .' He laughed. 'Cute name, that. Anyway, Freddie turned out to be her husband's child.' He laughed again. 'Much, I'm sure, to the window cleaner's relief.'

'Yes,' she agreed.

Simon Bracknell continued. 'This time, after the baby was born, she was followed up even more closely by the community psychiatric team and treated. Oooh,' he suddenly exclaimed, 'looks like you've got a problem. Bit of self-harm here. A cutter. Very disturbed. And very upset post-delivery. Again treated with the usual neuroleptics and chlorpromazine.'

'But not admitted.'

'Seems not, which is why she's stayed underneath *your* radar, Claire. They kept an eye on her in the community, but even though she had had one cot death there were no concerns about the second child. She'd never hurt him. But at two months old the little boy died, just like his big sister. It was put down as a cot death. Again, there were no signs that this was anything other than a second tragedy. Poor little Freddie. Heather was monitored in the community, counselled and eventually discharged.' He paused. 'Unlucky girl,' he said with typical antipodean understatement.

'As you say,' she responded drily, 'unlucky girl.'

That was when he showed some curiosity. 'And this time?'

'She's pregnant again and making another claim that the child is not her husband's. Again, the GP believes this is not true.' He didn't need to know any more than that – for now.

'Is it possible the problem lies not with Mrs Krimble but with her husband? She can't bear the thought that he's the father of her children so she substitutes?'

'It's certainly a possibility. I'm meeting her for the first time on Friday so maybe I'll get some idea. Thanks, Doctor.'

'Cut the formality, please. Call me Simon, for goodness' sake. Look, if I can help in any way, I'd be happy to.'

'Right. Thanks. Do you know how long you'll be filling in for Laura?'

'Looks like it'll be for the long haul.'

He was giving nothing away but prolonged sick leave didn't sound too good for Laura. Claire didn't ask. The jungle drums of NHS colleagues would reach her sooner or later.

'Maybe we'll meet up one of these days?' he added hopefully.

'Yeah,' she said, tacking on a banality to avoid sounding unfriendly, 'it's a small world.'

'Certainly is,' he agreed, and that was the end of the conversation.

But she had learnt useful facts.

Heather had plenty of history and Laura's notes had given it colour and some flavour. Soon it would be time to meet her.

SEVEN

Friday, 19 June, 3 p.m.
Clinic 5, Outpatient Department, Greatbach Secure
Psychiatric Hospital.
33/40

Claire's primary emotion, as she made her way down to the clinic, was curiosity. It is difficult *not* to form a picture of a patient when you know pieces of their history, even if her current view was lopsided as the facts she had learned so far about Heather Krimble had all come from independent sources. Now it was her job to try and make some order of these reports, using Heather's version. Then, possibly, she would start to separate fact from fiction, psychosis from neurosis, sift out any hint of deliberate malice and behind that any motive for lies manufactured purely to bring Charles Tissot's lucrative career crashing down around his ears. A doctor is taught to trust a patient's account, to believe their stories and not to question their version. A psychiatrist has a different method. Their patients may not be lying deliberately. They may believe their own untruths. They may not. But every statement has to be measured and weighed. Doubted, tested and finally evaluated. Fact, fiction or a subtle blend of both?

A psychiatrist needs to look into their patient's eyes as well as their brain, and for that you need insight plus concentration. As she sat behind her desk and opened the set of brand-new notes, she was focusing her mind and anticipating that first stare. How much of a clue would there be to the turmoil writhing underneath? Would the iceberg principle apply? One-tenth visible? The other nine well hidden. If hidden, how deeply? Well below the consciousness? Too deep to probe without the use of hypnotics? How aware was Heather of the fact that her stories were denied by others? A psychiatrist needs to be able to drill deep into the mind like a geologist, taking his sample not only from the surface but also from the underlying rocks. Then analyse it before dividing it into various categories. Not igneous, sedimentary, metamorphic, but truth, deliberate lies, delusions.

The mind is stripped down as a mechanic does an engine, observing the processes as they work. Only then can the visible symptoms be classified, a diagnosis made before treatment is instigated. Whatever Heather Krimble had on show, it was time for Claire to make her own assessment.

She looked at the blank page, already feeling her pulse quickening. *This* was why she had chosen psychiatry for her career. For what is life if not a challenge? So she sat and let her mind explore. Charles had portrayed the woman she was about to see as a vindictive madwoman. But why should Heather feel vindictive towards him? She hadn't even known him. The two men she had previously accused had at least had some ongoing contact with her. But Tissot? Of his own admission, they had only met briefly on that one occasion. How would she explain this?

And underneath her professional interest was a female perspective. What would she be *like*?

Her notes were sketchy so far, written on loose sheets. She'd made a rough *aide mémoire* while Simon Bracknell had been on the line but Claire had had little experience of this condition. She had only treated one case of erotomania before – an elderly man convinced a ballerina with a local company was obsessed with him. He'd sent her flowers night after night, believing that every time in the *corps de ballet* she turned towards him or tilted her head in his direction (no matter that her fellow *corps* members were making identical moves), it was nothing to do with the choreography but a secret signal to him alone in the auditorium, picking him out, in the dark, from the entire crowd. And when the dancer pirouetted or performed an arabesque, it was to entice him. It had been an extraordinary case. The treatment had been difficult and protracted, the seventy-four-year-old very hard to convince. She probably never had achieved this. His conviction had been too deeply rooted, too intransigent. Her suspicion was that the Heather/Charles case may well turn out the same.

And the case histories she'd spent the previous evening reading up on appeared to reinforce that idea. But at least she understood the main principles of erotomania: an unshakeable but deluded belief that a person, usually someone of higher social status or more attractive, was secretly in love with the subject. Charles Tissot certainly fitted that bill as did, though to a lesser extent, the boss of the printing company where Heather had worked. But the window cleaner? Younger. Perhaps he fitted the 'more attractive' criterion.

But as she prepared to call her in, Claire reminded herself that the accused this time was Charles Tissot.

She gave a final glance around her clinic office. Shared by all who needed it and less personal than her upstairs domain. Health posters Blu-tacked on to neutral walls. A desk, a computer, three chairs, little else. Anonymous.

She stood up. It was time to meet her patient. She walked out into the waiting room and scanned the upturned faces that turned to regard her, like sunflowers. Some she knew. Others were strangers. A couple of rows from the back, two women were sitting side by side, their heads almost touching. They were similar enough both in looks and style to mark them out as sisters. Both were neatly but quietly dressed in tailored trousers and loose shirts, one cream, the other pale green. Both had thin light brown hair cut in a fringed bob. She picked on the one in the cream shirt who had first looked up at her approach.

'Heather Krimble?'

She was wrong. It was the other one, the woman with the slightly shorter hair and the green shirt who stood up. She was small and slight, with a pale complexion, and her face was sweating.

Anxious brown eyes met hers. And, of course, as she straightened up, there was the biggest clue of all: a swollen belly.

Her pregnancy looked less advanced than eight months, hardly showing a bump in the loose-fitting shirt, but she was obviously conscious of it. Her hands were placed protectively over it as though she recognized the vulnerability and uncertainty surrounding the child inside. Her eyes were tawny brown, almost feline, with flecks of yellow. Her expression was bland but wary as an antelope. She wore no make-up and had a resolute air, squaring her shoulders and turning towards her as though facing her fate.

Claire smiled and extended her hand. 'I'm Doctor Roget,' she said.

Heather's eyes flickered over her, her expression guarded, with some suspicion just stopping short of hostility. After the briefest of pauses, she nodded. 'Hello.'

Claire's eyes moved to the second woman as she too stepped forward. 'I'm Ruth,' she said briskly, 'Heather's sister.'

As Claire turned her attention on Ruth, her own questions proliferated. What *was* her take on this? A shared delusion? There were few clues in the sister's face. Ruth was slightly less attractive than her sister. But she improved her appearance with mascara and pale pink lipstick, unfortunately clumsily smeared just outside her mouth. She was more confident, almost belligerent as she squared up to Claire with something approaching a challenge. Her expression, if not overtly hostile, was guarded, on full alert, like her sister's. But Claire sensed doubt too. She was not quite comfortable facing the psychiatrist with this latest story. On the other hand, there was a certain set about her mouth, combined with honesty in her eyes, which gave Claire confidence that she would not flinch from the truth. *As she saw it.* But balancing that, her body language was unmistakable – affection and protection towards her older sister. Claire nodded in the direction of the consulting room. 'Shall we go?'

Heather walked by her side, head turned towards her, smiling, questioning. *Making friends?* Or carefully appraising? Ruth remained two steps behind, with a heavier and more determined tread. Almost fatalistic. Claire ushered them both into the consulting room, observing her patient. Heather appeared placid now and a little smug, patting her pregnant stomach periodically as though to congratulate it or else reassure herself that it was still there.

Not a fantasy.

When Heather sat she pressed her knees together primly. Her stare, unblinking and very direct, could have been classed as unnerving except there was some confusion, a slight pucker between her eyebrows, as though she was unsure quite how she had ended up here. Already, Claire was finding her difficult to assess. *Take your time*, she told herself.

She opened Heather's notes to the page where she had left her loose sheets, already thinking that on the surface it would seem that Charles Tissot had little to fear. Heather's past history appeared to be letting him right off the hook. Shame.

She began the interview with her usual intro. Climb into the patient's perspective. 'Heather, do you understand why Doctor Sylas has referred you to me?'

The women exchanged glances, neither answering. Difficult to read, except for a faint line of worry which appeared simultaneously between their brows. It was Ruth who answered for her sister.

'Yes, Doctor Roget,' she said, quite firmly, 'I believe we do. There has been . . .' a necessary hesitation while Ruth floundered for a word, '. . . conflict about the parentage of my sister's previous babies. Somehow . . .' She was twisting her fingers together and frowning down at them while Heather looked on, Madonna-calm now, waiting for her sister to explain. Not a trace of anxiety or concern. 'Somehow,' Ruth resumed, 'things have got a bit confused. Not helped,' she continued with defiance and an upturn of her chin, 'by men denying their responsibility.' Her eyes flickered. Maybe she was recalling the DNA test on Freddie? 'This time, however, my sister has *no* such doubts.' Her eyes were locked on to Claire's. 'This time,' she said, 'my sister is quite sure. She does not have sex with her husband. This child is the result of a liaison with Mr Tissot.' She spoke the words with firm and deliberate emphasis, without ambiguity and a cold, challenging stare. Hostile now.

Claire made a note in the margin. *If a delusion, shared by sister, Ruth?* But she did feel like applauding. It had been a great performance and at least Ruth was getting straight to the heart of it. Without preamble.

Both women were watching her. Her turn now. So, feed them a cue.

'I know from Doctor Hodgkins' previous notes that claims were made against two men who subsequently denied any involvement.' She addressed her question to Heather. 'So this time you're saying it's different?'

There was a moment of wariness in her patient, who visibly tensed up. She knew she was cornered. The alertness was mirrored by tension in her sister's hands, which clawed the arms of her chair.

Heather finally spoke hesitantly in a soft voice. Less confident, less confrontational than her sister. There was something meek about it. 'I know I *might* have got it wrong before,' she conceded, speaking quite clearly. Then she looked straight at Claire. 'But *anyone* can make a mistake.'

Claire drew in a sharp breath. *So now she was calling the previous allegations a mistake? Sweeping them under the carpet with a few choice words? Got it wrong.* She avoided saying the obvious, pointing out the damage these 'mistakes' had caused. But while she would have to delve into Heather's past history, it was her *current* allegation with which she was concerned and which she would focus on. 'As I understand it,' she said, 'your husband . . .' *and why isn't* he *here today instead of your sister?* '. . . believes that both Eliza and Freddie were *his* children?' She waited before continuing. 'And in the case of Freddie, that was proven by DNA analysis to be the truth.'

Did she accept this?

She certainly didn't like it. Fists clenched. 'As I said, *anyone* can make a mistake.' Heather was licking her lips now, eyes darting around the room before she came up with, 'It is possible that someone switched the samples, isn't it?'

No, actually.

Time to block this particular avenue. 'Now you know, Heather, there are strict rules about labelling samples, particularly in the case of paternity disputes. There is no record of Eliza's DNA being tested but, in the case of Freddie, he was your husband's son.'

Her response was obscure. 'I can't help it if men think they can take advantage of me.'

'Quite,' she said, knowing the rules. The proffered possibility should appear to be considered. Time now to explore. 'As Eliza's DNA was never tested and she and Freddie are now dead, we cannot repeat the tests. But of course, when this little one is born, we will be able to ascertain his or her parentage.' She smiled to soften her words. 'Obviously there never is any doubt who the mother is.'

Heather leaned back in her chair and held her hands up as though shielding herself from this denunciation. 'I know who the father of my baby is,' she said. 'A mother instinctively knows.'

Claire's eyes dropped to the bulge.

Heather's expression became sentimental. And with her next statement came an air of dignity and confidence. 'I would *not* be getting a certain person into trouble just for the fun of it.' Her hands stroked the bump. 'Or out of spite.'

Questions were bubbling away in Claire's brain. Among them: *Why would you feel spite towards a man you'd hardly met? Was it something to do with her sister? Her sister's job?*

'But you were quite happy to . . .' she borrowed the quote, '. . . get other men into trouble when you *believed* they had fathered your previous children.'

'That,' Heather said, venom in her voice, 'was different. This time . . .' She stopped. 'This time, I am sure.'

Claire was wondering if Heather knew that Tissot would be in serious trouble if these allegations were made public. She poised her pen ready to write. 'Let's start at the beginning, shall we? Your two babies? Let's start with them.'

'Eliza and Freddie.'

'Eliza was the daughter of . . .?'

'She was *my* daughter.' Heather had her answer ready.

'And her father?' Claire was doing this deliberately. She had to assess how rational Heather Krimble was. And for that, she needed to look back into the past.

'Eliza's father was a man I worked for at the time, a Mr Timothy Cartwright.'

'You worked for him.'

'Yes. Before I was married.'

'How did the affair start?'

'I stayed late one night at the office. He told me he'd always fancied me. One thing led to another.'

Instinctively, Claire felt that Heather was deliberately setting this story. That was unexpected.

'So why didn't you marry Mr Cartwright? He was single. You were single.'

'He didn't want to leave his mother. I understood that. He's a very loyal man.'

'So . . .' Claire did a quick calculation. 'It was very good of Geoff to accept the little girl. He must have married you when you were already pregnant.'

'*I* was Eliza's mother. I *knew* who Eliza's father was. And it wasn't Geoff.' She was shaking her head in denial. 'But Geoff . . .' She tossed her head in dismissal. Gave out a great big, regretful sigh. 'Geoff took her and me on when Tim – Mr Cartwright – tried to wriggle out of his responsibility.'

'Why would he do that, Heather?'

She shrugged. 'I don't know,' she said. 'Embarrassment, maybe? He was ashamed his mother would learn his sordid little secret.'

It made sense, but not Geoff's docile contribution.

'And why did Geoff marry you and take on Eliza?'

Her answer was unexpected. 'He did what my father told him. Besides . . .' A toss of the head. 'He'd always had a thing about me.'

Ruth's eyes flickered. Claire sidestepped the issue and searched for a different angle. 'So when Eliza died . . . how did you feel about that?'

Heather glanced at her sister. For a cue? Ruth didn't give her one but continued looking straight ahead, burying her own thoughts and responses.

'Well,' Heather responded finally, 'naturally the death of a baby is sad.' She looked around the bland room for inspiration. Found none.

And Ruth came to her rescue in a fierce attack on Claire's question. 'What do you expect her to say? She was bloody well heartbroken. How do you *think* she felt?'

Her response told her just how fiercely protective of her older sister Ruth was.

But she had to squeeze Heather. Like a lemon, to remove the pips.

'What was Eliza like?'

The question appeared to throw Heather. Again, she scrabbled around for an answer. 'Well, she was just a baby.'

'What word would you use to describe your relationship with Eliza?'

Both women gawped at her.

Heather looked most taken aback. 'What word? What word? I was her mother. And she was my baby.'

Claire waited for something more but nothing came. The silence extended and Heather looked again to her sister for a cue. None came. Ruth, it seemed, could not supply it.

'I was her mother,' she said again.

It described nothing.

'Tell me about your husband, Geoff?'

Heather smirked. 'What do you want to know?'

Claire leaned forward to rest on her elbows. 'Well, for a start, I don't really understand his part in all this.'

Ruth took up the baton. 'Geoff and our father were in the same church,' she said slowly. 'Dad, our father, was an elder. He suggested Geoff might want to help Heather out.'

Claire leaned back and thought about this. It both made sense and it didn't.

Heather shrugged again. 'Water under the bridge,' she said carelessly. 'What does any of it matter now? Eliza is dead anyway. What difference would it make if Geoff *or* Mr Cartwright was the father? It wouldn't bring her back from the dead, would it?'

'Mr Cartwright?' Claire seized on the name. 'How did he respond when you told him you were expecting his child?'

'Huh. Said it wasn't true. Denied the whole affair.'

'Ah, yes, the affair.'

This affair that never happened.

'Had it been going on long?'

Ruth answered for her sister. 'Long enough,' she said waspishly.

Claire turned back to Heather. 'He was your boss, wasn't he?'

'*Was* her boss,' Ruth supplied, firing again into the action. 'She left.'

Claire was aware there was a subtext here. Much more likely she was sacked.

Both women waited now politely but warily, both silently preparing to repel her next question. So Claire kept it neutral. She was beginning to get a feel here for Heather's state of mind. She was a little more puzzled as to why her sister was taking so much on board.

How far could she insert the probe?

'And then your second baby came along.'

This time it was Ruth who supplied the name, with a smile. 'Freddie.'

'Yes, Freddie,' her sister agreed. Another big smile.

It didn't happen very often, but every now and then Claire felt she would like to wipe – yes, literally wipe, with a damp flannel or dishcloth – the smile off a patient's face. What did she have to smile about? Another dead child.

But her imaginary cloths weren't going to wipe the smile off Heather's face, stop her stroking her pregnant abdomen or mumbling to it.

'And you claim that Sam Maddox, your window cleaner, was Freddie's father. He denied it, said it was impossible, and the DNA test proved that your husband was Freddie's biological father.'

Ruth met her eyes square on. 'Men can deny stuff,' she said, 'but a woman has the child growing in her belly. *She* can't deny it. *She* can't walk away from her responsibility.'

Was it then as simple as that? Had Heather not wanted the two pregnancies?

'My sister and I know the truth, Doctor.' The statement was uncompromising.

'How do you know, Ruth?' *You weren't there.*

'My sister doesn't lie. That's how I know.'

EIGHT

Both sisters were sitting upright, alert. Neither showing any doubt or concern. Or compromise.

Ruth was going to be backing up her sister's story all the way. Because her sister didn't lie.

Claire focused on the small mound in Heather's abdomen. 'So,' she said, encouraging her with a smile. 'That brings us up to date and to this little baby.'

Heather sucked in a sharp breath and encompassed her entire abdomen protectively with her arms while Ruth turned towards her, watching. There was almost an electric exchange between the two women before Ruth turned her attention on to Claire, a challenge hurled down silently but its viciousness unmistakable for all that. *You think my sister's nuts. I tell you she is not. So which one of us is right, Doctor?*

It is the way of a psychiatrist, when the consultation is entering dangerous ground, to retreat and find refuge in some safer place. Only when the balance has been recovered can you try inching forwards again.

And so, obeying this silent diktat, Claire turned back to her patient and asked about the current pregnancy. 'Tell me, Heather, about this baby.' She managed to inject a congratulatory note into the subtext. 'Your third. Are you keeping well?'

Heather nodded happily. 'Yes, thank you.' The question had appeared to pacify her. 'That's right, Doctor Roget. It is my third pregnancy. Third baby.'

Fact.

No suspicion that her psychiatrist was edging into something concrete that would either disprove or confirm her stories.

'So,' Claire prompted. 'Tell me about this one's father?'

'This one?' Heather was giving her abdomen a fond look. 'You mean Charles.'

Her use of his Christian name startled Claire. She had said it so easily. So comfortably. So convincingly.

'It happened at a party,' Heather continued. 'In an instant. We just fell in love.' She snapped her fingers. 'Just like that.' She looked sweetly at Claire. 'Tell me, Doctor,' she whispered, 'do *you* believe in love at first sight?'

This was more difficult for Claire to answer honestly than could be imagined. Yes, as a woman. She had 'fallen in love' with Grant at first sight, knowing he would become something precious to her.

But as a psychiatrist, which was what Heather was asking her? 'I'm not sure.'

Psychiatrists are rarely sure about anything. They sit on a fence, seeing both sides of an argument with equal clarity and sympathy. Psychiatry is not a black-and-white science but all grey, consisting of guesswork, conjecture, ideas and acts of non-committal. They are listeners rather than talkers and they bury their own prejudices and opinions very deep.

They are certainly not judges.

Heather was still in her romantic reverie. 'I met him in November, at a bonfire party.' She turned to her sister for confirmation. 'Didn't I, Ruth?'

Her sister nodded, then eyed Claire warily. *Wondering how much of this she was going to swallow?*

Claire moved slightly forward, listening intently. This wasn't a window cleaner impregnating her through glass or a boss seducing her over the office desk without a single witness but something far more possible and rational. A bonfire party? Heather wouldn't be the first to err against that particular backdrop.

She glanced at Ruth, who was listening with rapt attention as though to a Mills & Boon. She was certainly not contradicting her sister's story.

Heather continued, 'I wasn't that keen on going but you persuaded me, didn't you, Ru?' Her focus was still on her sister, who nodded back affectionately. Sentimentally.

Heather turned back to Claire then and shot her a very direct challenge. 'And *he* was there. Watching me. He's got quite a stare, you know.'

Unfortunately Claire did know. She remembered that other night. Before . . . before they had drunk quite so much. That was exactly how she would have described the early part of that evening. Charles Tissot had stood, propped up against the wall, not talking to anyone, his eyes glued to her. Every time she'd glanced across, his eyes had not shifted. Not one centimetre. Not one fraction of a centimetre. It was an unnerving stare. He hadn't even seemed to blink.

Unbalanced, she returned to the present. Pretended to write. Thought furiously. What if Heather was telling the truth? At least as she saw it.

'Where did this party take place?'

'The surgeon Ruth works for, Mr Metcalfe, it was at his house. He lives at the Westlands.'

A fact tossed into the fairy tale. And the troubling thing was that this gave the story authenticity. A backdrop.

And was so much more plausible than a boss who lived with his mother and had never shown interest in her, or a window cleaner who could apparently impregnate through glass. But Charles? This was how he operated. And the story was about to become even more plausible.

'It was there.' The smile was permanently pasted on to her face now. Memories had stuck it there. It wasn't about to slide off.

'It was a lovely party. Huge bonfire outside and brilliant

fireworks. They've got a massive garden.' She sounded naive, child-like.

A quick glance at her sister confirmed the fact that she was nodding in agreement.

'It was a big house. Lots of rooms. I looked all around it, you know.' The eagerness in her voice made Claire feel that she almost anticipated a pat on the back for her reconnaissance work. 'The bathroom . . .' Her eyes were wide open as she spoke. 'Bath*rooms*,' she corrected. 'There were loads of them. Anyway, I was in a bathroom putting some hand cream on my hands.' Her voice was slow now and pedantic. She was relating facts. As she saw them. 'The bathroom was off a bedroom. *En suite.*' She pronounced the words with a deliberate and self-conscious pride at mastering a foreign phrase. 'The bedroom was gorgeous. A cream carpet and a silky bedspread. I'd been running my hands over it when he was standing right behind me.' She did a little shimmy, a little manoeuvre with her eyes, jerked her head halfway around as though he was there.

As acting, it was superb, but it had the unsettling effect of giving her story colour and credence. Claire almost felt she was witnessing it. A reality that surely couldn't be?

'I was startled. He was soooo handsome. Soooo tall and . . . he even smelt nice. Sort of tangy. Spicy. Anyway, he said something about it being stuffy and why didn't we go outside. And then . . . And then.' Her face was beatific, the face of a fallen angel who had once been blessed. She looked as though she was listening to some holy music. *Ode to Joy?*

She leaned forward, eyes bright. 'His car is a Jaguar, you know.'

Faking being impressed, no, Claire hadn't known. But it was an easily verifiable fact. Much easier than this weird tale of seduction. Something in her felt slightly sick at the recall. Not a Vauxhall Astra these days then, but a Jaguar. And that was when she first realized that although on the surface Heather Krimble's story appeared gross fantasy, whatever the MDU might say and Heather's GP had already said, whatever her history, Claire didn't quite, not a hundred per cent, not hand-on-heart completely disbelieve her. At least, not in this instance. It all sounded too possible. Too real.

She was stroking the plastic seat cover. 'Soft, soft, with white leather seats.' She stretched her arms above her head and gave another little shimmy. 'I just knew he wanted to make love.'

Claire took a swift glance at Ruth. How much of this account was *she* really believing? Her mouth was slightly open and she was frowning. Was a little doubt creeping in, like a mouse from a hole beneath the skirting board?

'I was tempted. I really was tempted.' Her hands ran down her breasts. 'And then I . . . I just lay back on the seat and gave in to . . .' A swift glance at her sister, who kept staring straight ahead. 'He lay on top of me and we . . .' A dirty red flush spread over her face. 'We . . .'

Her sister had turned her head to watch her, that slight, doubtful frown still there.

Heather licked her lips. 'We . . . you know,' she hesitated. 'We made love.' The phrase sounded awkward. Claire eyed her. This was a woman who claimed to have been made pregnant by three different men, none of whom had been her husband. No prude then.

Heather stopped speaking, apparently to gauge Claire's response. And seemed to feel she should add something more. 'I've worked it out,' she said quickly. 'I've worked out the dates. I know.'

Claire was silent. Whatever Heather Krimble's previous history, this story was plausible. And she did have that extra private knowledge. *This is the way he works.*

It was not only plausible, it was possible. The dates would match.

She dropped her gaze to the notes she had made prior to this consultation and picked up on one of the points she had highlighted from Dr Sylas's letter. *Each time, late in the pregnancy, Heather had doubts about the parenthood of the baby.*

'When did you realize?'

'When the baby began to move. It felt . . . different. Livelier.'

'And is it a boy – or a girl?'

'We want it to be a surprise. Charles says it is a son. I believe we have a daughter.'

'So there have been other encounters?'

'No.' A little smile. 'Now I'm pregnant, Charles wouldn't. You don't *do* it to a pregnant lady.'

'Plenty do.'

'Not Charles.' Said with pride. 'He's very particular.'

'But you've met up?'

'No. We have to be *very* careful.'

'But you asked to be referred to him as your obstetrician.'

She even had an answer for that. 'Naturally Charles would want to deliver his own child.'

'But he doesn't,' Claire said bluntly. 'With these claims, it wouldn't be ethical.'

'Oh.' Hand slapped over mouth. 'I didn't realize that.'

Time to trick her. 'You say that you have had further contact with Mr Tissot.' She was not going to use his Christian name. 'So how do you keep contact?'

At that, Heather turned nauseatingly coy, one shoulder turning away, pale eyelashes flickering. 'That,' she said, 'would be telling.'

Claire was ready to bring this initial consultation to an end. 'Just to recap,' she said bluntly, 'so there can be no misunderstanding, though we can't be certain about Eliza, that Freddie was your husband's child. The DNA proved it.'

Heather nodded but her eyes flickered away in the first indication that she had been caught out. She still had her answer at the ready. Almost bravely, she gave it.

'The sample was obviously swapped. I know what I know,' she said, eyes blazing. 'I know who I've had sex with and when. And a woman has an instinct about the child she carries in her belly.' With that, she gave her abdomen a hard punch.

'Please don't do that,' Claire said. 'It could hurt the baby.'

Heather had her answer ready. 'So what do I do,' she asked, 'if the baby – or its father – is being naughty?'

'Not that.'

Heather dropped her hands.

'Tell me one thing,' Claire said. 'The encounter with Mr Tissot. Was it similar to the affairs with Mr Cartwright and Sam?'

Heather blinked. 'I don't want to go into all that,' she said, pulling her shirt tightly around her, acting the prude now. 'This one . . .' Her fingers caressed her pregnant belly. 'This one was conceived in true love. Charles adores me. He couldn't keep his hands off me.' She looked up at Claire and this time her predominant expression was innocence.

'He denies this relationship.'

Heather's eyes blazed. 'Then he is a liar, both to me and to you.'

Claire tried again. 'So how do you communicate, Heather?' *Mobile phone? Internet? Facebook? Twitter? Snapchat?*

'At this point,' Heather said annoyingly, 'I'm not going to tell you.' She folded her arms, stuck her chin in the air.

And Claire's doubts started to multiply. Her story had too many holes in it. Was missing too many solid facts.

By her side, Ruth was statue-still, eyes trained on the floor. Tightly reined in as though any movement might cast a shadow over her sister's incredible tale of romance, lust and love.

In her body language, Claire read something very sad.

At some point, she was going to switch her focus to Ruth. Interview her alone and find out why she was so protective of her older sister. But for today, this was enough.

She closed her file.

NINE

Friday, 19 June, 4 p.m.

She'd arranged to see Heather in a week but after the two women had left, her feeling of uneasiness wasn't fading. Facts and fiction were too tangled. And it was a strange feeling to enter into a patient's world and not know where the boundary was between truth, lies and misconceptions. She paced her clinic room for a few minutes, before, still agitated, she picked up the phone. She needed to speak to Charles herself. See him face-to-face. Hear his denial again from his own lips. Watch as he formed the words.

He sounded relieved to hear from her. Succinctly, she related the essence of the consultation. 'The trouble is, Charles, we know that you were at that party.'

He made a sound like a cough.

'It just squeezes in under the wire of a plausible story.'

'Claire.' He sounded appalled. 'You can't even entertain the idea that she could be telling the truth. With her fantastic history? You cannot possibly . . .' There was a sudden silence as his mind caught up. 'Oh, fuck,' he said. 'That was years ago. And I fancied you like mad.'

She was supposed to say thank you?

'We should draw a line under all that, Charles,' she said briskly. 'It has nothing to do with this.' It was a thin lie and they both recognized it as such. 'Her story had so much detail. And she sounds rational.'

There was silence on the other end. She didn't fill it. She knew the way he worked. The question was how, also, did Heather? How did she know such detail? How did *she* know his *modus operandi*? The compliments, the flattery, the way he worked? His blinding stare?

On the other hand, there was a lot of detail missing. Particularly about subsequent contact. But DNA may neither prove nor disprove the story. Only the parentage of the child would do that.

'I can't keep this under my hat, Charles,' she said. 'It's going to have to come out – or we'll both be suspended, if not struck off. It's a very serious allegation she's making.'

The silence stretched. She heard him sigh. 'You don't have to point that out, Claire. It's all the most fantastic fable.'

'You may well be suspended pending a full investigation. So you should prepare for it.'

He came back fighting. 'I'll speak to the MDU myself, thank you.'

'Yeah.' He was cornered and they both knew it. She had to at least offer an olive branch. 'If they want to speak to me I'm more than happy. I can't give an opinion at the moment. It's too soon. I've only seen her once with her rather creepy sister.'

Further silence fell. Thick as felt.

'Charles . . .' She almost felt his whiskers twitching, rat-like. 'She *will* need to be seen by another obstetrician.'

'Of course. I never want to see the fucking woman again – not in my entire life. Anyway . . .' he was recovering, 'as her *obstetric* history is OK, there's no real reason for her to be under a consultant at all. The midwives can take care of her and the paediatrician can look after the infant.'

'I thought the community obstetric team could pick her up.'

That was when the knot became even more tangled. 'Community team?' It sounded like a groan. 'Oh, not Rhoda,' he said. 'Not my ex-wife. Put those pair of psychos together and they'd beat any three witches stirring their evil brew.'

'Your ex is in charge of the community midwifery services?'

'Yeah. They'll gang up,' he objected. 'They'll crucify me

between them. They'll feed off each other's paranoia. It'll cause sparks . . . Oh, no. Please, Claire. Spare me this. Rhoda doesn't exactly have a high opinion of me right now.'

'Why not?'

'Oh, let's just say . . .' His voice trailed away and Claire knew. She just knew that the reason Charles and his wife had split up was to do with his philandering ways. Some guys can't help themselves.

So now Rhoda was to be brought into play. Hardly likely to help his case, was it?

'Charles,' she said, 'we can't all skip around you. You're going to have to be at the very least investigated and cleared. In case you'd forgotten, Heather Krimble is claiming that you and she had sex and that you are the father of her baby. And she is a vulnerable adult with a history of mental instability. Now I know – we all know,' she hastily corrected, 'that the child's father can easily be ascertained. But, whatever her previous history, Heather is currently making these very serious allegations.'

'That's why I asked you to see her,' he said through tightly clenched teeth. 'To certify her as fucking insane.'

'It isn't as easy as all that. She may have a distorted view on things. Charles, I have to ask you again: is there any truth in it?'

She didn't even recognize the expletive he barked down the phone line. But she pursued its source. 'Did you have sex with her in the back of your car at a party back in November? She says it took place—' She broke off suddenly. 'What sort of car do you drive?'

'What the hell has that . . . A Jaguar.'

'White leather seats?'

'Well, yes, actually.'

Details. Little details growing like seeds.

'Has Heather ever been in your car?'

Instead of answering, he went on the attack. 'Whose side are you on, Claire?'

'The side of the truth.'

She paused to allow him to let off some steam. 'Her sister is backing up her story.'

He had his answer ready. 'Bonkers, too.'

But it wasn't strictly true so her honesty impelled her to add, 'Or at least, she isn't contradicting it.'

'Get Ruth on her own,' he advised. 'You'll soon get the truth out of her.'

'I intend to,' she said coldly. 'Heather's also claiming that you have ongoing contact.'

'How?'

'She wasn't specific.'

'I'll bet.'

'But until I get to the bottom of this—'

'With DNA,' he provided.

'Well, we'll see. Until I get to the bottom of this I'll continue to see her, speak to some of the people involved, her husband, maybe the two men she previously accused of having fathered her children. I have to say, Charles, I do still have an open mind but currently my suspicion is that this is a case of psychotic erotomania.'

'Phew,' he said, the confidence returning in his voice. 'For a moment there I wondered whose version you were believing.'

'As I said, I'm impartial.'

'Well, thanks,' he said.

'My advice at the moment is to speak to the MDU and explain your take on this. Trying to hide behind Heather's mental state and past history might be the worst thing you could do for you, for her and even possibly for me.'

His response was a sceptical and non-committal, 'Hmm.'

She tried to coax him over to her point of view. 'You'll almost certainly be let off the hook.'

That produced a dry, cynical laugh.

'Unless, of course, her story proves to be true.'

This time the response from the other end was a dialling tone.

Claire sat in her office fully aware of how critical an issue this was for Charles Tissot. It could well be the end of his career and the beginning of his descent into ignominy. Heather's story was just about plausible. True or not, the allegation of sex in his car outside a party would be damaging – fatally so if Heather changed her story and claimed that the sex had not been consensual. And Rhoda Tissot wading in would hardly help matters. The only glimmer of light was that at the time of the *alleged* encounter Heather would not have been his patient. The breach had been when she asked to be referred to him and he accepted her.

Claire was deep in thought, recognizing that she was in a unique position – probably the only person who knew just how plausible Heather's story was, how very neatly all those facts fitted in with what she already knew of Charles's past predatory habits. But as this neat collection of detail did not necessarily make it true, neither did the holes in Heather's story, including her previous history of false allegations, indicate it was untrue. It would take time and numerous interviews before she could sift fact from fiction and learn just what was really happening here. Instinct was pushing her towards rejection of Heather's account, and to classify her as a sufferer from erotomania or de Clerambault's syndrome. Her sister was sharing the delusion possibly out of a sense of misguided loyalty or a reluctance to doubt her sister's word. Claire was also fully aware that the story could take so much unravelling she might never find the truth. Unless the DNA test on the child proved that Charles Tissot was the child's father. She couldn't resist a smile. Now that would be interesting.

As she filled in her notes and dictated a letter back to Dagmar Sylas, she reflected that although she was ninety per cent certain that this third child, like little Freddie, would prove to be the offspring of Geoff Krimble, she would not have staked her life on it. And the child's life?

That stopped her in her tracks. The child's life. Two had died. What would be the fate of this one?

And then, as emotions do, her view shifted. In a way, she felt sorry for Charles. If he was innocent it was bad luck getting caught up in this woman's fantasy. He would be very lucky if the Medical Defence Union didn't suspend him. Even if they didn't, stringent conditions could be insisted on. He'd be very lucky if this episode didn't leave some sort of scar on his professional reputation.

The law governing doctors' behaviour is perfectly clear and aimed at safeguarding their patients, who are seen as vulnerable. Not manipulative, not liars, not deceivers. Innocent patients.

It is the patient who is seen as the victim, while doctors are perceived to be in a position of authority. And so doctors must keep to the strictest of moral and ethical codes when it comes to their patients. If anyone would know all these rules, Charles would. As a male obstetrician, he was particularly vulnerable. But, of course, this encounter had allegedly taken place at a party, outside his remit as a doctor, before Heather Krimble had become his most dangerous patient. Now her mind whirring round had got stuck on a cog. If Heather's version of events was true, they had had sex *before* she had been his patient. It was only when he had become her obstetrician that the rules had been broken, which had been by Heather's request.

And the parallels between her own experience and Heather's story were not helping.

Oh, she thought, picking up the next set of notes. She would play her part, assess Heather's mental state. The MDU would play their part and Charles Tissot would play his part.

But, like a broken record, a CD marked with fingerprints or a worn-out MP3 player, her mind led her to a question. For that drunken fumble years ago, did *she* think he was fit to practice? The thought haunted her. It would seem a harsh judgement. But what was making her uncomfortable were the little grains of incontrovertible truth. Heather *had* worked for Timothy Cartwright's printing firm. There had been some contact between them.

On the Internet site she had searched last night, patients suffering from de Clerambault's syndrome hadn't imagined the *entire* scenario – simply misinterpreted gestures or words, taking them to extremes.

Sam Maddox *had* been a window cleaner at Heather's house. Window cleaners were friendly people as they cleaned and scrubbed, peering in and smiling at those inside. He *would* have peered in through the windows, almost certainly given a friendly wave. To a healthy mind, they would realize this was a meaningless gesture, simple politeness. To a person with erotomania, it would be seen as an invitation, a seduction. That smile means that that man wants to . . .

Heather *had* been pregnant. Twice. Eliza's DNA might not have been checked for paternity but Freddie's had. And Geoff Krimble had been the child's biological father.

Still tolling in the background was the reminder. Both these babies had died.

The real puzzle was Ruth. Why was she backing up her sister's story? She had no mental problems. But she couldn't have been there, watching the coupling through the steamy windows of the Jag.

She scanned the GP's letter again, searching for something that might explain Ruth's assertion that her sister's story was true. Or at least why she hadn't contradicted it. And this time she picked up on a point she had previously glossed over.

She has a brother, Robin, five years older, but he left home when she was nineteen and she claims she has had no contact with him since. He has, to all intents and purposes, disappeared. No one knows what has happened to him. I understand the police were informed and he's officially listed as a missing person.

Was it possible that the mystery of their brother's disappearance united the sisters together in some abnormally close fashion?

And where did Geoff Krimble fit into all this? Was he an innocent fall guy? A non-participant? An amused, sceptical bystander? What was his take on this? Did he sympathize with his wife's delusions? Was he angry with her – or was his anger directed at the men she was claiming to have fathered *his* children with? Did he share Charles Tissot's verdict – that Heather was 'nuts'? And because she was a psychiatrist and psychiatrists ask questions, Claire asked herself one now. Was it possible that Heather's obsession with other men was masking some aberration in her husband's behaviour? Was Geoff Krimble abusive? Was that why his wife wanted to deny his part in the fathering of her children? Was she seeing this from the wrong angle? Rather than an accusation against other men, was this primarily a rejection of her husband?

What *was* his take on all this? His opinion would surely be of significance. She added him to the list. Maybe when she met Mr Krimble she would understand all.

She put her head in her hands. To sift through all this, sort out truth from fiction could be a challenge. Lying, so far in the shadows, were allegations that could stick like a burr to Charles even if the child proved to be Geoff's. And once the child was born and its paternity established, what would be its fate? Would it, too, die?

She closed the notes.

It was late by the time she left Greatbach, and she was too tired to do her usual run or spend an hour at the gym. By nine o'clock she had showered and, in her pyjamas, she was watching something so banal on the television that she couldn't remember the next morning what it was she had watched.

TEN

She had spent the morning at the hospital catching up on her reports, but by lunchtime she was free to meet up with her friend, Julia Seddon, and her partner, Gina Aldi. Julia was an old friend from medical school who was now a GP in Hanley, the city centre of the five towns. Her partner, Gina, was the diametric opposite of the pedantic, scientific doctor. She was an artist from the Potteries who was making a name for herself with some contemporary designs and pottery sculptures, mainly of fantastic animals derived purely from her imagination. Animals with tusks and long, snaking bodies, horses with beaks, birds with fabulous and frivolous crests like models' hairstyles, fish with hooves. They were instantly recognizable as her work. Claire had bought one, a sheep with a shark's fin on its back. It made her smile whenever she looked at it, which was possibly the key to Gina's worldwide success. The model stood on the windowsill of her study, at the back of the house, overlooking the garden and its ancient apple tree.

But for all their obvious differences, her two friends were similar, both full of enthusiasm, energy and sparkle and always up for a long, chatty lunch. It was a perfect way to spend a Saturday afternoon which was dull and rainy – nothing like the flaming June which now seemed as much a fantasy as one of Gina's sculptures. Her friends had been hugely supportive when Grant had disappeared and equally so when he had reappeared, like some genie with magical powers.

They had met at a small Italian restaurant in the centre of the city and settled down for a good old chinwag. The restaurant stayed open between lunchtime and dinner so there was no need to rush. They always had plenty to talk about. So many subjects, except one. Even though Julia was another doctor, Claire avoided mentioning Charles Tissot, although all those years ago she had talked to Julia about the encounter in his car. Then, she had desisted from giving advice, merely listening, and when she had come out later Claire thought she understood why. The subject of hetero sex was foreign to her.

But the rules on confidentiality were unambiguous and protected the patient, even when the confidant was another doctor. Sharing medical information with a colleague was only justified if the colleague had a medical interest. Under the law of need to know.

So instead they chatted about a holiday she was wondering about, a brief tour of classical Spain, the Alhambra, Seville (*Carmen*!), Cordoba and the famous cathedral/mosque. The minutes ticked away into hours, the conversation meandering like a stream, through meadows and fields, deep cuts and dark valleys, galloping across plains and climbing mountains. None of them was driving home. Claire planned to take a taxi home. Julia and Gina lived within walking distance of the restaurant so they had no need to watch their alcohol intake, and a bottle soon replaced the one they had just emptied.

Gina's talk was all of designs she was filching from Japanese folklore. Kappa, the water monkey. Heikegani, the crab with a face of a dead Samurai. Kasa-obake, adapting her themes to larger objects, goldfish bowls and garden seats and incorporating contemporary design. And often she'd slip images in of the Potteries, the Portland Vase, a piece of Portmeirion pottery, some Spode or Wedgwood. Bottle kilns, barges, even the red-and-white stripes of Stoke City Football Club. She delighted in making her clients search for the connection with her city.

Her wares were a unique combination of the contemporary, angular, bright, imaginative, bold colours similar to Clarice Cliff's traditional design. They were instantly recognizable as her work even before you saw the signature on the bottom: *Gina Aldi.*

As Julia listened and Gina talked, Claire watched her silver hoop earrings sparkle in the light, flashing in the tangle of her tumbling dark gypsy hair. The contrast between the two had never been more marked. Gina was all animation while Julia was quieter, more restrained, very polite. While Gina was all about movement, Julia was still. And because she too was a medic, she tended to ask more probing questions about Claire's work.

Claire kept off the subject of Charles Tissot's current little problem; she didn't feel she knew or understood enough of Heather's case to make it interesting – even without mentioning

her name. But Riley Finch proved an animating topic which interested all of them, even Gina understanding the potential for further
trouble. And the three of them touched, in a sympathetic way, on
Arthur Connolly's crime and the position of a male dominated by
a female, Julia and Gina laughingly making the comment that this
would be a problem they would never experience. There were
plenty of other subjects to keep the conversation rolling. And then,
halfway through the meal, the conversation having been intermittently lazy and desultory at times, and at others animated and
noisy, with them pausing only to refuel with food, Julia's gaze
wandered across to the other side of the restaurant. Mid-sentence,
she stopped speaking, her face frozen, her pasta slowly sliding off
her fork. She was looking over Claire's right shoulder out into the
room, focusing on a spot near the door at some newcomers.

Her eyes widened. She glanced at Claire, alarmed. 'Gosh,
Claire,' she said. 'Isn't that your ex?'

Something cold crept up Claire's spine. She didn't want to turn
around. Her head felt as though it was in a vice. Julia gazing,
transfixed, Gina watching her, silent now and immobile. When
Claire did finally turn her head, she was looking straight into Grant
Steadman's dark eyes. As luck would have it, he and his companion
had been placed on the table right next to them. She could have
reached out and touched his sleeve. Six months had gone by since
she had last seen him. It could have been six milliseconds.

It would have seemed puerile to have pretended she hadn't seen
him. She couldn't have done it anyway; neither could she stick
her chin in the air, make a show of ignoring him, pretend it didn't
matter. Besides, it wouldn't have fooled Julia or Gina – or even
Grant – for a moment. Her friends were watching her with a
mixture of anticipation and sympathy, mouths open, breath held,
waiting for her to . . .

Do what exactly?

She made her mind up, pushed her chair back and stood up,
crossing the two feet between them as he too scrambled to his
feet, eyes level with hers. She had just time to take in the fact that
he was sitting with a much older woman she took to be his mother.

'Hello.' She addressed both, hoping she sounded suitable –
detached but friendly. In control. Unlike Grant, whose eyes were
desperate. He leaned into her, gripped her shoulders, brushed her
cheek with his lips. She felt their heat, the scratch of his newly

grown beard, breathed in his tang, the spice and the soap, the shower gel and shampoo. Felt his presence. His inner circle.

'God, Claire,' he said, voice husky. 'It's good to see you. So very good to see you.'

'You too.' It had come out before she could stop it.

He extracted the full sense, the complete meaning behind the phrase. His eyes widened. 'Really?'

'Ahem.' The splinter of sound broke their contact and seemed to rouse him.

He moved away. Dropped his arms. Actions which told her everything.

'Sorry. This is my mum.'

The woman was eyeing her with curiosity and disdain. She gave a small jerk of her head. She was in her fifties, by the look of her, and had short hair, skilfully streaked blonde and beige. She was well made up but thin, with an aged complexion emphasized rather than disguised by an overambitious attempt to disguise it, heavy kohl around the eyes and a sharp, citrus-orange lipstick. She looked so unhappy, with sagging eyes and a guarded expression, that Claire could hardly imagine the expression ever fading. It was too deeply scored by chronic anxiety, presumably rooted in her daughter's poor health.

'This is Claire.'

The woman's expression turned even more hostile and she said nothing but regarded her as though she was an arch enemy. Claire managed to return a cool response and an attempt at a smile. 'Mrs Steadman. Hello.'

Her eyes searched the room and returned to Grant. 'And Maisie?'

The subtext was always there. *Maisie, your little baby sister with cystic fibrosis, the sister who needed you so much more than I. The sister who manipulated you into abandoning me, the sister who finally replaced me. Well – she won in the end, didn't she?*

Her eyes scanned the room again before returning to a direct gaze into Grant's pirate eyes. *Where was she?*

'Shit, Claire.' Grant's eyes were amazing; very, very dark, with almost girlish long lashes but unmistakably heavy masculine eyebrows. She knew from experience it could be hard to resist those eyes. Eyes that could reflect every single emotion, search so deep into your soul that he found dark places hidden to all – except him. She felt any resistance, hostility, resentment tumble straight into those eyes. And die. His mouth was equally expressive: hard, soft, full, tight, generous, angry, mean, pink, moist, dry. She knew that mouth in all its phases. She lowered her gaze.

'Maisie's in hospital.' His voice was husky, while his mother's face sagged further. 'We just came back to collect some of her stuff. Stuff she wanted.'

'I'm sorry.' She put a hand on his arm, watched his mother's shoulders stiffening even at this tiny gesture. 'Is she very bad?'

'They're talking about a heart and lung transplant. She's been on the list for ages.' He made a weak attempt at a joke. 'No one seems to want to give theirs up.'

As a joke, it was feeble. The weakness behind it was breaking her heart. As a tragedy for a young woman loved by her mother and brother, it was terrible. Whatever Claire resented about Maisie's domination and manipulation of her older brother, sending him on a guilt trip every time he had a life which didn't put her centre stage, Maisie was still a young woman. Not yet thirty but had a diagnosis which had meant a lifetime's ill health and a shortened life expectancy. Maisie had suffered more procedures and courses of antibiotics than most people would have if they lived for three hundred years.

'Grant, I'm sorry.'

'Yeah. Well.' He glanced at his mother. 'We're hoping . . .' He couldn't finish the sentence. His mother had given up trying to be brave and had dropped her face into her hands. Not before Claire had seen that her heavy black kohl was smudged, trailing dark, miserable rivulets down her cheeks.

She turned back to Grant. 'If there's anything . . .'

He simply stared at her. The silence between them extended until it became thick and embarrassing. Claire struggled for something to fill it. Grant seemed incapable. He half turned towards his mother, who was now sitting very still, rigidly watching them. He moved in to speak very softly in her ear. '*They* need *me*, Claire. And *I* need *you*.'

There was not a word in the entire English language suitable for a response. And now he had said it, Grant, too, was silent.

Then he did manage something. He stroked his chin and made an attempt at a mischievous grin. 'Do you like the beard?'

It was that watered-down look of mischief that finally did it, that reminded her of all that had been good between them. It would be this that she would remember. People talk about someone being a shadow of their former self. This Grant was not so much a shadow as a photographic negative. Light and shade in the wrong places.

She backed away. 'It was nice to see you.' It was all she could manage. Nice . . . to finish on a cliché. She could have bitten her tongue off. And that was that. Encounter over. She backed away, returned to her table and two friends, and behind her she heard him sit down again and muttered conversation between him and his mother.

End of. Except she had read the look in his eyes. Despair. Pleading. *They* need *me*, Claire. *I* need *you*. *She* needed *him*. Simple as that. She could not live her life without him, whatever the difficulties thrown at them.

The encounter had put a dampener on the afternoon, prevented it from stretching into a gay evening. The sparkle had gone. The rest of the evening was subdued. Julia had always been a sensitive person. She regarded Claire and said nothing, except she stretched her hand across the table and touched Claire's. 'Darling.' That was all she said.

And Gina's smile added her sympathy.

ELEVEN

Monday, 22 June, 8.45 a.m.

She was glad to return to work on the Monday, put distance between herself, Grant and his poison ivy family and start focusing on the case in hand. Heather.

How was she going to tackle it when *no one* was quite speaking the truth and every step could mean trampling on the eggshells of Charles's career and her own previous experience, which she had largely blocked out – until now?

So, sitting in her office, nibbling the nail of her index finger, she started to plan her campaign. To get at the truth, she needed to speak to three people.

Top of the list was Heather's enigmatic sister. Alone.

Then there was the acquiescent husband, Geoff. She couldn't

quite get a handle on this man, who appeared to have married his wife when she was already pregnant before tolerating her claim that her next child was not his but the result of an extra-marital liaison . . . with the window cleaner. A claim which was proved wrong. And now a third – again not his but the result of yet another affair. Was he so docile, so passive? Two children had already died. How had he taken that? Just as passively? Perhaps Geoff's take on this bizarre situation would shed some light on Heather's current claim.

And then there was Heather herself. Claire realized from a sudden, sharp pain in her finger that she had bitten her nail right down to the quick. Was Heather mad, bad, dangerous to know, or simply a sad fantasist? Did she really believe that Charles was desperately in love with her? Claire shook her head. Certainly she didn't appear to fit neatly into the little box of ICD classification of mental disorders. The edges were too ill-defined.

She decided to take a step or two further into the strange world of Heather Krimble, so she added two more names to her list: Timothy Cartwright, boss of the Cartwright Printing Company, alleged father of Eliza Krimble and Sam Maddox, window cleaner, proven not to have been Freddie's dad.

Her pen hovered over her list. It was incomplete, one name still missing – perhaps the single most important name. She realized she was reluctant to add it.

Was there any point questioning Charles about this? Something inside her shrank from any further contact. But even thinking about him had led her in a different direction. What had actually happened between him and his ex-wife to make him so apprehensive of a meeting between the two women? An exchange of confidences?

She smiled at a memory. *Claire. Will you ever stop asking questions? Will you ever get all the answers?*

Grant.

She squared her shoulders. She had to start somewhere. So she picked up the phone and asked Rita to make an appointment as soon as she had a free space.

Tuesday, 23 June, 10.30 a.m.

Ruth Acton turned up on time, neatly dressed in what looked like her work clothes, an A-line black skirt modestly touching her knees and a white blouse with a Peter Pan collar. She had her sister's rather prissy air as well her pointy little chin, but Heather was prettier. In her case, the pointy little chin nicely finished off a heart-shaped face, but the same feature in her sister made her look sharp and spinsterish. She wore little make-up except a tangerine-coloured lipstick that drew the eyes as she talked, changing shape to form words. She carried a large black handbag from which she produced a small notebook and a biro and laid them, closed, on the desk in front of her. There was something both businesslike and threatening in the gesture. It felt like a lawyer's action, waiting to record the interview verbatim.

Claire greeted her warmly and thanked her for coming. But she soon realized that sisterly loyalty was winning. Ruth was careful in choosing her responses, guarded in what she said and her eyes were wary and suspicious throughout.

Claire began by laying her cards down on the table, mentally flipping them over one by one as she covered her points.

'We need to get to the truth of your sister's account,' she began. 'I'm sure you understand that there are some serious implications, particularly for Mr Tissot, if her account is reliable.'

Ruth stared back at her, hesitating before she responded. 'I don't think you quite understand, Doctor. Mr Tissot and his career are not the issue here. My sister is not a liar.'

Not deliberately. Claire kept the comment to herself.

Ruth's eyes were now stone cold, her arms tightly folded. She regarded Claire with an expression just short of hostility. In the small, anonymous consulting room there was an unmistakable air of alienation, which Claire ignored as she ploughed on.

'Your sister has made allegations in two previous pregnancies.'

Ruth nodded. It was a staccato movement, neither a yay nor a nay. Just an acknowledgement, while her eyes remained cold, detached, guarded. Watchful. She offered no explanation. Claire was going to have to drag it out of her.

'So what do you make of that?'

Claire's eyes trained on her, Heather's sister shrugged. It was no answer.

Claire continued, 'Before we discuss the specific allegations surrounding this current pregnancy, let's focus on Eliza and Freddie's parentage.'

Again, something was missing. Ruth Acton had been the babies' aunt. She would have expected some semblance of grief. Some response. But there was nothing except a stony stare and apparent adherence to her sister's stories.

Claire waited before continuing again, 'In the case of Eliza, Mr Cartwright, your sister's boss, denied that there had been ever been any sexual activity between him and your sister. In fact, he said there had never been any sort of relationship between them at all.'

No visible response. Nothing except this brick wall. After a pause, which Ruth declined to fill, Claire ploughed on. 'In the case of Freddie and your sister's allegations against Sam Maddox, a paternity test *was* carried out. And as I'm sure you know, Freddie was Geoff's son. Your sister's husband.'

Straightaway, Ruth pitched in on the weak spot. 'That doesn't mean to say the relationships never happened.'

'No. But both times the men have denied it.'

Ruth stuck her pointy little chin forward. 'Well, they would, wouldn't they? That's men all over. Have their way and off they go.'

'You're not married yourself?'

Ruth shook her head and broke eye contact.

'In a relationship?'

Another firm shake of her head. Claire wondered. Did she have her own prejudices against the male sex? Some negative experience, perhaps?

'Well,' she said, 'I will be interviewing both Mr Cartwright and Mr Maddox.' Again, she waited. Again, there was silence.

'And so to your sister's current pregnancy.'

Ruth was now silent; lips pressed together, eyes evasive.

'What exactly do you remember of that night in November when you went to your boss's bonfire party?'

Ruth frowned.

Plotting a story or struggling to recall the truth?

'Mr Metcalfe always has a party,' she said, speaking slowly. 'Every year.' Her eyes flickered up to Claire's. 'Usually I don't go, but last year I thought why not? Why ever not? Why don't I go? But I didn't want to go on my own, so I asked Heather if she'd come.'

Claire interrupted. 'Her husband didn't mind?'

Ruth dismissed this – and him – with a shake of her head.

'We got there about eight. The party was already in full swing. Really noisy. People milling around all over the place. Mr Metcalfe owns a field at the back of his house and the bonfire was there, already lit.' Her eyelids fluttered and drooped. 'People were trooping in and out. It was a cold night, but . . .' Here she stopped and unexpectedly smiled. 'The fire was hot. You could feel the heat from it as you stepped outside the house. It was magical,' she said. 'They'd just lit the fire and there were fireworks going off.' She smiled. 'Popping off all the time. The fire was crackling and the fireworks shot brilliant stars into the sky, reds and blues and this bright, bright white. It was wonderful.'

Claire badly wanted to prompt her. *What about Charles?*

But she resisted the temptation and let Ruth Acton tell the story at her own pace, telling it her way. 'There were lots of people there. I don't know how many and most of them were strangers to me but I did recognize Mr Tissot. He was near the house having a drink. Standing on his own.'

'Was he near your sister? Speaking to her?'

She shook her head, frowning. 'Not then.'

She wanted to ask whether Charles had been watching her sister, as Heather had claimed. But it was too leading a question.

'Did you see them talking, maybe later?'

She looked up, thoughtful. 'I don't remember,' she said. 'I . . . I lost Heather for part of the evening.'

'For long?'

'I don't know. An hour, maybe . . .' She sounded dubious.

'And how was she when you met up again?'

'She seemed happy.'

Consistent with just having had a fuck on the back seat of a Jaguar?

She substituted that little crudity with, 'Did you form any conclusion as to *why* she seemed happy? Did she *say* anything?'

'Not then.'

Claire waited.

'Later, she told me about Charles. She said he'd been watching her all night and that she'd encountered him in the bedroom.'

Again, Claire interrupted. 'Did she use that word?'

'What word?'

'Encountered.'

'I think so. I can't actually . . . Why do you ask? What difference does a *word* make?'

A word plucked from a romantic novel is not the way a woman speaks just after the event. It speaks too much of fiction. She had to find a reason. 'A word,' she said, 'adds colour – authenticity. And when she found out later that she was pregnant?'

Ruth smiled. 'She was . . . overjoyed. She couldn't wait to tell him.'

'So she wasn't seeing him in the meantime?'

'Oh, I think they'd met up.' It was a vague answer, which she appeared to feel the need to clarify. 'If not physically, they'd kept in touch.' She waited for a moment before adding archly, 'You have to leave my sister a few little secrets of her own, Doctor Roget. I haven't pursued her story. If she wanted to tell me more she would have done. I've never asked for details.' There was a note of discomfort now, a little trickle of doubt, maybe?

'You've never disbelieved her story?'

'Of course not.' She paused before she crossed her legs and launched into an attack. 'You're only taking this line because it concerns one of your colleagues.'

Something flared inside Claire. 'I'm taking this line because your sister has made a habit of making allegations against men. Now I don't know what the consequences have been to the other two but I do know what will happen to my colleague. We're talking about an entire career here.'

'And my sister's life.' Something in the sharp defence and implied confrontation made Claire's skin crawl. This devotion between the sisters was pathological. There was absolutely no doubt that Ruth was convinced that, whatever anyone else said or science proved, her sister's version of events was the truth. She added with more than a hint of venom, 'And the dates fit.'

Claire studied the woman who held her gaze without faltering. Considering the chequered history, apart from family loyalty, what was it that gave her such blind faith in her sister's integrity? Maybe that was just it. Family loyalty.

'When exactly did she tell you about Mr Tissot?'

'When her period was late. That was when she told me.' Ruth frowned. 'That was when she told me who the father was. It was at the same time that she told me she wanted Charles to deliver their baby. She said that she would ask Doctor Sylas to refer her when she was a bit farther on. She said that he had said he would look after her. That was what he'd meant.'

I'll look after you. She'd forgotten he'd said that to her all those years ago until this very minute. She had felt sick and had sprung open the car door, told him she was feeling unwell, almost tumbled out. He'd called it out, at the same time pulling up his trousers, zipping up his flies. She felt herself stiffen, shook away the memory and returned to the present with difficulty pursuing the words. 'He said that? When?'

'When she told him she was expecting his child.'

'So when exactly was that?'

'I'm not sure of the exact sequence of events, Doctor.' Ruth was wary but perfectly in control. 'You'll have to ask my sister.'

'Did she give you any *other* details about the circumstances of that night? Perhaps earlier, the encounter in the bedroom?'

'I don't know.' Ruth was confused now. 'I'm not sure she told me.'

'OK.' Claire dropped it. 'So what about contact between them now?'

'She says he's been taking really good care of her and the baby. After all,' she challenged, 'who would take better care of a child than its father and mother? In their own home, together.'

Claire picked up on the implication. 'Are you telling me that your sister, the baby and Mr Tissot plan to set up home together?'

Ruth nodded.

Claire drew in a deep breath. This hardly squared up with Charles's desperate plea to her.

How much of these events had really happened? What did *he* remember of that night? Of Heather? What she had been wearing? Had they spoken? Or had he conveniently forgotten it all? She repeated her question. 'What exactly does your sister expect to happen now?'

'She and Charles – well, they're going to make a go of it.'

'He actually said that to her?'

The challenge made Ruth visibly cross. 'She wouldn't say it if it wasn't the truth, would she?'

Back to square one. 'What do you expect to happen next?'

'Well, he's divorced. His wife is a nasty, cold-hearted bitch.'

Aren't they all?

'So why shouldn't they get married?' Her eyes blazed. 'Why shouldn't my sister have some happiness in her life? She's put up with that oaf, Geoff, largely because it was what our father wanted. Why shouldn't she have someone decent in her life?'

It was a convincing version from her point of view but it was totally untrue – according to Charles. There were two different tableaux here – Heather's fantasy picture and Charles's sheer desperation – that she couldn't stitch together without the thread of a psychiatric diagnosis.

Ruth was watching her, waiting for her pronouncement.

'Would you describe your sister as amoral?'

Ruth's eyes flashed out fury.

Claire tried again. 'Has your sister had many lovers?'

This brought her to the edge of her seat and an emphatic and unambiguous response. 'No.'

'She doesn't sleep around?'

'Absolutely not.'

'Do you think this baby will prove to be Mr Tissot's?'

'Of course.'

'You must know him from the hospital.'

'Yes. He's a friend of Mr Metcalfe, the consultant I work for.' Her voice trailed away uncomfortably. 'I think they play golf together.'

That figured. She could well imagine Charles propping up the bar on the fourteenth hole. Gossiping, swapping private patient stories and crude jokes.

'Tell me more about Heather's husband. What sort of a man is he?'

'Geoff? Oh, he's all right. Just boring and never going to make anything of himself. When he drinks, he gets nasty.' She paused before adding, 'Not surprising really, considering it was our father who selected him.'

'Your father set up the marriage?'

'Heather was pregnant. Cartwright wasn't stepping forward. Dad didn't want her staying at home. She didn't have a lot of choice.'

'Is he violent towards her?'

'No. At least, I don't think so. Just verbally unpleasant. Rude. Boorish. He's not good enough for my sister.'

'And how did he respond to Heather's claim about Sam Maddox?'

Quite cleverly, Ruth parried the question. 'Well, he's his, isn't he? The test proved it.'

There was a challenge as well as anger in her response.

'And when Freddie died?'

'Heart . . .' She stopped before adding, *broken*. 'Very sad,' she substituted. 'Freddie was a lovely little chap.' She bowed her head.

And Claire sensed that the interview was over.

TWELVE

Thursday, 25 June, 3 p.m.
Outpatient Department, Greatbach Secure Psychiatric Hospital.

There was an advantage and disadvantage to this absorbing and interesting case. On the one hand, it was enough of a distraction to have stopped her brooding over Grant. But on the down side, she knew she was neglecting her other patients, in particular Arthur Connolly and Riley. She should have been completing her psychiatric assessment of them both and was well behind schedule.

But her priority at the moment was to get to the bottom of Heather's story. And so she asked Rita to send her another appointment slot only two days after the interview with her sister.

Something had been bothering her. It was that last episode of banging her abdomen, punishing the child for the perceived sins of the father. According to Laura's notes, she was a 'cutter'. From self-harm to harming a baby was not a big step.

And two children had died.

Again, Ruth sat in, quiet as a mouse, so unobtrusive she faded into the wall. Whether she had told her sister the content of the consultation they had shared, Claire didn't know and couldn't guess from the sphinx-like, impassive face of both sisters. Impassive but wary.

Initially Heather seemed positive, friendly, nodding and smiling, but in an automated fashion. There was no warmth behind it, nothing genuine. A strange lack of emotion. Almost of humanity. What Claire felt she was looking at was a robotic response.

Her pregnancy was more pronounced and she appeared increasingly aware of it, intermittently stroking her bump, looking down at her swollen abdomen, which she'd emphasized by draping a tent-like billow of flowery material over it, even giving little secret smiles downwards as though the child could peer through her abdominal wall and see its mother. It was bizarre and a bit creepy, in Claire's opinion. And the secret gestures between Heather and her child excluded both her and Ruth who sat, back ramrod straight, staring ahead, looking miserable.

Which made Claire wonder why was this having such an effect on her? Was Ruth's job threatened because of the poison her sister was spreading and her allegiance to Heather? Who knew why it was so intense? Why this bond so strong? But *Ruth* was not her patient; *Heather* was, and so Claire passed over the sister and focused on her patient, plunging straight in. She needed to find out how far Heather was from reality.

'Do you understand *why* we are doubtful that Mr Tissot is the father of your child?'

Heather lifted her gaze heavily and slowly to meet Claire's challenge.

'No,' she said. 'Quite honestly, I don't understand why I'm here at all. When I tell Charles that you've been interfering, he will be furious.'

Claire felt her mouth drop open as Heather continued her rant. 'You can't doubt that he is this . . .' a glance downwards and another stroke before staring back again at Claire, '. . . child's father.' She stiffened in her chair, hands now gripping the arms. 'Are you trying to say that we are not lovers?' She had just the right measure of incredulity in her voice. 'That *nothing* happened between us?'

Now that was possibly a step too far.

Claire's best ammunition was, 'And in the cases of Eliza and Freddie?'

Heather gave a little hiccup of a laugh. 'They can deny it all they like,' she said smoothly. 'Sam and Mr Cartwright can say it didn't happen.' She leaned in. 'But I have powers, Doctor Roget. Men tend to fall for me.' The words were accompanied by a flick of the eyes, as though she couldn't quite believe it herself. 'And then they feel ashamed and deny it. Or blot it out of their memories out of a sense of guilt or . . . something. In this case, Charles is simply frightened to come out with it.' A curving smile. 'After all, his divorce is recent. His ex-wife is vindictive and his own children are furious with their father for . . . succumbing.'

It was one way of putting it. But . . . 'You know an awful lot about him.'

'Of course.'

There was only one way of achieving anything here – follow Heather Krimble down the rabbit hole.

'But Tim Cartwright wasn't married,' she pointed out. 'He had no reason not to. He had no vindictive wife or angry children.'

Heather threw back her head and laughed. It was a high-pitched, hysterical laugh, almost a scream. 'He had a mother. Far more controlling.'

Claire blinked back her response. *Tell me about it.*

'Besides . . .' Another throw back of her head. 'Tim was a wimp. Weak. He couldn't face the truth, the consequences of what he'd done. He couldn't confess to his mother.'

'And Sam Maddox?'

Again, a secret smile that excluded both Claire and Ruth, who was still staring rigidly ahead but now looking slightly awkward. 'Sam was due to get married when he seduced me. He wasn't man enough to call the whole thing off so he pretended it hadn't happened.'

Always an explanation. Ready and logical. Heather's eyes were overtly hostile as she waited for Claire's next parry.

'But, as we've already ascertained, Freddie wasn't Sam's. The DNA proved he was your husband's child.'

The pointy little chin jutted forward and tilted upwards. 'And *I* say the samples were switched. People didn't want to acknowledge my power over men. They fall head over heels. And it was the same with Charles. He. Could. Not. Have. Resisted. Me.'

This was one of the paramount signs of erotomania: an unshakable conviction that you are irresistible to any man you turn your attentions on. Yet, by her side, Ruth was nodding her agreement. Though not without a brief, worried glance at her sister.

'How do you and Charles communicate, Heather?' She asked the question without any hope of an honest response. What she anticipated was some fiction of Heather's own invention.

There was no answer. No response. Not even fiction. Wary-eyed, Heather had shut down, so Claire left the question dangling in the air, spinning like a corpse on a gibbet, a warning to others.

To her, Heather was still a puzzle. She didn't quite fit into the criteria, though the borders of psychiatric problems are invariably blurred. Most people who experience erotomania are basically conceited. They have wrapped themselves up in shiny bubble wrap.

Heather was certainly displaying that. Erotomaniacs do not tell lies but the truth *as they see it*. The trouble is that their version of the truth is distorted by a kind of dysmorphia. But, unlike anorexia, dysmorphia is a halo of irresistibility that shines around them, drawing suitors in, moths to the flame. Iron filings to a magnet. A natural force. In Heather's mind, these bald statements were the truth. She was irresistible, which patently was a fantasy. What Claire had to find were the borders of Heather's psychosis. Did it make her a danger to herself, the wider community, the unborn child, or even to Charles himself when he continued to deny his role in the conception of the baby?

If Heather was a danger to anyone, including herself, Claire's role was clear. Heather Krimble should be admitted, detained and observed, and when the infant was delivered it should be kept under surveillance. She had to consider this option and make a decision. She focused back on her patient.

Heather was leaning back, eyes half closed, inhabiting some place of her own where she was Queen Bee. As Claire watched, her lips moved, forming words as her hands stroked her pregnant abdomen as though reassuring the child inside. And then her right hand reached out and stroked her left upper arm and her gaze flirted up sideways to her imaginary lover. At the same time, her legs parted and she licked her lips. The whole tableaux was strange, unreal and felt on the edge. Erotic. She gave a little curvy smile downwards, looked up through her eyelashes. Her hand stole up to her shoulder, fingers outstretched, weaving in with an invisible another's so convincingly that Claire could picture him. Charles Tissot, big, burly, looking down as Heather continued to tease and play as their hands slid down to her engorged breast.

Claire watched her for a while, noting that Ruth appeared excluded from the inner tableaux, looked uncomfortable and a little scared.

And Claire felt the same. Heather's actions spoke of psychosis. Claire tried to draw her back to reality by focusing on detail. 'Where did you and Tim Cartwright have sex?'

Heather didn't even hesitate, stop to think or look at her. 'In his office, of course.'

'What about his other staff?'

This earned her a look of pure contempt. 'After hours,' she said heavily.

'But physically . . .?'

'He has a sofa. It's red. Small but big enough. And there's always the desk.' Heather leaned in, spoke in a hoarse whisper, eyes flirtatious, right hand now dropped to her legs. Then, in a sudden and graceful movement, her back arched. 'You know? Legs apart, like this, and I lean back, like this.'

'And the window cleaner? How exactly did that happen?'

Initially, again, no response, so Claire tried a little harder to flush out the truth. 'You're aware that the window cleaner says he never came inside the house, Heather. So where are you claiming you and he had sex?' She leaned forward to press for an answer. 'Through glass?'

She received a look of contempt.

'In the garden? Did you go out to the garden?'

No response except a wary look.

'Is your garden overlooked?'

'In some parts,' she said haughtily.

Claire pressed again. 'So was it in the garden or in the house? Did Sam, whatever he said, come in the house? Was he lying?'

'Men always lie.' It was said contemptuously.

'In the bedroom? Is that where you had sex? In the bedroom? In the very bed where you and your husband slept?'

Heather was silent, eyes still wary as she thought about this one.

'To your husband's knowledge, you were at home for most of the time. Not gallivanting around the town, so if Geoff's . . .'

A little flicker at the mention of her husband's name.

'So if Geoff's right, sex must have taken place either in the house or in the garden, or else in *his* car – or van. What does he drive?'

'A van.' Her response was sullen. She hadn't wanted to give this detail.

'How many times did you make love? Often? Did he come round when he wasn't cleaning your windows?'

Heather frowned in anger, then drew in breath as though preparing her answer. But none came. Her frown deepened – as she struggled to remember? Or more likely hunt through her catalogue of fantasy to find a suitable response?

Claire prompted her again. 'Your time was largely accounted for. So . . .?'

Heather's eyes lifted and then her shoulders drooped. Answer? She didn't have one.

'Doesn't Geoff get cross with you for telling these tales?'

'He's always cross.' The statement had spilled out before Heather had had time to think. This then, Claire sensed, was the truth.

'Is he violent? Like your father?'

She shook her head. 'Not like my father. Not in the same way. Father was strict, wasn't he, Ruth?'

Her sister heaved out a big sigh. 'Oh, yes. Dad was strict all right.'

'In what way?' Claire addressed both sisters.

Ruth answered. 'Very religious,' she said. 'He had – rules.'

'So in what way is Geoff similar?'

'He's not above raising his fist to me if he doesn't like something I say.'

Alarm bells sounded, accompanied by a possible explanation for Heather's fantasy. Geoff? Violent? A man selected by her father? This could be the reason why she had to invent another father for her child. Ruth was looking troubled. Her hand reached out to touch her sister's arm The two women exchanged glances. Ruth was warning her sister to be guarded, stopping her from saying something. What? Whatever it was, Heather had read the message and taken heed.

'Heather,' Claire said gently. 'Are you saying that your husband is violent towards you?'

She was wondering about the two dead children.

Annoyingly, Heather's concentration seemed to drift away again. She opened her eyes wide to stare into space.

'Because if he is,' Claire continued, 'you should report it.'

No response.

She pursued the point. 'He can be charged.' This was useless. 'Was he ever like that to your babies?'

No response. Not even a flicker of a muscle. Just a strange, steady smile.

'Do you think your new baby could be in danger from Geoff?'

Heather relaxed and shook her head. 'Charles,' she said, 'will look after us. Protect us. He won't let anything happen to either me or our child.'

Claire almost groaned. *So it was back to Charles again, was it?*

She paused, sensing she was peering over the edge of a precipice, about to make a big, big leap. She had to tread carefully here. Maybe it was too soon, but she sensed she was getting somewhere. 'Do you think that is why you claim the baby is not your husband's, because you fear for the child's safety?'

Heather's eyes flickered in her direction.

And Claire was aware that she had just provided too neat and tidy an explanation, one which fitted the facts like a handmade glove. Of course damaged Heather would look to her boss, the kind window cleaner, the obstetrician she had fleetingly met at a party. They would protect her children from her husband who was not above raising his fist to her.

But there is a danger that, when you have provided an account, however well it fits, it doesn't necessarily mean it is the truth.

Heather stared out of the window and declined to respond now. But there was a new dignity in her silence, a squaring of the shoulders, a lengthening of her neck, a tilt of her head. An awareness that up until now had been missing.

It emboldened Claire. 'So,' she picked up briskly, 'let's talk about Mr Tissot. Charles.'

At this Ruth stepped in, vinegar in her voice. 'We know you're bound to stick up for one of your own profession.'

Claire turned her attention to her now. *Two days ago, when I questioned you, you said nothing about domestic violence, which gives us a more logical and less psychotic reason behind your sister's behaviour. You kept that back, didn't you, little sister?*

She addressed her in a low voice. 'Have you ever witnessed Geoff assault your sister?'

Hesitation. A fraction too long. Surely just a simple yes or no?

Finally Claire got her answer. A reluctant but emphatic shake of the head.

Heather spoke, picking up on the subject. 'Charles,' she said dreamily. 'It was *fate* that I went with my sister to the party and he was there. *Fate* drove us together. He was unhappy because his wife was being a shit about the divorce.'

How did she know that? Had it been common knowledge around the hospital, gossip her sister had picked up and passed on?

This is the danger. The fantasist weaves small truths into the fabric of their story. It throws you because then you have to unpick every single stitch to know which is authentic and which simply a story.

'I knew it was fate when he started kissing me. He has big, soft lips.'

THIRTEEN

Claire stared at her. After all these years she could still taste them, almost feel them, those big, soft lips pressing down on hers.

But surely these days Charles would not just dive in with a kiss when so much would be at stake? He would be subtler than that? But then Heather provided an explanation – of sorts.

'He was pretty drunk.'

And a drunk man is less predictable.

She was enjoying this reliving of her quite detailed fantasy. 'He pulled my knickers down. I wasn't wearing any tights.'

'Even though it was November and you'd been invited to a bonfire party?' Claire frowned. 'So what *were* you wearing?'

'I can't remember.' She was cross at the interruption and continued without answering.

'We had sex. It was . . .' lazy smile, '. . . enjoyable. He knew all the right places to touch.'

He would. He's an obstetrician. Oh, yes, Charles had the knack all right.

By her sister's side, Ruth was looking distinctly uncomfortable at this detail.

'And then? Afterwards?'

'I went back to the party. I knew I had him hooked.' She continued without prompting, 'When I missed a period, I waited for a while, and then I asked Doctor Sylas to put me under him. I pretended. I said that I'd *heard* he was very good and this time I wanted my baby to live.' She looked pleased with her performance. 'He pretended not to recognize me.' Now she was affronted.

'And since then?'

Heather stared.

'Since then, have you had much contact with Mr Tissot?'

Heather bit her lower lip in a gesture she might have imagined was coquettish. 'We've had to keep our distance,' she said. 'Now he's my doctor, we have to be ve-ery careful.'

Play along with this, Claire. 'At the party, did he know your name?'

Heather shook her head, smiling.

'Did he recognize you when you turned up at his clinic?'

'Of course he did.' Her eyes were wide open. 'But he had to pretend I was a complete stranger.'

'You realize if all this is true he could be struck off? Do you want Charles Tissot to be stopped from practising?'

A shake of the head. 'That won't do me any good,' she said, smiling. 'Or the baby. What would we live on if Charles doesn't carry on working?'

She had it all planned out. Every step of the way. 'But you understand that if your story is true he *must* be stopped? The Medical Defence Union will stop him practising while they investigate.'

She was watching Heather's face for a trace of realization at how the walls would come tumbling down. There was none. Only this evangelical conviction.

'I don't see what he's done wrong,' she protested. 'He just fell in love.'

'A relationship between a doctor and his patient is . . .'

Heather stood up then, fury steaming out of her nostrils while her sister watched with a wary eye, tension in her neck. *Ready to duck?*

'You're just jealous. You wish it was *you* he was madly in love with . . .'

The phrase jarred with Claire. Charles didn't do 'madly in love'. He did cynical, manipulative, careless sex with no payback.

Her patient ranted on while her sister played no part in the proceedings, just watched from the sidelines. 'You just wish a clever, rich, handsome man wanted *you* . . .' she jabbed her index finger towards Claire, '. . . instead of me.' Heather was panting now with the effort and emotion, her hand sliding over her breasts. 'I wasn't his patient *then*. It was only later when I knew I was pregnant with his child that we decided he was the best person to make sure I kept well and that our baby was born healthy.'

We decided? *Our* baby? The phrases found their target like a stiletto blade. And Claire almost felt like a knife-thrower's assistant. Standing there, waiting for the knives to miss – or else.

'Are you trying to tell me,' Claire asked very carefully, 'that the request for you to be put under his care was something you cooked up *between* you?'

The snooty, nose-in-the-air pose, pointy chin tilted back. 'I don't like the fact that you said *cooked up*, as though you don't believe me. As though it was a sort of fantasy game.'

Claire hesitated. This is the trouble. When you don't enter the fantasy world sometimes your patient becomes angry. And, in the psychotic, anger to violence is a very short step.

'I'm sorry. I should have said "decided".'

Heather accepted the apology with a regal bend of her head. 'How?'

'What do you mean?'

'How did you communicate? Did you speak on the phone? Internet? Facebook? Skype?'

Anything that can be checked on. 'How did you and he keep in contact?'

Heather folded her arms and pressed her lips together. She didn't answer.

She had taken refuge again in her own little world where she was adored by all, men falling at her feet, women green with envy at her irresistible charms. She was peering down at her swollen abdomen and then she appeared to jerk and freeze, leaning back in her chair, distancing herself from the pregnancy, making a face of sudden revulsion as though she saw something evil in there, behind the billow of flowered material. Her head shot up, eyes bulging, so she was facing Claire, and she appeared to have a moment of blind panic. Then she started to smack it. Punish it. 'Bad. Bad. Bad baby.'

Was this reality knocking at her door? Her husband's baby rather than Charles's?

Claire responded quietly and calmly, at the same time starting to fix her mind that this infant could well be in danger already. 'Don't do that, Heather. You don't want to hurt it, do you?'

'I do when it kicks. Too hard.'

'But it can hurt the child. You wouldn't want to do that, would you?'

Instantly, Heather's head shot up and she gave her a look of pure vitriol.

Claire simply observed, not reacting. The violence and sudden-ness of the action was concerning. And gave her good reason to admit her. To observe. Protect.

But she needed to play this her way and she'd come to a

decision. 'You need to be under an obstetrician,' Claire said. 'And it shouldn't really be Mr Tissot if you're having a relationship with him.' She could have added that if Charles had acknowledged the child as his he would have had every right to be in the labour ward.

But, interestingly, Heather hadn't responded to this. Claire persisted. 'And you also need to continue to see me.'

'Why?'

'Well, two of your babies have died. And I think we should keep an eye on your mental state as well as your physical state.'

'Then I'll see you *and* I'll see Charles,' she snapped.

'I've already said it wouldn't be appropriate and I'm not sure he'd want to continue to be your obstetrician in view of the circumstances.'

'If you say so.' The resignation made her voice flat.

Heather glanced across her sister, and in that look Claire read complete complicity. A conspiratorial exchange. These two were thick, in it together. All the way, right up to the hilt.

'So what next, Heather?'

'What next?' She gave a small, private little giggle, then put her hand in front of her face to hide it. 'Charles will deliver the baby. *Our* baby,' she corrected. 'And then we can be together. At last, without all this interference.'

'And the baby?' Claire asked quietly.

'Oh.' In her excitement, she had obviously forgotten about it. Her eyes dropped to the bulge. 'Well, of course,' she said, looking a little defensive. 'That too. He is divorced, you know. He is free to *marry* me. And I know that's what he wants.'

Ri-i-ght.

'I know,' she repeated with even more certainty.

'And then what?'

'Sorry?' Heather looked bemused. 'I'm not following you.'

'What then?' Claire repeated. 'Two of your children have died as cot deaths. Do you think this baby will be all right?'

Heather had her answer ready. 'Charles is a big, strong man,' she said. It was no answer, or else an answer of sorts.

Now Claire had to make a decision. There were no winners here. Heather was vulnerable, her sister colluding, Charles in trouble, the baby possibly in danger.

'You must understand, Heather. Mr Tissot denies . . .'

She got no further. Heather's eyes burned. 'But he *has* to say that, hasn't he? He *can't* admit it.' She laughed. 'You can see that, can't you? He just *has* to pretend it didn't happen or he'd lose his job.'

Her eyes narrowed then, cat-like, sharp and spiteful, gleaming as she mused over the point. 'He might *still* lose his job.'

FOURTEEN

C laire started filling in her notes, stating all that had been said, finishing with her conclusion:

It is possible that physical violence from her husband, Geoff, has translated to a rejection of his fatherhood and this has in turn led to substitute parenting furthered by erotomani. She can't bear to think a man who was violent towards her also had sex, possibly under duress, with her and fathered her children.

But . . . She sat back and half closed her eyes. What a huge word this was, the *but . . .* that you wait for after praise, knowing it will be tagged on, almost as an afterthought, but leaving the bitter taste of criticism in your mouth, and it is this bitter aftertaste that stays with you, not damning with faint praise. No, rather destroying it, erasing the memory of anything sweet that was said before. It is always the *but . . .* that you remember.

We can search for the truth. It exists. It is out there, somewhere, sometimes buried deep under a pile of debris, tantalizingly difficult to find. Sometimes you have to scrabble over shards of half-forgotten memories or the pointed barbs of long-ago events dealt with and discarded. Dig deep, Claire. Dig deep. And then dig deeper. Because it is down there, somewhere. At the bottom of the well lies the real truth. She was reflective as she wrote.

It is unusual for this circumstance to translate to erotomania, to find a substitute male role model. She stopped writing. Yes, it did happen, but in this case, three times? With three different men? Was she convinced that this was the true version? She continued writing. *She sought out Charles Tissot, probably after the chance meeting at the bonfire party.* Again, she stopped writing to think. *Heather Krimble shows some signs of psychosis – inappropriate movements, particularly directed at the unborn child. But she has a firm conviction, shared by her sister, that she is speaking the truth. In her mind, men want her. She holds an absolute certainty that all men will fall under her spell. But there are troubling aspects of the case. Namely, two previous cot deaths and the punishment she appears to mete out to the unborn child manifested by banging on her abdomen hard enough to cause the foetus discomfort if not actual harm.* She scrubbed out the final four words after a moment's thought. So how do you stop that? Bandage her hands?

She closed the file, mentally leaving it wide open and planning her next step.

It was time to meet the man she had mentally registered as the Monster, the villain of the piece, the cause of this particular mayhem: Geoff Krimble, not Charles. She would ask Rita to invite him in.

Pleased she was seeing a way forward, she could now focus on other responsibilities.

5 p.m.

She often met her registrar towards the end of the day to discuss cases. She was aware that her absorption with Heather had distracted her from her other responsibilities and possibly left too much to the rest of her team. Now she needed to catch up and check that all else was well.

Salena Urbi, her registrar, was a beautiful Egyptian who wore her hijab with tantalizing elegance, gold earrings flashing against her dark skin. But her superficial beauty did nothing to detract from the fact that she was an experienced clinical forensic psychiatrist who had worked in many other countries. Claire felt lucky to have her. Besides her professional competence and vast experience, she also had a delightful manner and mischievous sense of humour, finding aspects of many cases that brought breadth and balance to her diagnoses. Claire was interested to hear her 'take' on the odd case of Heather Krimble.

Hoping Salena might have some past experience in similar cases, Claire explained the situation and watched as she absorbed the facts without comment. Finally she turned her dark eyes with their finely shaped eyebrows towards her. 'I've never encountered a case like this before. It sounds most unusual. And potentially very troublesome to Mr Tissot.'

'Quite.'

'So what are you going to do next, Claire?'

'Apart from interviewing Geoff Krimble, I thought I'd delve a little deeper into Heather's previous allegations. See if I can get some clues there.'

'The other two men?'

'Yeah.'

'The fathers, she claimed, of the babies who died in infancy?' She looked concerned.

'The pathologist found nothing at post-mortem,' Claire reminded her.

It didn't erase the frown line from Salena's normally smooth forehead. 'Still worrying, though. Now she's carrying another. And you say she's hitting her abdomen?'

Claire nodded.

'I did have one patient. A paranoid schizophrenic. I looked after her during her pregnancy. It was in Lille.'

'Which only goes to show that medical histories are the same the world over.'

Salena laughed. 'Which is why we can get a job more or less anywhere.'

'Yeah. And is why, as Laura's off sick . . .'

'Nothing serious, I hope?'

'Well . . . I don't like the sound of it. Put it like that.'

'Oh, dear. So who's doing her work?'

'To prove your point about medicine being the same the world over, an Aussie.'

'Then maybe he has experience of erotomania.'

'Maybe. But what about your pregnant schizophrenic? What happened there?'

'She got worse during the pregnancy, claiming the baby was the Devil's and that she must destroy it. She got hold of a knife and tried to excise it. Luckily the staff were vigilant, though she should never have accessed a knife in the first place. We didn't want to sedate her in case it harmed the child. The stuff we use in psychiatry is pretty toxic, isn't it?'

'Yeah. So?'

'We kept a very close eye on her and did an elective caesarean section at thirty weeks, then had the baby made a ward of court and subsequently adopted.'

'So she didn't actually harm the child?'

Salena looked grim. 'After the knife attempt, we didn't give her the chance. We couldn't risk it. She was observed twenty-four/seven.'

Which gave Claire food for thought. 'Thanks, Salena. I think you've just made up my mind for me. We'd better admit her as soon as possible.'

'Here?'

Claire nodded.

'You'll get the community midwives in to see her?'

'And there lies yet another problem.'

'Ah.' Salena still looked concerned. 'I'm beginning to understand. Isn't Charles Tissot's ex-wife . . .?' Her eyes widened and her voice tailed off.

Claire nodded. 'She's the head of it.'

'Won't that be just a bit awkward?'

'Awkward? Explosive, more like. I'm hoping that Rhoda Tissot will send a junior so she won't be directly involved. And if she is, that her professionalism will kick in.'

'A bit optimistic if you ask me. I've heard she's fairly fiery.'

'Very.'

'And Charles Tissot himself?'

'I've advised him to contact the MDU. He's on a sticky wicket whatever.'

Salena nodded. 'He'll be suspended?'

'Maybe. They'll certainly impose conditions on his continuing to practice. But considering Heather's previous history they'll probably ask me for a report before they take action.'

Claire leaned back and took a sip of the coffee Rita had brought in for them.

'Now tell me about the ward patients. What about Arthur Connolly and that devious little minx, Riley?'

'Same as ever. They'll both be coming up for review quite soon.' Claire blew out a sigh of frustration and resignation. 'Where Arthur will be found guilty of attempted murder and have a custodial sentence – not in my opinion the correct way to treat him. He'll be bullied in prison, just as he was at home.'

Salena nodded. 'Except he won't be able to take such violent action. Not a lot we can do there.'

'No. And Riley? What do you think about her?'

'*She's* the one who should be locked up.'

'I couldn't agree more. She's a potential danger to anyone who gets in the way of something she wants.' Claire smiled. 'But you try proving it.'

'So.' Salena smiled and looked a little more relaxed. 'The law really is an ass?'

Claire nodded, laughed and stood up. 'Time I went home,' she said.

But home was an empty mausoleum. As she closed the front door behind her, the hallway seemed to echo its emptiness, the slam of the door reverberating and mocking her. She stood at the bottom of the handsome staircase, recalling Grant stripping gloss paint from it before staining and varnishing with, as she remembered, *Golden Oak*.

Claire had done all the things you're supposed to when a long-term relationship dies. She could tick them off on her fingers. She had joined a gym, taken up running, returned to cycling, which she loved, particularly the Stoke Ladies' Cycle Club which went out on long rides most Sundays. She had been on a singles holiday to Venice. Big mistake that. Wandering the art galleries, the Guggenheim, St Mark's Square, watching couples kissing on the gondolas. It had rubbed her single state in just that bit too much. She'd been glad to come home to unromantic Burslem. She had been on a couple of Internet dates, which had been an unmitigated disaster, and accepted three blind dates set up by well-meaning friends. But all the sparks were missing and reluctantly there had been no follow-ups. She had spent a few pleasant evenings with her colleague, Edward Reakin, the clinical psychologist. Pleasant, she reflected. Yes, she thought, pouring herself a glass of ice-cold Chablis straight from the fridge and sitting at the kitchen table, polished and stained in antique pine. Pleasant. That was the word. Pleasant. No sparks. No fireworks. No explosions. No Grant. She took big gulps of wine and reflected. No one measured up to him. Grant had been all sparks and fireworks. And unpredictability. Hot sex, warm lips, a voice that caressed and aroused.

Shit, she said out loud, and tried to focus elsewhere, searching for the advantages in her single state. And now she was determined to maximize them, ticking them off on her fingers.

She'd developed a much closer relationship with Adam, her

half-brother, and Adele, his girlfriend. No, she admonished herself with a smile. Fiancée. They were due to be married in six months' time, which would mean an uncomfortable and unhappy encounter with her mother. Her mother, who had hated Claire, the 'Frog', daughter of the Frenchman who had abandoned her, leaving her alone until David 'Superhero' Spencer had come along on his big white horse, married her and given her the perfect life and the perfect son, Adam. As a child, Claire had crawled into any hole she could to hide away from her mother, who so patently hated her, and spent long hours fantasizing about her father, whom she imagined as a cross between Eric Cantona and Maurice Chevalier. And one dark night, when her mother and stepfather had been downstairs watching a noisy television programme, Claire had crept into Adam's room, a pillow in her hands.

With malicious intent.

Thankfully, intent had been all it was. She had looked down at the tiny baby whose big eyes stared up at her and she had felt guilty, a reinforcement of her mother's pronunciation. Bad. Wicked.

The Frog.

She'd always wondered. *Did he remember?*

FIFTEEN

Friday, 26 June, 8.45 a.m.
34/40

She knew exactly what her next step *should* be. Move around the story, testing the water. Try and verify each little detail of Heather's account. And one thing she needed to do was set in her mind where the boundary lay. Which meant, in turn, however reluctantly, talking to Charles Tissot again. Of course, she told herself, Heather's story was fiction. But *something* was at its heart. Also, she had a professional duty to check that he was keeping the Medical Defence Union fully informed. This was potentially a dangerous situation for her as well as for him.

She got hold of him fairly easily on his mobile. He had probably been waiting for this call and recognized her number.

'Claire.' She could hear tension in his voice even as he spoke her name. He started off creepy. 'Thanks for calling. Have you . . .'

She cut in, speaking more crisply than she'd meant. 'I've spent some time with Heather and her sister.'

He gave an uncomfortable bark of a laugh. 'The Crazies. Nuts, aren't they?'

She responded warily. 'It can be hard to separate fact from fiction, Charles. Particularly when they're *both* suffering from the same illusion. Heather not only believes that you and she had sex in your car the night of the bonfire party, she is also absolutely convinced that you and she are in some sort of ongoing clandestine relationship. She is also convinced that the child she carries is the result of . . .' here she hesitated, almost embarrassed, before plunging in to recount events, '. . . that quick shag in the back of your car the night of the party.' *Did he remember?* She needed him to understand. 'The dates do fit. Her sister is backing up the story.'

He snorted. 'Says she was there, does she?'

'No,' she responded carefully, 'she just recalls that Heather went missing from the party, and when she returned seemed smug. Happy. On the surface, the facts fit. Right down to the detail.'

'Hah.' Even across the telephone, the laugh he gave sounded phoney, the response forced. A laugh extruded simply to convince her that this could not *possibly* be the truth. Nothing could be *further* from the truth.

She moved on. 'The MDU?'

'Yeah, yeah.' He sounded impatient. 'On my list.'

'OK. Apart from these shared allegations, there are other factors that disturb me about her case. She seems to bang her abdomen as though punishing the child.' She waited, giving him a chance to respond. Got nothing. 'She could actually harm the foetus.'

'Hmm.' It was all he could manage. A *see-if-I-care* sort of dismissal.

'Also, Charles, she wants to remain under your care.'

'Fat chance of that,' he said through gritted teeth.

'And her sister is in on the act, accepting Heather's story without question.'

She wished she could see him, read his face. Analyse his responses. Something here wasn't right.

'So what next?' His tone was terse.

'I've put her under the GP and the community midwives.' She practically felt him wince.

'Oh, thanks, Claire.'

'I had no choice, Charles.'

'Other than to expose this bitch of a nutcase to my vindictive and barking mad ex-wife.'

The thought swam in to her mind. All the women who surrounded Charles Tissot were necessarily bitches, vindictive. Mad. How so?

'And I will be admitting her as soon as I can arrange it.'

'That's good.' His voice was heavy now, weighed down with the lead weights of accusation as though he had divined her thoughts.

But his next sentence surprised her with its humility. 'Claire.' There was a note of desperation in his appeal. '*You* believe me, don't you?'

It was as though he'd shrunk, the balloon of self-confidence deflated. 'Yes, of course I do.' She kept her voice steady, hoping he could not hear the little warble of doubt which she tried to rectify with a hearty, 'Charles, of course I do.'

But his response was still the grumpy acceptance of a sulky teenager. 'I suppose that's something.' He paused but couldn't resist tacking on his mantra. 'The girl's obviously nuts.'

She had to smile because Charles had reverted to Charles. And the smile translated into words. 'Unfortunately, Charles, nuts isn't in my repertoire of diagnoses.' She had to prepare him for the weakness in her history. 'Charles, there is some bad news.' She quickly corrected. 'Well, not bad. Just not quite so good.'

'Hit me with it.' His voice was gloomy.

'Heather's previous psychiatrist, Laura Hodgkins, is off sick, which robs us of a very important and detailed source of information on her previous history, as well as Laura's professional support. I don't know when she'll return but it doesn't seem like it'll be any time soon. I have spoken to the locum but it isn't the same as actually discussing the patient with a colleague who's spent time with her, getting some weight behind the evidence with which to fight this case.' She had to warn him. 'Because it is going to be a fight to clear your name for certain. You know how blurred psychiatric diagnoses can be.'

'So Laura Hodgkins is off?'

'I'm afraid so.'

'Just my bloody luck,' he said gloomily.

'It doesn't help things,' she agreed.

A pause settled between them, which he finally broke. 'So where do we go from here?' The gloom had intensified in his voice.

She tried to inject some positivity into her response. 'I'll continue to see Heather and assess her mental state,' she said briskly. 'Admit her sooner if it becomes necessary, either for her or the baby's health.' She felt she must shine a ray of hope in his direction. 'It is possible, Charles, that once she's delivered and the baby proved to be her husband's, her psychosis might recede.' She avoided adding that equally it might worsen. She was trying to keep the conversation optimistic and cheerful. 'I'll try and find out from the locum what happened post-partum in the two previous pregnancies. For the moment, though, we'll watch and wait. I'll see her on a weekly basis, the midwives also, and . . .' The warning had to come. '*You* shouldn't see her, Charles. I'd get your registrar to monitor her and if it's a male, warn him to have a chaperone at all times. And that chaperone can't be her sister. The duo are potentially dangerous to *any* male professional. I'll go ahead and put her under the community midwives' care. And we'll just hope that it isn't Rhoda who attends her.' She hesitated. 'Charles, if she *does* decide to proceed to a formal complaint . . .' She stopped. Right there, feeling possible consequences collide into her. 'Actually,' she said, 'I'd be more worried if she *doesn't* decide to take it further.'

'Uh?'

'At the moment, she's not vindictive. She's convinced that you two are going to be setting up home together, happy as a pair of lovers.'

'God.' He sounded suitably appalled.

'Well, be glad of it. Because that means that complaining about you to your professional body is the last thing on her mind.'

Silence. Then, 'Really, Claire, how worried should I be? How nuts is she?'

'On a scale of 1–10?'

He waited.

'A nine.'

He took a moment to digest this, then, 'And if she realizes this . . . romance . . . is nothing but a fantasy, am I likely then to come under attack?'

'She's never done that before. Her allegations have never gone as far as the courts, but as I say, I only have a patchy history of her two previous episodes.'

'What does her husband think of all this?'

'I don't know. I haven't met him yet but he's on my list.'

'Thanks. Hardly reassuring but thanks anyway, Claire.'

'My pleasure.'

'I owe you one.'

Her response was a chuckle. She almost put the phone down then but didn't. Instead, she allowed him to see the one ray of hope that she believed might exist. 'There is the possibility of a rational explanation behind all this.'

'Oh?'

'Heather has hinted at abuse by her husband. If that is so, and we can obtain hard evidence, it would provide us with an explanation for her flights of fancy. A substitute father for her children. Someone other than her cruel husband.'

'O-o-h.' It was as though a dawn had peeped over his horizon.

Which she had to dim with a cloud. 'But then that viewpoint would be unusual for her sister to share.'

'Hmm.'

When she put the phone down, she glanced back at Dr Sylas's initial referral letter and wondered whether she would learn anything else useful from the GP.

There were potentially a few other points that she could pick up on which might point her in the right direction. She was starting to piece together a narrative. Beginning with the historic physical and mental abuse by her father. Mirrored by her husband? It happened so often. Strange that so many women did this – married their fathers' shortcomings. She grimaced. No danger of that happening to her. She could hardly remember her father, who had walked out on his baby daughter and her mother without a backwards glance. All she had left was her imaginary dad, 'Maurice Cantona'. Not her mother's version. Her father, *Monsieur* Roget, as she always called him, the venom in her voice making the title sound poisonous, was a filthy frog.

She left *Monsieur* Roget in his foreign land and returned to the present. Back to Heather Krimble and Geoff. She knew the drill as well as any other psychiatrist searching for domestic abuse. Look for hard evidence: unexplained cuts, bruises, a black eye. Controlling behaviour or mental abuse would be much more difficult to ascertain but here she had an ally. She could rope in Edward Reakin, clinical psychologist. He had a real talent for winkling out factual history as well as for putting patients at their ease. The bottom line was this: patients trusted him.

Then there was this Aussie guy, the locum who was filling in for Laura. What was his name? She glanced down at her notes. Simon Bracknell. Like Salena, he would bring a perspective from another part of the world. But mental illness, delusions, psychosis, depression, mania . . . Salena was right. They were the same the whole world over. Though how much insight would he have? Bracknell had never even met Heather, so anything he could tell her would necessarily come from Laura's notes. Second hand.

She could speak to Geoff Krimble herself. And she wouldn't mind interviewing Ruth alone again. When the baby was born, they could take a DNA test which would exclude Charles Tissot for ever. At least from being a father.

One step at a time. First, she'd better make contact with the community midwives. Get the obstetric team on board. She had to do that before she could admit her. But that meant explaining the situation to Rhoda Tissot. And this was when things were about to become a little more complicated.

Justice is a fickle fellow, elusive and unfair. Heather had, unwittingly, selected the right candidate for her allegation. Charles *was* a philanderer. Perhaps something in Heather had sensed this on that night. It would be just like him to seduce someone drunk or a rather naive woman, someone he'd just met at a party – lure her out to his Jaguar for a sordid little fuck. But just because he was capable of it did not necessarily make him guilty. Likewise, because Heather was a disturbed and deluded woman, it did not make her story necessarily fiction. Just because the cap fits, it does not mean you are committed to wearing it. These thoughts spinning around in her head, she glanced at her watch. The day was moving on. Heather Krimble was not her only patient, so she climbed the stairs to the top floor. She needed to work on the cases of her two other tricky patients – Riley, who deserved a custodial sentence and was about to be set free, and Arthur, who didn't have an evil bone in his body but would still be sent down on a charge of GBH and sentenced to a very long stretch.

Outside Arthur Connolly's room, she paused, her hand on the handle. What could she really do?

SIXTEEN

He was sitting in the corner, almost invisible. In a pair of dark trousers and beige sweater he practically blended in with the wall. Arthur was this sort of man. He never would stand out in a crowd, never act the hero, but would blend in with whatever background he was stood against.

Given only the bald history of a man who had apparently gone mad and stabbed his wife, when she had first met him, Claire had been unprepared for such a small, timid man.

He looked up and smiled, eyes watchful and intelligent. But meek, ashamed, a man who tried to shrink into the background, a man who wanted nobody to notice him. And usually his wish was granted. Nobody did. Except soon, when he would be Centre Court.

'The hearing will be in the next week or so,' she said, sitting down in the adjacent armchair. 'We need to present you in the best possible light.'

Again there was that eager, wanting-to-please nod.

'Arthur. You need to understand,' she urged. 'You were lucky to be sent here for assessment rather than to prison. Although I understand many things about your case, you have been charged with GBH.' She hesitated and continued. 'Grievous bodily harm, if not attempted murder. You understand that?'

His eyes flickered and he looked as though he was reaching for something deep inside his mind. 'I understand that perfectly,' he said quietly, 'but *you* must understand too. I *didn't* want to kill her. I just wanted her to stop.'

She'd heard this all before but she had to make him understand that there could be no plea of diminished responsibility. He would be held fully responsible for his actions. Unless . . . 'Why then?' she asked baldly. 'You've been married for almost thirty years.' She repeated the question. 'Why then?'

'It . . . just . . . happened.' He was choosing his words very carefully, rejecting some, selecting others like picking bones out of a fish. Setting them carefully around the rim of a plate in an invisible pattern. *Tinker, tailor, soldier . . .*

'Can you think of any reason why? Did something particular happen that day?' She was clutching at straws, knowing most of the time it was just like elastic that had simply been stretched too far. And snapped. Randomly.

His look changed. It became desperate. Arthur was hunting for a reason too, something that would give him a get-out-of-jail-free card. His eyes bounced around the room, searching for an explanation that took its time coming.

'She . . .' he finally said. 'My wife. Lindsay. She . . .' He looked as though he was about to give up. He couldn't find the words.

She waited. *Give me some clue, something I can hang a plea on.*

He began again. 'She . . . I . . . I found it difficult.' He was speaking very, very slowly. Words emerging, sluggish and hesitant. Testing the water. 'It was difficult,' he finally said, 'to be myself. I wanted to be myself.' His fists were clenched. It had been a very strong desire. Strong enough to almost murder her.

'Arthur,' she continued, 'I think you should be prepared for a custodial sentence.'

His eyes widened. 'But . . . Doctor Roget, surely that's why I'm here. I thought you would be able to help me.'

'I can only go so far, Arthur. My job is to assess your mental condition.'

'It was,' he said firmly, handing her the words at last, 'a temporary madness.' He gave a tentative smile. The first smile she had really seen. It was achingly sweet, trusting like a child. But she would have to let him down. 'That's what it was,' he said firmly.

It was not enough.

He looked up, eyes bright. Suddenly hopeful. 'My sister came to see me today,' he said. 'Mary. I haven't seen her for ages. It was nice. She says Lindsay's going to be all right. She's going to be fine.'

'Yes. I heard that,' she said. 'That is good news.'

He spent some time nodding, then, 'I wonder, Doctor,' he said. 'Should I send her some flowers? Or would that be inappropriate? Misinterpreted, perhaps?'

Patients always did this to her. Surprised her. They asked her impossible and inappropriate questions and expected some sort of rational answer to an irrational question.

But . . . What the hell? 'I don't see why not, Arthur,' she said, 'though she might not quite take them in the spirit in which you sent them?'

He chuckled. 'What you mean is that she'll probably just throw them in the bin?'

And patients did this to her too – proved they had insight. No easy answer came to mind. She shrugged and he attempted to explain. 'The spirit in which I'd send them would be a form of apology,' he said, 'for hurting her so badly.'

She had gone through this when he had been first admitted two months ago.

When you stuck the knife in her, did you mean to kill her?

He had appeared initially confused by the question. She had repeated it and he had finally said, 'I didn't care. I only wanted her to stop saying such horrible things *to* me,' he had raised his eyebrows, inviting her to see things from his perspective, 'and *about* me.'

'Did you want her to die?'

Again, he had considered the question carefully. 'If Lindsay had died she would never have been able to criticize me again, would she? So, yes. I suppose I did want her to stop for ever.'

Perhaps it was at that point that she started to realize just how out of touch Arthur Connolly was. But out of touch is not quite temporary insanity. It would not help his plea or shorten his sentence or gain him the sympathy of the jury who, however hard or skilfully she might try to portray the Connollys' marriage, would see yet another man assaulting a defenceless woman.

'Can I ask you,' she ventured now. 'We suspect you might have a custodial sentence but we can't even guess how long that will be. When you are free, what are your intentions?'

'I'm not going back to her,' he said, his mouth twisting in wry humour. 'I'd just do it again.'

So – for once in psychiatry – she did have a definite answer. Something tangible. Such a relief after the ghosts and shadows of Heather's claim.

She wandered along the corridor but Riley's room was empty. One of the nurses answered her query. 'She's with Edward Reakin,' she said, 'having one of her sessions.' She pulled a face. 'Rather him than me. She's a tricky little bugger, that one.'

Claire was still smiling as she returned to her office, where she spent the next hour collating the statements she had received about Arthur, searching for something that would lighten his inevitable sentence. Plenty of people had spoken up for him: Arthur's sister, friends, neighbours, relatives, acquaintances, people who went to the same Methodist church. All saying the same thing but in different words. Arthur was completely dominated by his wife, that if he put a foot out of line he would be publicly humiliated verbally, on occasions even physically by her slapping his head, his shoulder, his face or twisting his ear. Lindsay Connolly, they all agreed, was a monster, a twisted, vindictive woman. But, they all also agreed, Arthur was, in some way, responsible for his own fate. He should have been a man. He should have stood up to her. One particularly perceptive neighbour suggested that that was what Lindsay had wanted, for Arthur to act like a man, to stick up for himself, stand up to her. But, Claire had thought, if Arthur *had* stood up to her, *he* would have been the one labelled a bully.

People are more prone to being judgmental than sympathetic. It is easier to take a side, whichever side, rather than stand, piggy-in-the middle, or sit on the fence and wonder. And what outsiders see is what outsiders are meant to see. She leafed through the statements one by one.

'He should have stood up for himself', 'Shouldn't have let her get away with it', 'He brought it on himself', 'He should have acted more like a man'. All had added, 'But she was a devil to him.' While others had been more descriptive. 'Treated him like something you picked up on your shoe.'

But having responded to the cumulative effects of years of bullying, allegiance had shifted from Arthur to his wife. People always pity the injured party. Not one of them had condoned Arthur's assault. The aggressor rarely gets the vote. So now different words echoed round and around, the tables turned. 'Poor Lindsay, married to that maniac. What she must have put up with.'

Maybe even that would be just temporary. Once her injuries had healed and Lindsay Connolly had recovered her character, possibly finding someone else to pick on, perhaps the streams of sympathy would dry up and Arthur's friends and acquaintances would gather round him again?

Some hope.

Tattooed as a jailbird, a manslaughter/attempted murder conviction under his belt, he would be dropped by all except his ever-faithful sister, Mary. Like Ruth Acton, sisters can be close. For, after all, blood is thicker than water, and a prettier colour, too.

So, if blood really is such a bond, what about Arthur's son,

Saul? Their only child? She had him down as siding with his mother. But what was his true perspective?

Perhaps, if she spoke to him face-to-face, he could throw some helpful light on the case, help her arrive at a conclusion that was fair, some way down the middle. She was running out of chances and people to speak for the underdog, unless something unexpected happened.

In Claire's mind, there was only one cause for celebration. Arthur's action had been so completely out of character, so shocking and unpredictable that he had ended up in Greatbach Secure Psychiatric Hospital for assessment, finally away from Lindsay, albeit under an umbrella of temporary madness.

So back to Arthur's son, Saul. Surely he had witnessed the relationship between his parents? She made a note in her diary for Rita to make an appointment with Saul Connolly, aware that it was a last-ditch attempt at keeping Arthur out of prison. And, she supposed, she should interview the dreaded Lindsay at least once more. Recalling her square chin and tight lips, she was not looking forward to repeating the experience.

But she would dig deep to try and rescue her patient from prison, which would damage him even further, only too aware that if the narrative had been different so too would the outcome.

If this had been a *woman* claiming mental cruelty, complaining about controlling behaviour, if eye witnesses had come forward telling their stories of physical and mental abuse, Claire reflected, there would be a very lenient sentence. Maybe not even a custodial one. Harassment, domination – these were crimes. Against females. But who had sympathy for a male victim? Men were seen as physically stronger but Claire had often reflected that it was women who were psychologically stronger.

Just look at Grant, her ex.

His weakness and inability to stand up to a stronger force had been one of the things she had loved about him. Initially. He was so very amenable. So sweet-natured. So kind, so lazy, easy-going. Accommodating. And it was that which had led to his downfall. A mother and a sister manipulating him, pushing him into a corner and making bloody sure he stayed there. Claire realized her fists were clenched. She hadn't realized how angry she was over all that. The way she'd been robbed of a gentle, loving . . . She smiled. A sexy and wonderful bloke. The best.

And *she* hadn't helped. She had simply joined his sister and his mother in pinning him into that corner. Giving him an ultimatum. This was something she still found uncomfortable, a sense of guilt that she hadn't been fair on him. In fact, she'd sulked. Oh, for goodness' sake, she thought, exasperated, tempted to hurl something across the room. Leave it. Move on.

She didn't exactly. She moved back to her original thought, acknowledging that while the law recognized male-to-female controlling behaviour it had yet to be tested female to male. She looked up, startled at something. Maybe that was her role. To be the first to draw attention to it, recognize it, maybe even give it a name.

Roget's Syndrome.

She giggled and started writing her report with a lift of her spirits. *Arthur Connolly*, she wrote, *is not a danger to the wider society. While the assault against his wife was serious, there had been extreme provocation. Independent witnesses have affirmed that Mrs Connolly was controlling and belittled her husband in public on occasions, even going so far as 'slapping' him. With this affirmation, I would suggest a lenient sentence. However, there is no psychiatric diagnosis. And while agreeing that the assault on Mrs Connolly was serious and potentially life-threatening, it was a spur-of-the-moment act, a kitchen knife pulled from the knife block. It was to hand and the entire incident happened early in the morning when Mr Connolly – Arthur – had spilt some coffee and his wife, as was her wont, berated him. He has expressed remorse and, when he is free, he will not return to what he describes as an abusive relationship.*

What, she wondered, would be the courts' decision?

SEVENTEEN

She went home on the Friday evening still tussling with the problems of Arthur Connolly and Riley Finch. And, at the same time, she was considering her next move on the Krimble/Tissot case, which was intriguing and entertaining her at the same time. Something, long buried within her, was feeling that, after all this time, Charles Tissot was getting his just deserts. He might be a hundred per cent innocent this time, having just caught Heather's eye at the party. But, oh, what a fitting punishment.

As she drove, she was planning. Having to arrange midwife cover would mean a delay in Heather's admission as the weekend loomed. This was the complication of cross-speciality cases and two separate hospitals. But close monitoring by a midwife and/or an obstetrician was equally as important as her psychiatric assessment. God help her if anything went wrong in the final stages of this strange pregnancy. Claire hadn't yet finalized her obstetric care so in the event of a complication *she* would be the one hung out to dry by the MDU. But she was also realizing the task of protecting Heather's unborn infant was not going to be simple – even with midwives *and* an obstetrician in attendance twenty-four/seven. A paediatrician would also need to be involved. It was difficult and complicated. And Salena's tale of the schizophrenic attempting to excise her baby, *ex utero*, with a knife was a sobering one. It can be difficult to assess the depth of a psychiatric case's paranoia and delusions as many psychiatrists have learned – too late. And then there was the added complication of involving Rhoda. But Claire couldn't bypass her. Community obstetrics was her responsibility. The troubling angle was contemplating what dirt this contact between the two women would throw up. While Heather was in a dark place, Rhoda was probably in the next room. Ex-wives are notoriously bitter and, knowing Charles as she did, Claire suspected philandering was probably the reason behind the marital split. So another unknown was how professional was Rhoda Tissot? Would Heather's allegations against her ex-husband influence her care? Sense whispered surely not. But might Rhoda feed small worms into Heather's already sick brain? Worms, Claire thought as she flashed her lights at an ill-advised manoeuvre by a sporty Lycra-clad cyclist and received a middle-finger gesture in response. Worms. She couldn't have chosen a more appropriate analogy. This was, indeed, a can of wriggling worms.

And that wasn't all. Claire sat, waiting for the traffic lights to turn green. Something else was bothering her. It wasn't only the complexity of this case. Although her experience of de Clerambault's syndrome was limited to the elderly man and the ballerina, she was well used to tricky assignments, piloting the narrow channel between the proverbial rock and hard place. Psychiatry is an inexact science at best, often going no farther than venturing an opinion. Unlike a confirming blood test or CT in other specialities, there is no definitive blood test for most psychiatric diagnoses, though research into magnesium or other chemical levels in the brain was promising a new dawn. And with this added evidence, the future of psychiatry promised to be very different from its past; its treatments, too.

So why was there this background of unease? Was it her own past history with Casanova Tissot? She smiled at a sudden realization. There was only one thing that would absolutely prove the truth of Heather's version – and Ruth's backup statement: Charles's DNA matching that of the infant Krimble. And in a small flash of insight, she knew what was causing her discomfort.

Heather's past history was pushing them into an assumption. She wasn't quite seeing this square on as she should. The lights turned green and around her everything shifted, including her own point of view.

Freddie had been proved to be her husband's child. But not Eliza. Even Geoff hadn't claimed Eliza was his daughter. Hence the lack of grief. So whose daughter had she been? In spite of his denial, Cartwright's?

Maybe she should look at events through the other end of the telescope. What if Heather's claims were true? All true? Except that Freddie had been Geoff's son . . .

She spurted forward with a heartfelt sigh. More than ever, she wished she could have spoken to Laura Hodgkins. At least they could have worked together, pooled their ideas. Of course, on the surface Heather's stories appeared fantastic when the men concerned ridiculed her claims. Then reason kicked her doubts aside. Surely someone of Charles Tissot's stature would not be tempted to fuck a girl in the back of a car outside the party of one of his colleagues? Except she knew him. Charles was a risk-taker. And now Claire wondered whether she'd just scratched that itch. She was not hundred per cent convinced of his innocence. Never would be.

The traffic had come to a standstill. So now, stuck in a traffic jam on the A500, she mentally replayed Heather's account, searching for the same words she had used, the description of a secret love combined with the absolute certainty that Charles Tissot loved her and planned to be with her for the future. Maybe that was the most incredible part: not the sordid sex but the conviction that he loved her, planned to marry her, was delighted to be having a child with her, had lovingly accepted her as his patient. The traffic started to move and her mind unblocked. It was that romantic scenario that had the feel of fantasy, fitting much more with the diagnosis of de Clerambault's syndrome than a lucid, factual account of a clandestine love affair. So why was she analysing these nagging doubts when they spoke so clearly? Simply because of that drunken fumble all those years ago, way before he and she had climbed the greasy pole to become consultants in their different fields? Again, she pictured her patient, apparently meek, submissive, trusting, her voice soft and quiet as she related her story. The image resonated because it mirrored herself years ago – a medical student who did not believe in herself, had little confidence in herself. And now? She opened the window to breathe in traffic fumes, ran through sentences, words Heather had used, and knew what had clinched it. It was the corroborative evidence. Ruth, the loyal sister. Ruth, who held down a good job, was trusted enough by her employer to have been invited to his personal party. Ruth, who appeared so calm, so uninvolved, so unemotional, so rational. So sane. And *she* was backing up her sister's story. Trusting her account. Even though she could have seen nothing.

She trusted her sister's word enough to jeopardize her boss's colleague and friend. Why? Loyalty? Just because she believed her sister incapable of telling such a huge and fantastic lie?

Or was it sympathy with her married sister's plight? What was the glue that bonded these sisters so closely?

Or rather than a loyal bond, could the motive behind this be something completely different? Deliberate and organized destruction? Was the real motive for the wild tale to watch Charles Tissot tumble from his pedestal? Had he slighted *either* of them in the past? Should she be focusing not on her patient but on the loyal sister? Perhaps she, Claire, had not been asking the right person the right questions.

Bugger. She smiled at herself in the rear-view mirror. Her list of questions was growing rather than shrinking. And the list of answers?

So far, non-existent.

EIGHTEEN

After a weekend of gym, cycling and a long walk in the Peak District with Adam, her half-brother and his fiancée, Adele, followed by an extended pub lunch in Grindon, Claire felt fit enough to face the world, including Charles Tissot's murky little kingdom. And the feeling of optimism was intensified when Rita greeted her arrival with the news that she had made an appointment for Geoff Krimble to attend the outpatient clinic on the following day. Claire worked her way through the ward round and clinics with energy. Another piece of the jigsaw was about to slot into place.

Tuesday, 30 June, 2.30 p.m.
Outpatient Department, Greatbach Secure Psychiatric Hospital.

Geoff Krimble was a large, lumbering guy with long, ape-like arms and greasy dark hair that needed a pair of professional scissors. His trousers were slung low beneath a beer belly which wobbled as he walked, furthering the idea of the missing link. Around him clung the aroma of fried food and stale clothes plus the unmistakable stink of beer and tobacco, which seemed to ooze out of his pale pores. He had watchful brown eyes that met hers with a strange awareness. And considering the image she'd built up of him, she read there a simple honesty. He looked directly at her with a ghost of a smile. 'Funny business this, Doctor,' he said.

As she nodded her agreement and led him towards the consulting room, she took in other things.

Geoff Krimble had made an effort today. He had teamed a bright Royal Maddox tartan shirt buttoned right up to his thick neck with a red-and-black striped tie. It made a colourful, if not coordinated, combination.

He had a pleasant manner, a friendly, tentative smile and more worry lines than a man in his thirties should have. Claire held out her hand and shook the proffered sweating palm. He looked an unhappy, uneasy man but not unpleasant. His mouth was so dry that when he tried to lick his lips she heard a sticky, rasping sound. She gestured to the drinking water machine and watched as he filled a polystyrene cup half full, the water rippling as his hand shook.

'Mr Krimble,' she said, smiling, wanting to put this shifting, uncomfortable person at his ease. 'Thank you for coming.'

He dipped his head in acknowledgement but his eyes were still watchful and wary. If he was violent towards his wife there was, currently, no sign of it. He looked anxious to be of help.

Or perhaps, like many people, he was put off by the lanyard which hung around her neck. Dr Claire Roget, Consultant Psychiatrist.

She would need to move very delicately around the justification for her involvement, at the same time touching on Charles's role in all this.

He lumbered after her into the interview room and spread himself over the chair, looking oddly expectant now, as though she would wave a magic wand and all these strange tales spun by his mad wife would somehow melt away.

'You and your wife,' she began, watching his face quite carefully. 'You're aware that she has made some allegations about the parentage of her child?'

He nodded, his frown deepening. He looked puzzled.

She continued, 'You and Heather. You're happy together?'

He shrugged. 'Same as any married couple.' He had a broad Stoke accent. 'We have our ups and downs. You know.'

'Well, you've had your share of tragedy.'

'Aye.' He nodded, but if she had expected emotion from him about the two dead children, she was let down. His face remained impassive.

'The baby that Heather's expecting . . .'

He leaned forward in his chair so his stomach rested on his knees and his face was near. His teeth were yellow with nicotine and looked neglected, a higgledy-piggledy mouthful of untidy, stained dentition. 'Every time she gets pregnant,' he said, getting the words out with difficulty, 'she gets these fancies.'

So that was how he read them. A pregnant woman's fancies.

'You're saying there's no truth in them?'

Again, he dipped his head. ''Course not.' His voice was scornful. 'Nothing's happened.'

She was obviously going to have to find the delicate touch of a lace-maker. 'You're looking forward to the birth . . .?'

His face screwed up. Grief or puzzlement? She couldn't be sure.

'Aye. After the two we lost, 'twill be nice to have a bebbe around again.'

'I'm sure.'

She waited for him to ask a question, to offer some sort of explanation. Nothing came except . . . She could have sworn there was a tear in his eye.

She needed a more direct approach. 'Mr Krimble, Heather is making allegations against her obstetrician.'

'Aye.'

'You think there's no truth in this?'

'Phh.' He blew out fleshy lips. 'No. 'Course not. It's all nonsense.'

'You're aware that the consequence of these allegations could be quite serious for the doctor concerned?'

'Aye.'

'And you believe them to be untrue?'

'Aye. 'Course.'

'If you think she's imagining these events you must have asked yourself why?'

'Part of bein' pregnant, I suppose.'

'Most pregnant women are only too happy to have their partner's child.'

'She's peculiar,' he said. 'She's always been a bit . . . strange.'

She picked up on the hint he'd dropped. 'Strange? In what way? Any other way apart from these beliefs that other men are involved with the parentage of her babies?'

'No,' he conceded. Then added: 'But they proved Freddie was *my* son. Not some window cleaner's.'

'True.'

'Which proves that Heather's mistaken, doesn't it?'

'Not quite. Not necessarily.'

'Oh.' He looked flustered.

'Heather was pregnant when you and she were married.'

'Aye.'

'Were you Eliza's father?'

There was a pause while he considered how to answer the question, finally, reluctantly shaking his head. 'We never, you know . . .' He didn't finish the sentence.

'So who was?'

'I don't know,' he said quickly. 'I never knew.'

'It could have been Mr Cartwright.'

'I very much doubt it.'

Though the question of Eliza's parentage was of concern, she let it slide and moved on. 'I'll tell you what's puzzling me, Mr Krimble.'

'Aye?'

'Her sister's backing up her story. Ruth seems to believe her.'

'Oh, Ruth.' He dismissed her with a wave of his large hands. 'She thinks the sun shines out of Heather's . . .' He flushed, smirked and returned to his backup phrase. 'Well, you know.'

She inclined her head to one side to prompt him.

And he obliged. 'Ruth? She'd say black was white if Heather told her to. She'd say we lived on Mars or that grass was blue – not green. She'd say day was night and night day. She doesn't have a mind of her own, that one.'

She stored the phrase. *She doesn't have a mind of her own,* and returned to the main text. 'So the sisters are devoted?'

He simply nodded this time. And behind his eyes lay another story, which she tried to winkle out of him.

'Why?'

'Sorry?'

'*Why* are they so devoted?'

He met her eyes with a frank look and at the back of that was something very much like shame. 'Their dad,' he mumbled. 'Religious maniac. If they did anything he thought wrong he used to knock 'em about something rotten.'

And she knew then. The admission behind the story. It was the look of shame that told her, the dropping of the eyes, the flushing in his cheeks. It wasn't just her dad who *used to knock 'em about something rotten.* So did he. Not out of anger. This man appeared too bovine for hot, quick, violent anger. No, it would be more that he didn't have any other way of expressing himself. No words. Just fists. Geoff Krimble was a big man, more than double Heather's weight with big, meaty hands. Ball those up into a fist and they would be formidable weapons. Heather was a petite woman. *A tap*, he'd say. *I didn't hit her hard.* But a 'tap' from him would be a knockout punch to her. Geoff was a man who did not know his own strength.

She had to address it. 'Have you ever . . .?'

Innocent eyes. He didn't know how to answer but sidetracked. 'That's why Robin left.'

'Robin?'

'Her brother. It glued them sisters together. See?'

She nodded now. 'I'm going to admit Heather, Mr Krimble. I've noticed some slightly disturbing behaviour. She bangs the baby.'

'Aye.' He looked almost happy at this. Probably relieved to move away from the subject of domestic violence. 'Aye, I've noticed her do that once or twice.'

'Did she do it in her two previous pregnancies?'

He thought about this before nodding.

'So both for her protection and the protection of the infant, we think we should keep her in for observation.'

'Here?'

'Yes, here, but we will have midwives in attendance to make sure her pregnancy and labour are monitored.'

'But she'll go to the maternity unit when she starts to have it, like?'

'Oh, yes.'

'Then it sounds like a good idea. Thank you,' he said, apparently anxious to ingratiate himself with her.

She observed him. He seemed to feel something more was expected. 'When the baby's born,' he said, starting already to lift from the chair, 'she soon drops all that nonsense. Anyway . . .' He puffed out his chest. 'Anyway, the DNA . . .' he was proud of his grasp of scientific matters, '. . . proved that Freddie was my son.'

His eyes were challenging her to dispute this. And all she could think was that this little boy and his half-sister had died. Would this as yet unborn infant also die? Had the pathologist simply failed to find proof that Heather was a child-killer? Or was there something else?

She wondered what was going through Geoff's mind. Had he ever explored various theories?

'Why do you think Heather makes these claims?'

He looked at her as though she was the batty one. 'She's just ill, Doctor. That's all. Ill.'

The next batch of questions were a bit more difficult to ask Heather's husband but he might hold an explanation, of sorts. 'Had she shown any particular interest in her boss, Mr Cartwright, before she became pregnant?'

'Oh, I think she liked him all right.' There was no embarrassment in his voice. 'But not like that. He was just kind to her. You know. She had a bit of morning sickness and he'd bring her a cup of tea and a dry biscuit saying he'd heard they might make her feel better.'

A phrase from Dr Sylas's original letter floated helpfully into her mind . . . *late in the pregnancy*. This was an explanation of sorts.

Geoff continued, 'He'd chivvy her along, like. You know.'

And she thought she might. She smiled at him.

Which urged Geoff Krimble to add, 'There weren't nothing in it, you know. Nothing.'

She interpreted this. 'So you're sure that this was all fantasy on Heather's part?'

'Oh, aye.' He leaned in. 'And science has proved it.'

'And the window cleaner? Sam Maddox.'

That was when she saw the first flash of anger. 'She used to say how she thought he were good lookin'. I took no notice. Just a fancy, I suppose.' He rose in his chair. Angry now. 'She's just been making a bloody monkey out of me. I'm a laughing stock. No wonder I have a beer or two. Heather? She's not right in the head.'

'When she's pregnant,' she reminded him, following on with a question. 'Only when she's pregnant?'

He nodded.

'So . . . Why?' She let the question linger in the air.

Geoff leaned in even further. In confidence. 'It's to get back at me,' he said. 'To punish me.'

'For what?'

His mouth clamped shut.

She waited. People are like this. They bury secrets and all you see is the tip of the molehill pushing up through the earth, giving a hint of the network of tunnels underneath.

He eyed her for a moment without responding. Then his mouth started moving very slightly as though beginning to form words. In his eyes, there was no clue as to what this response would be. Finally he found an answer. 'Maybe it's because I find it hard to stick to a job. I don't have no qualifications, you know, Doctor.' He grinned, exposing more of his crooked teeth. 'Not like you. And I find it hard to go in day after day. They've said I have Tourette's.'

'Who said you have Tourette's?'

'Me old doctor.'

'Not a psychiatrist? You didn't have a formal assessment? Answer a questionnaire?'

'No. Nothing so formal.' His tongue moistened his lips before he managed, 'But sometimes . . . Occasionally,' he substituted, 'I have the odd day when I'm just not myself.'

What a useful phrase.

'Find it hard to get up in the mornin'. That's why,' he finished triumphantly, 'she goes a bit queer when she's pregnant,' he said, batting away the explanation with a waft of his hand. 'Worry. That's why she starts saying daft things. Inventin' stuff. Imaginin' things. Goin' a bit loopy.' He accompanied the word with a circular finger motion on his temple. It was a gesture Claire hadn't seen since she was a schoolgirl. His left eye twitched, which he tried to restrain with his middle finger. 'Sorry,' he said, rocking ever so slightly in the chair. 'She gets these ideas, you know.' He tried to laugh it off. 'Says they're not mine, that they're some other fellows'.'

Claire moved on. 'As Eliza wasn't your daughter, did you have trouble bonding with her?'

'No,' he protested. 'She were a nice little thing. I loved her like me own. But we lost her.'

There was no grief contained in the sentence. Claire simply nodded, gauging the situation. Just as things had felt wrong when she had interviewed Heather and her sister so this, also, felt strange.

He seemed to think he should add something. 'Couldn't believe it,' he said – no rancour. 'Two kids. Lovely little things.' He moved in to share a confidence. 'Cost her her sanity, it did, being pregnant. And then they go and die on her.'

There was no self-pity, no breast-beating, no grief or sorrow or any of the other emotions considered normal in this situation. Just

words. Plain and simple. And genuine. They could have held more
pathos but Geoff Krimble appeared to have accepted his own
version of events.

'I don't mean to be funny or sorry for myself,' he continued,
'but people should realize it was *my* tragedy as much as her. I'd
looked after Eliza like one of me own. And I didn't take comfort
by bleating on about Eliza and Freddie. They didn't suffer. They
just went to sleep and didn't wake up. They just weren't there any
more. End of.' His eyes were challenging her now.

She narrowed her eyes. Was this man-speak? 'When did you
first realize something was wrong with Heather?'

He frowned, shaking his head in confusion. 'Dunno.'

'When did she first begin to have delusions?'

His answer was a frown. 'Ever?'

'Yes. When you first met her, what sort of a person did you
think she was?'

The question foxed him. He swallowed, leaned back, appeared
to be deep in thought. It was only surface deep. 'Dunno,' he said.
'Quiet.' He frowned. 'Deep.'

All that thought and that was the best he could come up with?

She tried again. 'What did you like about her that made you
want to marry her even though she was pregnant with another
man's child?'

Again, this provoked puzzlement. *Please, she thought, don't
give me 'Dunno' again.*

'She were different,' he said finally. 'There was somethin' almost
mysterious about her.' His eyes focused on the wall behind her.
'Maybe that was part of it. The secrets,' he said. 'I couldn't make
her out.' He shifted his gaze. 'Intriguing,' he said, frowning, as
though finding the word had been an effort.

She persisted. 'When did she begin to imagine things?'

'When she were pregnant with Eliza. About halfway through.
Not long after we were married.'

'How did it manifest itself?'

'Sorry?' The word had baffled him.

'What did she imagine?'

He gave an almighty twitch and again she caught the unmistakable waft of beer, as though a pub door had opened. 'Stuff about
the baby being evil, stuff that it was cursed. Her dad said she was
goin' through a bad time and it would help. It would really help

if we was married. Up until then she'd been sort of ordinary. Nice. Quiet. Obedient.'

Claire winced at the word.

'But there was always something out of reach. You know.'

Claire nodded. She was beginning to have a picture. Not a nice one, of a woman, bullied as a child, glued to her sister by circumstances, married to someone who could not fathom her depths so swiped her.

'Do you find her claims strange, out of character?'

He nodded. 'The real Heather wouldn't say boo to a goose let alone go off with some bloke. Before we was married we didn't even . . .' A sweaty flush crept up his neck, reaching his forehead in a breakout of sweat.

'And her attitude to sex *after* you were married?'

That was when Geoff Krimble started bouncing his feet around, tapping a nervous dance, patently uncomfortable with the subject of sex.

'I can't say she liked it much.'

'But you don't think Mr Cartwright was Eliza's father?'

'I don't think so. After she'd got over the birth and left the firm she never mentioned him again.' He spoke with smug satisfaction. 'So . . . that proves it, don't it?'

'And Freddie?'

'Hah.' Geoff spluttered his mirth. 'That was even more bloody silly. Window cleaner. He never even came inside. Shagged her through glass, did he?' Veins bulged in his neck, giving him the look of an angry bull. 'Or in the garden when we're overlooked on three sides and the neighbours are nosey old buggers.' He forced accompanying laughter for a few seconds before sobering up.

'You discussed all this with Doctor Hodgkins?'

He nodded. 'She were helpful but Doctor Sylas said she's off sick at the moment so we can't be seeing her this time.' The phrase seemed to hold threat of further pregnancies, further allegations reaching for the horizon as well as the tacit implication, *So we're stuck with you.*

Claire felt almost exultant. This interview seemed, on the surface at least, promising – at least for Charles Tissot. On Geoff's evidence alone, Heather's allegation appeared to be yet another tale from an unbalanced mind. But while Cartwright and Sam Maddox had been men she'd already known for some time, the encounter between her and Charles had been a single brushing encounter at a crowded party. It was different. And it did fit in with Charles's hunting habits.

She tried to explore this aspect. 'Is there anything different about this pregnancy?'

'Same old,' he said, again wafting the question away with a limp wrist and spread fingers.

'But they only met at that one party? She didn't know Mr Tissot before?'

He shook his head. 'Normally Ruth and Heather would just go out for a curry or something, you know, Indian places. I'm not keen on curry, see. And to be honest I'm not over-keen on Ruth. She's a bit a snob, you know, and doesn't approve of me.' He spoke the words with an accompanying eye-roll. 'Heather's a shy bird. Not a great mixer.'

'So when she told you that Mr Tissot was the father of her baby, how did you react?'

'Gave her a spank.' He leered. 'Just a little one. Told her not to be so stupid.'

If only it was as simple as this. *A little spank and told her not to be so stupid.*

She sat very still. So, then, one of her theories had just been admitted. If a man admits to his wife's psychiatrist that he had given his wife a little spank you can be sure that there is something much more sinister going on behind closed doors. 'It's the same old thing,' he said, bored now. 'She's spinning the same old stories.'

'You're saying, then, that the child is yours and not Mr Tissot's?'

He gave her a sharp look. ''Course it bloody well is mine. Who else's would it be?'

'So you and your wife have regular sex?'

He nodded.

It had been a long interview. She felt this was the end of the road as far as Geoff Krimble went. She had got as far with him as was possible. She didn't arrange to see him again.

Sometimes the mistakes we make are the mistakes of omission. There was one word she should have picked up on.

NINETEEN

Thursday, 2 July, 8.50 a.m.

Her next plan was to speak to Simon Bracknell, to see if Laura Hodgkins' previous notes could firm up her diagnosis. Puerperal psychosis plus de Clerambault's syndrome. It would be interesting to write up in the Journal of Psychiatry and Neuroscience. She had plenty of other avenues to explore but first she needed to understand a little more of Heather's past. The next best thing to speaking to Laura would be to read her notes.

But, as often happens, in psychiatry, as in life, events took a sideways swipe. In many ways, it was her fault. It began when she decided to follow up another previous idea, have a conversation face-to-face with Charles. She knew exactly what she was up to. She wanted to convince herself of his complete and utter innocence. So she rang.

He sounded abrupt and vaguely hostile when she invited him to her office – at a time of his own choosing.

'Oh, for goodness' sake,' he said, patently in a bad temper over something. 'Let's go to a wine bar, make the chat informal. At least do that for me.'

As always, he was quickly dominating the encounter, drawing up his own battle lines and ignoring hers.

'OK,' she said reluctantly, already uncomfortable at his Alpha male position. But she agreed to it with only the faintest hint of discomfort and the proviso that she would make it early in the evening. They fixed on Saturday night at The Orange Tree, an up-and-coming pub along the A34 in Newcastle-under-Lyme. 'I'm not meeting in Hanley,' she said, slightly petulant at having been manoeuvred into being there in the first place. 'I got a bloody parking ticket the last time I parked there.'

Needless to say, Charles was totally unsympathetic. 'You should have fed the machine, Claire.'

'I would have done,' she retorted, 'if I could have made head or tail of the parking charges. They were the most ambiguous I've ever seen. Anyway, it puts Hanley out of bounds for me now.'

He chuckled, obviously delighted to be scoring points over her and, for the first time since he'd first made contact, she wondered what he was like now. Still preppy? Still humourless? Cocky and conceited? Predatory? Or had he settled down into a typical consultant, abiding by the rules, breaking none, behaving himself, putting on weight and playing golf?

His ex-wife would doubtless have plenty to say on the subject. But she had yet to make her acquaintance. She had tried to get hold of Rhoda on a couple of occasions, only to be told that she was away on a course with the exciting title: Pain Management in a Prolonged First Stage of Labour. It was being held in Scarborough and Mrs Tissot was not expected back until Monday at the earliest, so for that pleasure she would have to wait. And it further delayed Heather's admission. Claire couldn't risk admitting her to Greatbach without suitable obstetric care, but neither did she want to discuss such a complex case with the second-in-command. She wanted Rhoda, whose reputation was deservedly formidable. For competence.

Saturday, 4 July, 6 p.m.
The Orange Tree, Newcastle-under-Lyme.

The Orange Tree was one of those pubs which had, in the last couple of years, spruced itself up and suddenly become a gastropub with arguably some of the best food in the Potteries. Even though it was on the busy A34 south of Newcastle and parking could be a bit of a squeeze and forbidden in the nearby streets, it had become one of 'the' places to meet, dine and socialize.

Although Claire considered the evening an extension of work and her 'date' was with Charles, it had been nice to start getting ready for an evening out. Radio on, long bath, deciding what to wear . . . in this case smart black trousers, high-heeled boots and a multicoloured silk shirt. Make-up, perfume. Done. Time to meet the man. As she drove along the A500, leaving it to join the A34, she wondered. What was the real origin of Heather Krimble's potentially damaging allegations? Simply a deluded, sick mind or was there some substance behind them? A look, a flirtation, a compliment, a grope? What had happened at that party to set her mind on such a track?

The evening was warm enough for her to sit outside and she was early. Obsessional time-keeping was one of her private curses – she was invariably early for appointments, usually arriving well before time, on one occasion in danger of catching the train before her booked ticket. She sat outside in the beer garden, overlooking the car park, sitting under the shade and watching cars cruise through, searching for a space, seeing people come and go, greet each other, smoke, drink, eat, laugh. Like many people sitting alone with just a white wine spritzer for company, she fiddled with her phone, sending out the message that she might be alone at the moment but she had lots, hoards, queues, piles . . . of friends. She texted a few of them, including Adam, her half-brother, pleased at the way their relationship had thawed, acknowledging that it was partly, at least, due to his new girlfriend, Adele. Adele the peacemaker. Adele the forgiver. Adele who did not probe into an uncomfortable, dangerous past but looked forward to a pleasant, friendly future with her fiancée's half-sister.

She looked up from a friendly returned text – *Hi Claire, nice to hear from you. Yes, let's meet up again – soon? A XXX* – to see a maroon Jaguar slide in next to a Peugeot and Charles climb out, instantly recognizable. He was a large man, over six feet tall and these days burly rather than slim. Even as his eyes scanned the courtyard he oozed confidence, seeming to look down his nose at the patrons of The Orange Tree. Claire reflected that he hardly looked like a man whose career could, potentially, be about to swirl right down the plughole. She rose to meet him and he crossed the courtyard quickly, kissing her on both cheeks with the comment, 'Gosh, Claire, I don't know what you're on but you haven't changed a bit.'

What was the correct response to this particular cliché?

Coyness, honesty? Obviously she'd bloody well changed in fifteen years. She ignored the comment, instead studying him back. *She* might have changed but not as much as he. Her eyes exposed dissolution blooming in his face, weight, puffiness, worry.

Oh, Charles, your lifestyle is catching up with you.

'Drink?' He disappeared off to the bar for ten minutes, returning with a wine glass in one hand and a beer in the other, a big, confident grin almost splitting his face. Large, square, rugby-player's shoulders. Powerful thighs bulging through his trousers. Some things never change. He set the drinks down on the table and sat down heavily opposite her. Then he took a long draft of his beer, eyes warily observant over the rim of his glass, before saying mournfully – and insincerely, 'Oh, Claire, why didn't *we* make a go of it?'

Again, how does one respond to this clichéd set piece, so patently a play-act? Truthfully?

Because it was never on the cards. Never on offer. Because . . . All the reasons why romances never get off the ground.

He looked the same as ever but more so. More confident, more preppy, teeth whiter, physique heavier, but softer than when he had played for the varsity rugby elevens. In a cream open-necked, short-sleeved shirt and navy chinos, he emitted an air of confidence and the unmistakable scent of success. *God*, she thought, *he is so sure of himself.*

'Well,' he said, grinning and taking another slurp of beer. 'This *is* nice. Pity about the excuse for meeting up again but it really is great to see you, Claire.' His hand stole from the beer glass to touch hers. It was still chilly from the drink. 'Great to find an excuse to catch up.' He couldn't resist tucking a compliment in but as he had so obviously used it a thousand times it was worthless. 'You look fantastic.' The usual bit of bullshit followed. 'If I'd known how gorgeous you were going to turn out I wouldn't have got myself in a pickle with bloody Rhoda.'

He'd handed her the cue and a comfortable introduction. 'So tell me about . . .' she managed a smile, '. . . bloody Rhoda. What happened there?'

He leaned back in his chair, folding his arms. 'Bloody Rhoda,' he said, 'ensnared me. I fell into her trap mainly because I was a bit bruised after a previous relationship had, well, um, you know, gone the way of . . .'

She didn't *know* but she could guess. He'd cheated on her. It fitted in so well with all she knew about him.

He continued still with the same aggrieved air. 'Lovely girl, she was. Lawyer in London. Absolutely refused to come and live up north.' He looked at her mournfully. 'I had it all planned out, Claire. Nice big house, great job. Marriage and a family, but when I suggested it she turned me down flat. Said that was not in her plans. Accused me of all sorts of stuff. Shit,' he said, suddenly explosive, 'I'd even bought the frigging ring.'

No doubt a huge solitaire. And an even huger blow to his ego when he'd thought he could get away with it. Just one more time.

'Oh, dear,' she said, deliberately avoiding matching his insincerity with an *I'm so sorry,* at the same time knowing he'd half pick up on the sarcasm but would not be absolutely certain. Charles was not and never had been subtle. As predicted, he narrowed his eyes and looked at her suspiciously before continuing with his sad story.

'So I was very vulnerable when I took up the post in Stoke . . .' She was aware he was waiting for more sympathy. But . . . He looked nothing like vulnerable. Still cocksure – maybe a tad less so, but it hardly showed – and there was a large slice of self-pity. 'Rhoda was in charge of the labour suite then. Good legs.' He thought for a moment before acknowledging, 'Bloody good legs. What a looker, and tits like . . .' He suddenly remembered he was talking to a woman and had the grace to stop right there and look abashed, defending himself with a grumpy, 'Well . . . she did.'

Yeah, good decision, Charles. Leave it right there. On the doorstep.

But he couldn't.

'She trapped me,' he continued. 'Believe me, I did not stand a chance against those legs, that fantastic blonde hair. All wispy round her face. Bleached, of course. But I didn't find that out until later.' Truth prevailed. 'Well, a bit later, anyway. Like I said, I wasn't in the best of places. Emotionally.'

'Poor you,' she managed.

Charles looked at her quizzically, sideways on, until he decided to ignore the irony – if he'd even recognized it as such in the first place. He grinned. 'Yeah,' he said. 'Poor me. Anyway, Rhoda and I were married a couple of years later. No kids, thank goodness. She started imagining all sorts of things. Flirtation, accused me of affairs.' He still looked aggrieved but the phrase had struck home in a vulnerable place: *imagining things.*

He was still going. 'And the cow divorces me for half a million. That's over two hundred grand a year.'

The old Charles would have then said, *though I'm worth it*, but the new Charles simply peered ruefully into his beer glass before taking a further noisy slurp. 'I shall be more careful next time.'

She simply smiled. Unsurprisingly, he was not considering a lifetime of celibacy.

He continued, 'Bloody women, conniving cows.' He remembered

her sex again and tagged on politely, 'Present company excluded, of course.'

'Of course,' she echoed. 'Though you're right. Women can be conniving cows. Some women,' she finished severely. Which brought her neatly round to Heather Krimble and the conundrum. 'It's a shame Laura's off,' she began.

Charles looked uneasy. 'Yeah,' he said. 'I heard about it on the grapevine. Hospital jungle drums, you know.' He made a feeble pretence of beating a tattoo on the table but stopped when it didn't even raise a smile.

'Breast cancer, I'm afraid,' he said, wisely reverting to the serious. 'She'll be having treatment, radiotherapy, surgery, chemo. It'll go on for a while. She's under one of my colleagues and he spilt the beans – though he shouldn't have, really.'

It happened.

A jaunty grin obviously meant to ameliorate his indiscretion.

'But surely there's a locum covering her work?' There was an anxiety note in his voice. He'd obviously considered Laura an ally.

'Yeah,' she said, 'an Aussie guy. I've not met him yet. He sounds OK. But it's not the same.' She couldn't resist throwing him the bait. 'Is it, Charles?'

He wasn't sure how to take this and managed a quizzical glance but no other response.

She continued seamlessly, 'He's never met Heather. He'll just be reading out Laura's notes. I imagine she kept pretty good ones but I would have gained a lot more insight by talking to her.'

'What about the bitch's husband? Isn't he some help?'

'Geoff. Have you met him?'

''Course not.' He grinned again. 'Obstetrician? I treat women. Remember?'

She managed a laugh this time. 'Well, let's just say he's not the brightest button in the box. Openly admits he's not above giving her a slap every now and then.'

'Well, there you are, Claire,' Charles said, grin widening and looking pleased. 'There's your motive. A rubbish, violent husband so she fabricates substitutes.'

'Well, yes. I had considered that explanation, Charles,' she said coldly. 'Even apart from the "odd slap", Geoff Krimble is hardly the ideal husband. He has trouble keeping a job, there's a spurious and almost certainly misguided diagnosis of Tourette's and I also suspect he has an alcohol problem. He stank of beer at his outpatients' appointment. And that was at two thirty in the afternoon.'

Charles's ears visibly pricked up but he couldn't resist injecting native spite. 'He sounds just the sort of guy she deserves, if you ask me. Bloody danger to society. Women like that . . .' His eyes met hers and he shook his head. 'Destroyers,' he said.

She continued, 'Then there's the history of previous psychosis during pregnancy. But I could really do with Laura's take on that.'

The waitress interrupted their chat to take their order before Claire filled him in.

Charles's grin was ever-widening. He was practically rubbing his hands together. 'See,' he said, quite excited now. 'She's fucking nuts. No one in their right mind would believe a word of her wild and impossible tales.'

Claire continued without comment. 'The allegation she's made against you falls into the same category as the other two.' She was having to choose her words more carefully now but one question had been nagging at her right from the beginning.

'The question is, Charles, why on earth did she pick on *you*? I mean, both her boss and the window cleaner were men she had regular contact with you. So why you?'

He looked uncomfortable. 'Christ, Claire,' he said, his face almost frightened, 'I don't fucking well know.'

But she persisted. 'According to you, you only had a very brief encounter at a crowded and noisy party. So why *did* she pick you out?'

His face twisted. 'I don't suppose it could be my incredible good looks?'

But she wasn't diverted and stuck doggedly to her line of questioning. 'Did you make a pass at her that night?'

His face froze. 'No.' The denial had no weight behind it. 'No,' he said again.

She didn't insult him by adding, *Sure?* She moved on. 'Geoff Krimble claims that both Freddie and her current pregnancy are down to him and, of course, we can easily prove or disprove who is this child's father.'

He could see the hole in this argument. Now came the awkward bit. She delayed the moment with a sip of wine. 'While the allegations are being . . .' she scratched speech marks into the air, '. . . investigated . . . you can't really work.'

She was puzzled by his smug look. Only for a moment.

'Got you there,' he said. 'I've already discussed it with the GMC. And the MDU. I gave them the full story. They'll back me up on a few conditions.'

'A chaperone,' she guessed.

He nodded. 'Pretty obvious really. I'm not to see patients at any time alone, even in the clinic when they're fully dressed. It'll mean allocating someone to be alongside me day and night but I can accept those conditions. I can't see her; I'm to hand her care over to one of my colleagues,' he made a face, 'and the community midwives. I mean, there are the two previous cot deaths so a paediatrician will be involved in the birth.'

She let this all sink in before meeting his eyes. A mistake. Charles Tissot had lovely eyes. She remembered them now. They were a particularly bright blue and he had almost feminine long lashes but very masculine, heavy black eyebrows. Somehow his eyes melted into you, reassured you, deceived you, told you you're special just before he hunted down another girl to flirt with. She remembered those eyes a little too well.

'So . . .?' He interrupted her reverie.

'I'm not worried about *you*,' she said. 'You'll make it through. You're strong, Charles, and intelligent too. You'll see a way round this.'

His eyebrows expressed a mocking thank you.

'I'm more worried,' she said, 'about the child. Two have died. And there are signs . . .'

He held his hand up in a top sign. 'Not my problem, Claire. Not being funny but I don't want to be any more involved with that woman than I have to be. Hand it over to the paediatricians and Melissa.'

'Melissa?'

He gave a smug smile. 'My lovely colleague who will be taking over the bitch's obstetric care. Along with Bloody Rhoda. And then the child protection team can poke their noses in, in case she tries to hurt the baby.'

'I think she's already started,' she said.

'Uh?'

'Harming the unborn child. I've already told you, she punishes it when it moves *in utero*.'

'Claire . . .'

She never knew where that sentence had been heading. Their meal arrived and the conversation, between mouthfuls, moved to catch up on their years in med school.

But when they had finished eating and had moved to coffee and the bill had arrived, Charles returned to more serious conversation.

'Don't believe everything bloody Rhoda tells you about me.'

She'd hoped to avoid the topic. Safer for her, better for the ex and would possibly avoid muddying the waters further with her patient.

Charles huffed in an injured sigh. 'She won't have a single good word to say about me. I can promise you that. The divorce was *extremely* acrimonious.' Eyes wide, displaying self-pity. '*I'm* only just getting over it myself.'

She took this in and decided to change the subject completely.

'How well do you know Doctor Sylas?'

'Dagmar?'

'Yes. Heather's GP. She seemed to know you.'

He was on the alert. 'Why do you ask?'

'Just the PS she put on the end of her referral letter. It sounded personal. Almost impassioned.'

He smirked, and at that moment she realized what a Lothario he was. Nothing had changed. Charles was Charles. To disguise the hostility she could feel rising against him, she picked up her glass and twirled it around.

'She's a married woman,' he said. It was the nod-and-a-wink answer. She got it, all right.

Charles seemed to realize he'd lost her empathy as well as her attention. He drained his pint glass and slammed it down on the table.

'Get that DNA, Claire,' he said. 'Make the diagnosis. Get me off the fucking hook.' He moved his face closer. 'Don't let me down.'

Without waiting for her response, he threw three twenty-pound notes on the table and strode out of the beer garden, no one even looking up, leaving her realizing she'd been played like a fly on the end of his fishing line.

TWENTY

The baby was due (a notoriously moveable date) on 7 August. Just a few more weeks to wait for the DNA test to prove or disprove Heather's conviction that the child was baby Tissot. 'Charles'll love it whether it's a boy or a girl.' Claire could have requested a cord blood sample but there was no point. And the procedure was not without its risks. So there was a wait ahead. But Claire was impatient to learn the truth about that night way back in November. And one of the best ways to find out more would be to quiz Ruth again. See if she could unravel her story, possibly break it – at least find out what had bonded these two sisters so tightly.

Claire knew she would need every single piece of information to satisfy the GMC, who had a duty 'to defend their innocent member'. She couldn't help but smile at the pompous wording. Innocent member? Charles hadn't even been *born* with one of those.

And so, as she drove home from The Orange Tree, she was strangely dissatisfied with the evening and Charles's behaviour. But she had to agree with him on one score.

If his divorce really had been as acrimonious as he claimed and Rhoda got wind of the story Heather was spinning, she would have to be a saint to act as an impartial bystander. It was even possible that she would add to Heather's delusions, encourage her to see Charles as a predatory male, throw a spanner right into the centre of the works and exact revenge from her dissolute and philandering husband. But Rhoda was head of the community midwifery services. There was no way of bypassing her. And the sooner Rhoda attended her patient, the better. By Monday morning she was already preparing for a tightrope dance.

Monday, 6 July, 8.45 a.m.
35/40

Rhoda's voice on the answerphone was as crisp as a nurse's apron starched until it crackled, stiff enough to stand alone and white enough to make summer clouds look grubby.

Claire left a message asking her to contact her about a pregnant patient she was about to admit.

It was later on when she finally rang back.

Claire had never met Charles's wife but as Rhoda spoke, combined with Charles's description of her assets, she began to form a picture of a professional woman who probably stood no nonsense either from colleagues or patients. Or her husband.

Claire began with a brief resumé of Heather's history, about the three pregnancies, physically normal, but accompanied by delusions that crept in during the weeks, allegations that were hotly denied by all three men accused of being her lovers. She explained that this time the allegation was against her obstetrician.

Rhoda cut quickly to her role. 'But the pregnancies were *physically* normal?'

'Yes.'

'And the labour too?'

'As I understand it, yes. She wasn't under me but the community psychiatrist.'

'This time?'

'The allegation is potentially more serious and besides, Laura Hodgkins is currently off sick, her work being covered by a locum.'

'And that is why you're involved?'

Claire felt a prickling down the back of her neck. This woman was sharp as a box of needles. 'There is an issue of her trying to harm the foetus,' she said. 'It's a clear case of puerperal psychosis complicated by erotomania.'

'I see.'

'Her two previous babies died, one at six months and the other at two months.'

'Cot deaths?'

Here, Claire was cautious. 'Apparently so. Nothing was found at post-mortem.'

Rhoda listened without adding comment.

Claire filled the midwife in, waiting for Rhoda to pick up on the significant point, finishing with, 'I think she needs admitting and I hoped you'd agree to monitor her obstetric needs either at Greatbach or we can bring her to your clinics.'

Rhoda greeted Claire's history with a brief silence while she digested the facts. Then, 'I think, doctor, as we midwives are not psychiatric trained you should provide us with a bit more detail. Would my staff be under any threat?'

'Oh, no. Not at all. Heather is no danger to anyone else.'

'So what exactly happens in these pregnancies? The alleged fathers . . . are they real people? Or fantasies?'

'Oh, they're real people.' Claire was waiting for Rhoda to make the connection. But not yet.

'And the claims she makes against them?'

Claire could feel Rhoda edging closer. 'Well, the first two men have not been badly affected by her claims. This time, well, obviously, it's possible it could harm his career.'

Again, Claire held her breath, waiting for Rhoda to make the connection.

But she simply sounded interested. 'And you're saying there's *no* truth in *any* of her stories?'

Claire scooped in a long breath to answer. 'In each case the alleged father has denied there has even been a relationship and the DNA test proved the father of her second child to be her husband.'

'But only in the case of the second child.'

'That's right.'

Rhoda Tissot had picked up the history without a stumble. 'And I take it,' she continued crisply, 'that you'll do a paternity test in the case of *this* claim against . . .' another pause while Claire pictured the cogs clicking into their grooves, '. . . the obstetrician.'

'Correct.'

Claire paused, knowing that Rhoda Tissot was almost touching the tender heart of the matter. 'Obviously the person alleged to be the father is in a difficult position until we can prove otherwise.'

This was greeted with a long silence, as though Rhoda Tissot was working through a few variations on a theme.

Then, 'How many weeks did you say she is?'

'Thirty-five. Her EDD is the seventh of August.'

'But you're convinced it's just another . . . story?'

Skating on thin ice? Claire could feel it crack beneath her feet, almost feel herself fall into icy depths. Caution. Caution. 'It would seem so.'

'When were you thinking of admitting her?'

'As soon as possible.' Claire was forced to add, 'As soon as I have a bed.'

'Ah, the same old problem.' Now Claire sensed that Rhoda was smiling. Back on familiar territory.

She came to a decision. 'OK. Well, why don't you let me know when she's in Greatbach and, if you like, I'll come round myself.' She sounded pleased with herself but Claire was dismayed. She had hoped that Rhoda would keep her distance, send someone else. A minion. The membrane between the two women, patient and midwife, was too porous, too sensitive. Too thin. But Rhoda had patently made up her mind. 'Thirty-five weeks,' she said briskly. 'She could go into labour quite soon. Has she a history of premature labour?'

'No. She's always gone to term.'

There was a strange, unexpected silence. Claire could almost feel cogs whirring and clicking into place somewhere inside Rhoda's mind. Two and two making . . .

And finally she got it. 'Which consultant is she under?' *Click.*

Claire hesitated, which gave Rhoda a chance to fill in.

'Ah,' she said, her quarry sniffed out. 'She's a patient of that scumbag of an ex-husband of mine? That's who the allegations are against.' She snorted with laughter and echoed Claire's sentiments. 'Finally, he gets his comeuppance. Oh – and the real irony. Probably this time, for once in his randy little life, he's almost certainly innocent. What a hoot.'

Claire feigned ignorance. 'Sorry?'

Rhoda Tissot's voice trickled poisoned honey into the phone. 'Oh. You didn't know?'

'Know what?'

'Oh. That dear Charles and I are no longer . . .' Even the pause was poisonous. 'An item?'

'I'm sorry.' What else was there to say? She hadn't known them as a couple.

Rhoda's venom spilled out. 'Well, he banged everything in sight. Particularly when he'd had a few. Taking the hostess's bed in parties was his particular speciality. Or tempting ladies into his Jag. Didn't really matter who the woman was, as long as it wasn't me. Still, I've had my share of the pickings. Divorce lawyers these days are soooo good at arithmetic.'

Claire frowned into the telephone. She felt the danger intensify. Flashing red lights all over the place. Sirens screaming. She felt very apprehensive.

Rhoda spoke again. 'So when do you think you'll have a bed?'

'She'll be in early next week.'

Rhoda's response was careless and sarcastic. 'Like I said, do let me know when she's in and I'll pop over and make her acquaintance.'

'Thank you.'

She hadn't quite finished. 'Tell me, Doctor Roget – this time, is there any truth in your patient's allegations?'

'No.' But the single word must have sounded too weak.

'So, Charles really is in hot water.'

Claire kept her silence. Instinctively she knew that any comment she made would only make matters worse.

'Well,' Rhoda said, 'I'm just glad I took the money and ran. *This* won't help his career path or his earning potential. Although . . .' She paused, puzzled now. 'I wouldn't have thought Charles, even with his randy cock, would have been daft enough to break this ultimate taboo – accept someone he'd had sex with as a patient. Still . . .' And she chuckled again.

But Claire didn't join in. Much as Charles Tissot was not her favourite person in the world, she didn't want to join this hissing, triumphant spite. Besides . . . although there were obvious doubts, the bet was still on, even though the likelihood was that Heather's baby would prove to be the son or daughter of Geoff Krimble.

Rhoda gave another snort of laughter. 'I take it Charles is currently suspended?'

Claire felt her shoulders drop. 'In view of Heather's previously unfounded allegations he is not suspended, though certain conditions have been made and he has been removed from any responsibility or contact with her. That,' she said, more sharply than she had meant, 'is why we're anxious for you to be involved.'

No response. Claire couldn't tell whether Rhoda was pleased or disappointed that her husband was getting off so lightly and that, subsequently, she was being dragged in. Her voice was crisp and professional now. 'Let me know when you have her ensconced at Greatbach and I'll come over and see her.'

'Thank you.'

Claire waited but the phone was not put down. Instead, Rhoda asked another question in a humble tone. 'Tell me honestly, Claire. What do you think? Has Charles really . . .'

Maybe there was still some affection for the love rat?

And this time, Claire couldn't duck the question. 'I think she's deluded,' she began before altering the weak wording to something stronger. 'I'm *convinced* she's deluded.' She paused before adding, 'I can't see Charles falling into this trap.'

Rhoda didn't respond. The conversation had ended.

But when Claire had put the phone down that one word bounced her mind. She'd used the word without thinking, almost instinctively. Why? Was it a trap? A deliberate trap? Set to snap shut around Charles Tissot's career for some perceived slight? Mentally she ran over the other two cases, which posed different scenarios. Cartwright's business had suffered temporarily. Sam Maddox was still a window cleaner. But Charles's career – certainly any private practice he had – might not recover.

She sat still. What were her senses and her training telling her? Don't make assumptions. Listen hard to the words your patient is selecting. Above all, watch their body language and keep sensitive to inconsistencies.

She was increasingly sure of one thing. Heather Krimble needed to be watched and her unborn child protected. But from what direction might the threat come?

TWENTY-ONE

As the week rolled by, Claire was aware of a pounding urgency surrounding the troubling case of Heather Krimble. She wanted her and her unborn baby where she and her staff could keep an eye on her.

In her mind, the aura around Heather's romantic fantasy was slowly changing from pink to purple to black. Possibly even red. Maybe the core was not love but destruction.

By Wednesday, she was acknowledging something else. Her concerns were not purely professional. There was some curiosity, too. Her instincts were telling her something. That Heather might be disturbed, psychotic. But what if, hidden inside the labyrinth of her damaged mind, there was a kernel of truth? What if she and Charles really had had a brief liaison and she had simply misinterpreted it? And another question. What lay *behind* both Heather's fragile mental state and the absolute devotion of her sister?

Something in their past? Or was it simply a bond forged by paternal cruelty and maternal indifference?

It was this curiosity which had led her towards psychiatry in the first place. Not simply interest but a burning desire to know, to solve the mysteries.

Questions were pouring through her mind like sand through an hourglass. None of them answered *quite* satisfactorily. Nothing beyond the reach of doubt. Who? What? When? How? And as always, she was staggering along the wobbly cake walk that follows any statement made by a patient you have diagnosed as deluded. The old problem: what is the truth? Where is it? How do you recognize it?

But part of the urgency she felt was a drop in the barometer pressure, a sign of an approaching storm.

She could see the black sock whirling around in the washing machine drum of whites. Visible, invisible but always there, somewhere, staining. Something bad would happen. But would admission really avert that?

On Friday, a patient was discharged and Heather's admission finally arranged.

She did not demur.

Friday, 17 July, 2 p.m.
37/40

The call came in at two p.m. Heather had arrived on the ward, accompanied by her sister. And so Claire headed upstairs.

One thing struck her.

Ruth couldn't have fed her the detail: the make of the car, the leather seats, the colour of the leather, the scent all car owners know is peculiar to their own vehicle, could she?

She reached the top, pleased that her breathing rate hadn't even increased, and peered in through the porthole window.

Heather was sitting on the bed, legs tucked beneath her, back completely straight, eyes watchful as her sister fussed around the room, hanging up clothes, spreading out baby outfits, disappearing into the bathroom with hands full of toiletries. As Claire observed her, Heather didn't strike her as Charles's type. He liked them obvious – 'bits' on show. His comments about women were all about tits, arses and legs. Personality didn't cut much ice with him. Heather wore little make-up and looked coy in her maternity clothes. But eight months ago, tarted up for a party, made up, wearing party clothes? What then? Could she morph into something else, something different? Some*one* different? Charles's type?

The sticky snail trail continued as Claire continued to observe the sisters. If events had happened as Heather had related them, would Charles have recognized her name, if he'd ever bothered to learn and retain it following their encounter? Probably not? And then would he have picked it out from the tens of referrals he received in an average week? Again, probably not. Charles never thought about consequences. After their encounter, he had not shied away from her. It had been Claire who had secreted herself in the farthest, darkest corner. He had been oblivious. In Charles's convenient mind there were no consequences. Besides, a woman's name would be the last thing Charles would recall. Tits, legs, arse. Vital statistics. Those were the important things about a woman. These were the parts he would remember. Not her name.

And would he have recognized the party animal for the pale, quiet, modestly dressed pregnant patient sitting opposite him in his consulting room?

Possibly. Probably not. These liaisons were not something Charles retained in his mind.

But the Charles she knew would surely not be idiot enough to keep her as his patient, even directed by Dr Dagmar Sylas.

So, possibly not.

What would he have done when this inconvenient situation presented itself?

Answer: refer to her.

So now she had gone full circle and was disliking the way this case was forcing her to turn around and face her own past.

And even now, hand on the door, she troubled over the question all female victims ask themselves: what secret message did I give out? What pheromone vibes? What scent inviting men to do this?

Why did he pick on *me* at that party all those years ago? And the inevitable consequence: how can I stop giving out these dumb messages? By wearing uninviting clothes, less make-up, shoulders rounded, eyes on floor. Just like Heather.

She may be learning about Charles through this case. But what, exactly, was it telling her about herself?

She had always been slim and worn little make-up. Though her hair was light it was not and never had been peroxide blonde. Her skin was good and she had dark eyelashes and eyebrows which needed little to no enhancement. Her one vanity was lipstick. She often wore a fairly vivid shade of pink at work, leisure and to parties. Had that one fatal cosmetic invited Charles? Her normal outfits were smart without being either provocative or spinsterish. That night she'd been wearing tight black jeans and a flimsy white top. She *hadn't* led him on that night. She knew it. She'd been wearing jeans . . . and now she blushed. Underneath the top, she'd not been wearing anything. That still didn't excuse him.

Even with a tank full of shots and spirits, even way back then in her misspent student days, she hadn't been the sort to have casual sex. But Charles was a horny bastard. And sexy too with his male hormones stacked up. Drunk, he was quite capable of ramming a girl against a wall and trying his luck. But that was the Charles of then. Not now. Now he would have to be guarded in order to maintain his career and position.

But, by nature, Charles was neither subtle nor careful. His care might only extend to luring a girl into the back of his Jag, maybe wearing a condom. It wouldn't moderate his behaviour completely.

As she watched, Ruth moved towards the bed and kissed her sister, wrapped her arms around her then moved away. For a moment, the two women gazed at each other, exchanging something, until Ruth patted her sister reassuringly on the head and continued fussing around the room.

A negative DNA sample wouldn't let him off the hook.

Neither would Heather's messy past psychiatric history. Then Claire recalled Heather's hard, punishing blows on her pregnant abdomen and worried. At least part of her concern was not for Charles, who could look after himself, or Heather, who had invented a story behind the baby's conception, but for the unborn infant and his or her dead siblings.

Two of them.

Cot death is tragic and notorious because in most cases it is inexplicable. There is nothing for the pathologist to find except an absence of life. Perfect little bodies lie on mortuary slabs. Various theories have sprung up over the years, coming in and going out of fashion as regularly as hemlines: milk allergy, placing babies face down on their mattresses, having a pillow, bedrooms too hot, too cold, having a slight fever. An impending cold. A virus. The trouble is this tragedy is without reason and leaves behind it heartbreak and an empty cot. Numbers rise and they fall and mothers, fathers, grandparents, godparents, aunts, uncles, siblings – everyone is left behind to wonder and to suffer.

Before she finally pushed open the door, Claire reminded herself yet again of the very first rule of psychiatry: make certain of your own impartiality before you even start trying to unravel your patient's story. Analyse your own prejudices. Ask yourself this question: what do you *already* believe?

TWENTY-TWO

Friday, 17 July, 2.10 p.m.
37/40

It had been a while since she had seen Heather and her pregnancy had ballooned. Like many petite women late in pregnancy but before the baby's head had engaged into the pelvis, it was hard to imagine her small frame supporting anything bigger. There was simply no room for expansion. In any direction.

Claire greeted them both, aware that she must keep Ruth on her side if she was to have any chance to winnow fact from fantasy. For that she needed *both* women's confidence so she needed them both to relax, drop their guard, to see her as an ally. Trouble was that admitting Heather to Greatbach, even as a voluntary patient, cast her in the role of jailor rather than friend. So, reassurance before interrogation.

Heather swivelled around to face her as Claire entered the room to sit in the armchair, Ruth hovering, uncertain where to place herself.

Claire began with an explanation. 'I know you're here because there seems to be some confusion about the relationship between you and Mr Tissot.'

'No confusion,' Heather snapped. 'I'm quite clear in *my* mind. You'll see.'

Claire continued smoothly as though she hadn't spoken. 'I don't want you to have any concerns about the baby, Heather. Midwives will be in regular attendance here at Greatbach. I've already organized it. But at least we can keep an eye on you here, keep you safe until the baby is born.'

'As if I need to be kept "safe",' she scoffed. 'And afterwards?'

Afterwards? Two dead children cast a shadow behind her. Claire shuddered. *Was that what afterwards would mean?*

'Afterwards, too,' she continued, hardly pausing but still feeling her face stiffen. 'For a few weeks. Just until the situation is resolved and we think it's safe for you both to go home.'

Heather's eyes flashed but she didn't ask any of the logical questions.

Home?

To . . .?

Situation resolved? Her eyes narrowed as she tried to read Claire's attitude, fingers tapping out a staccato beat on her locker which intensified and speeded up before she moved them to dig into her abdomen.

Claire couldn't ignore it. 'Why do you do that, Heather?'

Her patient flashed her another look heavy with hostility but she did not answer. And then her eyes flirted upwards. It was as though she challenged Claire, asking her silently, *Why do you think I do it, psychiatrist?*

Then she dug her fingers in even harder so Claire winced for the child while Heather simply glared back, gloves off. There was an intensity both in her action and in the look, a cruelty and hatred about it that she'd successfully hidden, until now.

There was little doubt that in Claire's mind that she was punishing the unborn child for the sin of the father. The sin of denial.

She had never witnessed this sort of behaviour before though she'd read about it. But such hatred of the unborn was rare. Even after violent rape. Attempted abortion was not uncommon in the early stages. And even more common was behaviour that indirectly harmed the child: alcohol, drugs, risky sexual behaviour. Yes, all these would harm a foetus but the actions were at best careless, at worst deliberately neglectful. But this was destruction. Particularly when two children had previously died.

'Please stop doing that,' she said. 'You could harm the baby, you know. Is that what you want to do? Hurt Charles through harming the baby?' This time the look that Heather aimed back at her was unmistakably calculating, malicious, triumphant. *Just try and stop me.*

Claire's opinion of her shifted. This was a different act from the meek, pliant person who had first arrived at her clinic with her story of a party liaison followed by an intense love affair. This woman looked perfectly in control, rational and well able to look after herself. A quick check with her sister told her a different story. Ruth's eyes were wide. Frightened. And she looked shocked at this morphing of her sister from star-crossed victim to harpy. Families are a strange entity, roles reversing, siblings skirting around each other. Thoughts criss-crossed Claire's mind as she studied the two women and revised what she knew about Ruth.

She worked for Leo Metcalfe, a thoracic surgeon whose Christian name could not have been more apt. When his mother had christened him Leo, she must have imagined her son would one day be tall, well built, with a mane of tawny hair. In which case, she must have had a crystal ball, because that was a pretty good description of him.

Ruth bounced her gaze back defiantly.

Heather was smiling at her now, looking around the room with satisfaction. 'I'm happy to be here,' she said. 'I'll be glad of the rest.' She patted her bulge. 'So will he.'

Claire continued with her instruction. 'The community midwives will come in, probably daily, to keep an eye on you and the baby. And when you go into labour you'll be transferred to the maternity unit for delivery.'

Heather's eyes slid upwards as though she saw some heavenly vision. Or was it an eye-roll? As always with Heather, there was a text and a subtext. 'Will it be Charles who delivers his own child?' Her eyes were inspired, bright, her manner enthusiastic now.

Claire drew in a deep breath and shook her head. 'No, you

won't be under the care of Charles Tissot. It wouldn't be wise.' She tossed the statement back. 'Would it?'

Heather looked angry then, fury bubbling up. 'I want to see him,' she said, petulant now. 'I know he wants to see me and be involved with the birth and aftercare of his own baby. I must insist, Doctor.'

Claire couldn't let this pass. However much Heather might resist the truth, this was an undeniable fact. 'Mr Tissot denies any involvement in the conception of this baby.'

But the words didn't even seem to graze Heather. 'I don't believe you,' she said flatly. 'You're making it up. Just jealous. A father should be present at the birth of his child, Doctor Roget.'

For now, Claire could only work around this. 'In view of your allegations, it wouldn't be ethical for him to attend you as a doctor.' She took the opportunity of repeating, 'And as he denies the paternity of your child, he has no role in the labour room as father, either.'

A quick glance at Ruth showed her shrinking, eyes scared, the alarm bells ringing loud and clear. Claire could read her message clearly. *It didn't do to confront her sister with such a blunt truth.* Claire continued, 'A doctor and a team of midwives will ultimately take responsibility for your obstetric care. And I will be responsible for your mental well-being. A paediatrician will see to your baby's needs and check the child over.'

She was puzzled at Heather's sudden look of alertness.

Ruth was staring at the floor now, chewing her lip, frowning, looking as though she wished she was somewhere else.

But Heather was angry, her pale face red. 'You don't believe me now.' Her eyes blazed with hostility and fury and she jabbed her index finger towards her, straight as an arrow. 'But you will, Doctor Roget. You will. You'll see.'

The bang on her belly was hard enough to almost hear the baby cry out. After the bang the three of them fell silent, listening for an infant cry. But there was no sound. Nothing except Heather's hard breathing. She was glaring down at her swollen belly with hatred now, her face twisted as she sucked in a long, rasping breath. 'The father of this little devil, the little devil itself and I will be a complete family.' She gave an oddly triumphant, twisted smile, hands gripping each side of her belly, speaking to the unborn child. 'If he tries to deny it, I will destroy him. And if *you*,' the word was accompanied by a glare, 'try to stop us being together with your clever words and silly ideas, I will destroy you too.' She leapt forward, towards Claire, clawing hands grasping the air between them.

Every room in Greatbach has two alarm bells – one near the door and the other underneath the window. Claire had rarely needed to use either but it was a comfort to know they were there. To have to summon help would seem like failure. It broke the relationship between psychiatrist and patient and the patient came out on top. They were the winners; the psychiatrist, the so-called expert, vanquished. Claire's arm rested on the arm of the chair, her index finger stroking the small round button.

If she increased the pressure, even just a tiny bit, Security would come running. The patient would be overcome but *she* would be the one leaving with her tail between her legs. This fury directed at her had opened up a new situation. Not only was Heather a danger to the baby, Charles and his career, but also to her. She held her breath and waited.

After a furious glare, Heather dropped back into her seat and the crisis was over, the mood quickly normal. Ruth's chin dropped to her chest, shoulders bowed.

But Heather hadn't finished her assault. She held her head up high. 'You'll see,' she said. 'You'll soon see. I'll show you. Just wait till our child is born.'

Her hatred was directed all at Claire now. This is the moment a psychiatrist needs to be wary. Whatever the diagnosis, from schizophrenia with all its manifestations and variations to psychopathy with all its dangers and pitfalls, when the anger, the paranoia, is directed solely at you, it is as hot and dangerous as a laser.

It is *you* who are to blame for all that is wrong in this person's life, head, brain, current situation and problems. Everything is *your* fault. You are the evil psychiatrist, the Dr Jekyll, creator of this monster. The next step? Punishment.

Claire's finger remained on the small panic button.

She almost sensed that Heather Krimble could feel that gentle pressure too. There was triumph in her face. For the first time, Claire saw glimpses of the legacy of the bullying, violent father.

And began to understand a little of the place from where Heather Krimble came.

She stood up. 'Until I come to talk to you for a bit longer, there's something you can do for me.'

'Oh?'

'Write down details of your liaison, dates and places when you and Charles met up.'

'Why?'

'Just to clarify your claim.'

'But I've already . . .'

'We need more detail, Heather. Times. Places. Telephone conversations. I need you to write down his mobile number. Anything else you can remember.'

Claire closed the door behind her, shutting out the fury.

TWENTY-THREE

Monday, 20 July, 3 p.m.

She didn't doubt that Heather Krimble was deluded and she recognized that these were testing times for Charles. But until now she hadn't understood the wider danger to herself, the sole person who stood between Heather and her imagined nirvana – life with her beloved. And there was something else concerning her. In her book, cases of erotomania complicated by psychosis and pregnancy are often marked by deterioration and unpredictability following delivery. They needed to be prepared. Not only for the birth itself, but the aftermath. The baby would need protecting from its own mother.

In the articles there were also warnings about protecting the object of desire. Even under the circumstances, Claire smiled. Charles needed protection from Heather? Well, there was something to think about.

There was no treatment for Heather's condition apart from gentle counselling and a certain optimism that the sufferer will, at some point, move on. So rather than focusing on a 'cure', you talk about 'managing'. To have any chance of 'managing' Heather's case, they needed to delve deeper inside her psyche, reach the boundaries of her mind and try and plant a few seeds of truth. She would need help. And the person who sprang to mind was Edward Reakin, the clinical psychologist attached to Greatbach.

He'd already seen her once but Claire had had no feedback yet. Before she rang him, Claire felt her face warm.

He was a lovely man with a grave insight. Older than his years, polite, divorced, intelligent, with perceptions that dug deeper than any psychologist she had worked with in the past. Plus, he was fast becoming a real friend. They'd shared drinks together a few times after work, even the occasional curry, but he would never replace Grant. There was simply no spark between them. No romance. No sex. Just a valued and treasured friendship. And she believed that Edward felt the same about her. She believed that his divorce had proved so traumatic, played out in public, so humiliating and damaging, he would probably remain single and never again trust his life to a partner.

That stopped her short. Just like her? It was her private fear that she would never again trust her life to a partner. But she wasn't so different from the average woman. She *wanted* a partner, perhaps children, a home, love and security to return to. She thought she had had it with Grant. But now her fear was that that one relationship would prove a tripwire for any other she might have.

Bugger.

She picked up the phone and connected with Edward, who agreed to spend more time with Heather and then fill her in on his thoughts so far. She appreciated the fact that he made little comment, no judgement, simply agreeing to see Heather again later that afternoon on the ward.

'I'll just have another chat,' he said. 'Nothing too heavy. Just get to know her a bit better. So far, I thought she was a very closed book.'

'Did you see her with her sister?'

'No. I saw her alone.'

'Thanks, Edward. See what's happening.'

'OK, Claire. I'll give you a ring later, shall I?'

It was a relief to hand over the reins to Edward and let him drive for a bit. 'That would be great.'

She would be interested to have his perspective. She couldn't rid herself of the feeling that she was missing something and that perhaps her view was skewed by her previous involvement with Charles. Maybe she needed less focus, more breadth, more understanding, more of a picture of the complicated person Heather Krimble was.

Maybe Edward would reinforce some of her ideas. Perhaps he would find new ones of his own. Find a reason why Heather invented fantasy romances.

Husband rejection? A need to find love, even if it was imagined? Or was it something darker? Something else strewn across the path of memory, something unpleasant in her past, a fiction to block out a damaged truth? Substitution? If so, how conscious was Heather of this truth? Or was she completely deluded? Was there no basis in fact?

Was the fiction a deliberate attempt at destruction of another individual? In which case, was a possible motive spite? The result of a previous rejection? She might learn something more by talking to both Tim Cartwright and Sam Maddox. It was possible that they had searched themselves for a motive. Maybe they'd found one? Bubbling under was another question. Had Tim Cartwright been Eliza's father, or someone else?

Anyway, Edward would see Heather and they could pool their ideas. Still upbeat, she trotted along to the coffee shop and picked up a latte before heading back to her office, an idea sparking in her brain. Something she had neglected to do.

She might not be able to connect with Laura Hodgkins but she could stick to her original plan and speak to the locum who was filling in for her. Take a better look at Laura's notes.

3.50 p.m.

Needless to say, getting hold of a locum consultant was not quite instant. She'd drained her coffee cup by the time Simon Bracknell returned her call.

She got quickly to the point, explaining the bare bones of her case, and again, his response was bright and friendly. 'So how can *I* help you?'

'I could do with reading through Laura's notes myself.'

'I thought you might. I've got her notes out all ready.'

She smiled. This guy was making life that little bit easier. Particularly when he followed that with a suggestion.

'Look, I've been dying to take a look round Greatbach. Call it nosey if you like but . . . Why don't I bring Heather Krimble's notes over so you can read them through? We can kill two birds with one stone. *You* can take a look at Laura's notes and *I* can satisfy my curiosity by taking a peek round Greatbach. See how it compares with our secure units at home.'

'OK,' she said, liking the idea. 'I'm seeing a couple of patients this afternoon but I'll be free by five. Why don't you come over then?'

'Great,' he said, sounding as pleased as a child who'd just been promised a trip to Legoland. She put the phone down. Now she could give all her attention to her other patients.

She'd finished preparing her report on Arthur Connolly but knew she could not say enough to save him from a prison sentence. The assault had been too serious. His wife could easily have died. She'd had to have five major operations but was still left with life-changing injuries. Claire couldn't even use the defence that he had been of temporary unsound mind. Arthur had been perfectly aware of what he had done and freely admitted it. He'd been charged with GBH and he didn't have Riley's genius of plucking on the heartstrings as skilfully as a royal harpist. Riley, who had subtly adapted her mantra to the classical sounding, *I grieve for what I cannot have.*

Where on earth had she picked that one up?

It was a line which would have fitted into medieval poetry but Claire knew full well it was likely to bring out sympathy in the jury, who probably wouldn't recognize it was a borrowed cliché. Particularly when Riley accompanied the phrase with a flash of those sad little eyes and an almost clownish downturned mouth. So Riley would go free while Arthur would be incarcerated on the grounds of *his* robust mental health and *her* assumed sad case. Justice? No. Not in Claire's opinion. Quite the reverse. She knew that Arthur was not and never would be a danger to society. Not even to Lindsay any more – provided he did not move back in with her and she steered well clear of him. Something in her smiled at the thought of Lindsay – and Saul – welcoming him back into the marital home. It was more likely that stocky Lindsay and bulky Saul would block the doorway to prevent another disaster which might well have turned into a second tragedy. Maybe next time it would be Arthur who would be the victim of a physical assault. And then would the raft of sympathy change direction? The question intrigued her. Her smile stiffened. Lindsay would not be so insane as to invite him back. Instead, she would find someone else to dominate.

If Claire had learned anything about people and human nature it was that they did not learn from their mistakes, do the sensible or safe thing and change their ways, but threw themselves back into the path of danger. If experience was the school of fools they hadn't even attended kindergarten. Why, she had never worked out, but her patients returned to their damaging relationships, continued with the very acts that had made them unhappy in the first place.

Riley, on the other hand, was a quite different kettle of fish. What she wanted, she would have. Oh, yes, she would. But Riley was slightly cleverer than Arthur. Subtler. More deceitful. No one would ever manipulate *her*. *She* would be the one pulling the strings. She would conceal her emotions, airing them only when it suited her purpose and they would achieve something she wanted. Emotions for her were something to be used to her advantage. And she would hide her footprints as cunningly as a felon on the run. In Claire's opinion, whereas only one person was in danger from Arthur Connolly, *no one* was safe from spoilt little Riley.

But then what did she know? She was just a psychiatrist.

Which brought her neatly back to Heather Krimble. Merely labelling her as obsessed was not enough for Claire. It might be the title page of a book but it wasn't the full story. And that was what she wanted. From beginning to end. She didn't want to treat a symptom without really understanding its cause. So, work to be done. Questions to be answered. Was she a danger to society? To her baby? To Charles – apart from the destruction of his reputation? *Mud sticks, you know?* Claire's mind flicked back to her last interview with Heather. She had felt it then – hatred boiling over at anyone who came between her and her beloved, the man she was so certain adored her. Or was that simply a front? A pretence?

Was there any truth in Heather's version? Recalling Charles's account that night at The Orange Tree, the answer was an emphatic *no*. But was she missing something? Was that the whole truth? For a moment, her mind snagged on the two dead babies. Perhaps if Freddie and Eliza had lived, Charles would not have had this sticky mud of scandal slung at him. Watching Heather bond with them might have given her more of a clue as to her mental state. Would she be able to draw parallels between the three pregnancies and their accompanied allegations? Maybe when she had learnt more details about Heather's two previous claims she would be able to do so, to spot the diagnosis and find a resolution.

But at the back of her mind was always a darker alternative. What if, heaven forbid, the child's DNA proved Charles to be the father? That would be it. End of. Obstetricians don't survive an allegation of sexual assault on a vulnerable and misguided woman. Even a lengthy enquiry and subsequent exoneration would mean the end of his career, a career he had had for fifteen years. Longer than that. School exams had to be passed, the best results achieved to gain that treasured place in medical school.

She looked forward to hearing Edward Reakin's opinion. And reading Laura Hodgkins' notes. And, for that matter, meeting the Aussie locum.

Briefly, she wondered about him. He had sounded jaunty, confident, happy. Which led her to another curious thought: why *did* Aussies come over here? Why, for that matter, did so many Brits take the trip over to Oz-Land and stay there?

Maybe she should give it a try. She toyed with the idea for a minute or two before realism kicked in. She was on a good salary here, had a mortgage, a family – well, a half-brother. It had taken her a long time and a number of exams to reach consultant status. And she was thinking of giving this up? To take root on the other side of the world? Where she knew no one, had no family, no friends? No ex-boyfriend?

She picked up her files and left the room, smiling at the tiny glimpse of life someplace else, the way she had imagined when she was a little girl. Upside down.

TWENTY-FOUR

Monday, 20 July, 4.15 p.m.

Without any sense of foreboding, Claire climbed the stairs to the top floor. She thought she would check to see whether Heather had started compiling her diary of 'trysts' and whether Edward had continued his assessment of her.

The sun had finally made an appearance and streamed in through tall windows, lightening the grey, Victorian walls and drab decor. She met a few colleagues on the stairs and stopped to exchange stories: holiday plans mainly. Those who had school-age children were raring to go away and 'chill'. It rubbed it in that she a) had no children to talk about b) no partner and c) the one she could do something about – no holiday booked. But where does one go when one is alone? As she reached the top of the stairs, she made herself a promise. Once Heather was safely delivered and she had done her best for Arthur Connolly and her worst for Riley, she would book a cottage somewhere beautiful, perhaps near the sea, take her bike, a pile of paperbacks, running shoes and she too would 'chill'. On her own. It was an enticing thought.

She had reached the top floor and felt a draught of cool air, as though someone had left a window open. We pin moments of emotion on to one particular reference point, a place and time we revisit to remind ourselves what that extreme could be . . . In this case, the emotion was happiness.

Happiness was a damp and uninspiring April evening over a year ago now, returning home after a difficult, long and tiring day at work, exacerbated by an episode which some might call an occupational hazard. A young woman, twenty-three years old, with a severe forensic personality disorder, had run amok in the ward, wounding two members of staff with a knife filched from her meal tray and ultimately injuring herself. All, luckily, had only superficial injuries. The patient had been sedated and the members of staff treated but the episode had underlined the danger they ran the gauntlet of every day and she had returned home exhausted and a little depressed, closing the front door behind her with a sense of heaviness. And then . . .

Grant had been lying in wait for her. Without a word, he had picked up on her low mood, her despair, taken her hand and led her out to the garden where, underneath the ancient apple tree (which they should really have felled by then but hadn't had the heart to) a bottle of red wine and two glasses sat, and as he poured them each a glass he had looked at her with those beautiful dark eyes. Later, she had analysed every single word, the tone, the manner, the gestures that had accompanied them.

'I love you, Claire,' he'd said huskily. 'I love you. I love your intelligence and your steady ways. I love the fact that I can trust you and rely on you. I love your smile and your sense of fairness. I love your judgement and your lovely face . . .' She had tried to contradict him, tell him it was not lovely but plain, but he had stifled the comment with a finger on her lips. 'And that's what I love most about you,' he'd continued. 'The fact that you don't even acknowledge your beauty, let alone flaunt it.' A wisp of a smile had softened his face. 'Is that because your mother always called you an ugly little frog?'

Now she pondered those words too and answered in the affirmative, recalling the cruelty of her childhood. '*You, mademoiselle* (said in a scathing tone), *are an ugly little frog.*'

She left that moment to the past and returned to Grant and that feeling of happiness.

'God, Claire, I love everything about you . . .'

And so the day had been transformed from dire to dream, to something beyond wonderful, a jewel to be treasured, kept in a box and brought out to sparkle and dazzle, to transform dull days into magic. Kept for special occasions but always there, buried so deep in her heart it could never be removed or disturbed.

And she'd left that behind? Discarded it like worthless trash? All because he had kept secret the hold his sick sister and needy mother had over him. And because the seconds of missing him had stretched into minutes. And then to hours and days, to weeks and long months. Without a word?

But . . .

The draft chilled her. The locked ward was not actually locked – it was secured with CCTV cameras watching entrances and exits, the patients carefully monitored, the staff particularly vigilant. If it was necessary, patients could be confined to their rooms, but she preferred not to go down that route. It smacked too much of prison. She had no reason or justification for locking Heather Krimble up. She was not a danger to anyone except, potentially, Charles Tissot, his inflated ego and his financially rewarding career, as well as possibly her unborn child – whoever the father proved to be. Claire pushed open the swinging doors to enter the ward. A quick peep through the porthole window showed an empty room. She found Heather and Ruth in the day room, watching television. It was as she was escorting them back along the corridor that the chill engulfed her.

Another emotion took over. It was a moment that sticks to you as the spider's web does to a fly. Or napalm to a child's body, burning, scarring, frightening. As she walked along the corridor, the memory of that happy moment drained away as quickly as it had arrived and was replaced by fear. It was the precise moment when, as she was leading Heather back to her room, that they passed someone. Riley Finch, returning from the bathroom, a towel wrapped around newly washed hair, the steam and shampoo forming a cloud of scented vapour around her. As they drew parallel, Riley's eyes first met and challenged Claire's before sliding across to Heather and then slipping down to Heather's blooming pregnancy, which made her mouth curve. For a moment, Riley was only conscious of the child within Heather and her smile looked cruel.

If I can't have something, why should anyone else?

She quickly remembered herself, picked up her gaze to meet Claire's face and wiped the instinct away, but not before Claire had read it all. Riley wanted that child. Heather's arms stole over her abdomen. She'd read Riley's avarice too. Knowing Riley as she did, the triangle of glances chilled Claire. These two were both her patients. At the centre of this morass of illusion, delusion, accusation, denial and lies lay vulnerability – an unborn baby quite unable to ward off these toxic ingredients. Riley's character was ultimately selfish, Heather's deluded, the compound mix as poisonous as a volcano's sulphuric belch, as evil as Satan, as mischievous as Puck. They would be in close proximity for a period of time. Riley would be here for another few weeks while the courts decided her fate. During which time, Heather would have delivered. Put them together, baby in the middle, and . . . Claire felt the same dread as when she had been carrying out a chemistry experiment in the sixth form, knowing that the expected outcome was an explosion. Waiting for it had been a mixture of dread and anticipation, attuned to the flash and the bang. She could see it already, Riley's lust for what Heather would have, Heather's determination to cling to her mistaken beliefs. Waiting for Charles. And when Charles didn't come?

Riley Finch looked straight into Claire, met her eyes and smiled.

It was deliberately innocent but underneath both triumphant and challenging. An *I'm going to win* smile. A *just watch me get what I want* smile.

The three of them passed in the corridor, Ruth trailing behind. The moment was gone. Vaporized.

Claire didn't look back.

She ushered Heather and her trailing sister back into her room and was much relieved when Heather sat on her bed, gave one or two test bounces and looked around contentedly at her surroundings. 'It's nice here,' she said. 'It'll be a good place to wait for our baby.' There was no sign that the encounter between the two women had even registered. And yet there was a strain on Heather's face that had not been there minutes ago.

Perhaps, Claire thought optimistically, it was all in my mind.

Hospital rooms are reassuringly anonymous; they act as a sedative rather than a stimulant. Once the door was closed behind them there was a feeling of shutting out any threat, an atmosphere of calm, which soothed Claire. Inside here things felt normal – right up until the point when Heather lay back on the bed, tucked her hands behind her head and said, 'I wonder when Charles will visit.'

Snakes and ladders. Slippery slip. Back down to square one. Claire eyed her and swallowed the words. *Don't hold your breath, Heather.*

She needed to unravel this knot carefully, tease out the strands and cause the least amount of trauma. So she merely smiled. It is part of the training of a psychiatrist that you smile when confronted with a wall. Initially you agree with your patient. Or rather, you don't blatantly contradict their statements, however false you believe them to be. Confrontation is bad for a mind already heavy with misapprehension. Later on, you may introduce doubt. You plant this tiny seed of doubt deep into their mind. Then you wait for it to germinate. Now was the time to introduce that little seed. 'When do you think he will come?'

'As soon as he can.' Her tone was complacent.

'The midwife will be visiting you tomorrow morning, Heather.'

The hands stole down to her pregnant belly again. 'That's good,' she said. 'I'll look forward to it.'

Claire was keeping her fingers crossed that Heather would not discover her midwife's relationship with her beloved Charles.

Thinking about Charles, maybe she should keep him informed, let him know that Heather was now safely ensconced at Greatbach and from now on would be watched twenty-four/seven. She really should make that call, put his mind at rest. But she didn't. And she recognized that, in some small way, she was punishing him for his assault. Who said revenge is a dish best eaten cold? It's true.

Her feeling of optimism leaked and encompassed other areas. Perhaps Heather's delusions would melt away. Perhaps the child would be safe. Perhaps Rhoda would send one of her minions. After all, the community midwife team was large. On the balance of probability, the odds were about fifteen to one that Rhoda would not attend her patient. Whatever she had said, maybe she would be just too busy – particularly as she had been away on her course. Surely there would be plenty of catching up to do. Claire felt calmed as she observed her patient. Heather looked comfortable, content, relaxed, her pregnancy bulging. Through her loose top, Claire noted a twinge. Braxton Hicks. False labour, a trial run but a sign that birth was approaching. 'Heather,' she urged, 'if you need to be seen at any time, day or night, it will be arranged. If you go into labour early we'll transfer you to the maternity unit.'

The cunning look was back. The sly eyes slid over her. 'So will Charles be *there*?'

Something in Claire snapped. 'He *works* there,' she said.

That produced a smile. 'So he *could* be the one to deliver our child.' The pressure of her fingers was leaving indentations on her pregnancy, visible even through her dress. She spoke down to it. 'You will meet Daddy soon,' she said.

Enough was enough. 'No,' Claire said, 'that won't happen.'

'No?' Heather's eyes slid up to challenge Claire. 'And if I go into labour early – as an emergency? And everything is unexpected?'

Was that what was in her mind? Digging her fingers in, urging the child to make its appearance and 'meet Daddy'?

'You didn't go into labour early on your two previous pregnancies but we *are* getting near the date now so it's not impossible. The baby moves a lot?'

'Oh, yes.' The response was smug. 'All the time. He's going to be a rugby player – like his dad.'

How did she know that? Were the contractions Braxton Hicks tightening or pseudo labour? 'Have you had a "show" of mucous or blood?'

Heather shook her head. 'No. Not yet.' Ruth was pressing herself into the corner, making herself practically invisible as her sister rose from the bed and crossed to the window to scan the car park.

Claire had a nasty feeling she was looking out for the Jaguar. She didn't ask.

Heather turned back to her. 'Do you know what time the midwife will be here?'

'No. Just sometime tomorrow morning, so you'd better keep to your room then.'

And out of Riley Finch's way.

Heather nodded obediently.

Claire felt she needed to emphasize this. 'It's probably better if you stay in your room anyway, out of the other patients' way. And later this evening the psychologist, a lovely guy called Edward Reakin, will have another chat with you.'

'The psychologist, eh?' She was looking at her sister now, a twinkle in her eye.

What, Claire wondered, was she exposing Edward to?

'Very impressive.' The mocking tone in her patient's voice was unmistakable.

Claire felt bound to defend him. 'Sometimes,' she said, 'psychologists can be very helpful.'

'Really?' This time her tone was sharp.

'Have you written down any of the dates when you and Charles met up, spoke, had contact yet?'

'I haven't had time,' Heather snapped.

Surprise, surprise.

Claire spent a short while longer explaining parts of the treatment to Heather and Ruth, using the words discussion, psychotherapy, exploration. Then she left and had a word with the nursing staff on her way out, asking them to keep careful eyes on both Riley and Heather. 'I don't want their paths crossing.'

Astrid, the nurse in charge, gave her a challenging look. 'It's going to be difficult to keep them apart,' she said, 'unless we confine one or both of them to their rooms.'

'True, but I don't want them conferring.' Claire was frowning as she spoke. Something was in the air. That toxic chemical mix. Heather, Riley, the baby.

At least, she thought, as she passed Arthur Connolly's room, peering in to see him sitting with his crossword, puzzling over the answers, there was one patient she didn't have to worry about. He looked completely oblivious both to her and to his surroundings – even his plight. He looked what he was: a man who had been dominated all his life. Only once had he rebelled. And this was the result. The premature ageing of Arthur Connolly. This is what happens when the weak become suddenly and unexpectedly strong. They are not used to the power. As she observed him through the porthole, he made a gesture of irritation – a sharp jerk of his fingers, then his hands, the stiffening extending up to his shoulders as he reached for the rubber and obliterated his presumably incorrect answer. Claire moved away. Arthur, she felt certain, would play no active part in this drama. His day of adventure was over. If he and Lindsay were apart he would revert to his natural state, as meek and gentle as a lamb.

That was what she thought. How wrong can you be? *All* had their parts to play. And were already jostling into position.

TWENTY-FIVE

Monday, 20 July, 4.58 p.m.

Two minutes to go before she met up with Simon Bracknell. She left the ward, hurried down the stairs, deep in thought, confident of some facts, ignorant of others, fearful of still others and sensing yet others, the shadowy ones that hovered in the background like ghosts. With each step, she wondered what she was leaving behind on that top floor and contemplated her next move, aware of the people who swirled around her, drawn into the vortex. All featuring in their very own Chagall: 'Woman with Unborn Baby'. Watched by . . .

By the time she reached the bottom, she was feeling better. She had made the situation safe for now. Neutralized it. Taken the initiative. Admitted her patient, warned the staff and, hopefully, kept Riley away from Heather Krimble. It was five o'clock and she had an appointment.

She was looking forward to meeting Simon Bracknell. It would be a change. Perhaps coming from the other side of the world, his take on matters would be different. Refreshing. Inspirational. Enlightening? And it would be nice to be in conversation with a bloke again.

Since she and Grant had split she had had a few dates, spent
half-hearted evenings comparing all other men with him unfavour-
ably, knowing before she'd finished the first drink that this
encounter was a dead end, going nowhere. No replacement. It
wasn't only a matter of physical attraction, it had been buried deep
in their characters. Grant had been the perfect foil to her rather
intense, intellectual, analytical even, approach to life, work, everything really. Always doubting herself, feeling at her core that her
mother had spoken the truth.

Mademoiselle Roget, ugly little French frog.

She sat, waiting at her desk, thinking as she had done many
times before, chin cupped in her hands, and delved deep inside
herself to find her identity, analysing just why she and Grant had
worked so well. But behind the sweetness there was a scorpion
sting in the tail. Had Grant really meant what he had said in that
damp April garden he would not have abandoned her without a
word. He would not have concealed his sister and her illness from
her but would have confided in her. That day, he would have
explained that his sister was sick and needed him but that he would
be back. Soon. He would have asked. No, begged her to wait for
him. Instead he had simply vanished without a word, which
made *him* a coward and *her* a fool for waiting so long. The
fact was he had turned tail and run. And his explanation, six months
too late, that every day he had been gone made it harder for
him to come back seemed weak and insincere.

And yet, she still smiled at his memory. Glanced at her watch.
Ten past five. Simon Bracknell was late. She sat back in her chair,
returning to her previous thought. Her obsession with time-keeping
was just one symptom of her character that had been foiled by
Grant. She was always early, always stressed about time, which had
led to many gentle teases. Grant's lazy, laid-back attitude had calmed
her down, sedated her, helped her to accept the less-than-perfect.

Simon finally rolled in at five thirty, knocking on her door and
peering round in response to her curt, 'Come in.'

He began with an apology. 'I'm so sorry, Claire. I got lost round
the hospital.' He grinned. 'A nurse sent me round to the morgue.'
His grin broadened. 'Must have thought I was the pathologist.'

She stood up and held out her hand. How could she be annoyed?
She studied him and liked what she saw. He was nothing like the
perma-tanned, tousled-haired beach bum she'd pictured. For a start,

he was thin. Not athletic looking. Not a surf buddy but bony and pale skinned, with clusters of freckles on his forearms. She studied him. So where was the *Baywatch*, swaggering confidence? Nowhere to be seen. Plus he wore large, black-rimmed glasses that looked heavy on a rather delicate, fine-featured face. Hazel eyes hid behind the lenses. At least his accent was antipodean enough to convince her he was the genuine koala bear, marsupial article.

His grin broadened, displaying teeth which also fitted the bill. Big, white, straight.

'Hi,' he said, pumping her hand. 'I really am sorry about this. I didn't mean to keep you waiting.' He hesitated, must have felt he needed to say more. 'It's lovely to meet you at last, Claire. I've heard a lot about you.'

The comment provoked the usual silent questions: *What exactly? From whom?*

'All good,' he tacked on belatedly.

She smiled back, responding to his boisterous, awkward manner. 'Tea? Coffee?'

'Coffee, please. That'd be great. Thank you so much.' He waited while Claire picked up the phone and asked Rita to do the honours. 'I've brought Heather's notes with me. Thought we could go through them together.' He pulled the set of notes out of a man-bag before continuing eagerly, 'I've put a marker in the bits I thought you'd be most interested in. Generally, the letters back to the GP, a . . .' his fingers were already leafing through the pages towards the first of the pink markers poking out from the thick file, '. . . Doctor Sylas and before that Doctor Barker. They give out the story clearest.' He grinned again, his eyes meeting hers with a glimmer of amusement. 'And shortest. Weird but not unknown for a woman to fall in love with her doctor.'

'According to her version, Tissot wasn't initially her doctor,' she said. 'She asked to be referred to him *after* she was pregnant.'

'Right. So . . . what's the story? Fill me in.'

'Well, this is the third time she's made allegations about the parentage of her babies. All denied by the gentlemen concerned.'

'Right.'

'First it was her boss at work, secondly the window cleaner. Charles Tissot is in third place. They encountered each other at a party last November.'

He worked it out quickly. 'The dates fit.' He paused, adding awkwardly, 'Listen, Claire, I'll have to return the notes in the morning or there'll be hell to play. But I thought you'd prefer to see the originals than have me pick out just one or two letters I thought were relevant.'

'Yeah.'

The coffee arrived, which took their attention for only a minute or two, then she started scanning through marked passages. There was a lot to read. Simon kept up a patchy running commentary, peering over her shoulder as Claire tried to absorb the contents.

'I had a quick look. Laura saw her a few times during the pregnancy and after Eliza's death.'

They both took a sip of the coffee. Rita had got it off to a fine art with the new Krups coffee maker, a present from a grateful patient who knew about Claire's caffeine habit.

'It was only during the second pregnancy that she became more heavily involved. It's a shame she's off and you've just got me.'

Claire looked up. The comment invited a denial. *No, no, you'll do fine. Yes, it's a shame that Laura's sick but . . .* and so on.

She started but in a half-hearted way. 'No. It's . . .' before telling the truth, swivelling round in her chair and looking up to meet his perceptive eyes. 'Yeah. Laura would have been good but hey, you're better than no one.' It was a frankness which caused them both to laugh and had the result of relaxing them equally. There. The ice was broken.

She read on, absorbing the information, beginning with the initial referral letter.

Claire quickly realized that the GP had made up his own mind, using the words, *Deluded . . . Strange story . . . Appeared to believe . . . Recently married . . . Exacerbated by the baby's tragic death.*

It was a murky tale but Dr Barker had still managed Heather's case himself, right up to the point where he had been asked by a solicitor acting for an anxious Mr Timothy Cartwright to provide evidence of his patient's mental health.

A copy of the solicitor's letter was enclosed, dated a month after Eliza's death. And it gave a different angle from the one she had previously seen. This time it was Cartwright's view.

Dear Doctor,

Mrs Krimble is making a claim for unfair dismissal from Mr Cartwright's printing firm.

My client, Mr Timothy Cartwright, has been very much upset at an allegation of a sexual and romantic liaison which Mrs Krimble has made against him and which has almost resulted in bankruptcy for a previously successful business, a small, family-run firm which his grandfather began in the mid-fifties.

Mrs Krimble alleges that she and Mr Cartwright had been indulging in an affair and that her daughter, Eliza, is the result of this union. The little girl has, unfortunately, died quite recently, the result of a cot death. She has been cremated so it is not possible to ascertain the baby's paternity through a DNA test.

Mr Cartwright asserts that he has not and never has had any carnal contact or romantic attachment to Mrs Krimble. He was not attracted to her, and further claims that he has never had a girlfriend but is instead very happy living at home with his mother. Mrs Krimble has worked for him for a number of years as his secretary and she was perfectly competent at her job. Loyal was the word he used.

His statement had the ring of truth.

Around a year ago, he said, Heather started making suggestive remarks, asking him very personal questions about his private life. He tried to get her to stop but she continued, even making these claims to her work colleagues. It was not only untrue, it was embarrassing. He tried to get her to stop but she did not, simply mocking him for his embarrassment.

What was my client to do? Mr Cartwright further states that her actions then included suggestive remarks made in front of some of the workforce and included physical contact which became even more overt when she was pregnant and she alleged that the baby was his. He thought they were the result of a mind disordered by pregnancy. I asked him whether, prior to these incidents, she had any cause to resent him, to feel angry or slighted by him, whether he had discriminated against her, but he said absolutely not. In view of the situation, he felt he had no option but to ask her to leave.

I had no reason to disbelieve him. I may add that the subsequent distasteful gossip surrounding Mrs Krimble's allegations have had consequences. It has taken hard work and some skilful negotiation to save the printing company from bankruptcy. Also, two longstanding female employees have resigned, stating that they no longer feel comfortable working for Cartwright Printing Company. And while he extends his sympathy to Mr and Mrs Krimble for the tragic death of their daughter, he nevertheless intends to countersue Mrs Krimble for the defamation of his character, unless she:

1. Withdraws her complaint of unfair dismissal

2. Issues a confession that her claims of romantic entanglement were fabricated, or

3. Produces a statement from a psychiatrist testifying she has been diagnosed with a recognized mental condition.

'Phew,' Simon said. 'Scary stuff.'

'Yes. A tricky one for Laura to pick up.'

Any diagnosis would be well beyond the skills of an ordinary general practitioner. Dr Barker had had no option but to refer her. And so Laura and Heather had been set on a collision course. It had been a brave decision by the GP to try and manage her condition himself. Claire remembered Roy Barker as an unimaginative, traditional doctor. Very good with physical illness, its signs and symptoms. Less so with mental disturbances. If he couldn't see the disease, touch it, feel it, read it on a CT scan or do a blood test to prove or disprove it, he didn't believe in it.

An old-fashioned view, one Claire might not sympathize with but could understand. Laura had begun her own assessment with notes that were crisp, clear, concise and easy to read. Cleverly, she had focused initially on Eliza's death rather than the actual reason for the referral.

Heather appeared less emotional than I would have expected, almost detached from her six-month-old baby's death. I questioned her how Eliza's father was taking it, to which she didn't respond. But when I used her husband's name she first of all became angry and then started laughing. 'He isn't the father. My boss at work, Mr Cartwright. That's who the father is. Was,' she quickly corrected.

Claire glanced at Simon. 'She set the trap.'

He nodded. 'Probably a good way round,' he said, 'rather than tackling it head on.'

Claire bent back over the notes and continued reading Laura's account of that first interview as she had written back to the GP.

I asked her how Mr Cartwright was taking the baby's death. She became disturbed, jumped up and banged her fist on the desk. 'He's denying he's the father.'

'Why would he do that, Heather?'

She had her explanation ready. 'He's embarrassed at his love for me.' She had a strangely inappropriate smile as she continued. 'He's crushed under the weight of it. Afraid of his mother's reaction if she finds out we're lovers.'

'And are you still lovers?'

'No. Not any more, although he is still very much in love with me. I've had other things on my mind.'

'You don't work for him any more.'

She shook her head. 'No. He thought it better if I left.'

'So how do you know he is still in love with you?'

'He sends me messages.' She was smiling all the time. A smile I would describe as smug.

'How does he send you messages? Over the Internet? Mobile phone? Do you meet?'

She shook her head. 'We communicate.'

I already knew that no contact between them was documented and that Cartwright himself absolutely denied that he had ever had any communication with her other than work details when she had been his secretary. Therefore, this was either a deliberate and conscious fabrication or an illusion or a delusion. When I asked her why she thought he had asked her to leave, she had her answer ready.

'Well, it's impossible, isn't it? Being infatuated with someone and working alongside them. Employing them.'

As is often the case, her answer was logical. I had no doubt that she believed her allegations absolutely.

But her description of their liaison was peppered with inconsistencies. Notes, phone calls, flowers sent, secret, coded messages. And the other question that bothered me was why had she married Geoff Krimble? It was all very bizarre.

'Nice lady,' was Simon's comment, 'but dangerous, eh?' He'd pulled a chair up now and was reading by her side.

Claire glanced across at him, conscious of his nearness. He smelt of soap and, inexplicably, of the sea, a sort of briny, salty smell like the breeze that strokes the sea, not stiff enough to whip up waves but fanning the air landwards. The sea? Eighty miles away? His sea was over 10,000 miles. A little far for a scent to travel. Maybe it was on his clothes.

But, quite apart from the fresh, briny air Simon emanated, this was a treat, being able to share a confidence with a colleague, someone of equal status and similar outlook but with such a different background. The saying is sickness and health are the same the world over. It is how we view them and then treat them which is different. And that was what was interesting her at the moment: how to treat this deluded woman who was causing such mayhem. At that moment, apart from her professional role, she still felt some sympathy towards her patient, seeing her as victim of a mischievous Puck, that *shrewd and knavish sprite*, the love affair as ridiculous as Titania's obsession with Bottom. But at the back of her mind she had to wonder whether this entire drama could be a calculated way of paying people back for perceived slights. Her boss? Her husband? Charles. She smothered a smile. The window cleaner for leaving smears on the panes? She bent back over the notes, trying to find the clues and wondering whether Laura had tracked along the same path.

The question for me is how pathological were Heather's convictions? There is no doubt in my mind that Heather truly believes that her ex-boss, Mr Cartwright, is truly, madly, deeply in love with her; in other words, she is suffering from erotomania. I'm quite happy to write to the solicitor and explain that Heather is suffering from a mental illness.

Her documentation was careful but unmistakable. At the bottom of the letter was the Greek triangle Δ. Then D for Diagnosis where she had written her conclusion: *An apparent case of erotomania, otherwise known as de Clerambault's syndrome.* With an added note: *Further complicated by the death of the infant, Eliza.*

A brief note written a month later stated that the GP had informed her that Heather was taking no further action in her claim for unfair dismissal and that Cartwright had subsequently dropped his counterclaim.

A few weeks after that, Laura had written again to Dr Barker, advising that if Heather became pregnant again and displayed similar symptoms it would be a good idea to refer her early in the pregnancy. And, just to be certain, to check any subsequent child's DNA against that of her husband.

During one of the consultations, Laura had also interviewed Geoff Krimble, who claimed that his wife had been '*strange*' since they'd married halfway through the pregnancy.

'*Load of old nonsense*,' he'd insisted. He didn't believe '*for a minute'* that his wife and Mr Cartwright had had *'any sort of affair. It's all in her mind, Doctor'*.

'And as for Eliza?'

'I never knew who her dad was. She weren't mine but Heather always said she were Cartwright's. And that weren't true either. She has her fancies, Doctor.'

And Laura had agreed with him, making the dry comment that Geoff Krimble was a bluntly spoken Potteries native who *'told it as it were'*.

Claire could picture her smile as she quoted the words verbatim, adding *sic.* to the side.

She had followed Heather up on four separate occasions and come to the conclusion that this was an odd presentation of erotomania and puerperal psychosis, complicated by the death of the child.

After one of the consultations, she had written: *There were peculiar gaps in her stories which she was unable to fill. How had Timothy Cartwright reacted to Eliza?*

She said he loved her but couldn't give me time, place or circumstances for when he had seen her.

Just like now, Claire thought. Short on detail. It being impossible to shake Heather's conviction and so treat it, Laura had referred her for some psychotherapy and cognitive behavioural therapy (which she had failed to turn up for), given her a mild anti-psychotic and finally discharged her.

'So she didn't really get anywhere with her,' Claire commented.

'No. Maybe . . .'

'Yeah?'

'Well, just a thought. A suggestion. Sometimes . . . you know . . . ladies who aren't particularly attractive sort of make things up?'

She had to smile. He'd been so polite, so tentative and so careful in making this simple suggestion. 'Yes, but it doesn't go *this* far.' Claire tapped the notes. 'The question is,' she said, '*why* she has these delusions of men being in love with her and having affairs when she has a husband who appears so loyal?'

'Maybe she didn't think he was much of a catch?' His eyes had a mischievous gleam behind the thick glasses.

She laughed. 'Maybe. But then Cartwright doesn't exactly come over as Adonis.'

'Oh, really?'

'Yeah, really. Tell me. Have you ever encountered a case like this before?'

'No. Most Aussie guys would admit to anything if a lady said they'd been having an affair.'

She scrutinized him. 'You're joking, right?'

'Yeah. And to answer your question – no, I haven't ever treated a case of de Clerambault's. At least, not to *this* degree. But then neither have I had patients who've lost *two* babies to cot death.'

'Well, it happens.' She leafed through the notes, finding the next referral.

All was quiet for almost two years. And then, during her second pregnancy, slightly earlier than before, in the twenty-fourth week, Heather's stories had started again, resulting in the second referral.

This time it was Dr Sylas who referred her at 24/40, saying that Heather was claiming that the child she was bearing was not her husband's. This time, the GP wrote, Heather was convinced the baby was the window cleaner's. Claire read through Laura's initial assessment, almost forgetting Simon sitting beside her, also scanning the psychiatrist's notes.

And again, the GP's history detailed that both Geoff and the window cleaner were categorically denying that this was true.

But this time, bearing in mind Heather's previous claims and the tragedy of Eliza Krimble's death, the professionals were wary and it was decided to keep a much closer eye on Heather both during the pregnancy and during the puerperium. Also to involve the entire team: district midwives, health visitors, social services.

This time, Laura had had the opportunity to speak to Heather *during* the pregnancy and question her about the child's parentage. Most of it she already knew so she picked out the salient facts.

She told me that on a Friday morning (apparently he always comes early on a Friday morning, waiting until just after her husband has left for work) he climbs in through the bedroom window and on more than one occasion has had sex with her. She did not use the term rape, or the police might have been involved. She tells me that he has been obsessed with her ever since he first visited her home and spotted her in her underwear. Since then he has been making 'suggestions'.

On the surface, this would seem a similar case as before.

I have spoken briefly to the window cleaner over the phone. Sam Maddox, thirty-three years old, is engaged to be married. He assures me not only that he has absolutely no designs whatsoever on Mrs Krimble and that the incident of him glimpsing her in her underwear never happened, but also that he has never been inside her house as he only cleans the outside of her windows and she does the insides herself. He also said that he couldn't climb in through the bedroom window as only the top bit opens. I invited him in to speak with me at my office with his partner if he so wished but he declined.

Underneath, again, was her conclusion: *Considering Heather's previous claim, I am convinced this is another case of romantic delusion. But I still feel that for the sake of clarity and a possible future court case, the child's DNA should be checked against Heather's husband. And only if it is not a match to Mr Krimble then Heather's claim should be checked against the DNA of Mr Maddox, the window cleaner.*

Signed with a confident flourish, *Laura*. And underneath: Laura Hodgkins, MBChB, FRCPsych. Claire sat back. 'She's very good at describing the people and the interviews. I almost feel I was there.' She thought for a moment. 'I don't think I would gain anything by interviewing them face-to-face.'

'No.' Simon Bracknell was nodding. 'The notes made easy reading and she's covered the case well.'

She turned to him. 'Thank you for bringing them, Simon. They've been invaluable. Really helpful.'

Simon cleared his throat. 'Interesting, eh?'

She nodded. 'Interesting and incredible,' she said.

There was a last letter clipped in with the brief note that the baby's DNA had proved a match to Geoffrey Krimble. And so, like Timothy Cartwright, Sam Maddox had faded into the background.

Freddie's death had resulted in a further batch of letters, post-mortem report, counselling, the involvement of social services. Laura's observations were similar to her previous involvement: that Heather appeared detached from the tragedy, Geoff had been stoic and that Heather, ignoring the evidence of the DNA result, continued to claim that Freddie was the son of Maddox. Eventually Laura had again discharged her. Case closed.

Until . . . They exchanged looks. This time it was not a window cleaner or a confirmed bachelor. This time the stakes were higher with a divorced obstetrician whose career could be blown away by just a puff of scandal. As she closed the notes, Claire felt a twang of worry, a strange sense of impending doom, an approaching storm.

Perhaps this child, too, would die.

TWENTY-SIX

Claire turned away from the notes, instead meeting Simon Bracknell's eyes. 'Murky waters, eh?'

Simon's face was animated and eager as though unravelling a particularly intriguing detective novel. 'The plot thickens,' he said, leafing through pages. 'Let's go back to some of the earlier consultations.'

'Laura saw Heather during her second pregnancy,' Simon said. 'She started with her claims against the window cleaner. Here.' He'd found the place, marked with a shocking pink Post-it note, screaming for attention. 'Three months later, Laura re-interviewed her.'

This time Heather attended with her sister, Ruth. The sisters are necessarily close, their brother, Robin Acton, having vanished at some point.

Claire was thoughtful. The name Robin Acton was beginning to haunt her. The brother who had disappeared. She looked at Simon Bracknell. 'I wonder how significant he is.'

'The brother? We don't know much about him.'

'No, but there's something else I'm missing: Heather's family history. I could do with a bit more information on that.'

'Mmm.'

They continued reading until Claire found what she was looking for. 'Ah,' she said. 'Here it is.'

The sisters were bonded by a shared damaged childhood, a violent, short-tempered father and a mother who seemed to make no active intervention in her children's upbringing, or to protect them from their father's tendencies. Both parents were very religious and the girls were punished if they did not conform to a strict religious code.

It verified what she already knew. But what part was Heather's family playing in the drama? Claire scanned the pages, trying to read between the lines, still searching for some clue. Had there been any sexual abuse? That could explain these weird imaginings, fantasies. Substitution for the crime of incest. Had Laura explored this? She scanned the text again.

Simon had anticipated her focus. 'I didn't find any mention of sexual abuse. It seems that it was more with corporal punishment. You know, spare the rod?' He blew out his cheeks. 'At least a bit of heavy discipline as well as a short temper.'

'Mmm.' Claire bent back over the filed letters. This one was dated May 2012, two months before Freddie was born.

Heather seemed on edge, suspicious and defensive. I asked her again who Eliza's father was and she stuck to her original story. Her boss at work, Mr Cartwright, she said, was in love with her, but he had initially held back his infatuation not only through a sense of duty and propriety but also out of loyalty and love for his mother. He had finally succumbed to her charms and had sex with her in his office, which had been the beginning of a steamy and surreptitious affair. She was rubbing her legs as she spoke and was visibly aroused.

'No one from the office even guessed,' she said smugly. 'We were discreet and clever.'

She had subsequently found out she was pregnant, knew that Tim Cartwright was the father of her child and told him.

'How did he react?' I asked.

Her response was strangely disturbing. She leaned forward in her chair and crossed her legs. 'He tried to wriggle out of it,' she said, smiling indulgently and speaking as though her ex-boss was a naughty child. When I reminded her that Mr Cartwright had flatly denied her allegations she initially became very angry, thumping my desk and shouting. But then she settled down; she and Ruth exchanged secretive looks and both smiled. Then Ruth said rather tartly, 'Well, he would say that, wouldn't he?'

'It's a useful stock phrase,' Claire said. 'That's exactly what she said to me.'

And now she is pregnant and making claims again. And, in spite of having no hard evidence, nothing but her sister's story, Ruth is agreeing with her.

Just the same. The words jumped out at her. Claire could just picture Laura's face sparkling at the challenge presented. She would not only have risen to it, she would have relished this odd picture. A rare case. But, for the three men involved, it was potentially seriously damaging.

We either had a case of shared delusion or was it possible that Heather was telling the truth? I had to continue to consider that option. One must always give a patient's account – however bizarre and apparently unbelievable – the benefit of the doubt. At that time, I had already decided that Heather was suffering from puerperal delusions, possible de Clerambault's syndrome or erotomania and her sister was suffering from shared delusions possibly encouraged by a sense of loyalty, sibling bonding . . . But this is unlikely. Has Heather threatened her? Why is the bond so absolute? Why is Ruth, who is an intelligent woman, holding down a responsible job, so trusting of her sister's version? Perhaps there is a clue there to Heather's erroneous claims. All possibilities have to be considered.

Claire leafed back to Laura's assessment after Freddie's death.

I advised the GP of my findings. Freddie was born July 2012, deceased September 2012.

Heather claimed that the window cleaner was engaged at the time, just as Mr Cartwright couldn't confess the affair to his mother, so both affairs had to be 'big secrets' between them. Just like Charles. Each had something to lose by acknowledging the affair, Claire thought.

A troubling pattern was emerging but this time I had a head start. I had the history. And when the child was born I would have the child's DNA. But something else was troubling me.

Eliza Krimble had died at six months old of a cot death. A cot death is an unpreventable human tragedy which unfortunately does happen. But when you factor in Heather's apparently unstable and unreliable state, you must ask the question: is it possible the child's death was no accident of nature? I had a bad feeling and requested a copy of Eliza's post-mortem report, which was reassuring. I could tell by the detail that, knowing Heather's history, the pathologist had searched for evidence of infanticide and found none. But the truth is I was still fearing for this unborn child's life. I rang Dr Sylas and shared my misgivings.

Claire looked up. 'Me too,' she admitted. 'Tell me, Simon, have you spoken to Laura at all?'

He shrugged. 'Only briefly. I met her just before she went off sick. But we didn't discuss individual cases. Only duty rostrum and stuff like that.'

'Nothing about this case?'

He shook his head.

'Goodness. I have so many questions.'

'Like?'

'What was she like with the babies? Devoted? Neglectful? Did she reject them? Or accept them? Did she appear to love them? And . . .'

He supplied the next question. 'Was there sexual abuse from her father which would have distorted her view of lovemaking, children, romance?'

'It would certainly explain a lot but apparently not.' She retrieved the word that she had felt she had so far missed: brother. 'Then there's Robin. What part has he played in this? Why did he go? Where did he go? Exactly when did he go? I bet *he* could unlock some of our questions, particularly why the sisters seem to be so joined at the hip. Or was that a *consequence* of his vanishing? I wish I could speak to him.'

'Me too.'

They both bent back over the page to read on.

My next move was again to invite the window cleaner, Sam Maddox, to come in for an informal interview. I needed to meet him face-to-face rather than interview him over the phone.

He attended with his fiancée, Shirley, a hairdresser, a very glamorous and attractive woman, two months pregnant herself. The couple were obviously very fond of each other and walked in hand in hand. Sam insisted he never even went inside the Krimbles' house, that he found Heather quite strange. 'A bit disturbing' was the phrase he used. He claimed he had never even met the sister, Ruth. Geoff always paid him in cash as he returned in the evening to collect the money. He said that Heather was making the whole thing up. 'Just to get attention,' he said. I asked him why she would need to gain attention.

'Because Geoff's a bit of a waster,' was his answer. And Shirley nodded.

On the surface, Heather's story did appear a complete fantasy with no basis in fact. Shirley, Sam Maddox's fiancée, seemed quite unperturbed, actually laughing at the story of his supposed infidelity. I had the impression that to her the entire fiction was derisible. In her mind, it had never happened.

Subsequently, I monitored Heather throughout the final months of the pregnancy. Her story never wavered. But all the verifiable facts were missing. Times, dates, places. Nothing to back it up except her sister. When Freddie was born the DNA paternity test proved that Freddie's father was indeed Geoff Krimble.

But Laura hadn't quite finished. Her next observations were a warning to Claire.

Immediately post-partum and throughout the puerperium Heather remained psychotic, becoming distressed when Sam Maddox failed (as she saw it) to live up to her idea of fatherhood. She complained he never visited her or (again as she saw it) showed any interest in his child. When faced with the result of the DNA result she spiralled into psychosis, depression, self-harm and harm to the baby.

Claire was thoughtful. So this was what was ahead.

She tried to scratch his eyes out, to thump him. We removed Freddie from her sole care and all her contacts were supervised. After six weeks Heather's mental condition stabilized and she was discharged with social services, community midwives and health visitors all involved. But Freddie died of a cot death at eight weeks. Naturally the index of suspicions was very high considering Eliza's death and his mother's mental state, but again the pathologist found absolutely no trace of assault. There was nothing, he insisted, to make him doubt the initial findings. Nothing to suggest anything other than a tragic second cot death in one family. He even ventured an opinion.

Perhaps the death of little Eliza contributed or even caused the psychosis during the second pregnancy. I would have bought that had it not been for Heather's initial allegations against her boss which had emerged late in her first pregnancy, at around 30/40.

But I decided not to lecture the pathologist on the complexities of de Clerambault's syndrome complicated by pregnancy. Freddie was subsequently also cremated, like his sister.

Claire was only too aware of the warnings hidden behind the words. Advice tucked between the lines. She was silent as she planned her approach, Simon Bracknell watching without interrupting.

When Charles Tissot had roped her in to clear his name, he could not have imagined what a hornet's nest he was stirring up. But, Claire warned herself, make no assumptions, take nothing for granted. Supervision of mother and baby was obviously vital. But, first of all, she wanted to separate fact from fiction. The trouble is that hidden in the sulci of psychosis could lie vital facts. Maybe there was some basis of truth behind Heather's claims that these men had paid attention to her. She knew Charles. She didn't know the other two men involved but her picture of them was clear enough. And most of all, whatever the pathologist said about the two babies both having been the victims of cot death, she could not afford to leave Heather alone with her baby. But for how long? When would the child be safe? Ever?

For a short time, she worried at the problems that lay ahead while Simon maintained a respectful silence. The burden of Heather, her allegations and the unborn infant felt heavy across her shoulders, like the twin buckets on a milkmaid's yoke. Only later would she realize she had focused too specifically. She should have reminded herself that Heather and her baby were not her only patients. She should not have forgotten the wider picture.

Simon, at her side, remained patient, quiet and still, frown lines between his brows. At last, she started to formulate a plan. It involved him. She turned her head slowly. Studied the pale, intense face. She would rope him in as a colleague. Use him as a sounding board.

'How much do you know about Heather's current allegations?'

'Not much. I mean, she's your responsibility now, Claire. Doctor Sylas obviously believes that this time she shouldn't be managed in the community but in supervised care. In that, she agrees with you.'

'Well, this time the object of her allegations is likely to face more serious consequences.' She explained just who Tissot was while Simon sucked in his cheeks.

'Whew,' he said. 'Dangerous place to be. Dangerous for him. I wouldn't like to be in his shoes, Claire.'

'No.' She leaned forward and decided to come clean. She liked the guy's frank manner. 'There is a slight issue,' she said awkwardly.

'Oh?' Obviously a man of few words.

'Charles Tissot and I have a bit of history. Heather's story . . .' She began again. This was proving a bit more difficult than she'd anticipated. 'Heather's story has a ring of truth about it.'

Simon managed to look both intrigued and confused in equal measures. 'Go on.'

'Unlike the other two objects of her attentions, Tissot is neither a sexless man uninterested in any relationship like Timothy Cartwright, nor is he a devoted partner like Maddox. Tissot really *is* a bit of a Lothario. Quite capable of . . .' She felt suddenly embarrassed, particularly as Dr Bracknell was looking at her, amused, his mouth visibly twitching at the corners, eyes warm as toast. She knew he was picturing a scene. And however much she tried to sanitize it, that scene would still appear sordid and tacky. A drunken tryst in the back of a car? For goodness' sake.

But if she was going to get him on her side, maybe take over some of Heather's care when she was finally discharged, she was going to have to come clean. She couldn't expect him to work blind. Full disclosure was what the legal beagles called it.

'He sort of . . .' She was squirming. 'The story she gave of him having sex with her in the back of his car. It's the way he works. He is a predatory . . .'

And then Simon Bracknell got it. He took in her reddened face and awkward words, chuckled and touched her hand with the tips of his fingers. 'Hey,' he said. 'Claire, it's OK. Don't worry. I think I can fill in the gaps without your having to colour the picture in.'

But she continued doggedly. 'If I confided this to anyone . . . told anyone else about this . . . I think Charles would be suspended. Although it was a long time ago.' She stopped. 'We've all changed since then. As it is, the MDU are prepared for him to continue working but under supervision. He's not to be alone with a female patient; neither is he to see Heather professionally.'

'And Heather,' he asked. 'How is she taking all this?'

'She's convinced he'll be visiting her at Greatbach.'

Simon lifted his eyebrows at that.

'Whatever his past,' she added, 'I wouldn't like to be in his position. He's on a tightrope.'

'So are there any other clues from Laura?'

'Let's have a look.'

They bent back over Laura's account. *I asked Ruth whether she had ever seen them together and she said no. I waited for her to enlarge but she remained silent. When I pointed out that she only had her sister's word that there had been any relationship between Maddox and her sister, she simply nodded but seemed undisturbed. When I challenged her with the fact that her sister could be making the whole thing up she said no, that wasn't possible, that Heather was truthful. When I asked her if she ever doubted her sister's word she got upset, said that their father had beaten them if they told lies so they never would. When I asked whether their mother had ever intervened, she said no. Their mother would stand motionless while he beat them, as though she approved. She mentioned their brother, Robin, five years older than Heather and a disappointment to their father. He smoked cannabis and drank cider. 'He's thoroughly bad,' their father told them. 'Wicked' was the word he used. She said that her father used to beat Robin and they were forced to stand by and watch. They loved Robin. He used to stick up for them, sometimes take the beatings for them. Then he'd finally run away from home.*

One phrase leapt off the page. *When I reverted to Eliza's death, she claimed that the Devil had taken her as punishment for the sin. I had an odd feeling that she and I were talking at cross purposes but when I asked her if she knew who Eliza's father was, she clamped her mouth shut. When I asked her what the sin she referred to was she picked her bag up as though to leave and made no attempt to answer the question.*

Claire was thoughtful. Laura hadn't really reached the heart of the matter. The answer was not, as she had written: *We put her on a course of Haloperidol.*

Even though the problem had appeared solved. *Her condition improved markedly until she was virtually normal. She was advised against further pregnancy but, of course, this is not something we have any chance of enforcing. After the ten-week period we discharged her from our care. By that time her mental state was reverting to normal.*

Simon was looking dubiously at her. 'Shit,' he said. 'She sounds a tricky one. So how are you going to manage her this time round?'

'Keep her in longer, supervise her contact with the baby. And I thought I might delve into her family history, try to see where all this comes from. Is the cause her upbringing, her husband, have the men given her some reason to believe they wanted sex with her? And what about her brother? Where exactly does he fit into this bizarre picture?'

Simon nodded and glanced down at her notes before meeting her eyes. 'There may not be answers, Claire. You know what psychiatry's like. Not always logical or reasonable. Just a ragbag of oddities.'

It was a good description of the fuzzy world of damaged brains.

He grinned. 'Well, if you want any help, any support, I'm your man.'

'That's really good of you, Simon. I guess you have quite a workload yourself?'

He shrugged. 'Nothing I can't manage. Anyway, I'd like to help. She sounds interesting.'

'Yeah.' She laughed that one off. 'She is that, although when you meet her you'll think nothing of the sort. You'll think she's bland. Plain and ordinary. No hint of the turmoil going on beneath.'

'Whatever.' He shrugged that off too.

She stood up. 'I promised you a quick tour of Greatbach.'

He jumped to his feet. 'Great stuff.'

TWENTY-SEVEN

They trotted around the wards and the outpatient department for a little more than an hour, Simon asking questions and making comments. Most things were, unsurprisingly, similar. It was a pleasant way to spend the early evening, almost seven thirty by the time they'd finished the tour and made conversation outside Claire's office. She'd enjoyed his company and was reluctant to see him go.

'Where are you staying?'

He made a disgusted face. 'A nasty little place in Etruria,' he said. 'It's noisy and dirty, nothing like it sounds. Classical Greece, my word. More like the slums of ancient Greece.'

'Oh dear. I hope that isn't colouring your entire view of the Potteries?'

'I'm sure there are nice places here, Claire,' he said, 'I'm just hoping that dump sure isn't representative.'

'No. Definitely not. So will you be doing Laura's locum for long?'

'Well.' He heaved out a big sigh. 'It looks as though Laura will be off for some months. And then they have intimated there could be another long-term post going. I'd like to stay in the UK for a minimum of a year or two, if that's possible. It'll look good on my CV. When I get back to Oz I'll be going for a consultant post but I can't stay in that shithole in Etruria for all that time. I'll have to find somewhere else. Somewhere a bit cleaner, for a start.'

She was thinking of her four empty bedrooms in the newly decorated house, the unused bathrooms. The yawning emptiness of the place which was easily big enough for a family home but instead housed just her. She had plenty of room for a lodger. She'd hardly notice him. But this was a big step. If she was working with Simon Bracknell, the most important thing was that they didn't fall out. And, as everyone knows, sharing a house, however big, carries risks.

He was eyeing her, waiting for her to speak, and she had the feeling that he was reading her mind. However, he stayed respectfully silent and she needed to think about it for a little longer.

'Are you heading back there now?'

'What – to that poky, smelly little room?' His face distorted even more, then brightened. 'I don't suppose you fancy a curry? On me?'

'Why not?'

And so, half an hour later they found themselves at the local curry house studying the menu, and she learned a little more about him.

His father ran a vineyard in the Barossa Valley, his mother was a nurse. 'She's the one that rooted for me to go to medical school,' he said. 'Ambitious lady, my ma.'

'And the psychiatry? What's made you choose that as a speciality?'

'I could ask you the same question.'

He was a great sparring partner. 'You first.'

'That was all me. Actually, I had a friend at school who committed suicide. Shot himself.' His face was far away, still pained, still troubled. 'Looking back, I suppose it was fairly obvious the poor guy was depressed but God, he hid it well. I felt guilty. I felt I'd failed him. I used to wonder what I should have picked up on, what I *could* have picked up on. What was there? What signs there were? I became more than just interested. I became intrigued. And that was that. Psychiatry seemed to be drawing me towards it, like a magnet.'

Another self-effacing grin, chin cupped in hand as he bit into a poppadom which shattered, spreading crisp shards over the table, making them both laugh like naughty schoolkids. 'So what about you?'

It pulled her up short. She'd never really given it much thought. 'I don't know,' she said. 'I had an inspirational teacher in psychology. And then my predecessor here, Heidi.'

'She was the one that was murdered?'

'Yeah. That was a real shock. I suppose if anyone you know is murdered it pulls you up short. Particularly as my chosen speciality is forensic psychiatry. I've met murderers, rapists, extortionists, child killers, analysed their personalities, assessed whether they're a danger to wider society or just some specific person. But to have actually known the victim . . . Heidi, Heidi Faro. That's something else.' She speared a gherkin marooned in the pickles. 'And the wrong guy went to prison for it. The whole thing took some unravelling. But, a little like your story, knowing the victim makes you feel responsible somehow. Makes you want to be able to intervene. It made it worse that as a teacher Heidi was special. Inspirational. A really clever woman with unique thoughts and ideas. I used to watch her during lectures and wonder how it was she could peer so deep into people's souls. She had an instinct for evil.'

'Wow,' he said. 'Deep stuff indeed.'

'Yeah. So did the suicide of your friend result in a special interest?'

'Have a guess. Depression, I suppose. Suicide attempts. Self-harm.' He frowned. 'Self-destruction. Treatments, drug therapy. Prevention. Counselling. CBT.' He hesitated before adding, 'I wouldn't mind doing some research into post-traumatic stress disorder. Stuff like that anyway.'

Her ears pricked up. 'For the military?'

'We-ell, we don't send a lot of our forces into conflict. No. I was thinking more broadly. Any sort of flashbacks, maybe into assaults and accidents.' His grin was appealing. 'Try and heal the mind. You know?'

They spent some time discussing various trends and current papers as they polished off the poppadoms and the curries arrived together with naan bread and rice, and then he asked her about her special interest.

'Personality disorder,' she said, feeling herself warm to her subject. 'That manipulative, dissociative evil. Each case so subtly different. That cleverness, sizing each other up like wrestlers in the ring. It intrigues me. And worries me.' She leaned her elbows on the table, met his eyes and told him a little about Riley Finch, the way she found excuses for her behaviour, disguising a manipulative and selfish character. 'You know, Simon . . .' her thoughts were finding words, '. . . I don't know where she'd stop. She recognizes nothing but her own needs, her own desires.'

'You think she'd murder?'

Claire shook her head. 'I don't think so,' she said slowly. 'Because the consequences to her would be too serious. That's the only reason. When I spoke to her about the suffering of the mother whose baby she stole, her eyes were quite blank. She genuinely didn't understand what I was talking about.'

'Trouble is, Claire, there isn't really any treatment. You can't alter someone's personality, can you?'

'I don't know about that,' she said through a mouthful of curry, index finger waving. 'I think something along the lines of CBT might work.'

'How so?'

'I think if they were shown clips of people suffering as a result of their crimes, it might teach them about the emotions they ought to be feeling.'

'Wow,' he said. 'That's pretty groundbreaking.'

She laughed to lighten the mood. 'And completely unproven. Most psychiatrists are more likely to say some people are evil, like Riley Finch, and others are not.' She gave him a potted version of Arthur Connolly's story. And, like her, he believed that Lindsay was a monster.

Claire's curry was a bit hot and she ordered yoghurt to cool it down, taking a spoonful before she was ready to continue the conversation. Simon looked up, his face worried. 'Hey,' he said, 'I just had a thought. I hope I'm not keeping you from your boyfriend.' He laughed. 'He's not about to beat me up, is he?'

It was half worry, half joke. Claire spluttered at the thought of Grant beating anyone up. His pirate looks did not extend to pugnacity. He was more the sort to cry at the plight of Syrian refugees than pick a fight with anyone. That was not to say he was a pushover. He was not. Grant Steadman could and would stand up for himself and protect her and anyone else he considered too weak for the job. But only if he deemed it absolutely necessary. An unavoidable requirement.

She was aware that Simon Bracknell was waiting for a response. And she had to supply one. She took a deep breath in. 'My boyfriend is an ex. We split up a while ago.'

'Leaving you heartbroken?' It was simple curiosity rather than anything else. Behind the glasses his eyes were kind.

But she didn't even try to answer, and diplomatically he didn't pursue the subject, perhaps understanding that she hadn't responded because she couldn't. She couldn't because she didn't know the answer herself. She felt her face crumple before deflecting his probing with a return shot. 'You?'

'I'm married,' he said shortly. And surprisingly.

Surprise which she couldn't hide. 'What – married? And you've left a wife back in Oz.'

'Umm, yes.' His eyes behind the glasses were now evasive, lids dropped, a film concealing his expression.

'What's your wife's name?'

'Marianne.'

Even the name was unexpected, sounding more like a Disney princess than a wife halfway across the world, dropped, discarded, to be picked up at a later date. He hadn't mentioned her before, even when he'd spoken of hoping to stay in the UK for a year or two. No, *I'm hoping my wife will join me,* or *my wife's hoping to get a job over here.*

But if she was only giving him half the story, Simon Bracknell was obviously equally reluctant to give up his secrets. The conversation appeared to have hit the buffers but, just before she left it, she allowed herself one stab at a question. 'Have you any children?'

He shook his head and pressed his lips together. A sure sign.

They'd finished their meal. Claire was still hanging back on telling him she had rooms to spare. She'd relegated it to the back of her mind but she had already worked it out. He could have the top floor. All of it. Bedroom, bathroom, study. She hardly ever went up there. And as for his rent . . . well, she didn't really care. She didn't need it. But it would help to pay off the mortgage that bit quicker. She actually opened her mouth to speak and then clamped it shut.

But she still heard the voices. *Why not offer it?*

Answer: because it was a situation easier to dive into than to climb out.

Think about it. Don't be impulsive. His wife, this Marianne, might be planning to fly over and join him. Would you like a couple up there, over your head, maybe rowing? Even children running around?

And so she obeyed her sensible voice. Shoved her impulsive and generous nature to the back of the room and slammed the door on it, allowing suspicion and pessimism and caution to take precedent. 'Coffee?'

'Yeah. That'd be nice.'

It was late by the time they left the curry house and parted. Past eleven. The evening had flown by and she couldn't remember when she'd last enjoyed someone's company so much. Conversation, outlook, even humour. Outside the curry house, she shook his hand and said, 'Keep in touch.' It was nice, friendly but not overly so – neutral but still ultimately dismissive. And she thought that behind the thick lenses she read disappointment. Regret?

He did make a small effort. 'Would you mind if I sat in on one of your clinics?'

She felt a rush of pleasure. 'No, of course not. Any time. You'll be welcome. Just arrange it with my secretary.' She scribbled Rita's number down on a scrap of paper. 'And thank you so much for bringing the notes over. They've been really helpful.'

That was it. She dragged herself back to the car park, reflecting. He seemed nice. Polite, quieter than she'd imagined, pleasant. And if he already had a wife, well, that was fine too. At least she'd know where she was with him. Already taken. No entanglement. It was just a bit strange that he seemed reluctant to discuss his wife. Most men with a 'Marianne' tucked away halfway across the world are only too happy to talk about their missing half. Claire imagined her to be glamorous, the sporty, tanned blonde she'd expected Simon Bracknell to be. Or maybe she was wrong on this count too. But still, wasn't it also strange that he'd come to UK, leaving her behind apparently without a backward glance? For a year?

Oh, well, it was none of her business, she thought as she drove home. People pursue their own lives and careers. They don't always sit too comfortably with married life, or at least the conventional image of married life. There was still nothing to stop her putting her idea of him becoming her lodger in front of him, see what his response was. It would only be for a year and no possibility of any romantic entanglement on either side. Her mind flipped over the issue and considered it afresh.

Now, what would be a realistic rent?

TWENTY-EIGHT

Tuesday, 21 July, 9 a.m.
37/40

The day began with a note on her desk to say that the community midwife would visit at 12 p.m., before there was a knock on her door and Edward Reakin's face peeped round.

'Sorry I missed you,' he said. 'I tried to get hold of you yesterday evening but you were with that locum guy from the community. I didn't want to interrupt.'

'That's OK. Come in. Sit down. So tell me. Did you get to see Heather?'

'I did.'

'What did you make of her?'

'A conundrum. I couldn't quite work out how real the entire fantasy is to her. She kept jumping to her feet, peering out of the window. *I wonder when Charles will be here.*' His mimicry was excellent. Heather's bland voice and vague Potteries accent sounded as though she was in the room with them. 'She must have said it fifty times.' His grey eyes were musing and perceptive. 'In fact, every time she couldn't think of an answer to my questions.'

'Go on.'

'I pressed her for more detail. Dates, times, places. What was Charles wearing that night? I think she realized I was sceptical and became defensive.'

'Aggressively defensive?'

He nodded. 'There's more behind that head of hers than you'd think.'

'Her thought processes?'

'Not so much damaged as crossed wires. Or rather twisted wires so she thinks one thing and then everything gets confused and changes her story.'

'Tell me more.' Claire was intrigued. She had always respected Edward with his steady, truthful insight. But this clarity was helping even more than usual.

'She plays it,' he said, 'like a virtuoso. She is so convinced he'll be delighted to meet up with her.'

'So why isn't she ringing him?'

'Truth?' Edward had a kind face. In his forties, mild-mannered and balding, he was the sort of man who was hardly remembered. You met him and forgot him. But underneath a bland exterior was the searing perception often found in quiet men. They sat. They watched, they observed, they drew their own conclusions.

'She doesn't have his number.'

Claire nodded. 'Did you mention the two children who had died, apparently as a result of cot death?'

'I only touched on it. The subject makes her very defensive.'

'Defensive,' she said. 'Not exactly grief-struck.'

'Yeah.' He stuck his long legs out in front of him. 'She didn't seem exactly heartbroken. Says there must have been something wrong with them. Almost discarded the two that died. Like she didn't care. Or . . .' again he thought about it, '. . . that it was inevitable.'

'So where exactly does that fit into the bigger picture?'

He shrugged. 'Who knows?'

'Anything else?'

He shook his head and looked a bit embarrassed. 'This is outside my remit but I think she'll be going into labour fairly soon. She's definitely getting some firm contractions.'

'Yeah, I noticed the Braxton Hicks. Well, I have the community midwife coming to assess her this afternoon so they can probably see if she's going into labour, check the foetal heartbeat, cervical dilatation, etc., etc. She'll be thirty-eight weeks on Friday so they may want to induce her then. Did you notice her banging her abdomen?'

He nodded. 'Quite hard.'

'Edward . . .' She almost hesitated to ask this. 'I've been wondering what's behind all this. Why all these phantom romances? Quite apart from her odd response to the deaths of her children.'

She stopped, suddenly thoughtful, while Edward Reakin waited for her to continue.

'I've spent some time delving into her family background.'

'And?'

'I've formed a theory.'

'Go on.'

'Did you touch on abuse by her father?'

'I did. She hotly denies sexual abuse, Claire. I don't think that's the answer. She does say he was a strict disciplinarian. Religious. No hint of sex. If anything, she hints that he found sex a sin.'

The word resonated to Claire, the sound loud and insistent, but she couldn't find its source.

'Did you get the impression that . . .' She scratched quotation marks into the air. 'The lady doth protest too much?'

He didn't answer straight away but thought about it before responding as was his way. 'No,' he said finally. 'I got the impression she was telling the truth. As she sees it.'

'Anything else strike you?'

'Yeah. Her delusion seems to be only in that one area – lovers, child. All other responses were perfectly rational. I mean about her life, her work, her sister. Even, to some extent, her marriage.'

'Geoff?'

He chuckled. 'She seems to have a sort of friendly relationship with him, a sort of disparaging affection.'

'Mmm,' she said. 'I might well try and see him again. So your conclusions, cause, effect?'

His eyes sparkled. Edward Reakin, clinical psychologist was polite, thoughtful, contemplative, intuitive and very, very clever. And divorced after his wife flaunted an affair which she'd never thought he'd respond to. But he had. In a swift and uncharacteristic action, he'd thrown her out of the marital home and divorced her almost in one rapid, smooth action. Quite against the grain when normally he was a gentle, easy-going guy, given more to thought than action with bland features: neat mouth, grey eyes. But once he'd made up his mind, that was it. Action.

'She supplies a need,' he said slowly. 'A need to be loved, cherished, protected.'

'Go on.'

'Her father was strict. A religious person who believed in upholding his values. There were three children – Robin, Heather and Ruth. During Heather and Ruth's childhood, to the best of his ability, Robin tried to protect his sisters. She spoke of him with very real affection.'

She nodded, picturing this family damaged, as so many are, by a father with rigid beliefs who tried to beat his children into submission and a wife who was probably afraid to speak up.

'But when Heather was nineteen, her brother vanished. She says her father told her he had run off.'

She saw his face change. 'That equation bothered me, Claire,' he said, face preoccupied. 'A father who regularly beat both his son and his two daughters. An older brother who felt he needed to protect his younger sisters.' He was frowning now. 'Just vanishing? Not even trying to get in touch with them to see if they were all right? *Never* getting in touch with them? I asked myself, why not?'

She felt a ripple, as though a great wave was about to wash over them. 'Did she offer any explanation for Robin's apparent abandonment of them?'

'No. But I got the impression that she's both damaged and hurt by his silence as well as feeling vulnerable. And so she substitutes.'

'That makes sense. And Geoff?'

'The traditional reason behind a swift marriage. Pregnant. A way of escaping her father. Funnily enough, Heather's father approved of her choice of husband. Practically arranged the marriage. Apparently, before Geoff fell off the wagon and took up drinking again, he was a member of the same church.'

She pushed on. 'How much of this is conjecture, Edward?'

He leaned back, thought for a moment, then half closed his eyes. 'I'm just filling in details, Claire.'

'But you agree that these romances and sexual experiences are all fantasy?'

'Oh, yes,' he said. 'I've little doubt.'

'Then that'll do. When are you going to see her again?'

He'd moved to stand up but instead dropped back into the chair. 'Soon. But to be honest, Claire,' he said, 'in these days of social media, mobile phones, Skype and whatever, I'm focusing more on what's happened to Robin Acton. I will see Heather again but I have the feeling it's the reason *behind* her stories and allegations where the truth lies.'

'Edward,' she said, 'thank you so much for this. I knew you'd have plenty of insight. I've been too directed by Charles, seeing it too much from his perspective rather than hers. You're right. I should have looked harder at Heather and her reasons for the allegations. Perhaps,' she continued slowly, 'we should ask the police for some help tracking down Robin Acton?'

'Do you know anyone?'

'I do.' It wasn't exactly on her list of things she'd like to do – she had had contact with DS Zed Willard of Burslem police before and it hadn't ended particularly well. 'I'll see what I can do,' she said.

'Keep in touch.' And he was gone.

She was well aware that to get Tissot off the hook she would need to formalize Heather's diagnosis and back it up with evidence. To arrive at that she should interview more people around her. But Edward's astute observations had set her thinking. Perhaps she should focus more on Heather's family history and less on recent events which could be simply a manifestation of some trauma in the past. And the name that sprang to mind was Robin Acton.

Edward's contribution had been really helpful, mostly to point her in the right direction. Maybe she owed a certain amount of professional loyalty to Charles Tissot. But nothing more than that.

In her heart of hearts, she felt that he was unchanged, the same person who would take advantage of a drunk woman. It was over-optimistic to believe that this episode would have taught him a lesson. For predatory men like him, there was no cure.

It didn't help that, from her perspective, Charles Tissot's behaviour was encouraged by a belief in *Droit de Seigneur*.

He was upper class, she nothing but the French frog, an image she could never shake off.

Somewhere at the back of her mind, behind the figure of Heather, her allegations and her family lay a niggling responsibility, a soft voice whispered warnings into her ear. *Other patients.* The uncomfortable memory of that brief encounter: Riley Finch's eyes caressing Heather's swollen abdomen. She'd seen that look and read in them Riley's dangerous message. *I want . . .*

And the last time she had spoken to Arthur Connolly, she had been overwhelmed with pity, an awareness of his vulnerability and inability to cope with either his past life, his violent response or the future that waited for him at HMP.

She shook herself and grabbed at a current buzzword. Outcomes. The NHS was fond of the word. Outcomes. And so she focused, right there, on the desired outcomes.

For Charles Tissot? Absolute acquittal, the very shadow of suspicion removed from him, continuance of his career unhampered by scandal.

For Heather? That was a bit more complicated. But a safe delivery and return to mental health, relief from her delusions.

The child? Heather and Charles could look after themselves. Not so the infant. The temptation was to make the newborn a ward of court. But they would need more evidence than a history of two apparently natural cot deaths and mental instability on the mother's part. Courts are not keen on snatching babies from their mothers' arms. And offering a plea of instinct or past history would be similarly unimpressive. As a psychiatrist, yes, she could attest to erotomania, give it the dignity of calling it by the obscure French name, but there would be an outcry if she either failed to protect the neonate or robbed Heather Krimble of her sole surviving child. And for how long could they or should they protect the child? Until the child was strong enough to protect itself? And what about the father, who would probably turn out to be Geoff? Good old Geoff, who had failed to protect Eliza and Freddie and seemed untroubled by their deaths.

Claire's instinct was that the baby would be in danger. How to protect it was a much more difficult question. Maybe she should follow Edward's instinct and involve the police.

Before she could change her mind, she picked up the phone and dialled the number she had for DS Zed Willard. He sounded more than surprised to hear from her. The surprise was tinged with anxiety, the subtext, *What the hell does she want? This is where the personal treads on the toes of the professional.*

She began with an apology. 'Sergeant Willard.' Her voice sounded awkward. 'I'm really sorry to bother you.'

He made an attempt to sound friendly. 'That's OK, Claire. It's lovely to hear from you. How are you?'

'Not bad. And you?'

'Fine.' It was the classic answer which told them both absolutely nothing.

Sensing her reserve, he hesitated before, 'Is this a professional call?'

'Yes.'

'So . . . is there something you want me to look into?'

'Yes, there is. I have a patient whose brother vanished about eight years ago. I wonder if you could investigate.'

'Sure. Be glad to. Give me the facts. Dates last seen, age, description.'

It was then that she realized how little she did know. 'Can I ring you with them – later?'

'Yeah. Sure.' He sounded friendly enough. He gave her his mobile number and hesitated. 'That boyfriend of yours resurfaced?'

'No,' she said, giving the word a little less emphasis than she'd meant. It still sounded too uncertain and DS Willard obviously picked up on it. 'OK. Right. Well, when you've got the detail of this misper let me know and I'll see what I can do.'

11 a.m.

She had an hour to spare before the midwife was due to arrive and she hoped it would not be Rhoda. She didn't fancy putting a bitter ex-wife into the melting pot. She had enough in there already.

But she could use the time wisely. She climbed the stairs to the top floor and knocked on the door of Heather's room. She was sitting, looking forlornly out of the window. When the door opened she jumped to her feet, her face eager. But as soon as it registered who it was, disappointment dropped her shoulders and sucked the anticipation out of her. She sank back in her chair, saying nothing but pleating and re-pleating her skirt. 'I don't understand it,' she said. 'I don't understand why he isn't here.'

Claire sat down opposite, glad that for once she was alone with her patient without the limiting factor of her sister's presence.

'Heather,' she said gently, 'tell me about Robin.'

Heather's eyes were wide but unseeing. 'Robin?' She sounded puzzled.

'Your brother.'

She stretched out her palms towards Claire. 'But he's gone.'

'I know he's gone,' Claire said. 'Where?'

Heather was frowning. 'We don't know where,' she said. 'We just know he isn't around any more.'

'What was the last thing he said to you?'

Heather's frown deepened.

Claire tried again. 'Was it goodbye? Did he say goodbye?'

'I don't remember.'

'Did you go to the police?'

She shook her head.

'Did anyone in your family go to the police?'

'I don't know. I think maybe. Maybe someone did. Probably Dad.'

'Not you.'

Heather dropped her head and shook out a definite *no*.

'Did Ruth speak to the police?'

The question appeared to confuse her. 'I don't know. I don't think so.'

'Your mother?'

That made her eyes flick up. 'Oh, no. Not my mother.' She almost laughed. 'Not her. She does nothing.'

'So . . . your father?'

'Maybe. I don't know. Perhaps. Probably.'

'What was Robin's full name?'

'Just Robin Acton. He didn't have a middle name. Dad always said they were unnecessary.'

'And his date of birth?'

'Second of February 1985. Why are you asking all this?'

Claire ignored the question. 'So he was twenty-four when he went missing?'

Heather nodded. 'I suppose he must have been.'

'He was five years older than you.'

Again, Heather nodded.

'When did you last see him?'

'I don't know. It was winter. Dark. Cold.' Again, she asked, 'Why are you asking me all these questions about Robin?'

And again, Claire ignored the question. Something else was troubling her. Heather and her sister had watched as their brother

was beaten. What else had they witnessed? She left the room with
the usual feeling of confusion.

She couldn't wait to fill DS Zed Willard in.

As she peered in through the porthole two doors away she could
see Arthur, the small man bent over his crossword, and felt
desperately sorry for him. What the hell would happen to him
in prison?

Overwhelmingly, she knew he did not belong there. He was no
criminal, no knife-wielding homicidal maniac. He was just a man
who had been pushed too far. In HMP he would be bullied and
assaulted. His life inside would be no better than his life had
been on the outside. Lindsay had put him there. She pushed the
door open.

He was sitting quietly in the corner, seeming to take up no space
in the room. He looked up when she entered and she was touched
to see how glad he was to see her. His smile was shy and warm,
yet she had nothing to offer him. No handy diagnosis on which
to dispose of a prison sentence. She sat down.

'I didn't mean to hurt her,' he said softly. 'You know that, don't
you?'

His voice was barely more than a whisper. To her ears he
sounded sincere. But however much he expressed regret for what
he'd done, she doubted it would lighten his sentence. The ruling
on psychological manipulation male to female was new, the
goalposts not quite set out. It was still something to be vaguely
swept under the carpet, something shameful. Few men would admit
it. The ruling from female to male was almost unheard of in the
courts. Untried and untested. However softly spoken, however
diminutive, however much he tried to shrink against the wall,
Arthur was still a man. She doubted he would gain a jury's
sympathy.

She swallowed the comment that not a single member of the
jury would believe his statement that he had not meant to hurt
his wife. She could almost hear the derision if she'd even
mentioned it.

*He had a fucking six-inch blade in his hand. That knife was as
sharp as a sword. He stabbed her four times. Only missed vital
blood supply, her heart by less than two inches. But for the Grace
of God his wife would have been lying there dead. Did you see*

the crime scene pictures? A blood bath. That's what it was. Slaughter. Even his own son won't testify for him.

The man is a monster.

Oh, yes, she could hear it echo around her ears. However much she protested that Arthur Connolly was a good man, no one would believe her. She'd kept interviewing him, trying to find a way to prove to the courts, to his lawyer, to the sceptical jury that this had been an impulsive act committed by a man who had been pushed too far.

But Arthur was giving her few clues. He'd never really gone into detail about the way Lindsay had treated him and the biggest blow of all was that no one from the church was willing to testify to Lindsay's treatment of her husband. Not the verbal abuse, not the slap, not the insults. It wasn't fair. But however soft, unusual and pliable a character Arthur was, his next question still managed to take her by surprise. 'Will Lindsay ever forgive me?'

She stopped to consider before she responded. Forgiveness, that Christian quality. Why was it so important? Why did it matter at all? Who cared? Why did he want her absolution? Once he'd come out of prison he wouldn't be returning to the marital home. Lindsay wouldn't have had him anyway. Too bloody scared. Claire couldn't help the sad smile spreading like butter across her face. Forgiveness? Was Arthur hoping his wife's forgiveness would earn him a place in heaven? After prison? If he survived it?

'Arthur,' she said gently, 'you know I can't answer that. Only Lindsay can.'

And I wouldn't hold my breath if I were you.

'Do you know how she is?' was his next question.

'More or less recovered,' she said. 'She's out of hospital but will need further operations. I'm sure she'll be fine. Saul is with her.'

His look changed to one of resignation as he nodded, donkey-like. Then brightened. 'They'll be glad to be home. Together.'

She spent the next ten minutes discussing the imminent gaol sentence. He took it all on the chin until she asked him that one final question. 'Have you seen Saul?'

It was at that point that Arthur's face crumpled.

And Claire left the room, struck by the sheer inappropriateness of it all.

TWENTY-NINE

Tuesday, 21 July, 12 p.m.

With half an hour before the midwife was due and only a vague idea of her purpose, she approached Riley's room. But it was empty. No sign of her at all. Bed neatly made up, no clothes strewn around the room, no one in the chair. It was as though she had vacated it. Which worried her. Like an active toddler, Riley was at her most dangerous when out of sight.

She asked the nurses, who looked unconcerned. 'She'll be in the bathroom. She spends a lot of time there.'

But, reassured, instead of searching her out she entered the staff room and pulled out her mobile phone.

She had a bit of a conscience that she hadn't kept Charles up to date. She should inform him of all the developments: Heather's current inpatient status as well as the imminent arrival of the community midwife, possibly Rhoda. She found his number but just before she pressed the call icon she hesitated.

'Oh, come on,' she said to herself. 'You're a psychiatrist. You have the story. You've met the people concerned. Work it out for yourself.'

And that was the problem. She hadn't met *all* the people. She was missing some.

The two male subjects of Heather's previous allegations and Heather's parents. And last of all, another person who must once have been close to Heather and Ruth, someone who would have known them as children. Someone who would have known Heather's parents.

The missing brother. She hadn't spoken to him. And neither had Laura.

There were other people who featured on the edge of this story. Charles she knew. And it was possible that she was about to meet Rhoda. But first Charles. She pressed the call button and prepared to speak.

He answered the phone with a weary, 'Hello, Tissot here.'

This debacle was taking its toll. 'It's Claire. Are you all right?'

He gave a mirthless laugh. 'Stressed, knackered, and yeah, a bit worried.'

'About Heather?'

'Oh.' He gave a long sigh. 'That and a long list of other things. Work's busy, Claire. Divorce is complicated, bitter and expensive.' He gave another long sigh. 'Whoever would have thought a quick shag could prove so fucking costly.'

And whoever would have thought that a man as talented and intelligent as Charles M Tissot, consultant obstetrician, would have proved so obtuse in learning such a simple lesson? All actions leave baggage just as all operations leave a scar, however invisible.

But she tried to sympathize – on the surface at least. 'Patient care?'

He gave another mirthless laugh. 'If only it were that simple. Patient care? They teach you that at medical school. No, what they don't teach you is hospital policy, how to make things sound better than they are. How to massage your figures for caesarean sections or lie about infant mortality. How to keep one foetus alive at eighteen weeks and watch another die because it is unwanted. How to stick to guidelines written by governments who know fuck all—' He halted mid-flow. 'Sorry, Claire. But meetings, directives . . . they're what's wearing me out. Not the work itself. Obs and gynae are a dream compared to the rest.'

'Same here,' she said, without much sympathy. 'It's the price we pay for a well-paid, stable, enjoyable and interesting job.'

'Hmm,' was his huffy response.

'Charles,' she said, concerned, recalling Simon's comments on suicide and depression, 'are you all right?'

And with a flick of phrase and a split-second pause he reverted to Charles the letch. 'I could do with a holiday,' he grumbled. 'Somewhere nice and hot where the women wear bits of string instead of clothes, where the beer is cold and with piles of dirty paperbacks when I stretch out my hand. Say, Claire, I bet you look hot in a bikini.'

And because now she was angry that he appeared to be just playing about his troubles, she didn't rise to the bait. After a brief pause, possibly but unlikely realizing he'd said anything wrong, he added, 'You do wear bikinis, don't you?'

She didn't even bother to respond to that, instead reverting to the original subject. 'If you want a holiday, Charles, why don't you go on one? Now would seem like a really good time. Get away from it all.'

'I know. I ought to but I feel I have to watch my back, Claire. I may need to be here to defend my name.'

At least he hadn't said the word honour.

'Against . . .?'

'Well, Rhoda's poisonous, and with Heather's little contribution, I probably need to stick around. Besides . . . going on holiday on your own isn't a great deal of fun. Sure you won't . . .' She could almost see him frowning at the thought that maybe he was missing out on some fun.

'No.' It came out a little more vehemently than she'd meant.

'Hmph. I suppose you're still shacked up with . . .' He sounded grumpy now. Lotharios dislike competition.

She tried to laugh it off and failed miserably. 'Not any more. We broke up. He had family problems and they sort of impinged on our relationship.'

There – packaged up neatly. Nicely put.

Not quite.

'Sorry about that. Had you down for the settling down sort, two point four kids.' There was a pause while she guessed he was considering his next move. 'Maybe we'll meet up professionally again?' And in spite of herself, she couldn't prevent a smile. He didn't give up, did he? But he couldn't know she would rather have met up with a king cobra looking for his next dinner than Charles Tissot on the razzle. She kept that one to herself.

'Anyway,' he said, 'what did you ring about? Anything special?'

'Just to keep you up to date really. I've admitted Heather for the remainder of her pregnancy and probably for at least part of her puerperium to protect both her and the . . .' How to put this? 'I'm a bit concerned she may harm her baby.'

'And I care?' He'd let it slip out.

'No. No, of course not.'

He *would* have the last say. 'Fucking woman's near as destroyed my career. If it hadn't been for . . .' He changed his phrase. 'If you hadn't stepped forward, come to my rescue, believed my story . . . backed me up . . .'

Hang on a minute, she thought. *I haven't done any of this yet.* He couldn't know that every ounce of gratitude was another nail in her hand attaching her to the cross.

Another pause, then, before he snapped. 'If you're really worried about the brat, make the child a ward of court.'

She responded coolly. 'I could do, but there *is* a husband. Presumably the father of the baby.' Which brought her round to a thought: where *was* Geoff in all this? Fathers bring up children. Protect them. But he hadn't saved the other two. They had still died.

Of natural causes. The post-mortems had proved it. There is no known way to prevent cot death. Minimize the risk, maybe. But you can't stop it happening. And pathologists don't miss out on obvious causes of death.

Suddenly she wanted Charles's take on it as a fellow professional, so she began with a small baiting. 'You must have formed your own opinion.'

'Sorry?' His tone was stiffly formal, as though he believed she might be recording the conversation.

'What do you think happened to the two babies, Eliza and Freddie?'

'I don't understand why you're focusing on *them*.'

She ignored the comment and continued. 'I've never heard her talk in any meaningful way about them, which could be seen as both a symptom and a cause of her current mental state. And in cases like these of puerperal psychosis, you must know as well as I do that with each pregnancy the condition worsens. Intensifies.'

'I take it she's still alleging that *I'm* the father of this child?' Now he was sounding injured.

She smiled and couldn't resist a subtle jab below the belt. 'She's waiting for you to visit her, Charles.' She smiled. 'Looking out of the window every few minutes for your . . .' she couldn't resist it, '. . . flashy red Jaguar.' When he didn't respond, she added, 'Yes, Charles, she's waiting for you. She hasn't changed her story. But I don't think, with her past history, anyone is going to be taking her allegations too seriously.'

'They don't have to. Mud sticks.' His response now was gloomy and defeatist again. Had it not been *Charles* on the end of the line but a girlfriend, she would have suggested going out for a drink or a curry. Or both. Cheer them up. But with Charles she knew it would be a wrong move. So she chose a middle road. 'There are singles holidays.'

'Yeah. Somehow doesn't appeal, but maybe when all this has

blown over I can hustle a few of my old buddies together and we can go golfing or something.'

She might have known he would be into golf. Anything that would further his private practice. 'OK, well, keep your . . .' she rejected the word pecker and substituted with, '. . . spirits up.'

'OK. Thanks. And if you reconsider my holiday offer . . .'

She put the phone down.

12.30 p.m.

Unfortunately for her, it *was* Rhoda who turned up as community midwife. Crisp and smart in a maroon dress, she turned up bang on time. Claire had to acknowledge that she was a beautiful woman with a good complexion, although her features were hard and her voice similarly so. She would be a good midwife. Efficient, clever, decisive. Able to control a woman in labour as well as her nursing and medical colleagues. But, Claire soon decided, if *she* was in labour she would have preferred someone a bit softer, someone with some sympathy, someone who would comfort her, hold her hand. Rhoda Tissot's response, she felt, would be of the pull-yourself-together school. For Charles, she must have made an uncomfortable and slightly unpredictable trophy wife. As concisely as she could, she brought her up to date.

Rhoda was quick. 'Wouldn't it have been better for her to have been admitted to a maternity unit and you come and see her rather than admit her . . .' she couldn't prevent a shudder, '. . . here?'

Claire managed a smile, trusting she too looked serene, confident and in control. 'It seemed better this way. Heather suffers from delusions. She is, on occasions, psychotic. And, two previous cot deaths added to the fact that she is sometimes antagonistic towards this child, we wish to observe her developing relationship with the new baby. Here seemed the best place.'

She accompanied Rhoda into Heather's room. She was alone, sitting, as usual, staring out of the window. There was no sign of Ruth, who must have either gone to work or gone home. Heather turned as they entered but, as usual, her shoulders drooped when she saw who it was.

Claire almost felt sorry for her as she began with the introductions and Heather's complete lack of interest registered. 'Heather, this is Rhoda. She's the midwife who will monitor your progress while you are here in Greatbach, right up until you are ready to be admitted to the labour ward.'

A sharp, rebuking look from Mrs Tissot, who must have wondered at the informality. No surname?

Claire hurried on to cover up the omission. 'She or a member of her team will keep an eye on you until you and the baby are ready to be transferred back here.'

Heather lifted her face towards Claire and Claire was struck with a sudden realization. For a moment then Heather had looked beautiful, almost transfixed. She nodded her thanks to her and turned her attention to the midwife as Rhoda stepped forward. 'Now then, dear,' she began. Claire excused herself. It felt voyeuristic to be standing there with no role to play apart from bystander.

She left and waited for Rhoda Tissot at the staff desk, checking up on Riley Finch, who had tried to slide past her unnoticed.

'Riley. I came to see you earlier. You weren't in your room.'

'No.' The girl's response was casual and confident. She tucked a strand of hair behind her ear. 'Must have been in the shower.'

Bad luck that that was the moment Rhoda emerged. 'Well,' she said brightly. 'Won't be long now. Her cervix is already dilating. I would say she'll go into labour in the next day or two.'

Behind her, Riley Finch melted away as though she hadn't even been there in the first place.

Rhoda continued in her crisp voice, 'I'll come in daily and, when we think she's about ready, we'll transfer her. Now then, you say she has a history of normal deliveries but two cot deaths. Oh dear.'

Claire was fully aware that although she couldn't see her, Riley was not far away, listening. For privacy and on instinct, she ushered Rhoda Tissot into the staff room and closed the door behind them.

Rhoda took the initiative. 'Just remind me of her psychiatric issues.' She was taking copious notes, writing quickly, jerkily, on a reporter's notebook. 'She believes that her husband is not the father of her child. And she's gravida three?' She looked up. Arched eyebrows framed the question.

'Yes.'

'So?' Her question was straight to the point, pen poised.

She answered slowly and very carefully. 'She's alleging that this child is the result of a casual liaison at a party.'

Rhoda's smile was mocking.

Claire continued, 'This has happened twice before with her two previous children – allegations of a relationship with men who deny it and a claim that the child she bears is the result of this "liaison". We don't know for sure with the first pregnancy as no paternity test was taken. She was six months pregnant when she married her current husband. He denies that the child was his and says he doesn't know who the father was.' She was reflective. 'No one seems to know. The second child proved to be her husband's son.'

'And both were unfortunately cot deaths?' Rhoda's response was like an arrow, flying straight to the centre. And suddenly Claire was surprised that this brittle and apparently callous woman looked distressed. 'Oh, my word. That's awful.'

'Yes.' Claire looked hard at her. *Was there some history here?*

'I don't have children,' Charles's ex said abstractedly. 'I'd have loved at least one. But Charles was never ready for it. Permanent child himself.' Then her eyes looked straight into Claire's. 'Of course,' she said with a brittle smile, 'you know him, don't you?'

'Only at medical school.'

Rhoda picked up her bag, interest lost. 'Yes. Well. Let's hope this child is a candidate for a better future.'

'Indeed.'

Claire let out a huge sigh of relief. This initial tricky interview was over.

THIRTY

Friday, 24 July, 4 p.m.
38/40

Claire had not exactly been looking forward to interviewing Heather's parents. She anticipated a stiff and uncomfortable experience. But she wanted answers which they could possibly provide.

And time was running short. The baby would soon be born, so she'd asked Rita to arrange an interview as soon as possible.

Heather's mental state was deteriorating. She slept in a chair now, refusing to go to bed, worried she'd miss his visit. She spent the entire night watching, waiting for Charles to arrive. She looked exhausted. Her distress was palpable and no amount of talking, explaining or counselling was helping, even with Edward Reakin's contribution. Another worrying feature was that she was paranoiac against the nurses, accusing them of stopping her 'lover' from visiting. Once or twice she had been violent towards members of staff. Added to that, her punishment of the unborn infant was gradually becoming increasingly unpredictable. One minute she would be furious with it, the next stroking and crying, apologizing. Geoff Krimble turned up faithfully every day, sometimes with a box of chocolates which his wife never ate, believing them to be poisoned, intended to kill both her and what she now called *the cuckoo baby*. At other times the poor, confused man arrived dangling a bunch of petrol-shop flowers upside down by his side. He looked both bemused and resigned at his wife's protestations, sitting by her side, holding her hand and saying little to nothing. The situation was beyond him. He would stay for about an hour. On his way out he usually commented that she'd be better when she'd had the baby.

'She's always like this, late on.' The staff would nod and smile.

Claire had gleaned nothing of use from him during two further interviews. Ruth was too loyal to breathe a word against her sister. Robin was absent and so she had turned to Heather's parents and now waited in her clinic room for Mr and Mrs Acton who had finally, under stiff protest, agreed to attend.

'They took an awful lot of persuading,' Rita had said. 'They didn't want to come at all.'

But Claire felt it was important enough to insist. They were a Little and Large couple, Bailey tall, burly and strong looking, his wife diminutive at his side. He had very dark hair and a powerful physique while she was pale, ghost-like with sandy eyelashes. Claire ushered them into her clinic room.

Bailey Acton sat rigid, his back ramrod straight, staring ahead, keeping his eyes – and his fury – directed not at her but at the wall behind her. Win, by his side, sat silent and shrunken, listening to her husband explaining their three children's upbringing. Mr Acton did all of the talking, Win simply nodding periodically.

'We're religious people. Follow the Bible's teaching of spare the rod and spoil the child. We have high standards and we expect the same from our children. If not, we'd punish them.'

Claire listened before asking if they had any idea whose child Eliza had been.

They looked at each other. 'Her husband's.' Win's voice was squeaky. Bailey nodded his agreement.

She swallowed the fact that Geoff denied they had had sex before their marriage. Substituting with, 'So not Mr Cartwright's, then?'

Win looked anxiously at her husband for a cue. Then both shook their heads.

Bailey Acton scowled. 'The Devil must have got in her brain somehow,' he said angrily. 'She imagined that. It's all a load of nonsense.' The fury brought veins standing out to the side of his forehead, though Claire wasn't sure whether the anger was directed at her, his daughter, Geoff, who appeared to be the victim, or the Devil himself.

'Some people might say we were too strict as parents,' he conceded, thick eyebrows beetling together in rank rejection of this opinion. He folded his arms and stared at her, uncompromising. Challenging her to disagree. 'But we have our morals, Doctor. That is certain. We brought our three children up to respect *standards.*' The word was produced with emphasis and a proud flourish as showy as a bullfighter's *capa.*

'Standards,' he barked again, puffing out his chest like a bullfinch. 'Heather was soon married. Who else's could the babies have been but Geoff's? The test proved it in respect of Freddie.'

Bailey had dressed to impress. He wore his shiny Sunday suit, trousers a little too short, jacket a little too long, gaping over a bulging stomach. His shirt, though, was purest white, perfectly ironed with not a wrinkle, though the effect was spoilt by plump chins spilling over a tight collar. But his tie was tasteful, a modest, muted burgundy and grey stripe. A scent of mothballs clung to the air around him. The suit was little used. But overall he made a rigid, unbending figure. A biblical patriarch – a description Claire thought he would have been pleased with. She glanced at his wife but Win didn't even raise her eyes. She remained silent now, haunted, hooded eyes muddy green, studying the carpet. But though she *said* nothing, her mind must have been forming thoughts. Her mouth worked incessantly, perhaps shaping the very words she would not or could not speak. Or maybe she was quoting the Bible. Claire read painful suppression in the woman's expression. Once or twice, when her husband raised his voice, her mouth twisted in pain and she flinched. But she was not going to share her fears or her grief. Was she the only one to grieve the two dead babies or was there someone else?

Families, Claire thought.

Even without her husband's physical presence, she guessed Bailey's influence would reach far enough keep his wife's mouth shut. She would have been no match for him either, physically or mentally. Claire breathed in and caught the woman's personal scent. Slightly musty, mothballed fear and lavender, though she was tidily dressed in a plaid skirt which reached halfway down her calf and a cream blouse with a fussy bow at the neck, low-heeled brogues and thick stockings. A little like her daughter, Ruth, Win Acton spent most of the interview studying the floor, shoulders bowed in acceptance of the situation. Claire read something of *both* her daughters in her demeanour and immobile facial expression: tight control over any emotion combined with an acceptance of the status quo and a failure to challenge it. She might have been pretty once but, like a rose that has sat in the sun too long, she was dried out, the colour bleached out of her, leaving her pale. Skin, hair, eyes, teeth, lips all faded to a uniform shade of white sand. Had she ever been vivacious? Noisy? Colourful?

Probably not. And it had probably been her acquiescence that had attracted Bailey Acton to her in the first place. Bullies are skilled at recognizing potential victims.

But Claire did pick up on one thing. Win Acton had respect for her husband. When her eyes left the floor to fasten on him she sat as though he was some guru, some oracle, someone wise, someone to be revered. The prophet. And she, worshipping at his feet.

Claire thought she might learn more by addressing her directly. 'You're close to your daughters, Mrs Acton?'

As before, Win Acton took her cue from her husband via a swift glance. *His* reply was a bluff, 'Of course.' Hers a non-committal shrug.

'And your son, Robin?'

That was when, unaccountably, fear entered the room, sneaking underneath the door like a poisonous gas. Win gave an audible swallow, a noisy gulp before managing, 'Why do you ask about him?'

'What happened to him?'

'He left.' She pressed her lips together.

'Why?'

Bailey stepped in then. 'He was bad. He didn't fit in with our beliefs.'

'So where is he now?'

Both Win and Bailey shook their head. 'We don't know.'

'Have you tried to find him?'

Bailey frowned. 'Yes and no. We asked people. Our people.' By which Claire surmised they meant their fellow churchgoers.

She pointed out the anomaly. 'But he wouldn't have contacted other churchgoers, would he? You say he didn't fit in with your beliefs.'

The statement seemed to throw them. Bailey Acton frowned and his dark eyes searched the floor for an appropriate response. Which he didn't find. 'No one's seen him.'

'The police?'

'Couldn't find him neither.'

Mistakenly, Claire abandoned the subject.

'And what about your grandchildren, Eliza and Freddie?'

A flicker passed across Win Acton's face. Something nervous, a little frightened. She shuddered and again looked to her husband for a cue.

Claire could have sworn Win Acton's lips moved to form the word, *Punishment*, but she couldn't be sure.

'God's will,' Bailey Acton said without emotion.

Claire wanted to say, *You think?*

But she desisted.

Win put in, 'They said natural causes.' And then something like anger spilled out. 'What difference can it make what they died of?' A swift glance at her husband followed, as though she was expecting a slap. Her husband's response was a noisy clearing of the throat. Enough to make his wife press her lips together in case another word slipped out.

Claire pressed on: 'So you believe there is no truth in Heather's claims of other lovers?'

Win Acton twitched but her husband answered smoothly, his

anger, in front of a psychiatrist, well under control now. 'Of course not. The Devil's infected her mind. Heather is a married woman, may I remind you. Married. Her husband is a good and honest man. He was a member of our church.'

But not now.

'They have a normal marriage even if they did . . . anticipate the ceremony. Those poor little things.' Just in time, he remembered to inject some grief into his words. 'Those poor little things, Eliza and then Freddie. Double tragedy. Well, it was God's will but they were both her *husband's* children.'

So now Geoff was added to the list of lovers in denial.

Bailey banged the desk to give his words increased emphasis. 'There is no doubt about it.'

'No – at least, not in Freddie's case.'

'*Both* their cases.'

'And Heather and Ruth? Did they share your religious beliefs?'

Bailey and Win both nodded.

'But not Robin.'

Both seemed to falter. Interestingly, it was Win who responded. 'No,' she said. 'He was . . .' she looked to her husband for help but came up with her own word, '. . . different.'

Bailey came storming in. 'Wayward. He did not keep the faith,' he said and pressed his lips together. Subject over.

Win Acton continued while her husband, this time, listened. And in the thick-set face with coarse features, Claire saw respect. Perhaps she had read this couple wrong. Mrs Acton might be obedient to her husband but there was a steely strength behind her, well hidden from view. Like a woman behind a veil. But it was an acceptance.

'We trust Geoff with our daughter,' Win Acton finished while her husband nodded his approval.

'What about Ruth?'

'Adores her sister. They've always been close. Particularly since . . .'

A warning shot across the bows. Bailey's head shot round. Again, Win was silent.

So what, Claire wondered, as she thanked them for coming and ushered them out of the room, had she learned from that?

How deep the religious influence was, something she had, until now, underestimated. So surely, that would have made Heather's allegations against all and sundry even more shocking? No, for they had passed over that with equanimity and the simplest of explanations. Likewise their son-in-law's defection from their church. But it was the subject of their missing son, Robin, which had exposed them. So, the answer to what had she learned? Not as much as she should have done.

THIRTY-ONE

Tuesday, 28 July, 11.26 a.m.
38/40

Claire had meant to contact DS Willard earlier to follow up on any information on the whereabouts of Robin Acton but events had kept pushing this to the back of her mind. Besides, after so many years, there was hardly any urgency about it. It could have little bearing on Heather's mental condition.

Rhoda Tissot had been as good as her word. She or one of her colleagues attended Heather daily, even over the weekend. But ten days before her estimated date of delivery it became clear, by Heather's actions, holding of her back, sudden exclamations of pain and general behaviour that she was about to go into labour and would soon be transferred to the maternity unit.

Claire watched and waited and left this part of events to the midwives. Her only involvement was to speak, either directly or through the nurses, to find out how her mental state was. She called a meeting of the nursing staff and asked them to pool their ideas, which came thick and fast.

Astrid gave the clearest picture. 'She's at the window all the time. Waiting for Charles. It's pathetic.'

Another nurse, Juno, an import from the Philippines, said, 'She actually asked me to ring "Charles" and invite him to come in and see her, be present at the birth.'

'Imagine,' Astrid said with a dazzling smile. 'Imagine if she had.'

'And how is she towards you?'

'Aggressive, accusing us of not passing on enquiries, phone calls. A few times she's said she's heard him in the corridor begging to be let in but we've stopped him.'

So auditory hallucinations. 'Has she been violent?'

Both Astrid and Juno shook their heads. 'Not recently. Just verbally abusive.'

Edward had had two more sessions with her, trying to learn more about the family dynamics. In the end, he confided in Claire. 'She's not saying much,' he said. 'It's as though she's built a wall around her, family on the inside and anyone else firmly locked out.'

'So are we to surmise that the psychological pathology is there, inside the family unit?'

'It's tempting to think so,' Edward said. 'But that's always an easy pit to fall into.' He smiled, the warmth lighting his eyes with friendliness. 'You know as well as I do that there isn't always a neat and easy reason behind bizarre behaviour. But other questions came to mind, Claire. Questions she's just as reluctant to answer. For instance, why Tissot? Why did she pick on him? The other two men were, at least, known to her. But Tissot – they at most had a very fleeting acquaintance. But the specifics – the car, the detailed description, the professional man are all correct. It's only the other details – telephone numbers, details of actual contact, that are absent. Why the request to become his patient when even in her deluded state she must have realized that the result could have been catastrophic for him? Why did she want vengeance on him?' He paused for her comment.

'That's what it feels like?'

He pressed on. 'And then there's Ruth. I've had two interviews with her. Not an unintelligent woman. She does a good job in the hospital. She's well thought of but she just won't give anything up. Robin's disappearance is a puzzle and I wonder if it is perhaps the missing piece?'

'I'm heading that way myself,' she said. 'I think I should at least do some looking into it. Did you have any ideas . . .?'

'I was thinking of the dates,' he said. 'Although nobody can seem to remember exactly when Robin Acton was last seen it does appear it was round about the time that Heather was married. And Eliza was born three months after she became Mrs Krimble. I just wondered if there was any connection?'

'I need to think about that one.'

He stood up. 'Must go,' he said. 'But I hope I've given you plenty to think about.'

She nodded. And after he'd gone, she sat for a while. Yes, there was Ruth. Yes, there too was the absent Robin and the righteous parents. There was the slippery eel, Charles. And soon an unborn child who needed protection. The midwives had said, on their last visit, that it was a toss-up whether Heather would go into spontaneous labour this week or need induction early next. So it was possible that Heather would be transferred within the next twenty-four hours.

She climbed the stairs to the locked ward and found Ruth in the corridor. A midwife, not Rhoda, was in Heather's room, assessing the progression of labour.

Ruth looked suspicious at the request to *have a word*. 'What for?' The response was almost rude.

'I want to talk to you about your brother,' Claire said, sitting beside her to make it less of a formal interview. More of a chat. 'Tell me what happened.'

'He left,' she said flatly.

'Yes, I know that,' Claire said patiently. 'But what were the circumstances?'

Like her mother's, Ruth's eyes slid along the floor. Eyes downcast, frowning.

'I don't remember.'

'Remind me of the dates.'

'I don't remember.' Her voice was louder this time.

'The sequence of events. When did you last see him?'

'I don't remember.' Said through gritted teeth.

Claire changed tack. 'Was your sister pregnant before he left?'

Ruth blanched. Her eyes flew towards Claire's face.

Then she recovered herself, drew up her shoulders, gave a silly, girlish laugh and a fluttering gesture with her hands. It's a good way to avoid answering a question. Act silly. Pretend you're stupid when you don't want to answer a question. But Ruth wasn't stupid. This was an inept act. Finally an answer squeezed out. 'It's a few years ago now. I can't remember the exact sequence of events.'

Claire felt her eyes narrow. *So why is it so important that you don't tell me?*

Ruth smiled, stood up and peered through the porthole window into her sister's room before turning. 'I really can't remember, Doctor.'

As an interview, it was completely unsatisfactory and meant to put her off her guard, stop her asking questions, making the responses so fuzzy they were unhelpful. But it had the result of pushing Claire into finally following up the lead with DS Zed Willard.

'Sorry I didn't get back. I meant to ring you, Claire.'

How many times have you heard this one? I meant to ring you. My finger was just on the dial pad when you rang. What a coincidence.

She swallowed the *yeah yeah* of scepticism.

'You did say Robin Acton of eighteen, The Pike, Brindley Ford?' DS Willard sounded puzzled.

'Yes. That's the one. The brother of my patient.'

'He's never been reported missing.'

'What?'

'There's no record of a Robin Acton having been reported missing,' he repeated.

'But he left eight years ago and has never been seen again.'

'Be that as it may, no one's reported him missing.' Willard was doggedly sticking to his guns. 'I did do a bit of digging around.' He sounded aggrieved now. 'According to our records, he has no mobile phone, no bank account. No driving license.'

'He does have a birth certificate?' Claire was alarmed. Was this just another of the strange sisters' fantasies?

'Oh, yeah. He exists all right. Or has existed but there's no footprint since 2010 and no missing persons' case file has ever been opened. As far as the force is concerned, he's not on our radar.'

Claire knew Zed Willard well enough not to reinforce the question: *Are you sure?*

When she put the phone down she was more confused than ever. This was all about men disappearing and the appearance of other men who denied they were ever there.

It was with real difficulty that she tore her attention from the puzzle of mystery men and focused on her other patients.

As she'd anticipated, in spite of her testimony, Arthur was

awaiting trial for grievous bodily harm, one step down from attempted murder. It was something to be thankful for. Perhaps. But hopefully, after Claire's impassioned description of his family life, assessment of the causes of his outburst and, most importantly, her conviction that he was unlikely to be a danger to others, Arthur would receive a lenient sentence.

And, also awaiting her final discharge, this time in spite of Claire's assessments, Riley Finch was preparing to return home. Back to the one-bedroomed flat she owned and, presumably, back to her wicked old ways. When the words *absolute discharge* were uttered, Claire had felt herself tense. Leopards don't change their spots; neither do folk with severe personality defects. The defects do not heal. Ever.

What, she wondered, would be Riley's next project? And who would be the next to suffer through it?

She watched her leave Greatbach feeling nothing but apprehension. She could not forget those long, sly eyes sliding down a pregnant abdomen. While Riley was an inpatient she was watched and Heather protected. But out there, in the big wide world, no one would be keeping an eye on Riley Finch. Claire couldn't forget the way she had smiled.

A carnivore contemplating her next meal.

Wednesday, 29 July, 5 p.m.

Late afternoon brought a distraction in the form of an unexpected but not unwelcome invitation. Rita rang through to her office where she was dictating clinic letters, uncomfortably aware that there was a certain repetitiousness in her phrases.

Disturbed, repeated episodes, unpredictable behaviour, treatment CBT, medication, major tranquilizers, unable to offer an inpatient bed due to staff shortages.

Hmm. It made her feel she was offering a less-than-satisfactory service. And then the phone rang and her day changed.

'Don't suppose you have a fancy for another curry or even a drink or something?'

She was taken aback.

He continued, 'Only the thought of going back to that hovel is just so awful I might just jump on the next plane back to Oz.'

Smiling to herself, she accepted the invitation. But this time she chose the small Italian just round the corner from her home. They could meet up in her office.

He was there fifteen minutes later as she was dictating the last of her letters. The tape would go to Rita for typing and then back to her for checking and signing. And then off to the GP with a copy to the patient. Neat and tidy. Done and dusted.

As he stood in the doorway she was already questioning her sanity – her motive for the words that were about to spill out of her. She really hadn't thought this through at all. Not even considered what would happen if it didn't work out. It was an impulse, not sensible. Never sensible to get involved with a work colleague. Luckily . . . and this was her perceived safety net . . . she didn't fancy him. Not at all. Not one tiny little bit. Tall, skinny guys with specs and gingery hair, even if they did have nice eyes and teeth, were not her type at all. She was more into . . . Oh, stop that. She wasn't into anything. She was Miss Celibate. That was her name, her aim.

And even if he had been a newly freed Brad Pitt or gorgeous Simon Baker, Tom Hiddleston, Aiden Turner or Daniel Craig, he was off-limits, a married man. 101 per cent taboo. So why invite him to be a lodger? Why get involved at all?

She didn't need the money. She wasn't short of cash. She managed the mortgage easily on her wage. Houses, even ones as large and beautiful as hers, were under-priced in Burslem, which had both a chequered past, a chequered present and probably a chequered future. Its fortunes had gone down and up and down again like the Big Dipper in Alton Towers. It was proudly and publicly multinational. Saris merged with jeggings, hijabs with turbans, shalwar kameezes with jeans and plenty of bright kanga wear and great mops of material balanced on beautiful ropes of hair, the Jamaican dreadlocks. It was a town where anything went. Even Arnold Bennett.

Here all religions not only lived side by side, they nestled, mosques and churches, a synagogue, Presbyterians, Methodists and a lovely Roman Catholic church. She loved Burslem for that openness, that acceptance, the welcome it gave to people from the far and troubled corners of the earth.

She smiled. Even untroubled Australia. But the question remained stubborn. Why invite trouble? The real reason? Because the house was too big for one and seeming more than twice as big since Grant had gone down the plughole. But, on the other hand, she was getting used to her own company.

She was still analysing her motive behind the impulse when he stood in the doorway, grinning and giving out a scent of clean, fresh soap and still that inexplicable scent of briny air. None of the cheap boarding-house aroma. No tobacco, no fried food, no three-day-old socks. He seemed a genuinely nice guy. He'd come halfway across the world to study psychiatry, stuck a pin in a map and ended up here, right in the centre of the UK, in Stoke-on-Trent. He'd openly said that his interest was in forensic psychiatry. Like hers. This was a shared interest. Her focus was personality disorder and his was depression. Neither of them had ended up on nature's dangerous doorstep by accident. It had been part interest, part medicine, part law, part a life experience that had spurred them both on. And this she could identify with.

But he lived in a hovel? Not a great spur for him to gain positive images of the UK and Staffordshire in particular.

'Sit down, Simon,' she invited, thoughts completed and stuffed in a drawer. He sat down comfortably and now her office seemed less than half the size. He might be skinny but he still took up space. *That*, she thought, *was a warning*. Which she ignored.

'Great idea of yours,' she said. 'And I do fancy a meal out. But first . . .' She realized he was looking expectantly at her. 'There's something I want to discuss with you.' She found it difficult to begin. 'I split up with my partner almost a year ago. I live on my own in quite a big house.'

He blinked.

'What I'm trying to say is you can have the top floor for a peppercorn rent.' She laughed it off as a trivial, meaningless offer. 'I'd hardly notice you were there. It's newly decorated and is, I'm sure, not as horrible as the place you're staying in.' She waited for him to respond.

'You really mean it?'

'Yes,' she said, 'really. It consists of two rooms and a bathroom.' Now his eyes, behind the glasses, lit up.

'Would you like to come and have a look and then, if you still fancy an Italian, we can walk into Burslem to the local trattoria. It's really quite good.'

'Wow, Claire . . .' He touched her hand. 'I don't know what to say.'

'Just come and have a look at the place,' she urged, 'before you decide.'

'Wow,' he said. 'Fantastic. I'm tempted to kiss you.'

Mmm, she thought. *Maybe this would be a bit trickier than she'd anticipated.*

She shoved the thought aside. It would be months before she came to terms with the fact that there was one question she should have asked but didn't. *Is your wife intending to join you?*

He followed her back to Waterloo Road in his hire car and they drew up outside. Something in her felt proud of the lovely Victorian houses, built for pot-bank owners but many now sadly neglected. Burslem went through cycles, sometimes regenerating, at others decaying like a sugar-coated tooth.

But as he climbed out of the car, long legs first, stood upright, looked up and said, 'Wow,' she knew it was a *fait accompli*.

'Now this,' he said, 'is what I call a lovely traditional house. Is it Victorian?'

'It is.' And she felt that small burst of pride one feels when displaying your home and it is admired. As she looked at the solid Victorian walls, the bay windows (all neatly painted thanks to Mr Mudd), opened the front door to encaustic Minton tiles and ushered him in, she knew he would share her love of it. He stepped into the hall where she had a Victorian settle covered in tweed, above it a copy of a Stubbs – a shiny horse being led out of the stable by a well-dressed Regency man, hunting jacket over tight cream jodhpurs. 'Here,' she said, leading him straight up the wide stairway with shallow steps, holding on to the mahogany rail – carefully stripped and polished, again by Paul Mudd. She passed the first floor, her bedroom, spare bedroom and bathrooms and led him up to the second floor, which she had done little with so far apart from putting emulsion on the walls and installing the basics of furniture. Simon Bracknell's eyes swept around the generous proportions of the two rooms, one with a double bed in it, the other containing a desk, bookcases and chairs, the pristine bathroom never actually used. And he started laughing, which changed his face into something different. A Jolly Swagman.

'It's a deal,' he said, grinning and holding out his hand.

'There's no kitchen up here,' she warned.

His response was, 'When can I move in?'

She shrugged. 'Whenever you like. I'll sort you out with a key.'

'Rent?' he asked tentatively.

'Oh, goodness. I hadn't thought of that. How about you pay me what you gave for . . .' she felt the smile steal across her face, '. . . the hovel.'

They both laughed at that, Claire until tears ran down her cheeks, sooted with mascara. It was such a relief.

'So,' he said. 'Let's celebrate.'

And they did. At the local Italian, a favourite of hers. A hundred strides from her own front door.

THIRTY-TWO

Monday, 3 August, 2 a.m.
39/40

Even though they thought they had prepared for all eventualities, Heather's labour still took them by surprise, typically starting in the middle of the night. Luckily a vigilant nurse with obstetric experience called Trudy Winters was on the ball. She realized what was happening when Heather rang her bell to say her waters had broken and she was getting almost non-stop contractions. Trudy wasted no time, summoning an ambulance and ringing the maternity hospital. Heather was on her way to becoming a mother – for the third time.

At the busy maternity unit there was no duty social worker and no psychiatric support. The midwives would be on their own. The labour ward was staffed by a trained midwife, a pupil midwife and a registrar who was so knackered he could hardly keep his eyes open and had only wanted to be called if there were complications.

'I don't know why I have to be here,' he was grumbling. 'Previous normal deliveries, third child. What's the problem?'

'That's why you're here,' the midwife snapped. 'That is the problem. This is the third child. None of them, she claims, her husband's. Three children. And how many of them are still alive?' She peered at the head crowning to the accompaniment of Heather's groans. 'Only this one. Do you know where she's been transferred from?'

The registrar was well awake now. He shook his head.

'Greatbach Secure Psychiatric Hospital.'

He swivelled his head around to look up at her and she nodded. 'That's right.'

After that she practically ignored him, moving round instead to the woman's head. 'Come on, Heather. Push.'

The exhausted woman hardly looked at her but she grunted and the registrar saw the baby's head crowning.

And then it was gone. They had a bit of time yet.

The midwife moved down to him to whisper in his ear. 'Two cot deaths.'

'Has the husband been called?'

'The pupil's on to it now.'

With difficulty, Heather lifted her head from the pillow and spoke weakly. 'Is Charles here? Has he come?'

The doctor was puzzled. 'I thought your husband's name was Geoff.'

Heather looked at him blankly. He tried a joke. 'Not another . . .' He read the midwife's look correctly and added his voice to the chorus. 'Come on. Push.'

'Come on, Heather. Push. We're nearly there.'

The crown of the baby's head loomed again, larger this time.

The grunting eased and Heather gave one final push.

The registrar controlled the head, checked the cord was not about to strangle the baby, eased out the shoulders and in a rush of liquor and blood, umbilical cord trailing, the baby was born.

They were silent. There is something so magical about this moment. So overawing. So inspiring. So wonderful, beautiful, the wonder of a new life that even those who have witnessed it hundreds of times are still struck silent by its beauty. And then the baby was crying. 'Wonderful,' the midwife said, quite unashamed of her emotion and placing the child on Heather Krimble's abdomen, an area that now looked like a deflated balloon. 'You have a beautiful daughter.' She clamped the cord and delivered the placenta to be weighed and inspected.

Heather lifted her head. 'Where's Charles?' she asked weakly. 'He should be here by now.'

It was the registrar who asked, 'Who's Charles?'

Heather simpered. 'You should know. He works here.'

The registrar, whose name was Andrew Simpson, gave a swift,

worried glance at the midwife. It was a look that dismissed Heather's words. A look that said, *Loopy! Let's get her back to Greatbach asap!*

Heather sank back against the pillows, exhausted now. 'I shall call her Caroline,' she said, 'after the dead princess.'

Another look was exchanged between the midwife and the registrar. The urgency to return her to the psychiatric unit was intensifying.

Heather's voice was feeble now. 'Is he here yet?'

And when no one answered, she repeated the question. 'Is he here yet?'

The midwife tried to restore logic. 'Do you mean your husband?'

'No.' The anger in her patient's voice and face was palpable and unnerved them all. They were used to dealing with different problems. The midwife's response, given the busy unit, understandably echoed the registrar's. *Get her back to Greatbach asap.*

After they'd taken a sample of cord blood. There was some dispute over the baby's paternity.

Monday, 3 August, 10 a.m.

The first Claire knew that Heather had delivered was when she arrived on the ward. She'd planned to arrange her transfer to the maternity unit and labour induced anyway. Nature had beaten her. She peered into Heather's room and saw the empty bed, a cot standing at its side in readiness. And someone had put a small pink rabbit and a neatly folded pink blanket, which told their own story. Following her glance, Astrid couldn't prevent a smile spreading across her face like jam on a crumpet. 'A little girl, Caroline.' She screwed up her face. 'After the dead princess.'

'When?'

'In the night.'

'Mother and baby? How are they?'

Astrid Carter shook her long dark hair. 'Fit as fleas,' she said. 'They're sending them back later today after the paediatrician's had a look at the baby and taken some cord blood.'

'And they're both all right?'

'Apparently fine.' Astrid was a highly trained nurse who had worked at Broadmoor. Initially on her arrival she had appeared arrogant, a know-it-all who had looked down on the staff of what she had seen as a provincial hospital. But lately, and Claire suspected it was something to do with a mystery man named Tom, a subject which Astrid seemed to be able to slip into almost any conversation, Astrid had changed. Gone was the snooty nurse who looked down her nose at both colleagues and patients, replaced by a competent nurse with vast experience and the rough edges polished off to a shiny smooth surface. As they walked along the corridor back to the nurses' station, she added, 'But I think the maternity hospital is judging her condition on her safe delivery rather than her mental state.' Her eyes were merry. 'When they rang me to do a verbal handover there was mention of anguish at the fact that her husband, whose name is apparently Charles, wasn't there to see his daughter being born.'

'Shit,' Claire said. 'Was there any mention of Charles's surname?'

'No, luckily. So there was none of the prurient curiosity which would have come down the line if they had realized who Charles really was. They've sent some cord blood for a paternity test.'

'Good. That should move things along. We need to get her back here quickly. Bleep me or ring Rita when she's arrived,' Claire said. 'I want to see her, assess her, see how she is now the baby is born. She'll need watching. Make sure that no harm comes to the baby. I think we'll be more used to protecting our patients than the maternity unit.'

'Will do.'

Claire wandered back down the corridor, wondering. Would Caroline's fate follow that of her brother and sister? At that moment, she didn't even consider the possibility that the little girl was anything but Geoff Krimble's daughter. She ought to speak to Charles, at least tell him that Heather had delivered and the DNA test already arranged. He'd already submitted one himself for comparison. With a bit of luck, his ordeal would soon be over.

But she didn't ring. At the back of her mind was a naughty thought: *Let him suffer just that little bit longer.*

Simon Bracknell rang at noon and got straight to the point. 'Claire, if it's OK with you I wondered if I could move my things over this evening?'

She chuckled. 'You don't waste much time, do you?'

'I can't wait to move in, Claire. That's the truth.'

'Well, that's fine. I've had a spare key cut. Shall we meet outside at about six-ish? You remember the address?'

'Of course. Great.' His enthusiasm was infectious. 'See you then. Maybe I can treat you to dinner?'

'Maybe,' she responded, laughing. 'But *I* should really be treating *you* with the first week's rent.'

They both laughed at that and Claire put the phone down with a feeling of bonhomie. It was going to be OK. No strings attached. Just like her student days, she'd be living with a bloke. All platonic. She told herself she didn't want complications. This suited her fine. He was a nice guy and she didn't fancy him. He was a colleague, someone who would understand her point of view. Goodness, she thought. She might even be able to discuss cases with him, learn something from his upside-down geography.

Yes. On the whole, she was looking forward to the evening.

But events intervened. Snowballed.

At two o'clock in the afternoon, Zed Willard phoned. And he sounded puzzled. Once the niceties were over he too got straight to the point. 'This Robin Acton, Claire. Did you say they lived at Brindley Ford?'

'Yes. I have the address here somewhere. The Pike. Number eighteen.'

'I thought that was what you said.' He paused before plunging into his next point. 'Do you know the place?'

'No. I don't know the area at all.'

'I went out there, Claire, to take a look. The Pike is a row of old miners' cottages. They're quite rundown. They have large gardens and back on to a slag heap.'

Now she was the one who was puzzled. 'What are you getting at?'

'Wait a minute,' he said. 'Hear me out. There's been nothing from him for eight years. No national insurance number. No bank account, no mobile phone. Nothing. He's off the radar.'

'He could be living rough, unemployed.'

'Yes,' DS Willard said. 'That's perfectly true. He could. But . . .' He laughed. 'Call me a suspicious copper if you like, but I'm curious as to why Mr and Mrs Acton didn't report their son missing.'

'I gather he left after a family row.'

'Well, we'll look into it. But Claire, if I were you, I'd be asking your patient about her brother who went missing. Find out from her or her sister the exact circumstances surrounding the last time they saw him.'

'Right. I will.'

When she'd put the phone down she sat and stared for a while. Like peering into a tin full of writhing worms, she could not separate head from tail. All she could see was a muddle. Then she started doodling, writing dates, years. Robin had been five years older than his sister. And now the questions were *all* about dates. When, exactly, had Eliza been born? When had Heather married Geoff Krimble? And when, exactly, had Robin disappeared?

She didn't have time to sit here and ask questions. She had work to do. But her mind was only half on it. The rest was trying to pick out the facts and set them in order.

At four o'clock, Astrid bleeped her to say that Heather was back from the maternity hospital and was very disturbed.

They didn't have a specific mother and baby unit at Greatbach but they did have baby equipment for the odd cases of puerperal depression and psychosis. Anything from the post-baby blues to full-blown hallucinations.

But as she made her way towards the ward where Heather had been readmitted, she had the feeling that she was holding the strands of something other than these false allegations against men in her hand. She had the facts but she was not connecting them properly.

She could hear the baby's loud wail right along the corridor. It was a lusty sound for a newborn. Echoes bouncing along the walls, bare except for a few framed black-and-white photographs of bottle kilns, pot-banks and potters in clay-stained aprons lined up and smiling for the cameras. She pushed the door open. Heather was sitting up on the bed, cooing over the tiny pink bundle in her arms, tears in her eyes. Before she registered Claire's presence, she was sobbing. 'He wasn't there. He missed her birth. He wasn't there. I thought he could deliver his own daughter.'

Geoff was sitting on a chair by her side, head in hands, his attitude one of despair. He simply didn't know what to do – cradle the baby, put his arm around his wife or simply sit there, frozen, immobile. He looked up at Claire's entrance but his face was mournful, blank, hopeless.

Heather's expression changed when she realized it was Claire. She still looked pale and weary but furiously angry with her. 'Someone,' she said, jabbing the air with her index finger, 'is keeping Charles from me. *You* . . .' accompanied by another jab,

'. . . *you* are conspiring to prevent him from seeing our beautiful child.'

Geoff didn't even bother lifting his head but his shoulders gave a little shake. When he looked at Claire, she knew he wanted to talk. At last. She caught his eye and nodded.

But her concern was primarily for the baby. Heather was clutching the neonate, holding it against her breast. But the baby wasn't sucking. Or even fixed on the nipple; it was squashed against the engorged bosom. Heather was not focusing down with love at the infant but was glaring at her. 'He hasn't even seen her yet,' she said, fury making her eyes round and bright. She was now gripping the baby's head. The baby's soft little head with its two tiny fontanelles, protected during delivery by the registrar's guiding hand.

By Claire's side, Astrid moved forward and held her hands out. 'Be careful, Heather,' she said in a gentle tone Claire had never heard her use before. 'You'll hurt the baby.'

'But I'm feeding her,' Heather said, though patently she was nearer to suffocating the child. 'She'll die if she doesn't drink . . . my milk,' she continued, looking first at Astrid and then, longer, at Claire.

Without protest or comment, Geoff left the room.

Claire responded. 'That's true, Heather, but she's a newborn. And tiny little babies are often a bit slow to take to the breast. You just wait. Just wait and she'll be fine.'

But Astrid's look of alarm mirrored her own feelings. This baby needed protection.

Astrid took Caroline from her mother. 'Give her here,' she said. 'Take a rest.'

Heather looked at her with a vicious stare. 'Don't you dare give her a bottle. I want to breastfeed her. And when Charles comes you must let me know.'

Astrid nodded.

'Promise?'

Again, Astrid nodded and took the baby away. So now Claire and Heather were alone. Heather turned her head very slowly towards Claire. 'I want to know,' she said in a voice icy with hatred, 'why you're stopping Charles from coming, from seeing his daughter. And why . . .' Her finger pointed towards the door and the corridor beyond, '. . . why you let Geoff, that . . . oaf in.'

'That oaf,' Claire said, 'is your husband. And . . .'

Heather anticipated her words. 'Oh, no,' she said sweetly. 'That's where you're wrong. Soooo wrong. He is *not* the father of this child. And he was not the father of either Eliza or Freddie.'

Claire didn't respond.

Heather continued to rant. 'Geoff Krimble has no right to see Caroline.'

Claire was silently assessing the situation. At least the child was safe for now. And her patient? Sedation?

But Heather had finally given way to exhaustion. She settled down against the pillows and closed her eyes.

Geoff was waiting outside. She led him into one of the interview rooms and offered him a coffee. He, too, looked exhausted.

'Mr Krimble,' she began, 'I think so far you've told me some half-truths, haven't you?'

He paused as though on the edge of a precipice. Then nodded.

Her turn. 'Tell me,' she said, her tone deceptively casual, 'how well did you know Heather's brother?'

'I knew him through the church. But not well.'

'And you're not a member of that church any more?'

He shook his head.

'Why not?'

'Let's just say I lost my faith.'

'In the religion or the people who belonged to it?'

'People.'

'You and Heather were married . . .?'

He got twitchy at that. 'January.' His knee started bouncing up and down. He didn't want her probing further.

'2010?'

He nodded.

'Eliza was born in April,' she said gently. 'Who was her father?'

There was something endearing about Geoff's inability to tell a lie. He simply looked at her with those sad eyes, a horrible truth dulling them.

She tried another tactic. 'When did Robin disappear?'

'Some time . . .' He tried again. 'I don't really know.'

She let him think for a moment before asking softly, 'What happened to him?'

He looked mystified. On firmer ground now. 'No one knows,' he said. 'He just vanished.'

'When?'

'Sometime late in 2009. Just before Christmas.'

And something gave an audible click in Claire's brain.

'Eliza was born . . .?'

Geoff flushed and, in that rush of blood to his face, Claire heard a second click.

And now? Facts spun past her brain. Spinning out of control. She felt cold. Wait for the DNA sample. Partly out of pity and partly because even if he knew the answers she didn't believe Geoff would ever tell her the truth. Not out of loyalty to his wife but shame at having been involved. She left the room.

Someone was walking towards her, her face in shadow against the light. Ruth Acton drew level. 'You should have believed us, you know,' she said quietly. 'My sister doesn't lie. She tells the truth as she sees it.' She put a photograph in her hand. For a while, Claire did not recognize the sexy, beautiful woman who laughed into the camera.

And then she did.

And then she knew.

Some people have luck heaped on them and other people don't. There is no logic, method or reason behind them. Who knows why life's problems pile up against one person and spare another? Who knew why Heather Krimble had gone through life with these burdens? Who knew why two of her children had died the sleep of the innocent? Who knew why Grant's little sister had been born with an illness that made her so desperate to keep her brother close that he had been faced with an awful choice? Who knew why he had left her without a word to be at Maisie's side? Who knew any of it?

Claire stood still in the middle of the corridor, rooted to the spot, because her mind, in turmoil, was asking questions which had no answers.

Except now she was beginning to have a fragile framework of understanding.

Already she was wondering if it would ever be safe to allow Heather Krimble home with her little daughter. Would her nirvana ever happen? But even she could not have foreseen the reasons why it might not.

THIRTY-THREE

She made it back to Waterloo Road at five to six but Simon's small Nissan was already in the drive, his car packed, full of possessions. As he climbed out she felt the warmth of his grin and his gratitude. 'You've just made my stay in the UK quite a bit more pleasant.'

She wanted to respond with an equal expression of gratitude, maybe even a hug, but instead brushed it away with an almost churlish, 'That's OK.'

He handed her an envelope. 'First month's rent,' he said with a burst of laughter. She took it. It felt good. Not the money, the friendship. The beginning of a new era. They both glanced at the small car which looked as though it could not possibly hold one more thing.

'Here,' she said. 'I'll give you a hand.'

'Believe it or not,' he was saying as they dragged stuff into the house, 'I was thinking I don't have a lot. Most of it's still in Oz. How wrong can you be?'

'Stuff just accumulates,' she said.

The next hour was spent climbing stairs with arms full of random possessions, from a tennis racquet to arms full of clothes. But as he distributed them around the rooms she felt the top floor was transforming into a small home.

'Look,' he said when they had finally lugged his possessions right up to the top floor, 'I don't want to creep into your space. Intrude.'

It was time to set the ground rules.

'The two rooms are yours,' she said. 'Exclusively. I shan't be coming up. A cleaner comes on a Tuesday, a Polish girl called Matylda. If you want, she can do your room too.'

He sniggered. 'Room with a cleaner? It gets better.'

'But maybe tonight,' she suggested tentatively, 'we could order a takeaway and have a chat.'

'Yeah,' he said enthusiastically. 'Great, if you'll let me treat you.'

'I thought you could provide the wine,' she said with a glint in her eye.

'It's a deal. I've brought a bottle. Australian,' he added.

'Barossa Valley,' they said in unison.

'Just give me forty minutes to sort my things out.'

'And I'll order the takeaway,' she said. 'You'll be doing me a favour. I hate eating alone.'

He half bowed in an old-fashioned gesture. She wasn't sure whether it was mockery, charm or the way he thought the English said a polite and formal thank you. Anyway – whatever – she liked it.

When he came down he'd showered and put on a clean shirt, and very politely knocked and hesitated at the kitchen door. So far so good.

They served out the food and sat round her kitchen table. Claire liked traditional design but not in the kitchen. She did have a solid walnut Swiss table at one end bought from a local dealer but the other end of the kitchen was space age. Gadgets, cream units, a black marble surface, stainless-steel coffee maker, kettle and a wonderful food mixer. Simon looked around with appreciation. 'Great,' he said. 'This is really nice.' Then, looking at her, 'And I'm allowed to use it?'

'As long as you leave it like this,' she said. 'There's a kettle and a microwave upstairs that you can have so you're not constantly . . .' And then she was embarrassed. It sounded like she was banning him from here.

He poured them both a glass of wine and handed her one. 'I'm not a great cook,' he said as they clinked glasses. Claire laughed too. 'Neither am I,' she said. 'This is all for show.'

A knock at the front door announced the arrival of the food. She set the table, spooned some of the chicken and rice on to the plates and eyed him.

'You look troubled,' he said. 'So . . .?'

She took two mouthfuls of the chow mein before she answered. She wanted to get this story straight. And who better to bounce it off than her lodger? But it wasn't even straight inside her head. There was the missing brother. The loyal sister. The family dynamics. Two dead babies. A deeply troubled patient. A dangerous allegation. A vulnerable newborn. And on the periphery, peering in? Riley Finch, now free, and Arthur about to be incarcerated.

Somehow or other she managed to cobble it together like a very messy, irregular patchwork quilt while Simon listened, almost without breathing, his concentration so intense. And somehow, something recognizable emerged. A sequence of events. Finally, he spoke. 'You know what I think, Claire?'

She already knew what he would suggest. Knew where all the facts would be unearthed.

'I suspect your detective is already doing some digging of his own.'

'I wouldn't be at all surprised.'

'And then there's the sister,' he said. 'She might have all the answers.'

'If I can persuade her to talk.'

He nodded.

'So, how do I get her on my side, break her loyalty?'

'That's a difficult one,' he agreed.

'She seems almost brainwashed. Indoctrinated. Agreeing or at least not contradicting any of her sister's statements even though they're patently bizarre.'

'Have you done the DNA test on the little baby?'

She nodded. 'Took some cord blood. We're just waiting for the result. It'll take a week or so.'

'Which you think will be?'

'It won't be Charles's baby, Simon. That whole story is a bucket-ful of nonsense.'

'You think?' His eyes looked too perceptive. Too all-seeing.

'Surely . . .?' Her voice faded away weakly.

'Let me put a scenario to you.' He broke off to pour them both a second glass of wine. 'We have a brother they apparently adored who's missing. Yet neither Ruth nor Heather is showing any concern about that. Instead, they're focusing on a cock and bull story about "other men". When Heather is actually married and, according to her husband, having sex with him. Why is she doing this? What element is she too damaged to face? Think about it, Claire. There is another thing. Heather and her sister are focusing more on these so-called liaisons than the death of two little babies. Why?'

'Go on.'

'She was pregnant when she was married.'

She felt the smooth satisfaction of a piece of a puzzle completing the first recognizable picture since Charles had made that first phone call.

'The child she's carrying dies. No DNA test is performed. In fact, at that point no one realizes that this is anything but an allegation, an episode of puerperal psychosis, a woman misguided, deluded. She insists. Continues spinning stories.' He grinned. 'In other words, de Clerambault's syndrome.'

Claire was rapt at the way Simon, looking in from the outside, was putting the facts into something like a progression of events. A natural consequence rather than a rag bag of odd occurrences. She listened, elbows on table, cupped palm supporting her chin, food forgotten but taking the odd sip of some very good Australian Shiraz.

'Heather becomes pregnant for the second time. This time she blames another man, the window cleaner, who almost certainly never touched her and has his own partner and life plan. And that, almost certainly, does not include Heather Krimble.'

But Claire was remembering the photograph Ruth had pushed into her hand of her sister dressed and made up ready for a party.

'It's possible that the poor chap never even looked at her as anything but the lady who gives him ten quid for cleaning the windows. The child is proved to be her husband's. Unfortunately this second child dies too, aged just two months. In both cases a post-mortem was performed but no cause of death found.'

Simon topped up both their glasses. 'And then we come to your guy.' She bristled at the phrase but wisely said nothing. 'While I'm not wholly convinced Charles Tissot, with his murky, seedy little history, had sex with our lady in the back of his car, I do think it's perfectly possible. But then it's just as possible that the whole thing never happened and yet again was a figment of a mind damaged by real events.'

Simon Bracknell moved in a little closer. 'The real question, Claire, is what real events? What damaged her mind? What was she blocking out by insisting that her employer was the father of her child? And the last question: why did she ask to be referred to the very man she's accusing?'

She blinked. It was a lot to take in.

'And Freddie?'

'Maybe . . .' He was frowning. 'You know one of the generally held explanations for a cot death? Maternal involvement?'

She shook her head slowly. 'That won't do, Simon. While Eliza's was performed by a general pathologist, when Freddie died the

PM was performed by a specialist paediatric pathologist. He won't have made a mistake or missed anything he should have picked up on.'

'Well, in this case it probably was a cot death.'

She nodded her agreement. 'It's a notoriously difficult and sensitive subject. But unless there's clear and incontrovertible evidence, the pathologist will always err on the side of caution.'

She thought about this one and Simon Bracknell pressed on. 'I suggest,' he said, very gently, 'that you don't leave her alone with the baby.'

She shook her head, appalled at the vulnerability of a child. This helpless baby, danger homing in on it from all sides.

And her new lodger was patently following her thoughts. 'Babies are fragile little things,' he said. 'All it takes, Claire, is just one short minute.'

She looked at him sharply. There was a subtle meaning tucked behind these words, something personal, something that had touched this seemingly pleasant, uncomplicated man. Why had he really come to the UK without his wife? Questions she wouldn't be asking, answers he may well not want to give.

Give it time.

'So . . .' she pondered. 'What next? I can't keep her in for ever. Neither can I insist she have only supervised access to her child. I have no evidence. And from what you're saying, maybe the baby isn't at risk.'

Her mind was seeing Heather's fingers squeezing her pregnant abdomen, the hand raised for a slap.

'How was she when you saw her?'

'Odd. Knackered.'

'So . . .?'

'In her two previous puerperium her mental condition's improved after a few weeks. My plan was to wait for that and keep her in until we were certain she and the baby had bonded.'

He nodded.

They chatted until ten, when Claire decided it was time to run a bath and Simon disappeared up the stairs.

So far, so good.

THIRTY-FOUR

Tuesday, 4 August, 8 a.m.

She'd had a restless night and woke with a feeling of impending doom. She was anxious to reach the hospital before anything happened. She had no idea why, just knew she had to be there. As she'd left the house she'd heard Simon moving around and called up to him that she was leaving.

Down the stairs wafted, 'Have a good day, then.'

But as she slammed the front door behind her she had the feeling that she would not. She would have a bad day. A very bad day indeed.

School holidays invariably meant a reduction in traffic this early in the morning so her journey was suitably speedy. When Claire had first arrived at the Potteries there had still been Potters' Fortnight when everything had shut down. Stoke-on-Trent had become a ghost town. But these days there were too few potters for the title to make any difference. Maybe it was the same in Yorkshire, where they had Wakes Week.

But old traditions die hard.

Her first act was to bury herself in her office with Heather Krimble's notes and study the dates.

Some were missing, one of them an exact date for Robin's disappearance.

She picked up the phone to speak to Ruth Acton and even over the line heard fear in her voice as she questioned her about her brother's disappearance.

Too many questions answered with a *don't know* or *I can't remember*. Every now and again she remembered her manners and managed an *I'm sorry I can't help you more*.

But even the lack of information told her something. As pieces moved together to lock into position, she started to see the whole picture.

And by chance, as though he was tracking along the same path, at ten o'clock Zed Willard rang. 'We have a warrant to search the Actons' property,' he said.

And even though the information made her heart give a little skip, she still questioned it. 'On what grounds?'

'Robin Acton has disappeared,' he said, his voice sounding stern. 'Not been seen for eight years. We thought we'd do a bit of digging around as he *hadn't* been reported missing by his *loving* parents.' She caught the twist of Angostura bitters in his voice. 'He had a job locally helping to run a betting shop. He turned up sometime early in December 2009 but was only employed on a casual basis. Apparently his father came in just before Christmas and said that they had argued, that Robin had left home and wouldn't be returning. According to fellow members of their church, he was a rotten egg. He'd left after a row and Bailey Acton had said he would not be returning and his name was to be taken off the register. Put it like this, Claire: would your parents have covered up for your disappearance quite so well?'

Bad question, Zed. Having buggered off himself, my father wouldn't even have known and my mother couldn't have cared less – that is, if she'd even noticed my absence.

So she didn't answer the question.

'We're taking sniffer dogs to the property,' he said, and she knew.

Inching closer. I'm inching closer, she thought.

And climbed up to the top floor.

Heather was alone, sitting up in the bed. No sign of the baby. 'He still hasn't come,' she said, patently furious. 'He hasn't come.'

Claire glanced across the room. The windows didn't open very far and there were bars across, inches apart. 'Heather,' she said, 'where is the baby? Where is Caroline?'

Claire looked at her patient, saw hatred and fury. In her anger, was it possible she had killed her own child? 'Heather,' she said, 'where is Caroline? What have you done with her?'

But Heather was too distracted to respond, too mad with rage. And her focus now was on her missing 'lover' not the child. 'You're keeping him away from me. You're stopping him from coming. I hate you. You deserve to . . .' and she launched herself at Claire.

'I don't think so.' A miracle appearance. Edward Reakin was holding her back and two security officers had also arrived.

'Where . . . is . . . Caroline?' Claire repeated. She moved towards the window, which was open the regulation six inches.

Even though common sense told her otherwise, half of her still feared what she would see. But there was nothing, no tiny flurry of pink blanket. No baby. Just the quadrangle, too enclosed for sunshine to reach, benches occupied by patients chatting, some of them smoking. Two of them looked up. At last, Heather answered her question. 'One of the nurses has taken her for a bath.'

She went outside to the nurses' station.

Claire moved along the corridor, her footsteps echoing. There were three bathrooms on this floor. One was occupied by an irate elderly lady, the other two were empty.

The nurses were sitting at their station and responded blankly to her asking them where Caroline was. 'With her mother.'

'No, she's not. She said that one of the nurses has taken her for a bath.'

Both jumped to their feet and followed Claire back to Heather's room. 'Where is Caroline?'

'I already said,' she responded with dignity. 'A nurse has taken her for a bath.'

'Which nurse?'

'The pretty one,' she said dismissively. 'The one with lovely red hair. She took her. And she's giving her a bath now.'

Claire's heart almost stopped. There was no red-headed nurse on this ward. The only redhead she could think of was . . . unthinkable.

In psychiatric hospitals nurses, in general, do not wear uniform. It is thought that it is more calming for the patient if the staff are casually dressed. But this has its downside. Who can tell who is staff and who a patient? So even if Heather recognized Riley Finch as the woman who had passed her in the corridor, she might have assumed that she was another nurse.

She roped in the two security guards to search the ward as well as Edward. But this was all down to her. She should have taken better care. She'd recognized the threat when Riley's eyes had drifted down to Heather's pregnant belly. She'd seen the lust in her eyes, the naked desire. And done nothing. She'd almost foreseen this and not done enough to prevent it. And her fear was that no search would find little Caroline. Riley would have her until she grew bored.

And then what? And who was in a position to stop it?

A frantic search of the ward, Security darting into every room and then the entire hospital, revealed nothing. No sign of Riley. No sign of Caroline. Claire alerted the porters' lodge but her fear was that it was too late, an almost literal shutting the stable door after the horse has bolted. To make it worse, some of the patients picked up on the general panic and were wandering around, confused and anxious. And to top it all, in the general confusion, Arthur Connolly had disappeared too.

Through all this, Heather sat centre stage, cross-legged on her bed, enjoying the drama and waiting for her hero, Charles, to find his baby daughter.

Claire went down to the porters' lodge and saw the CCTV, which was when her heart sank. There was a clear picture of Riley Finch walking out almost an hour before she'd arrived, pushing the pram, baby presumably inside.

She rang the police.

And waited.

Inactivity can be the most exhausting way of spending time. Claire watched the hands of the clock crawl round to two p.m. Time for the clinic. She stood up – and sat back down again.

She'd pushed Arthur Connolly's disappearance to the back of her mind so far. But now she worried. What if he'd used the distraction of the baby's disappearance to abscond? What if, in spite of the peace offerings of flowers, letters and cards, he was heading back towards his former home?

This time, he'd do it properly.

Wearily, she connected for the second time with the police. Gave them a description and suggested they send some officers round to Arthur's former home and stay with his wife and son. Just in case . . .

She reached her outpatient office but instead of calling in her first patient she bleeped Salena Urbi and asked her to take the clinic. She couldn't concentrate on her work.

But what else could she do?

She headed back up to the ward to speak to Heather, who blamed her for everything.

'Everything,' she said viciously, jabbing her finger at Claire, 'is your fault.'

And Claire knew she was right. Her focus had been so much on Heather's story, she'd lost her peripheral vision. Heather's last words were ringing in her ears as she headed back to her office.

'You get her back.'

The afternoon dragged, time only filled by images that popped through Claire's imagination. She could protect Lindsay and Saul, but an invisible baby held by an unpredictable psychopath?

It was small consolation that this time, surely, Riley would be convicted?

It wasn't so much that Riley would *deliberately* harm Caroline. It would be an act of neglect. She would forget her or leave her or simply fail to protect her.

And this was a newborn. A baby whose umbilical cord was still a vulnerable, open wound. Baby Caroline had so many needs. To be kept warm. To be fed. Regularly.

The abduction of a baby from a so-called safe place, particularly when the safe place is part of the NHS, generates if not a mountain then a very large hill of paperwork.

Slowly, Claire began writing the report that would soon be demanded of her.

Critical event analysis. Even she could see where the failures had begun. She could point her finger at herself.

THIRTY-FIVE

Tuesday, 4 August, 3.30 p.m.

Arthur Connolly was a man on a mission. He walked with purpose, feeling determined. He could do this.

His target was ahead. He kept her in his sights. Arthur Connolly knew exactly what he must do. He would wait for his opportunity, then strike.

Lindsay was at home watching a soap on daytime television when the knock came. She justified sitting around all day, receiving flowers and attention, her son dancing in attendance – as his father had once done. She'd just been very, very poorly. Nearly died. She'd never be right again. Her podgy hand reached out for another chocolate. *Lucky to be alive*, the surgeons had said.

Another visitor, she thought.

3.32 p.m.

Claire couldn't resist ringing the police again only to hear the unwelcome news. No sign of baby Caroline. The forces were doing all they could to find her. Accusation soured their voices.

If you'd done your job properly, Doctor.

4 p.m.

Just be patient, Arthur told himself. *Your opportunity will come.*

4.45 p.m.

'He wouldn't dare,' Lindsay scoffed. 'Come here? With Saul here?'

'All the same,' PC Stephanie Bridges said, 'I'm instructed to stay here, with you.'

Saul Connolly stood in the doorway, arms folded. 'There's no need. I'm here.'

But Stephanie Bridges was used to carrying out orders.

5 p.m.

When he needed to, Arthur Connolly could move very quickly. If he didn't do it now the opportunity would slide by and he would lose it. Arthur recognized good and evil. He'd been married to Lindsay. He knew spite, and this woman was spiteful. He watched her hover outside the door, glance at the baby then back at the door again, tempted by the bright lights and promise of a pub meal.

The baby was ominously quiet.

And that worried him.

She put the brake on. Arthur sensed her moment of indecision, her attention away from the pram, foot inside the door.

Arthur moved. He grabbed the baby. And then he ran again.

A man on a mission.

6 p.m.

She couldn't, wouldn't go home. She needed to be here. In the centre of events. But there was nothing to do.

6.10 p.m.

The first sign of relief was a knock on the door. Rita came in, a big smile on her face. 'Good news,' she said. 'They want you up on the ward.'

Good news?

Astrid met her in the corridor, a huge smile on *her* face too, her manner bright with relief. 'Thank God,' she said, unexpectedly adding, 'for Arthur Connolly.'

Claire pushed the inevitable enquiry to the back of her mind and could only manage. 'Arthur?'

'He was keeping his eye on her.'

Claire's eyes swivelled round.

Arthur was standing in the centre of a crowd, patients, staff mingling, admiration on all their faces. And so the story came out in fragments as people interrupted.

'I saw her go into the ladies' room. I had a bad feeling.' He gulped and continued. 'Then she came out with . . .' And he held up baby Caroline as though displaying a trophy. No one took the child away from him.

'Instead of stopping her, I thought I'd do a bit of spying.'

Claps from two of the dementia patients.

'I followed her to the bus stop. And then she got on to the bus. She couldn't manage the pram, so I helped her.' He looked pleased with himself. 'She didn't recognize me.'

On cue, another patient asked, 'Where was the bus going?'

'All the way to Fenton.' Arthur couldn't resist a beam of pride. 'She called on one of her friends. They went off to The Queen Victoria.' Now he was frowning, speaking with a sort of focused intensity, trying to get his facts exactly right.

'But . . .' He looked down at Caroline. 'It's against the rules to have a baby inside the pub. Her friend went inside, left her with the pram. I waited.' He grinned. 'She didn't notice me nearby. You see, no one ever notices me.' For the first time, probably in his life, there was a touch of pride in his situation, bravado in his voice. 'When she'd almost followed her in, I saw my opportunity. And then . . . I caught the bus back here with her.' A couple of cheers were raised from the back row and Arthur bowed and handed baby Caroline back to her mother in a formal presentation.

So Arthur turned from villain to hero with a bus journey to Fenton. Claire could hardly wipe the smile off her face.

Astrid put her arm round her. 'We've rung the police,' she said. 'They found Riley still in the pub, just as Arthur said. They've picked her up.'

Friday, 7 August, 11 a.m.

Claire looked at the contents of the envelope in disbelief. And sat frozen. She needed to think about this one. When she looked at her calendar, she realized that if nature had played its course, this would have been the day that the infant would first have made her appearance. Yet she'd already been born and abducted.

It looked as though Caroline Krimble's life was set to be eventful.

On Wednesday, 12 August, Zed Willard rang. 'We took dogs trained to sniff out cadavers to the Actons' garden. We'll be excavating over the next few weeks but . . .' He cleared his throat. 'He's there, Claire. Not missing any more.'

Ruth remained tight-lipped, giving nothing away even when Claire suggested that her brother had been the father of baby Eliza. Claire was very gentle with this traumatized woman. 'There is a reason behind the ban on close relatives having children,' she said. 'Any genetic defect is magnified.'

Ruth covered her face with her hands.

'That's possibly why Eliza died,' Claire said, feeling sorry for her. 'Not strictly speaking a cot death but the result of consanguinity.'

Ruth shoulders shook with sobs. 'He made us watch,' she said. 'He made us watch as he . . . And he . . .' She couldn't say any more except . . . 'We had to dig.'

'Robin's grave?'

Her head nodded and nodded. 'And Heather had to marry Geoff. Geoff always had a thing for her. He was glad to rescue her from . . . Otherwise . . .'

The trouble with a deep cover-up of lies and deceit is that sometimes it is the truth which remains buried.

Thursday, 13 August, 10 a.m.

Claire was in her office, fingering the phone and savouring the moment. This was one phone call she was looking forward to making. Charles would probably already have forgotten about the case. She had difficulty tracking him down, waiting for his secretary to find him. She obviously wasn't number one on his caller list any more. His voice, on the other end, was suitably irritated. 'I thought this beastly business was done and dusted.'

'Not quite,' she replied, still relishing the moment.

'So . . .?'

'I need to congratulate you.'

Absolute silence on the other end. In the background, she could hear hospital sounds. Bleeps, trolleys being wheeled, muted conversation. No words. No *what do you mean?* Or *what the hell are you on about?* Nothing but a stony silence, waiting.

'You have a lovely daughter.'

THIRTY-SIX

Thursday, 20 August, 2 p.m.

One week later, Heather, smug now, was cradling the child. 'You should have believed me.' She dropped a kiss on to her daughter's pink forehead.

Claire settled down in the chair by the window. 'Believed you about what?'

And again, Heather hid behind her fantasy. 'He loves me, you know.'

'Who? Mr Cartwright? Sam Maddox? Or is it Charles we're talking about here?'

Heather was silent but watchful, waiting.

'Or do you mean Robin?'

And Heather froze like a statue. Mouth opening and closing. No words came out. But her eyes held pure horror. 'You know,' she whispered.

And Claire nodded.

Heather touched her arm. 'I loved him,' she said. 'He protected us, looked after us. I owed him my love. He paid a terrible price.'

For once, Claire was stuck for words.

She moved along the corridor.

There was still Arthur to consider. He awaited sentence and this time around Claire had good reason to be optimistic, because he was a hero now. Last week she had stood up in court, noting the rapt attention the jury had given the video evidence of a woman wheeling a baby out through the archway of Greatbach Secure Psychiatric Hospital, Arthur Connolly creeping along behind her. She'd tuned to face the judge. 'This man,' she said, 'is not a danger to society. He just wanted to be loved. Respected. And what did he have? He was despised, ridiculed by his wife and son.'

At the back of the courtroom Claire had caught sight of Lindsay Connolly, eyes starting in fury at this turn of events. Was she to be robbed of her rights? Saul, by her side, inching away from her, watching the video evidence with eyes wide open as though he was seeing something he'd never seen before, his father acting with bravery. His father a hero.

Claire had finished giving evidence. There was only one way this should go.

'I respectfully request that Arthur Connolly be given a non-custodial sentence with the proviso that he is never allowed within fifty feet of his wife, Lindsay Connolly.'

Wednesday, 26 August, 10 a.m.

And then it was Riley's turn. Again. And again, Claire could speak.

'Riley has what is commonly called a narcissistic, sociopathic personality disorder. She wanted the baby so she took it. In my opinion, she is and will continue to be a danger to society at large because of a diminished or non-existent sense of empathy or responsibility for the victims of her actions.'

And this time, Riley received her just deserts. She went to prison to try and lie and charm her way out of whatever mess she managed to generate inside.

Zed Willard unearthed the remains of Robin Acton. The shattered bones and fractured skull told their own story. Easy enough to lay the murder at Bailey Acton's door when his wife and two daughters turned Queen's evidence. Deciding exactly where, on the scale of accessories, his wife and two daughters lay, would be another case for Claire to offer an opinion on. Ruth had been crushed, her sister had been damaged and Win Acton silenced by the brutality of events. It had only been through clinging on to the elaborate fables that Heather and her sister had constructed around them, that they'd protected themselves from the horror of their brother's murder. Heather was calm, still focusing on her lover. Charles had not come to see her, she said, but his lawyers had been in touch.

There was no argument even such a consummate liar as Charles Tissot can conjure up against incontrovertible DNA.

Saturday, 29 August, 10 a.m.

The postman had been. Just one envelope dropped on to the mat.

She knew the writing. Scrawled, spidery letters, large and crawling across the page in a slow tarantella. Inside were a couple of short sentences.

Maisie died last Thursday. The funeral's set for Friday, 12 September, 11 o'clock at Carmountside. Please come.

G